A dream made flesh . . .

Suddenly Andrew knew the girl was there. He could feel her. He concentrated as hard as he could, harnessing his mind's strength until he was able to visualize her. He focused on her eyes, which held his like magnets. He saw her soft lips and slightly upturned nose with the sprinkling of freckles across its bridge. He pictured the waves of brown and gold that framed her face.

The vision grew from his thoughts, becoming so clear it seemed she stood in front of him. Her eyes were round with wonder. She looked as surprised as he felt, and she reached out her hand, close enough to touch him. Andrew's heart pounded and power streamed through him, fueled by the chunk of gray stone. He used all his strength to channel it through his arms so finally, impossibly, he reached her hand and gripped it between his own. He could feel the softness of her fingers, the warmth of her skin. He could smell her clean, earthy scent. And then he heard her.

"You can do this!" she exclaimed, her voice ringing like a bell in his ears. "*You* called *me* . . ."

Under the Same Sky

Genevieve Graham

BERKLEY SENSATION, NEW YORK

THE BERKLEY PUBLISHING GROUP
Published by the Penguin Group
Penguin Group (USA) Inc.
375 Hudson Street, New York, New York 10014, USA
Penguin Group (Canada), 90 Eglinton Avenue East, Suite 700, Toronto, Ontario M4P 2Y3, Canada
(a division of Pearson Penguin Canada Inc.)
Penguin Books Ltd., 80 Strand, London WC2R 0RL, England
Penguin Group Ireland, 25 St. Stephen's Green, Dublin 2, Ireland (a division of Penguin Books Ltd.)
Penguin Group (Australia), 250 Camberwell Road, Camberwell, Victoria 3124, Australia
(a division of Pearson Australia Group Pty. Ltd.)
Penguin Books India Pvt. Ltd., 11 Community Centre, Panchsheel Park, New Delhi—110 017, India
Penguin Group (NZ), 67 Apollo Drive, Rosedale, Auckland 0632, New Zealand
(a division of Pearson New Zealand Ltd.)
Penguin Books (South Africa) (Pty.) Ltd., 24 Sturdee Avenue, Rosebank, Johannesburg 2196,
South Africa

Penguin Books Ltd., Registered Offices: 80 Strand, London WC2R 0RL, England

This book is an original publication of The Berkley Publishing Group.

Cover illustration by Gregg Gulbronson.
Cover design by George Long.
Cover hand lettering by Ron Zinn.
Interior text design by Laura K. Corless.

PRINTING HISTORY
Berkley Sensation trade paperback edition / January 2012

Library of Congress Cataloging-in-Publication Data

Graham, Genevieve.
Under the same sky / Genvieve Graham.—Berkley Sensation trade pbk. ed.
p. cm.
ISBN: 978-0-425-24523-1 (pbk.)
1. Americans—Scotland—Fiction. 2. Scotland—History—18th century—Fiction. I. Title.
PR9199.4.G723U53 2012
813'.6—dc23 2011036631

PRINTED IN THE UNITED STATES OF AMERICA

10 9 8 7 6 5 4 3 2 1

For Dwayne

ACKNOWLEDGMENTS

I would like to say thanks:

To Dwayne, the love of my life, for reading my very first page and saying, "You know what? That's not bad!" (and trying not to sound surprised). Thank you for putting up with this strange new lifestyle of "Author" and assuring our kids, "Mom's *writing*, not playing." For building my confidence and my office and for giving me plot ideas both brilliant and ridiculous. You led me back when I lost my way, put up with more than any man should have to, consoled me when I was inconsolable, and you were always my rock. My very huggable rock. I love you, Dwayne.

To our beautiful and incredibly talented daughters, Emily and Piper, who reminded me that dreams are to *work* for, not *wait* for. Thanks for being proud of me, and thanks for making me proud of you every day.

To my mom for giving me great books to read and inspire me. Dad, I wish you were here. I bet you would have loved all this. Especially the Scottish stuff.

To Diana Gabaldon for unwittingly helping me discover my passion for writing; to Connie Kostash for being my original critic; to the amazing Rona Altrows for telling me, "Yeah, you've got it, kid"; to Guy Sheldon, Laird of all Knowledge Highlandish, www.historichighlanders.com; to Sabine Hope for her insights and warm friendship; to the man with Cherokee wisdom and patience, Iron Head Vann, www.cherokeebyblood.com.

To my fantastic new community of online writer friends—I learn every day from you.

To my wonderful agent, Jacques de Spoelberch, who believed in my potential as well as the story, and who did so much more than just "sell the book." And finally to Wendy McCurdy and Katherine Pelz at Berkley, who took my hands and patiently led this rookie author every step of the way.

PART 1: MAGGIE

From This World to the Next

CHAPTER 1

A Dubious Gift

He has always been there. That fact is as important to me as my own heartbeat.

I first saw him when we were children: a young boy with eyes as dark as rain-soaked mud, staring at me from under a mane of chestnut hair. I kept him secret, invisible to everyone but me. He should have been invisible to me as well, because he was never really there, on the same windblown land, under the same sky. We never stood together, never touched as other people did. Our eyes met, and our thoughts, but our bodies were like opposite banks of a river.

When I was little, I thought of him as just another child. One with a slow smile and gentle thoughts that soothed me, as if he held my hand. When he didn't fade with my childhood years, I began to wonder if he were a spirit, communicating through my dreams. In my heart, I knew he was more. His world was the same as mine. He was as human as I.

I was born in the year of Our Lord 1730 on a patch of grassland in South Carolina. Our pine-walled house, dried to an ashy gray, stood alone, like an island in a sea of grass. Its only neighbours were a couple of rocky hills that spilled mud down their sides when it rained. They stood about a five-minute run from our house, just close enough to remind us they were there. The house barely stayed upright during the mildest of storms, and we had no neighbours to whom we might run if it ever collapsed. When winter struck, the wind sought out gaps in the walls, shrieking around bits of cloth we stuffed into the holes. The cold pierced our skin as it had the walls, and we wrapped our bodies in dried pelts that reeked of tanned leather. Our barn offered even weaker shelter to one aged horse and a few poorly feathered chickens who, fortunately, were good layers. My father owned a rifle, and he occasionally chanced upon a prize from the nearby forest. He also ran a tangled line of traps that provided most of our meals. Beyond that, we had little. What we did have we mended many, many times.

I was never a regular child, spending my days with nothing but play and chores on my mind. How could I be? My dreams showed me what would happen an hour, a day, a year before it did. I had always dreamed. Not symbolic imaginings of flying or falling, but dreams that showed me where my life would eventually go.

I could also see what wasn't visible, and hear what made no sound. When I was a toddler, my mother encouraged my odd abilities through games. She would pry a toy from my grip and hide it somewhere, then return and say:

"Go, Maggie. Go find your toy."

I ran to the target and came back every time, prize in hand.

Mother said I had "the Sight." I never told her there was more. I never told her about the boy I could see, who spoke to me without words. I wanted to keep him safe within secrecy, as if sharing him might make him disappear.

My dreams introduced me to people I had never seen, and took me to places I could never have known existed. Most nights they appeared and vanished, leaving vague memories in the back of my mind. Other nights I awoke bathed in sweat, drowning in images I didn't understand: hands flexing into fists, bristled fibres of rope chafing my skin, the thunder of horses' hooves. And blood. So much blood.

Mother didn't experience dreams like mine, but she knew I had them. Their existence terrified her. Mother was a small woman of few words. When she saw me awake from the dreams, my head still fuzzy with half memories, her face paled and she looked away, helpless and afraid.

Her mother, my grandmother, had had the Sight. Mother both respected and feared its power. My grandmother saw her own death a week before it happened. She felt the hands as they tied her to a stake, smelled the smoke as the tinder beneath her bare feet caught fire, and heard the jeering of the crowd as they watched her burn as a witch.

Mother told me the story only once. That didn't mean it couldn't repeat itself.

Mother did the best she could. Many nights I awoke in her arms, not remembering her arrival, only knowing she came when my screams jolted her from sleep. She held me, rocked me, sang lullabies that ran through my body like blood. But her songs held no answers, offered no way to chase the images from my mind. She did what she could as my mother, but I faced the dreams on my own.

Except when I was with the boy no one could see. Sometimes he would brush against my thoughts like a feather falling from a passing bird. Sometimes we conversed without words. We could just *be,* and we understood.

As an infant, I lived with my mother and father and our decrepit horse. My sister Adelaide was born two years after I was. When I first saw her, wrapped like a pea in a faded gray pod, I stroked her little cheek with my finger and loved her without question. We were best friends before the newborn clouds faded from her eyes. Two years later, she moved out of her crib and my bed became ours.

Our brother was born that year. He died before he drew his first breath. We named him Reuben and buried him next to the barn.

Little Ruth arrived on a cloudless day in March when I was six. Ruth Mary Johnson. She was soft and fair and filled with light. Even my father, a man with little patience and less affection, gentled at the sight of her.

Neither one of my sisters had the Sight. Like my mother, they were slender and delicate, like fair-skinned deer. My mother's skin was always so pale, even under the baking sun, she looked almost transparent. The only way to bring colour to her cheeks was to make her laugh, and my sisters and I did our best to paint them pink. I took after my father, with his brown hair and plain face, though my hands weren't as quick to form fists as his. My arms and back were built for lifting.

By the time I turned seven, my dreams had become more vivid, and more useful to the family. I was able to catch Ruth before she tripped down a hill, able to find a scrap of cloth my mother sought. One winter I dreamed of a corn harvest, and my mother, daring to believe, planted a garden of it that spring. Her gardens never provided much food, because the ground around our home was either cracked by drought or flooded by heavy rains that stirred the dust to mud. That summer, though, the corn grew high.

Usually my dreams came when I slept, but sometimes they appeared when I sat quietly on my own. They weren't always clear. Most of the time they had faded into wisps of thought by the time I came back into focus, but they never fully disappeared.

My mother and I never talked about my dreams. Neither of us acknowledged them out loud.

Just like we never talked about my father's death.

It happened on the night of my seventeenth birthday.

I dreamed of a wheel from our wagon, its spokes blurred to a quick gray. Our ancient gelding pulled the bumping wagon over a moonlit ridge as my father returned from a late trip to town.

He slumped on the wagon bench, his weary body jiggling over every bump. I saw him lift his chin and glance toward the sky. Low-lying storm clouds glowed in the light of the full harvest moon. Everything around the wagon took on a strange orange tinge: the sparse patches of spring grass, the heaps of boulders casting pointed shadows in the dark. Tufts of salted brown hair peeked from under my father's hat, and he tugged the brim lower on his forehead. My father was not a patient man. He clucked to the horse and snapped the reins over the animal's back. In response, the gelding tossed his head and picked up speed just as they reached the peak of a long hill. My father should have known better. The pitch was too steep. Once the wagon started racing down the hill, the horse couldn't slow. The wheels spun out of control, bouncing off rocks and jolting my father so he barely stayed in his seat. He leaned back, lying almost flat as he strained against the reins, but couldn't slow the panicked horse.

The wagon clattered downhill, too fast to avoid a boulder in its path, and the front wheel smashed into splinters. Jerking in reaction, the wagon staves twisted from the horse's harness, ricocheted off a solitary oak, and hit the ground with a sickening crack. The horse screamed and ran faster still. My father struggled to loosen the reins tangled around his wrists, but couldn't do it fast enough. He was yanked from his seat and tossed into the air like a sack of flour. He hit the ground. Hard. His body crashed against rocks and shrubs as he struggled to free himself from the reins, tearing his clothes and scraping long gashes in his skin. The horse raced down the hill, eyes white with terror, chased by the screams and the body that thumped behind him like an anchor.

After a while, the screaming stopped. The horse checked its wild run and trotted to a stop, sides heaving, the insides of his back legs wet with white foam. His nostrils flared, and he bobbed his head nervously at the scent of fresh blood. But he sensed no imminent danger. He dropped his head to a patch of grass and began to graze. My father's lifeless body rolled to rest a few feet away.

The dream ended and I sat up, gasping, the neckline of my shift soaked with sweat. I twisted toward the window, but all was silent, silver under the moon. I threw back the covers and stood, shaking, on the cold floor.

I knew where to find my father's body. Not far—the horse had raced past a familiar oak my sisters and I often climbed.

I woke my mother and we ran without a word along the dimly lit path, faded nightgowns flapping around our ankles.

My father's body was little more than a heap of bloodstained rags. The horse stood nearby, chewing, glancing at us before dropping his head to the grass again. Scraps of cloth fluttered along the pathway the wagon had taken, bits of clothing caught on rocks. My father's tired gray hat lay at the top of the hill.

I stared at what was left of him and wasn't sure how I felt. He hadn't been a kind man. The only thing he had ever given us was beatings.

Still, I should have been lost in grief beside my mother, but my mind was on something else. My dreams had changed. For the first time, they had occurred simultaneously with the event. My dreams were no longer limited to vague messages forecasting the future.

Burying a man in hard ground is difficult work. It took two full days for Adelaide and me to manage a trench large enough for his mangled body. Even then, we had to bend his knees a bit so he fit into the hole. My mother read from her Bible, then nodded at me to shovel the earth onto his body.

Our father had never spent much time with us when he was alive. Even so, the house seemed eerily quiet after his death. It was strange not hearing his heavy footsteps, not hearing him gripe about the sorry state of his life. We mourned, but not terribly. When he left the living, my father took with him the stale reek of alcohol, a sullen expression, and a pair of overused fists.

My mother, my sisters, and I were forced to take on my father's duties, which included driving the wagon to town for buying and selling. The ride took over two hours each way, but once we arrived, we forgot every bump. My sisters and I never tired of the activity in town. The painted building fronts with fine glass windows, the people who walked the treeless street, kicking up dust as they visited the stores. Dirty children watched like sparrows on perches while fancy ladies strolled the boardwalks under parasols, protecting their faces from the sun, tucking their hands into the arms of stiff-backed men in suits and hats. Sometimes they were shadowed by people whose eyes gleamed white out of sullen black faces. My mother told us they were from Africa, brought to America as slaves.

The town of Saxe Gotha boasted more than two skin colours. Fierce tattoos and feathers enhanced the bronze skin and black hair of men who moved with the casual grace of cats. They avoided the plank walkways, preferring the dust of the road under their feet.

My father had told us stories about Indians and their bloodthirsty ways. We had stared open-mouthed as he regaled us with violent tales. So when I saw the Indians in town, they both frightened and intrigued me, but I never saw them attack anyone. They were in town for the same reason we were: to trade. An uneasy peace existed between them and the white men while business was conducted. They brought deerskins and beaded jewellery and left with weapons, tools, and rum. No one spoke to them on the street, and they offered no conversation. Business complete, they leapt onto the bare backs of their horses and disappeared into the shadows of the trees beyond the town.

I felt an odd connection to these men. When my mother led my sisters and me into the local shop to trade eggs or small hides for blankets or whatever else we needed, the other customers avoided us as if they were afraid our poverty might touch them. At the end of our day, we climbed onto our clumsily rebuilt wagon, pulled by the only horse we'd ever owned, and were gone.

We crossed paths with the Indians, but never came close enough to make contact. And yet their images began to appear in my dreams, to emerge from the trees and surround me with purpose, the tight skins of their drums resonating with the heartbeat of the earth.

CHAPTER 2

Battle Dream

There was so much blood. My senses reeled with the unfamiliar heat of it, the stench, the sticky weight of it.

It was more than a dream. It had to be. The images were real, but hadn't come from my own thoughts. It wasn't my bloodstained hand that gripped the slick hilt of a sword.

But I knew whose it was. He was perhaps twenty, two years older than I, with deep brown eyes. I had seen him my entire life. We had grown together since I was a little girl, in dreams as clear as waking days.

Usually when I saw him, he was at peace. Not this time. His dark hair was pulled back from his sweat-streaked face, tied into a tail. His teeth were bared. He was weak with injuries and exhaustion, disheartened by the sight of an endless tide of red coats pushing toward him through a field of smoke. Muskets and cannons boomed in their wake.

Every one of his muscles ached. I rolled over in my bed, feeling the tension between my shoulders though I was cradled within my mattress. His head thrummed, echoing the drums in the field, the crack of guns, and his racing heartbeat.

I felt what he felt, but my body was miles away. My eyes burned with gritty tears. My limbs were heavy, weighted down by defeat. The stink of sulphur singed my nostrils, and my feet squelched through ice-cold muck while my body slept in my warm, safe bedroom, the air sweet with baking bread.

The sensations roaring through my veins were unlike anything I'd felt before. Fear forced the blood through my veins at an exhilarating speed, but I had to control the panic. He was in grave danger. He needed more than encouragement from me. He needed me to be a part of him. My senses were alive, my body untouched. I gave him all I had, despite the fact I couldn't touch him. Where he felt pain, I brought a healing touch. Where there was dizziness, I gave him strength.

A grunt alerted me to someone approaching from behind. In my mind I thrust out an arm, and the body I inhabited followed. He jumped, reacting to my unexpected presence, and I felt his sense of surprise. But of course I was there. I would never let him die. He took the strength I offered and turned it to rage. He roared, fighting for his life, twisting and moving with the violent grace of a wolf. His sword blocked a strike, although the smoke was so thick I almost didn't see it happen. Steel sliced through the air on his other side, and I turned to foil its attack, knowing he would turn with me. Again and again he blocked killing blows and struck out, cutting through the attacking soldiers. His strength was returning, his confidence back in place. I felt a surge of power as it filled his body and mind.

All the silent communication from our childhood had brought us to this point. I would never leave him. I would be wherever, whatever he needed me to be, if only in his thoughts. I would give him courage and strength and love. And he would give me the same whenever my mind called to him.

Close enough that our minds were like one, far enough that we never felt each other's touch. We were what we had always been.

CHAPTER 3

Beyond the House

For nearly two years I spent my days looking forward to falling asleep. For me, the darkness was full of life.

The dreams that comforted me the most were the ones featuring him, the boy from my childhood, now grown into a man about the same age as I. He was tall with a solid build and ruddy complexion. Dark hair fell in loose waves to just past his shoulders, and sometimes a short beard framed lips that curled slightly at the edges. When we saw each other in dreams, his smile felt so warm I thought I might burst into flame. But it was his fathomless brown eyes that spoke to me the most.

He usually visited when I slept, but if I could find a quiet place and relax, I might see him under the light of the sun. He appeared in my thoughts as if to watch me, as intrigued by me as I was by him. Sometimes I sensed his presence, but couldn't see him. Occasionally the spectre of a wolf loped through my thoughts, but somehow I knew the spirit of a man lived within its coarse dark coat. The eyes were the same: unflinching, deep wells of intelligence. So, without any other name to give him, I took to calling him Wolf.

I had dreams where I walked without him, seeing images I didn't try to understand: colours that swirled and left me breathless, streams of voices shining silver as they passed, featureless faces shadowed by unfamiliar trees.

Then something changed. The dreams went dark.

Nightmares invaded my sleep the summer after I turned seventeen. It was the hottest summer anyone could remember. Weeks passed with no rain, and the air grew fragile with need. Dead grass lay flat on the cracked earth with no hope of resurrection. Cicadas screeched from the faraway forest, a constant trill from dawn until dusk. And at night apparitions stole my sleep—bulky shadows creeping closer or retreating at their whim, like creatures hunting.

Everyone has nightmares, but mine were different. They showed me my future. Except they were unclear. All I knew was something horrible was coming. Something I couldn't see, but knew. I could do nothing but wait.

I found it hard to fall asleep in the heat, but I didn't mind. When sleep finally claimed me, I wished it hadn't come. My nightmares became darker every night, oppressive with growing urgency. Their menace accompanied me constantly, even creeping into my waking hours.

When the need for waiting came to an end, I knew. On the morning of that day, sunshine flooded the walls of the bedroom I shared with my sisters, but I saw only blackness. Fighting dizziness and nausea, I rose from our bed, needing to escape the grasp of the dreams. My legs were weak, and I clung to the yellowed wall. I stared at my sleeping sisters for so long they awoke and returned my stare.

"What is it?" Adelaide whispered.

My mouth opened and closed, but words were trapped in my throat.

"Get Mama," Adelaide said to Ruth, keeping her eyes on me.

Ruth ran to our mother's room, next to ours. Mother came and stood with me, letting me cling to her as if I were a small child. Slightly steadied by her presence, I dressed in the same dress I wore every day. I only had one other, and I kept it folded in our wardrobe, saving it until this one was too dirty to wear. On the table by our bedroom door sat a large tin bowl and a small ewer half full of precious well water. I dipped in a cloth and used it to scrub my teeth, then wet down my hair with my fingers and tied a neat blue ribbon around my braid. My mother had given me the ribbon a week before, in celebration of Adelaide's fifteenth birthday. Blue for me, pink for Adelaide, and yellow for Ruth. To distract myself from the pounding fear in my head, I kept busy, mending torn clothing and cleaning the house. I wove a thin bracelet for Adelaide out of the dry grass that brushed our house's walls, and pieced together a little dress for the black-eyed rag doll Ruth carried everywhere.

The day seethed with heat, trembling in distorted waves over the baked grass. There wasn't even a hint of breeze. The late afternoon sun bubbled low on the horizon, and its glare painted black silhouettes of our small barn and listing fence posts.

From out of the silence came the sounds of horses' hooves, heavy on the dried earth, coming toward our house.

My mother had never been a hunter, but I had seen her use our father's rifle against coyotes that pestered our hens. She had never hit one while I'd been watching, but the crack of a shot scattered the predators and urged them to seek easier meals. At the sounds of the horses, she grabbed the rifle from where it hung on the wall. My mother, my sisters, and I crowded through the doorway and stood on either side of its crooked frame, squinting into the light and watching the black profiles of men on horseback as they rode toward us. She held the rifle across her body like a shield, resting the end of its barrel on our faded wooden doorstep.

Before their faces came into view, I knew who they were. I started to shake. Adelaide took my hand and clung to it.

The strangers had ridden here from town. I half remembered their slouching figures from the last time we had been there to trade. They had tracked us like wolves might follow a flock of lambs, and we were just as helpless. We had no neighbours to come to our aid; no man had come to champion the tattered household of women.

I counted twelve men. They were scruffy and unshaven, tobacco juice staining their beards. Their apparent leader looked perhaps in his forties and wore a blue shirt, the only colour that stood out among the group's worn gray clothing. He looked us over, then touched the brim of his hat in greeting.

My mother shepherded us behind her and straightened her shoulders, standing a little taller. An unexpected breath of hot, dry air moved through us, lifting her apron in a halfhearted wave and tickling strands of golden hair that hung around her ears.

"Good afternoon, gentlemen," she said. Her voice sounded unnaturally loud to my ears.

Blue Shirt's lips widened into a smile, but he said nothing. My mother tried again.

"My husband will be here shortly. Is there something I can help you with?"

Blue Shirt grinned through his remaining teeth and spat beside his horse's front hooves. The animal shifted its weight and the saddle creaked.

"Well, now, missus, we all know that ain't true, don't we?" he drawled. He smiled wryly at his men for confirmation.

"Ain't no husband, 'less you's married to a ghost," called one, and amusement rippled through the circle of men.

Blue Shirt slid from his horse, reached up to his saddle, and grabbed a coil of rope. Four other men did the same.

"Hold it right there," Mother said. She lifted the butt of the gun to her shoulder and aimed it at the men. I saw a tremor pass through her, and I heard the rustling of her skirt against the door. "Get right back on those horses, please. I've no wish to shoot any of you."

Blue Shirt drew his mouth into a tight line, his eyes cold. When he took a step toward us, my mother cocked the trigger, and shut one eye, focusing.

"Chandler?" Blue Shirt said, glancing over his shoulder toward a young man still on horseback.

"Yes, sir," said Chandler. He drew a pistol from his belt, aimed it at my mother, and shot her through her head.

She died in that instant, but the echo of the gunshot went on and on. My sisters and I stood frozen to the spot, not breathing, watching my mother's body slide down the wall. The back of her skull smeared an uneven path of red down the gray wood.

"Aw, Chandler," Blue Shirt said. He made a clucking sound in his mouth and shook his head. "I wasn't going for the kill. What a waste."

"Sorry, boss," Chandler said, sliding his pistol back into his holster.

We stared at the men, speechless. It wasn't until they began stepping toward us again, ropes twisting between their fingers, that we jerked out of our daze.

Everything moved very quickly. I shoved Ruth through the door and grabbed for Adelaide, but someone yanked her away. Her screams were terrifying, but I couldn't stop to help her. I had to get Ruth away. My baby sister ran into the house ahead of me, blond curls bouncing against her back. The cellar, I thought desperately, shoving Ruth through the narrow hall as I ran, needing to get to the back door. If we could get there, if we could fling open the heavy doors in the earth, if we could pull the bolt down in time—

One of them cinched a thick arm around my waist, forcing my breath out in a grunt.

"Run, Ruth!" I screamed. "The cellar!"

I dug my nails into the man's arms and kicked against his shins with my bare heels. He flung me to the floor and my forehead banged it hard. He flipped me onto my back so I saw the gleam of sweat leaking from his sunburnt pores. He sneered and slapped my face so my cheek burned and my vision went momentarily white. I thought I heard something crack in my nose. Tears flooded my eyes, but I fought as hard as I could. He pinned me beneath his body, grabbed both my wrists in one big, calloused hand, then tied them together with a rough rope. He tightened the knot, yanked me to my feet, and dragged me toward the door.

I looked behind me and saw Ruth, slung over a man's shoulder like a madly wriggling sack of corn. She was sobbing and calling my name.

"I'm here, Ruth!" I cried. I needed to give her something to hold on to, if only my voice.

Sunshine flooded through our open door, blinding me as my captor shoved me outside. My mother's body slumped against the outer doorframe, her head tilted to one side. Her eyes were open, staring, faded blue crystals going dark beneath the black hole in her forehead. The wind tickled the loose strands of her hair, blowing them back and forth across her face. A few got stuck on the thin line of blood that snaked down her neck and into the top of her gown.

Adelaide sat on a horse, her face twisted in terror, her hands tied to the pommel of the saddle. She saw me and tried to scream, but a rag was stuffed in her mouth and tied tight over her cheeks, muffling her voice. A man sat behind her, keeping her from sliding off. My captor carried me toward a different horse and handed me, kicking and screaming, to another man on horseback. My back met the solid wall of his chest and I pulled away, but he stopped my struggles by anchoring me against him, shoving his hands between my thighs and gripping hard enough to bruise. When he released my legs, I started to look around at him, but he shoved a cloth in my mouth and tied it tightly. My lips stretched until I thought they would split, but I managed to work my teeth over the gag so at least I could breathe through my mouth.

Blue Shirt strode through the group of men, pausing to look at each of us, ignoring our sobs. He studied me through squinted eyes, then reached up and ripped out the blue ribbon I had tied in my hair that morning. I yelped and tried to lift my hands to my head in reflex, but the man behind me shoved them down again. Blue Shirt stepped toward Adelaide, who sobbed through the gag. He grabbed her wrists and twisted off the bracelet I had made for her that morning. Finally, he turned toward little Ruth, also bound but not gagged.

"Leave her!" I tried to yell, but my words were swallowed up by the putrid fibres of the cloth in my mouth. I couldn't bear the thought of his hands on her, of any kind of pain inflicted on my baby sister. I tried again, even though no one would understand what I said. "She's just a little girl!"

He paid no attention to me. From ten feet away I could see Ruth's body shake. Her eyes were focused on our mother, lying still in the doorway. Ruth's tiny doll was tucked into her apron, and it moved with her, quivering like a hummingbird's wings. Blue Shirt yanked it free, walked to his horse, and shoved the three items into his saddlebag. His horse took a half step forward as he swung onto the saddle, then Blue Shirt turned to the men.

"I'll head in to make the 'rrangements with the cap'n," he said. "I'll join y'all at the meetin' spot."

The men nodded and Blue Shirt's gaze focused on each of the remaining riders. There were twelve of them in all, most about the same age as their leader, but a couple were younger, their long, tangled hair untouched by gray. Words of warning rumbled through Blue Shirt's tight lips, and I saw how they all listened with wary respect. Like a pack of dogs.

"Y'all need to remember the profit we stand to gain on these three. We already lost the mother. Mind there's no marks on the rest of the merchandise, fellas."

He adjusted his hat and, signaling with his chin for one of the men to follow him, rode off toward the east, away from the sun.

The rest of the men whooped and kicked their horses into a gallop. They ran across the dry brown land, the three of us helpless on the saddles. The wind obliterated the sound of our weeping and smeared our tears back into our hair. We raced through clouds of dust and headed toward the shadowed forest, where the world offered a hint of cool green. The horses thundered over a grassy knoll, travelling farther than my sisters and I had ever gone, their hooves pounding like thunder.

As we entered the closely knit trees of the forest, the animals were forced to slow and bunch together. The man who shared my saddle shoved aside branches that stung my skin. There were four horses ahead of me, and I could hear the others behind me, but I didn't turn to look. I didn't want to see the face of the man whose thighs pressed firmly against my skirt. Remnants of sunshine dappled the men's hats in front of me, then vanished as they disappeared into the shadows. The air cooled under the trees, but not enough to dry the sweat that rolled over my face and down my neck.

We rode for about an hour before the men stopped the horses in a small clearing. Spruce and ash trees had blocked the sunlight with their massive limbs, and the resultant bald ground beneath was black and hard, flecked with gray by the occasional rock and fallen twig. The man behind me swung off our horse and reached up to pull me down. My legs wobbled when my feet hit the dirt, and I grabbed the saddle to still the ground beneath me. He tugged me to the base of a balsam and forced me to sit. The tree's sap caught and smeared the back of my dress. It tugged at my hair. The man tossed a coil of rope upward until it looped over a branch. He pulled it until my bound wrists were suspended over my head.

"No, please," I begged through the gag, shaking my head wildly. "I won't run. I promise. Please, please—"

He said nothing, only checked to ensure the knot was tight. Then he turned and walked toward the other men.

Adelaide stood nearby, tied to a horse. Her eyes flickered around the clearing as if seeking a friendly face, but she didn't see me. A man came from behind and grabbed her by her arms, leading her to the opposite edge of the clearing. I could barely see her from where I sat.

Little Ruth sat alone on a horse. She sobbed and pulled against her restrained hands in disbelief, looking so much younger than her ten years. The man who now seemed to be in charge hoisted her over his shoulder and carried her into the trees, away from the clearing, far away from me. I heard her whimper, and a while later I heard a muffled scream, then I heard nothing more.

I slumped against the tree and hung my head, but the rope tightened around my wrists, yanking my arms straighter over my head. My fingers felt cold. My arms were so heavy I thought they might tear off at the wrists. I tried to twist my hands, to loosen the knot, but nothing moved. I stared at a tree across from me, trying to distract myself. Tears poured silently down my cheeks, blurring the lines of the forest.

The world is rich with scents and smells: the promise of supper, the sweet, musky smell of animals in a barn, the heady aroma of daisies blanketing a summer field. Around me the pines emitted a fresh tang, faintly reminiscent of our hearth fire. The pungent balsam at my back seemed strong enough to choke out any other smells. The ground where I sat had its own perfume: earthy, musty, solid as a grave. That smell will stay with me for the rest of my life.

I recognised another stink. My father had breathed the same fumes after each trip into town, brought them into our room on those nights he beat us without warning. Whisky. Amber liquid that burns men's throats and sets them free to follow their darkest natures. Whisky mixed with the sweat running down our captors' skin and mingled with each man's sour musk.

The men paced the clearing, then split into three groups. Three men walked toward me, chuckling amongst themselves, rubbing their hands together as if they were preparing to feast on a magnificent meal. In the end, the largest of the three stood before me: a bearded, middle-aged man, fumbling with his belt. His nostrils flared briefly as he straddled my skirt. I saw the hunger in his eyes, the lust moistening his lips. I could practically feel the tension in his fingers as he opened and closed his big fists in anticipation.

I shook my head, whimpering, trying so hard to convince him he was wrong without ever saying a word. *No, no, no,* I screamed silently. My arms burned, my wrists were rubbed so raw I thought the bone must be showing through. I couldn't feel my fingers anymore. Beneath my burning eyes, my nose throbbed, swollen and blocking my breathing. But all that pain paled against what I knew was coming.

I told myself it would be over soon.

I couldn't have been more wrong.

Over the span of a few unthinkable hours, those men changed everything. They climbed onto me, one after another, dulling my pain and revulsion until I no longer registered anything. A piece of me died on that hard ground beneath the sun-peppered trees, and I wished the rest of me would go as well. I stopped crying, stopped fighting, tried to stop breathing.

At one point during the day I noticed one young man with dirty blond hair, shifting from one foot to the other, standing slightly apart from the others. He seemed unsure of how he fit in, as if he watched the depraved group from somewhere inside himself. I wanted to cry out to him, but the gag had stolen my voice. I pleaded silently when he came to me, begged for pity, but my thoughts fell solidly, uselessly onto the ground between us. When he knelt on the dirt and entered my body, I looked up at him with a cold penetration of my own. Moisture glistened in the corners of his eyes for an instant, and then he closed them.

Someone had lit a fire, a pale orange flicker in the shifting sunshine. Its smoke curled and crept toward me like a curtain. I could neither see nor hear anything from my sisters. The silence terrified me most of all.

The smell of seared meat wove into the smoke, and my mouth automatically filled with saliva. Would they think to feed us? Would we ever eat again?

My wrists were still tied and suspended over my head. I no longer felt them. My nose had stopped bleeding sometime during the day, and the blood had hardened into a tight crust over my cheeks and lips. My tongue was dry and tasted like copper.

Nothing before that day had given me any reason to feel hatred. Now it pulsed through me, blackening my blood. I would remember these men. Their faces and features were burned into my brain. They would die and I would watch. I made it a promise to my mother, my sisters, and myself.

The peaks of evergreens loomed over me, their tips swaying with the breeze, bending toward and away from each other as if they were talking, whisky on their breath. Sleep came and went, ragged snatches of escape that blurred the line between reality and dreams. Fear melted to apathy, pain dulled to hopelessness, escape became an illusion.

The sun finally set and the men's voices rolled into snores around the dying campfire. Exhaustion consumed me and I slid into the relative safety of my mind—not asleep, but trying to find that place between sleeping and waking. I needed peace. Without peace I had no hope of dreaming. Without dreams I had no hope.

I lay on the hard ground, shivering and blinking at the stars. The shiny black eyes of a raven peered down at me from a branch overhead. Ravens. I have always seen ravens. In both my dreams and my waking hours they have been nearby, watching, voicing opinions in rolling squawks. This one perched silently above me, strangely awake in the night hour. It studied me closely, angling its head.

"Take me with you," I begged silently, then brought Wolf's face to my thoughts. *"Please, please find him. Find the wolf who is a man."*

The raven turned his glossy profile and seemed to consider the firelit faces of the sleeping men. After a final glance, the bird spread its wings and disappeared into the darkness.

I felt more alone in that moment than ever before in my life.

Gradually, I began to feel a warm pressure building in my chest, completely different from the ugly weight of being crushed beneath a man's body. And I knew Wolf had come, his gentle brown eyes bottomless with sorrow, nostrils flared, lips pursed tight. Without dreams, I had been unable to call to him. Now he saw my bruised, ragged body. His expression spoke of helpless fury.

"Help me," I whispered.

For a moment his eyes lost their focus, as if he heard something, as if he sensed the air around us both. Then something moved behind his eyes, and I felt the warmth of his fingertips brush my cheek.

"At the river," he murmured. That was the first time I had ever heard his voice. The words curled off his tongue, soothing as a touch. *"I will be at the river for ye."*

I turned my head, distracted by the sound of one of the men relieving himself in the woods near me. When I looked again, I lay alone, in my mind and on the ground. But now I could sleep. And I did. Without dreams.

CHAPTER 4

Damaged Goods

The morning brought no sunshine, only the ominous pressure of another sweltering day. Cicadas screeched from the trees. My cheeks were sticky with sweat before my eyes had opened.

Thirst was the first thing I felt. Thirst that felt like sand in my throat. Thirst that blocked the air when I tried to swallow. I struggled to sit, using my heels to push back against the tree. The skin of my face felt tight; sweat and filth pasted hair to my forehead and cheeks. My bloodied wrists hung lower, the rope having been tugged on repeatedly the day before. I was too weak to move them. At least the gag was gone.

They had moved Adelaide to a closer tree, so now I could see her. Her face was bruised almost beyond recognition, and smeared with dried blood. One of her eyes had been bashed into an ugly purple bruise. Like mine, her gag had been loosened during the night and hung like a thick necklace around her neck. Her hands were unbound and lay motionless at her sides. Her braids hung in tangles, matted with leaves and mud. In my memory I saw us as we had been the morning before, alone in our room while I wove those braids for her. They had been like cords of gold.

Of Ruth I saw no sign.

"Addy?" I called, but my voice was hoarse and too soft for her to hear. She made no sign that she heard anything.

Across the clearing the men were moving around, and I smelled the hint of coffee in their tin cups. My mouth flooded at the sweet smell of meat frying over the fire, temporarily easing my burning thirst. One of the men walked across the clearing near me, then bent to pluck something from the ground. My body began to shake. Seeing the men, smelling them, hearing their noises made my heart race. Would it start again once they'd finished their meals?

The sounds of hooves made everyone turn. A dark horse pushed through the leaves on the edge of the clearing, carrying the man in the blue shirt. The man's young cohort rode in behind him, astride a lighter-coloured horse. Blue Shirt swung off his saddle before his horse had completely stopped. He removed his hat and scratched his head, then jammed it back on and strode purposefully toward where I lay.

Not again, I thought, feeling tears sting my eyes. My body shook so violently I yanked involuntarily on my wrists. *Please, not again.*

I dragged myself as far away from him as I could, mewing, "No, no, no, no, no," but he grabbed my chin and lifted it, peering into my face. Without a word, he dropped it and headed toward Adelaide.

Adelaide whimpered when he did the same to her, raising her bruised face to his. Releasing her chin, he spun toward the men and growled like a dog, lips pulled back from his teeth. The men avoided his glare, but Blue Shirt's eyes found their mark. The short man to whom he had given instructions the day before shifted from foot to foot, staring at the ground. Blue Shirt glared down his nose at the shorter man.

"I said no marks, Leonard," Blue Shirt said through clenched teeth. Leonard's chin hung on his chest as if he were a small boy being disciplined. "I see marks, Leonard. I see big fuckin' bruises, Leonard. Those are marks folks don't wanna pay for. Tell me, Leonard, did I say to make marks? No, I'm pretty fuckin' sure I said no marks. Jimmah?" He turned to the man he had ridden in with and lifted his eyebrows. "What did I say about leavin' marks?"

"You said no marks, sir," the younger man assured him.

Blue Shirt made a sound of disgust in his throat, then paced between the other members of the gang, railing at them, shoving them out of his way.

"Where's the li'l 'un?" he demanded, and I stopped breathing, needing to hear.

Leonard lifted his chin and looked around, his eyes darting toward the wood. Blue Shirt strode back and grabbed Leonard's shirt front.

"The li'l 'un?" he growled, nose to nose with Leonard.

Leonard's eyes were wide, unblinking in the face of Blue Shirt's fury. He made a short grunting sound, then swallowed hard. His eyes flicked to the side, away from the men.

"Over there," he muttered.

Blue Shirt disappeared into the woods in search of Ruth. He didn't come back for what seemed to me a very long time. When he returned to the fire, his face pulsed a violent shade of purple. What had he seen? Where was Ruth? Panic bubbled up and stuck in my throat. Blue Shirt walked to Leonard, whose chin still drooped and, without hesitation, punched the side of Leonard's jaw. Leonard staggered sideways with the blow, then recovered his balance and spat to the side without looking up. He returned his chin to its earlier position. Blue Shirt spun the other way, throwing his arms in the air, kicking the dirt, swearing and yelling at each man in turn. I listened hard, but I couldn't make out any of his ranting.

Blue Shirt's eyes returned to my face, and he started walking toward me. I was pressed so tightly against the tree, there was nowhere for me to go. I sat, shaking, waiting. His eyes raked over me, taking in my bloodied dress, the finger-shaped bruises that coloured my arms and partially covered breasts, and finally my face. I blinked up at him, too tired, too resigned to bother looking away. He took off his hat again, scratched his head, and put it back on as he turned toward the other men.

"This one'll do," he said, then jerked a thumb toward Adelaide. "An' maybe the other one if you clean her good. But goddammit, boys!"

He spat on the ground by my feet then walked toward his horse, shaking his head. He threw himself into the saddle and turned the horse toward the path.

"Hurry up and git this all together. And Leonard," he growled, "take 'em to the river. I want 'em clean and ready. You got me?"

Before Leonard could respond, Blue Shirt gave his horse a hard heel. The animal reared back in surprise, then bolted into the woods. The younger man followed without a word.

Low-keyed grumbling and nervous laughter rippled through the group. A man with a jagged pink scar on his neck came toward me, and I squeezed my eyes shut. He grabbed my wrists and I cried out when he tugged me to my feet. He fumbled with my hands and I stared at him, dazed, not sure what he was doing. I felt the rope release and my hands fell to my sides. The blood that had been dammed by the ropes roared back into my limbs, ripping the vessels wide open, stabbing like thousands of needles. It burned and throbbed and from far away I heard myself sob. My knees wobbled and I leaned against the man's arm for support. He waited for me to regain my balance, then pushed me ahead of him, toward the tethered horses. I was tossed onto the saddle, and I gasped at the impact on my bruised and torn body.

"Drink," he grumbled, passing me a tin cup. The water smelled of sap, but I gulped it down.

"More?" I asked. He squinted at me, then stomped off toward the fire. He was back in a few minutes, cup in one hand, a chunk of charred meat in the other.

"Can't promise any more than this today," he said. "Enjoy it while you can." He thrust the food and cup toward me, then turned and walked back to the fire.

Camp was being packed up, the fire sizzling and smoking as the men extinguished it with their dregs of coffee. Adelaide was thrown onto another horse, where she sat as still as her deadened eyes. I slumped over the saddle, feeling nauseous, like something was churning in my gut. But the man had probably told the truth. I might not eat again all day. I watched the men work while I chewed on the tough piece of meat he'd given me.

The pink-scarred man swung his bulk onto the saddle behind me and clicked his tongue at the horse. We started moving slowly through the trees and my nausea got worse with every step, until I bent over and rested my forehead on the pommel.

Something was missing. Gone. One of the horses whinnied, restless. Its voice was high, like a child's. It made me think of Ruth, shrieking when we played tag, running wild through the goldenrod—

Ruth. My stomach dropped, my nausea frozen into a solid block of ice.

"My sister—" My voice strained through a throat torn by screams.

He grunted. I couldn't see his face, but one of his thumbs jerked toward Adelaide.

"No," I whispered, "my other sister."

"Oh," he drawled, "the li'l 'un."

He let out his breath in a low whistle. Then he tore what was left of my world to shreds.

"She's gone, sweetheart." He cleared his throat. "But we gave her a proper Christian burial."

My throat closed, crushed within a terrible fist. Fairy-like sparkles danced in front of my eyes, spinning faster and closer until I lurched toward the ground. I think the man jerked me upright and kept the horse moving, but in truth, I was unaware of anything around me. My mind filled with Ruth: her golden curls and trusting eyes, cherubic face and voice. She was gone, and I hadn't been able to say good-bye.

Air rushed unbidden into my lungs, and my senses returned in a flood of rage. Grief emptied my soul, and hatred gushed in. My fingers burned with the need to claw at the man behind me, to hurt, to kill. But even if I reached inside his chest and ripped out his still-beating heart, he wouldn't have died. How can you kill someone who has no soul?

CHAPTER 5

At the River

I knew where we were headed, and this knowledge helped me sit taller in the saddle.

Blue Shirt had said, "Take them to the river."

Wolf had said, "I will be at the river for ye."

Somewhere beyond the trees, the river waited. The horses plodded through rough deer trails, where there was no breeze, no soothing touch of coolness, only whining bugs who didn't mind sweat and dirt on their meal. My captor's chest pressed against my back and I could smell his shirt, drenched with sweat like the withers of our horse.

I wanted to sleep. The continuous steps lulled me, weighting my eyelids, but I forced them to stay open. We would reach the river soon. I wanted to be awake when we arrived.

"Matheson!" someone called from behind us.

My captor reined in and turned in his saddle.

"What?" he yelled.

"Get back here."

"Aw, come on, Richie. I got my hands full, don't I?"

"Come here, Matheson. And leave the girl there."

Matheson let out a resigned breath, glared at me, then grabbed my waist and dropped me to the ground. I landed with a thud on the earth. My hip struck a small rock, but after all I'd been through, I barely felt its edge.

"Don't move," he growled. I didn't argue. Where would I go? I could barely stand on my own. Besides, I could never leave Adelaide alone with these men.

Matheson turned his horse toward the others and stomped into the trees behind us, swearing under his breath. Finally alone, finally motionless, I fell asleep.

In my dreams I heard it first, then saw the hint of silver trickling through the trees, flowing downstream, as clear in my mind as it would be in reality. A wolf stood on the banks, tongue lolling from his muzzle, brown eyes searching for mine. When I looked again, the figure was no longer the animal, but the man. Wolf was almost camouflaged in a dark green wool that draped over his shoulder and around his waist. His eyes spoke of an aching sadness for me, but he offered a reassuring smile. There was hope ahead.

Then he was close enough to touch. He took my face in his hands as tenderly as one might hold a baby bird fallen from the nest, and the depth of that simple contact joined me to him. This was how we were, he and I. We touched, we saw, we understood, but we never shared the same air. I knew his hands held my face, and yet they weren't there.

His fingers traced the lines of my face, and his calloused thumbs touched the dark patches beneath my eyes, the bruises on my cheeks. Then his eyes shifted and he glanced behind me, concern momentarily hardening their depths. His nostrils flared as if he were a beast of the forest, scenting the breeze for threat. I felt no fear. Nothing could harm me as long as I felt his nearness. He narrowed his gaze, then his face relaxed. He recognised whatever, or whoever, was approaching. When his eyes returned to mine, they were smiling. Tiny specks of gold floated in their depths, winking in the sunlight.

My captor's hands jerked me from my dream and hoisted me back into the saddle. Wolf was gone. I glanced behind me as the horses began to walk again, searching for Adelaide. Her limp body was still propped up against one of the men. She must still be alive. They wouldn't have bothered carrying her body otherwise.

I knew when we were close to the river. I could hear the liquid wall of sound. The forest thrived closer to the riverside, thick with saplings that reached through the decaying remains of their elders. The sticky musk of pine clogged the air. Birds flicked from branch to branch, and I caught the flicker of a red squirrel's tail as he leaped from one tree to the next, always one step ahead of our group.

We entered a clearing, a rough circle edged by pines and boulders. The cool, clear breeze from the river cut through the heat and I breathed it in, feeling my heart quicken. The river. Wolf would be here.

The men slid from their saddles, groaning as their boots hit the dirt. They tugged the horses' reins toward the water, but the animals needed no encouragement. They ambled into the shallow river, with Adelaide and me still on their backs, and splashed relief onto their bellies. The spray tickled my feet, and goose bumps lifted the hairs on my body. The men pulled off their boots and stood knee-deep in the current, bathing their feet. They plunged their hands into the water, drank deeply, and splashed their grimy faces.

My throat was dry as dust. I thought perhaps my nose had been broken back at our house. I was having a lot of trouble breathing through it. Sweat tickled between my breasts and down my back.

Leonard and another man finally pulled Adelaide and me from the saddles and carried us to the shore. They stood Adelaide up, but her legs collapsed and she dropped like a stone without uttering a sound. I don't think Adelaide was aware she had fallen. Her eyes stared at nothing, as if her mind had been abandoned along with our little sister.

Leonard caught my eye and gestured toward the stream. "Go wash up," was all he said.

I hobbled back to the river, braced myself, then dropped into the freezing water. The level was high enough to cool the undersides of my breasts, barely hidden within my torn dress. I splashed water over my face and body, rinsing mud and tears from my face and filth from beneath the remains of my skirt.

Adelaide lay motionless at the edge of the water. Her face was horribly swollen, and her body was painted with thick strokes of blood and dirt. I forced myself to stand and shuffled through the river toward her, careful on the slippery pebbles beneath my feet. I lay beside her on the rocky shore and rolled onto my side to face her. She didn't even blink. I pulled her head against my chest, holding her there when her body jerked instinctively away. She shrieked and flailed in blind panic, but I hugged her close so my mouth was at her ear.

"It's me, Addy. Shh. It's Maggie."

I repeated myself over and over, rocking her against me until her sobs lessened into hiccups. Then I laid her back on the rocky shore and sat up.

"I need to clean you, Addy. I'll go slow. I promise."

I tore a strip from my wet skirt and gently dabbed at her purpled face, wanting to see the blue of her eyes. We were close enough to the water I could dip the rag in to rinse it. I squeezed out the dirt and the water bloomed with rusty clouds. I rinsed the cloth again and again until I finally saw the pale pink of her cheek. The length of her neck was blotched with bruises. One of her eyes was swelled shut.

The other eye watched me closely. A single tear rose to its surface and rolled down her cheek, disappearing into the pillow of stones under her head. I put my hand behind her neck and raised her just enough that she could swallow the water I cupped in my hand. It trickled through her lips, and her tongue slipped forward to greet it. After a while, she began to make small whimpering noises, but no words.

"Shhh, Addy," I whispered. "It's almost over. They're taking us somewhere, and we'll be done with them."

Her eye blinked.

"It's true," I said, trying to convince us both. "They said we need to clean up before they take us to wherever we're going. Someone will help us there."

She sighed and closed her eye.

"Sleep, Addy," I whispered. "I'm going to clean you while you sleep. You'll feel better when you wake up."

I didn't think she could sleep, but at least she relaxed under my hand. The rag stroked her neck, her shoulders, the soft skin of breasts and belly. I lifted her skirt discreetly and moved the cloth over her bruised thighs and the place where they met.

Exhausted as I was, I couldn't stop cleaning her. I forced myself to move slowly and keep my hands gentle, fought the urge to scrub her entire body, to clean away everything they had done to her. But she would never be truly clean. There was nothing anyone could do to purge her deeper scars.

I wondered if she knew about Ruth. How could I tell her? Not now. Not until she was more aware of herself and everything else that had happened. The thought of our baby sister made me dizzy, and I breathed in deeply, trying to clear my thoughts. I needed to be strong, to take care of us both. I couldn't allow emotion to distract me.

I could grieve later.

The men led the horses from the water and tied them to the nearby trees, then lit a fire on the other side of the clearing. I smelled smoke and tried to remember what comfort a fire was supposed to bring.

A while later, Blue Shirt rode into the clearing. He dismounted, grunted at the others, then walked toward Adelaide and me. He stopped a stone's throw away and stooped to examine the hoof of a gray mare who stood dozing a few feet from us. The horse didn't move when he picked at it and removed a stone. Apparently satisfied, he dropped the hoof and slapped her neck affectionately. He glanced our way, then turned back toward the other men.

That was when one of his fellows made a noise like a crow, grabbed his throat, and fell face first into the fire. The men were suddenly on their feet, pistols aimed into the forest, eyes searching the shadows. A short *thwick* came from the trees and another man fell, clutching at his belly and howling in agony. The throat of a third man was pierced by an arrow and he collapsed, hitting the earth with a dull thud. The clearing filled with men's screams and the hissing of arrows.

I watched with dread as a moving wall of dark-haired men advanced into the clearing. Their faces were painted in black stripes, their hands swung axes and knives. Over their shoulders hung the fragile curves of bows. The shrieking noises they made sounded wild, like the forest around them. Indians.

The horses near us stamped and snorted, yanking at the ropes. The gray mare tossed her head and Blue Shirt, eyes wide, sprung up from behind her. He lunged toward me, grabbing my arms and wrapping his rough sleeve around my neck.

I made a garbled sound of protest, but his arm was tight. His voice was scratchy in my ear. "Godammit," he muttered. "I ain't leavin' empty-handed."

He dragged me backwards into the trees, barking at me to be quiet. Adelaide still lay on the riverside, her open eye wide and liquid. I couldn't let him separate us. I kicked at his shins and dug my shredded nails into his arms. The sound of thunking axes and dying men drove Blue Shirt forward and he tossed me, sack-like, over his shoulder. Adelaide disappeared from my view. The momentum knocked his hat off, and I saw he was mostly bald, save for a ring of curly red and silver hairs. He stumbled through the trees, swerving in and out of branches, following the winding path of the stream while I bumped against his back. I lifted my head to see what was happening, but the brush blinded me.

I could hear, though. The air was alive with death.

As much as I feared and hated our captors, I had been brought up to fear Indians more. The stories were always the same: Indians killed and tortured white people for entertainment. They dined upon their victims' still-beating hearts. Indians were barbarians, barely more human than the animals with which they shared the forest. For those reasons I didn't struggle as Blue Shirt carried me away. At least I understood this man and had some vague hope of survival with him.

Eventually he stopped running and dumped me onto the ground. His pock-scarred face was streaked with sweat, his shirt a patchy blue. His hands shook, either from exertion or fear, and he panted so loudly I was sure the Indians would hear us. He staggered ten feet to the river's edge, where he crouched and plunged his hands into the water, splashing his face and body. My mouth was so dry my tongue felt swollen. I longed to taste the water, but could barely move my legs. I closed my eyes and breathed deeply, trying to ignore the thirst.

Then something in the air changed. My legs, my tongue, the water—nothing mattered. It all disappeared with the realisation that Wolf was there, waiting for me. I opened my eyes and saw him standing halfway between Blue Shirt and me, more lucent than solid in the sunlight. His hair was tied back into a tail, exposing his cheekbones and his mouth, which was set in a tight line. He tilted his head, motioning me closer. I hadn't been able to stand before. Now rising to my feet felt effortless, and I felt no pain. He filled me with his strength, and my fear melted into relief.

I glanced toward the river's edge, where Blue Shirt had collapsed onto his back, eyes closed, chest rising and falling in quick breaths. One of his hands dipped into the current, soaking one sleeve to the elbow. I could see the sweat on his cheeks, the lines of strain cutting across his forehead. Pale, almost invisible lashes rested on his cheeks.

I stepped toward Wolf, walking easily, as if he held my hand. In fact, his hand was open, gesturing toward a large boulder beside him. On its surface lay a broad hunting knife, long forgotten by an anonymous hunter. Time had whitened its handle, rust had dotted its blade, but it was still sharp. When the breeze stirred the leaves overhead, the knife's edge glinted in the sun, winking with encouragement.

The knife offered both escape and vengeance. But at what price? I had never killed anyone—nothing beyond the small creatures we hunted for food. Could I do it? Could I kill this man whose band had ended the lives of both my mother and my sister? Who had left Adelaide and me forever scarred? I glanced toward Wolf, questions in my eyes, and he nodded. Yes, he thought I could. He pressed his lips tightly together, then gestured toward the knife again. I reached toward it and closed my fingers around the smooth wooden handle, staring at it with uncertainty. Wolf's hands folded over mine, curling around my fingers, reassuring. I felt a sense of both losing myself and finding a strength I never knew existed.

I could tell Blue Shirt didn't see or hear me approach. If he had, he would have leaped to his feet and grabbed me. But he still battled for breath, still closed his eyes to the sun. He never saw the knife. In one swift motion I drew the blade deep across his exposed neck, pressing hard, allowing no room for error. Blood arced from a severed artery, shooting two feet away, and Blue Shirt's eyes flew open in disbelief. His hands jerked to his ruined neck, one arm springing from the river, trailing a sparkling curtain of droplets in its rush. The wound widened swiftly, filling with blood. His breaths bubbled through the chasm in his neck. The dark red blood overflowed, looking almost black as it soaked into the faded blue fibres of his shirt.

I backed a few feet away and squatted, watching him die, feeling a sort of detached fascination. Death didn't take long. His hand splashed back into the water and began to ride the endless ripples, darkening the current with the liquid remains of his life.

I inhaled a combination of smells: the metallic tang of blood, the sweet, soothing breath of surrounding pines, and the lingering scent of his panic. I held my breath, stretching my lungs until the ground beneath me wobbled. Every one of my muscles began to tremble at the shock of having killed a man.

But while my body reacted, my mind felt nothing. No regret, no disgust, no horror. Nothing except perhaps a vague pulse of satisfaction. One day had changed everything about the person who had been me. Because of him, I had killed. Because of me, my life continued. Any evidence of this was stiffening on the grass beneath his neck.

The wolf stood before me now, watching. I dug my fingers into the fur on his cheeks and gazed into his dark eyes, flecked with gold. I closed my eyes and let him go, then summoned the faces of my mother and baby sister.

"They're gone," I whispered into the breeze.

I had to find Adelaide. The last time I had seen her, she was lying helpless by the shore. I turned toward the trees, holding the knife tightly against my body and trying to find the vague path Blue Shirt had followed. When I lost my way among thorny clumps of brush, I stopped and strained my ears for direction. That was when a raven sang out, calling me.

I followed the bird's voice without question, and it led me to the remains of the camp. I squatted behind a bush, listening to men talking in a strange, singsong language. I barely recognised the camp. The bodies of our captors lay scattered and motionless, blood-streaked in their filthy shirts. Indians had taken their place and were busy retrieving arrows and wandering the site.

The courage that had carried the knife to Blue Shirt's throat deserted me, though I still held the weapon. Adelaide lay on the other side of the bush, but I couldn't call to her for fear of being heard. She seemed untouched, though in plain view of the Indians. I wanted to pull her away, drag her somewhere safe. I gripped my knife tighter and looked for a possible break in the bushes. Getting to her was going to be difficult. I tried to see a way around the Indians, but they seemed intertwined with the trees.

Large hands grabbed my arms from behind, and I swallowed a shriek. The hands forced me to stand, urged me ahead, and sat me firmly on the ground beside my sister.

I looked up into the face of an Indian and my stomach dropped, weighted by fear. He returned my gaze, wearing an expression of calm interest. Strong cheekbones framed a full mouth, and he had deep, dark eyes. His skin wasn't red as we had been taught, but a kind of dark honey brown. He motioned with his hands that I should stay where I was and uttered some short words I couldn't understand. He left us there and walked toward the fire, where the others had gathered. They glanced toward us, their expressions attentive, but not threatening. I took Adelaide's cold hand in mine and she gave me a weak squeeze.

The sun slid farther to the west, dipping fingers of light through the tangled branches as it passed. The Indians didn't try to move us. Instead, they built a small shelter over us using animal pelts, and brought us water to drink.

A while later, two women arrived at the camp and knelt beside Adelaide and me. Their hair was drawn from their weathered faces, braided into cords of black and silver that hung down the backs of their deerskin tunics. They leaned in, examining our wounds with a gentle but frank approach. One of the women looked into my sister's swollen eye, lifting the lid as gently as if it were a butterfly's wing. Adelaide looked back into the woman's eyes, and tears began to flow down her bruised cheeks.

The women brought out balms and herbs from small leather bags at their waists and tended our wounds with infinite care. The ointment was soothing, as were the reassuring caresses of their fingers. So were their jumbled words, tripping through my head like a child's rhyme. Between sips of tea, the women spooned a kind of porridge into our mouths that warmed our bodies and filled our stomachs. When they were done, they smiled, touched us gently, then left.

I rolled onto my side so I faced Adelaide's profile. Her eyes were closed, but I could tell from her breathing she was awake. I needed to speak with her, to talk about what had happened. She and I had shared a bed for so many years I knew she could sense the questions spinning through my mind.

"Sleep, Maggie. We'll be all right now," she whispered. The words sighed through her swollen lips, whistling in my ears like a song.

Hours later I awoke and shivered. Darkness was settling over the clearing, bringing with it the first cooling breaths of air. Adelaide slept beside me, her long lashes resting on her cheeks, small tangles of hair lifting with the breeze. The shadows camouflaged most of her bruises and cuts, leaving only the image of an innocent, sleeping child. The picture was a lie. Her innocence was gone.

And our mother was gone.

And somewhere in the forest, in a nameless grave, was the body of our baby sister, destroyed and abandoned.

I had no more tears. I closed my eyes and burned the impression of Ruth's sweet face into my heart.

"Don't forget me," she whispered.

"That would be impossible," I assured her, smiling weakly at the thought.

That had been Ruth's gift: the way she could coax a smile from even the bitterest person. I thought of how she had once brought me a broken bird, trusting me to fix the damage. She had wept for its tiny soul when I explained I couldn't save the creature. I remembered so many things and let the memories trickle like a river through my mind. How she laughed, how she sang, how she danced. Her murderers were dead, but their lives could never be equal payment for hers. They were nothing. Ruth was everything.

I looked up as the leaves near my head crackled under the feet of an Indian woman, about the same age as I was. She smiled and sat beside me, then smoothed the hair back from my forehead as if I were a child. She hummed a strange lullaby, and the forest voices of early evening joined her. I thought I heard Ruth's sweet voice singing among them, but couldn't be sure. I closed my eyes and let the music rock me to sleep.

PART 2: ANDREW

The Search

CHAPTER 6

Childhood Dreams

Sunny days like this were rare in the Highlands, and the beckoning warmth made indoor work almost unbearable for a twelve-year-old boy. The air inside Invergarry Castle's stable was hot and sticky, something that didn't often bother him. Usually the weather was so cold it wasn't a problem. Today, though, he couldn't help wondering why the builders hadn't had a tiny thought for the poor stable boys. After all, it was 1738. Over the past hundred years, they'd already rebuilt the place twice after the English had taken it apart.

Andrew's mouth was dry from working in the dust, and the midges were biting terribly, buzzing over his head in clouds as he cleaned the stalls, lighting on his neck and cheeks. He considered running to the other side of the castle when he was done, just so he could climb down the rocky shelves and jump into the freezing, bottomless waters of Loch Lomond. Then he remembered he had other plans.

He finished mucking out the last stall, then tossed in fresh straw with a pitchfork taller than he was. A chestnut mare lolled against the wall on three legs, waiting for him to finish.

"That's better then, is it?" Andrew asked her. "Certainly smells better."

He spread the new layer of straw across the floor, then leaned his flat wooden shovel against the wall, finished at last. Reaching his arms over his head, Andrew stretched onto his toes until he heard his back pop. He always waited for that sound after a day working in his uncle's stables. It was like a confirmation that he'd worked hard. Like his da did. Like his brother, Dougal, did.

Andrew took a step toward the horse, and put out an empty palm. She filled it with her velvet muzzle.

"That's it for today, Macalla," he said, petting her smooth copper neck. "I'll be in to see ye in the morn. Sleep well." He picked up his shovel and left the stall, careful to close the latch behind him.

The other stable boys were already outside, playing in the sunshine. Andrew caught a ball one-handed, then tossed it back, grinning.

One of the boys called out, "Come on, MacDonnell. We're going fishing."

Andrew shook his head, leaving his shovel with the other tools by the door. He could imagine the stream by his house, sparkling with sunlight, the trout rising like bubbles to the bait. It would be a fine day to fish. But not for him. He was tired. He'd been up most of the night, his sleep broken by dreams.

He always dreamed, but some nights the dreams were more vivid than others. This time he'd seen the girl again. She was in a meadow, her long brown hair falling in a veil over her face as she reached down and plucked a handful of wildflowers. When she rose, he could see how she was growing, how the oft-mended dress she wore was beginning to pull tighter around her chest and hips, though she was still slender. As if she could feel his gaze, she glanced at him and smiled. It was a gentle smile of contentment, and he wished he could have taken the flowers she held out for him. He'd seen her in his dreams for as long as he could remember, felt as if he knew her, but he'd never seen her as clearly as he had that night.

"I've things to do," he called to the boys, thinking only that he wanted to lie in the heather and catch up on his sleep. "Tomorrow, aye?"

The boys nodded and ran off, cheerfully tossing insults back and forth between them. Andrew turned in the other direction, knowing exactly where he wanted to go. He'd gone there before, when he'd wanted to be alone. Beyond the castle wall, down the windy slope, then past a jagged wall of rocks. Once he'd scrabbled over them, he found himself in a clearing and stepped into waist-high grass, dotted with small patches of heather. It was a beautiful place, alive with butterflies.

In the centre of the meadow Andrew sank into purple blooms, sitting so the flowers were even with the top of his cap. He felt safe, hidden away from prying eyes. With a sigh, he lay back, linking his fingers behind his head for a pillow.

The sky was so blue Andrew didn't want to close his eyes. A solitary cloud puffed into view, wispy and disintegrating as he watched. He wondered what it might feel like to touch it. Would it be soft to sleep in? Would it be warm? He blinked, then let his heavy eyelids close, still seeing the sun's red glow. He rolled to his side and curled into a ball. The soft, sweet scent of heather tickled his nose, and he fell asleep.

His rest wasn't deep. It rose and fell with the motion of his dreams. The girl materialised while he slept, one moment distant, the next an arm's length away.

"Who are you?" he asked, wondering if she could hear him. The girl said nothing, only curled her lips into a smile. A little girl's smile, like that of any other little girl he'd ever seen. Except this one was only for Andrew, and he knew it. He grinned back, and his hand felt warm, as if she'd entwined her fingers with his. In the way that dreams are, they walked through the meadow, though it wasn't thick with heather anymore. She led him through a place where there were no purple blooms, only sun-baked yellow grass.

The sound of a bird calling from nearby startled him awake and he sat up, rubbing his fists over his eyes. How long had he slept? Maybe an hour? The sun hadn't moved far. Long enough that he felt refreshed. He always felt more energised after he'd seen her. He pushed to his feet, suddenly hungry, and waded out of the meadow, disappearing into the trees on his way home. The dream had ended, but he held her face in his memory. He carried her smile along the path to his home, kicked pebbles aside and hopped over sprawling oak roots. Who was she? Did it matter? She was his secret, and that was the most important thing.

He stopped in the path and slid off a shoe, shaking out a tiny pebble. A rustling in the bushes had him turning to check, but there was nothing there. He slid the shoe back on, wiggled his foot to make sure it was all cleaned out, then resumed his walk toward home and supper.

Sometimes he wished he could talk with his mother about the girl. But he thought she might laugh, or one of his brothers might overhear. So he kept his dreams private.

Just as Andrew stepped from the trees onto the field where his family's cows grazed, he heard a terrifying roar. He spun toward the sound, but a solid weight bowled him over before he could defend himself. His back hit the ground with a thump that knocked all the wind out of his lungs, and he shoved his hands up, reaching for his attacker's throat. The man was strong, anchoring Andrew's shoulders with big hands. Andrew knew those hands, knew the chuckle that came with them. He glared up at the victorious expression on his big brother's face and combed through his memories, looking for possible escape techniques that had worked before.

"Daydreamin', were ye?" his brother Dougal asked. He was on his hands and knees over Andrew, bright blue eyes sparkling.

Andrew managed to hook an ankle behind Dougal's leg. He yanked to the side, forcing Dougal flat onto the ground with him. The cows didn't pause in their chewing, but stepped to a safer distance and stared at the boys. Andrew socked Dougal in the head, making Dougal howl, then hoot with laughter. The brothers rolled on top of each other, over and under, yelping like oversized puppies. Tired at last, they collapsed beside each other, laughing and breathing hard.

"I got ye fair an' square," Dougal said, swiping the back of his hand across his sweaty forehead. Andrew noticed a hint of a beard starting on Dougal's chin and felt a pang of jealousy. Well, Dougal was fourteen, he told himself. Time enough for Andrew's own beard to come in.

Andrew frowned at the sky and gave Dougal a low grunt of assent. "Willna happen again," he muttered.

Dougal laughed. "Oh aye, it will. Race ye home?"

Dougal was on his feet running before Andrew had risen to his. He chased gamely after his brother, shouting insults and threats. Dougal's laughter rolled back over his shoulders, along with the long black tail of his hair.

Their mother was sweeping outside the front door when her two eldest arrived, covered head to toe in mud and cow patties. She eyed them with disapproval.

" 'Tis a good thing tomorrow's wash day. For it'll be the two of ye that'll wash these filthy rags, ye wee rascals," she said, sweeping a large beetle out of her way.

"O' course, Mother," Dougal said, still grinning. He leaned in and kissed the little woman, whose smile fought to emerge. Both of her older sons were already taller than she was. She tended to stand closer to their ten-year-old brother, Ciaran, because, she told the family, Ciaran still made her feel tall. Dougal gave her a hug. "Andrew would be pleased to do the wash tomorrow, Mother, all on his own."

"Hey!" Andrew objected, then shook his head when Dougal winked at him.

"You lot stink!" said a young voice, coming around the side of the cottage.

Ciaran and the boys' father, Duncan, emerged, looking well pleased with themselves. They had been hunting, and their father's hand rested on his youngest son's shoulder. A brightly plumed pheasant hung from Ciaran's grasp, almost as tall as the boy.

"See what yon Ciaran's brought for supper while you two were busy doin' naught?" their father said.

"A fine catch," Dougal said, nodding.

Ciaran's grin was huge. "The wee bugger never heard me coming."

"Pheasant will be lovely for this eve, son," their mother said, reaching over and ruffling Ciaran's hair. His blue eyes twinkled with pride.

The family ate when it was still light out so they wouldn't have to waste too many candles. Afterwards their mother brought out books. Duncan taught the boys the way of the woods: hunting, trapping, and how to survive should the need ever arise. He taught them swordplay and how to handle the dirk that was always in their belts. Their mother taught them reading and writing, as well as basic arithmetic and history, using whatever books she could find. Not all the boys at the castle could read, and Andrew was proud that he could. He liked when the other lads came to him asking for help, asking him to read this or that.

Ciaran was the best pupil. Andrew's parents had plans for all of them, but Ciaran offered the most promise. His understanding of numbers amazed Andrew, though he would never admit that. Dougal, on the other hand, had little interest in his mother's lessons. He learned the basics. At the slightest hint that studies might be over for the day, Dougal ran outside to be with his father.

The brothers' strengths and interests varied little over the months and years, though Dougal began paying more attention to the lassies than he had before. The lessons intensified as the boys grew, in particular those lessons of their father, since the bodies of boys were swiftly being replaced by those of men.

A couple of years later, Duncan showed his sons the proof of how much their parents believed in them. He took them to the fireplace built into the stone wall of their house, traced his thick fingers around the chipped mortar, and showed them a hidden cache. He reached inside and pulled out a leather sack, then shook the contents into his hand. The boys had never seen coins before. They stared, captivated by the thought of anything that existed outside of these woods.

"My sons, one day ye will make me proud," Duncan told them. The boys stood tall, shoulders back, staring at him. "Ye will make yer way in the world and tell all ye meet ye are MacDonnells from Invergarry, sons of Duncan, nephews of Iain. Ye will become men of education as well as warriors." Duncan turned and his wife curled under his arm, smiling broadly. "No one has lads like ours, do they? Lads with brain an' brawn, more than they need."

The boys looked at each other, unsure of what to say. As usual, Dougal broke the silence. He nodded. "Aye, Da. I am a man to be reckoned with. But these two? I'm afraid ye might have made a wee mistake—"

Andrew's open palm smacked his brother's head and Dougal grinned. Their father, still holding the small sack in his hands, gave his boys a wry smile. He knelt to put the money back in its safe haven, and Andrew watched it disappear.

"Ye will have a future, each of ye," Duncan said. "Should ye be in need, ye will have this."

Duncan slid the stone back into its slot and wiped his hand over the surface of the wall as if to erase any evidence of its location.

The future, Andrew thought. If his life could continue as it always had, living in the woods with his family and friends, riding horses, fishing, hunting, he would be content. But he didn't think it would. He still had dreams he never told anyone about. Sometimes he saw the girl in those dreams, but other times he saw much darker images. He smelled smoke and heard the clashing sounds of battle. When he woke some mornings, he thought he could feel wounds burning in his arms and legs. Just like the girl, they seemed too real to be mere figments of his imagination.

There was a strange old hag in the next village who claimed to dream of the future. Andrew had seen her twice and looked away with something akin to disgust each time. The woman was filthy, and the one time he came close enough, he could almost see her skin move with lice. Her hands were partially covered by fingerless gloves, her sunken chest layered with strange beaded necklaces, and she smelled like rotten meat. Her ridiculous gray hair billowed out like a sail under her kertch, and her back arched in such a curve her knobbly knuckles nearly touched her ankles.

Andrew didn't know if she really could see things that were to come. On the other hand, he thought he could. He had never seen much proof, other than he always seemed to know where lost things could be found or where game was waiting to be hunted. But a few times he had warned his mother not to hang the washing because he knew it would rain. He found a lost calf that had wandered through his dreams the night before. Andrew said nothing about any of it. He didn't want his brothers—or anyone else—to link him in any way with that horrible old woman.

As Andrew grew, so did the detail in his dreams. Over the next four years he began to catch glimpses of events farther in the distance. The visions he had of the girl lasted longer, became more clear.

A great clan Gathering by Invergarry Castle took place the autumn Andrew turned sixteen. He and his brothers had never seen so many people in all of their lives. Over a hundred Highland families came together, a few billeted in the castle, most living in tents that dotted the side of a nearby mountain. Dougal took to the crowds like a duck to water, introducing himself to everyone, flirting shamelessly with every woman he met, singing at campfires of strangers he made into friends. Ciaran, fourteen, also wandered, meeting people with interests similar to his own. Andrew wasn't as quick to leave his family's fire. Not because he was timid, but because he preferred watching people, observing their lives from a distance.

And because he found if he sat quietly enough, breathing in the cool night air and letting the muted sounds of humanity wash over him, he could sometimes see the girl. She would stay with him, touching without contact, speaking without words, her little girl's face and body beginning to mature into those of a beautiful young woman.

The final night of the Gathering was a glorious evening, with dancing, singing, and games that set the group's strong men in competition. Andrew spent the day with Dougal, and as a result found himself constantly surrounded by women. Neither could be considered to be a boy anymore. Both boys were broad-shouldered and handsome, exuding masculinity and charm. They were young men now, well on their way to becoming warriors like their father. Intelligence sparkled in their eyes, and laughter was easy for them both. Matchmaking was not rare at Gatherings, Andrew discovered, but he avoided those entanglements. It wasn't that he didn't enjoy lassies. He stole a kiss or two over the few days, but he had no wish to become part of anything more permanent.

"I am only six an' ten," he reminded his mother, who broached the subject after another mother came to her, canvassing for her daughter.

"Ye'll no' be six an' ten forever, my lad. An' then ye'll wish ye'd a lass to tend ye. I'll no' be here forever."

"I'll be fine. An' I'll be young for a while yet. Plenty of time," he assured her.

Her brown eyes, so like his, softened and she shook her head, touching his cheek with her calloused fingertips. "No, Andrew. Ye dinna have all the time ye think. Ye grow so fast I barely see my bairn in ye anymore. Ye're a man. An' a good man at that." She pulled him to her and held him as if he were much younger.

On the final night of the Gathering, Andrew and his mother sat by their fire, watching the harvest moon. It rose from behind the castle and spilled its orange reflection over the southern tip of Loch Ness, giving an eerie sense of daytime to the night. Time for the Scots to return to their farms, to reap what they could before winter.

A small torch appeared out of the woods twenty feet away from where Andrew sat, and his mother placed her hand on his arm, holding him still. Her face bore a broad smile, and her eyes danced with the firelight.

"Watch, lad. 'Twill be many a year afore this happens again."

"Before what happens?" he asked.

"Hush, son," she said. "Watch."

One by one, the clan chiefs emerged from cover of the trees, lighting the mountain with their fires. Andrew watched, spellbound, silent as the rest of the observers. The first voice came from a man down the mountain, and it sent chills racing down Andrew's spine.

"The MacCallums are here!" called the man, and all eyes shifted to see his profile, lit by the torch he held. A loud cheer roared from below, spirited cries for "MacCallum!"

"The Gunns are here!" called another, and his clan thundered their approval.

"The Camerons are here!"

"The MacLeods are here!"

The voices of the chiefs boomed across the mountain, answered each time by their clansmen. Andrew's skin prickled as he waited for his Uncle Iain to appear.

Then he saw him, standing on the edge of the trees, twenty feet from Andrew's fire. Iain MacDonnell was a large man. Dressed in his best kilt and bonnet, his sword shining silver under the moon, he was an impressive sight. He stood quietly, waiting for the MacLeods to finish cheering. His torch lit the dark lines of his face and flickered over a silver brooch that fastened his plaid over his shoulder.

"The MacDonnells are here!"

The power in his uncle's voice resonated through Andrew. He had heard the man speak many times, but this was something new. It filled Andrew with pride. He thought he understood what his mother meant. He was a boy no more. The heart of a man beat within his chest.

CHAPTER 7

The Battle Lost and Won

Three years later, at the age of nineteen, Andrew set out with his brothers on their way to war, along with their father and the rest of the Jacobite army. Prince Charles Stuart was intent on enforcing his claim to the British crown, as the direct heir to the last Stuart king, his grandfather, James II. The MacDonnells were loyal to the cause, as always. Andrew, Dougal, and Ciaran walked with the other younger men—the youngest being no older than twelve—heads held high, trying to contain their eagerness lest it be taken for childish enthusiasm.

This was real. This was war. This was honour, bravery, and skill. This was where all their childhood practice with wooden swords would be put to use, fighting alongside seasoned warriors, led by their uncle and chief, Iain MacDonnell.

There *was* honour, bravery, and skill in battle. But as Andrew discovered, there were also miles and miles of trekking on hard ground. There was waiting, so much waiting, while Iain MacDonnell and the other chiefs discussed strategy.

Some of their earliest encounters with the English army had been almost comical. The Highlanders fought as they always had, roaring in Gaelic as they plunged down hills toward the waiting troops, swinging thick-bladed swords and axes as they came. These were mountain men, unaccustomed to regular bathing routines, indifferent to shaving or trimming their unruly heads of hair. They wore nothing but their plaids and their weapons, and many of the Highlanders simply discarded the plaids, finding them too cumbersome. As a result, the English were presented with the sight of thousands of hairy, naked beasts converging on them from the trees, screaming foreign curses, the whites of their eyes vivid from across the battlefield. The English, unprepared for this type of confrontation, got into the habit of turning and running from this maniacal tide.

Without an English army to contest the Scots, there were very few true confrontations until they reached Prestonpans in September 1745. That was Andrew's first experience with battle. He stood beside Dougal, exhilarated, almost trembling with anticipation. When at last the call for the charge came, the Scots were a seething beehive, waiting only for their release. The English stood their ground, but were no match for the Highlanders.

Andrew felt his knees churning beneath him, felt his feet hit the ground as he ran with the others, but his mind felt numb. He didn't know if it was fear, or simply how one felt on a battlefield, but it was as if he watched from somewhere beyond, witnessing the furious wave of tartan as it engulfed the red jackets of the English. Shots rang out and men on both sides fell, their screams jerking Andrew to the present. He focused on the soldiers around him, fighting back to back with Dougal, swinging his sword in one hand, dirk in the other. They were big men, good fighters, and both relied on the other's strengths.

Andrew was always one stroke ahead of the oncoming soldiers. Ever since childhood, he had known what was coming just before it did. It was like his dreams. The images were a physical pressure against his skull—not painful, but reassuring. As if he pressed his hand against his brow in concentration. His sword moved: block, block, slash, then a heavy thrust with his dirk and men fell dead at his feet.

Battles rarely went on for more than a half hour or so, after which time there was an opportunity for both sides to collect their dead and dying. Andrew, strong and energised by the conflict, helped carry the injured from the field to the surgeon's tent. But beneath the external strength, in a place so deep he could almost ignore it, Andrew's soul convulsed. He tried to ignore the way his feet slid on the gore. He blocked the fact that the smoky air he breathed stank of burnt flesh and hair. He shut his ears to the agonised cries of men and did what he had to do.

Ciaran sat at the side of the field, head in his hands. Andrew went to him and they sat in silence together, trying to erase the sights they would never forget.

After Prestonpans, the Highlanders waited for someone to make a decision as to what to do next. Many became restless and returned home to their families, unwilling to wait for Prince Charles's Scottish Council in Edinburgh to decide whether or not to invade England. Week after week, Andrew's father listened to rumours of the debates in the Scottish Council, and reported back to his sons. There was money coming from France, they were told. Thousands of new recruits were ready to join the Jacobite army along the way.

After six weeks, the Council, by a narrow margin, decided to strike south. They marched despite the fact the money never materialised. Their ammunition stocks fell miserably, as did their spirits. The chiefs argued among themselves, and not only did the new recruits fail to show, but more and more Highlanders left and headed home. Winter was moving in as they entered Derby, three days' march from London. The capital city was strongly guarded, and two English armies were fast converging on them. It had been the wrong decision.

The Jacobites had no choice. They turned back.

Andrew was relieved to be headed home, but was also slightly disappointed. They had been so close—imagine the Highlanders conquering London! But the men were exhausted. They stopped in at small cottages along the way, asking for food, but the people of the land were already going hungry.

The Jacobites marched north as far and as fast as they could. But on April 17, 1746, they could go no farther. Andrew, his father, and his brothers waited at Culloden Moor, near Inverness, with over thirty-five hundred shivering clansmen. The Highlanders huddled in the miserable bog at the edge of the field, waiting for orders from their chiefs: Camerons, Stewarts of Appin, Frasers, Macintoshes, Maclauchlans, Macleans, Farquharsons, and more—too many to remember. The continuous sleet masked the small white puffs of their breath, pelted their plaids, and reddened their bearded faces. Even wrapped in their heavy wool *breacon an fheile,* the big men shook, shivering against each other in their need for warmth. They were past the point of exhaustion and dizzy from near-starvation, living on rotted bits of oatcakes and little else.

Across the frozen field, over eight thousand well-rested English soldiers stood in disciplined rows, five men deep, their crisp uniforms the colour of freshly spilled blood. The yawning mouths of their cannons were gray under cloaks of frost. They vastly overpowered anything the Highlanders had. Unlike the Scots, the English muskets would have fresh, dry powder, and their bayonets would be razor-edged.

But the Highlanders were men of honour and ferocious loyalty. They had pledged their lives to Prince Charles's cause. Andrew understood his duty and would follow through. But that didn't stop him from being afraid.

Aye, it was cold. But Andrew knew something much colder. He had dreamed of this place. He knew of the slaughter that was to come. He knew most of these men would never leave this miserable field alive.

Andrew's father saw the impending defeat. Duncan MacDonnell, his cheeks purple from the cold, lifted his bearded chin in defiance. His glistening eyes held those of Andrew and his two brothers, and for the first time, Andrew saw fear in his father's expression. He also saw sadness, regret, and love.

"I'm proud o' ye, my lads. An' I'm proud to be here wi' ye," Duncan said.

He slapped them companionably on their backs, and Andrew's empty stomach dropped. He felt suddenly older, somehow elevated in status. The feeling terrified him.

A thunderous *boom* shook the earth as the English cannon began to pound the ragged groups of Highlanders. The air was pierced by an eerie whistling, and a three-pound cannon ball tore through the mist, blasting everything and everyone with grapeshot. From where he crouched, Andrew watched the iron hailstones shred a chestnut pony who had stood a few feet away from him. He witnessed the looks of surprise on two big Highlanders' faces as one cannon ball tore through them both. A constant pattern of artillery sprayed the Scots, punctuated by thick booms of the cannon, but Duncan held his sons back. The orders were to wait for the command, though they all wondered if they would hear it through the screams of those who hadn't died in the initial blast. Smoke sent tears coursing down Andrew's face; his ears rang with explosions and desperate cries.

"We'll hear the pipes soon, an' it'll be time," Duncan said, his voice like a growl, somehow audible over the guns and screams. "Go for the English throats like wolves, aye? Like I taught ye. Damn all the *sassenachs* to hell. Every one o' them."

Duncan put his hand on Andrew's shoulder and in that moment Andrew saw his father die. He saw how the bullets would catch the big man. How the bayonets would finish him. How his father's blood would mix with the blood of so many great men.

"Don't go, Da," he wanted to say.

Duncan turned to speak with the chief, sitting nearby, and Dougal gripped his brothers' shoulders. Even Dougal looked paler than usual. His mouth, so often drawn wide with laughter, was a tight line beneath his black beard. Andrew saw Ciaran swallow beside him, and Dougal gave Ciaran a shadow of a smile.

"Try to keep up, will ye?" Dougal teased. "I'll no' have time to come back an' pick ye up, aye?"

Andrew snorted and lowered himself into a squat, ready to run. Ciaran's blue eyes, the same colour as Dougal's, were wide.

"I'm—" Ciaran said, then stopped. His voice was hoarse, and he swallowed hard again. "I'm no' ready to die, Dougal."

Dougal's confident grin wavered, then returned, though it never quite reached his eyes. "No, baby brother," he said, giving Ciaran's shoulder a gentle shake. "I dinna suppose ye are. Dinna fash. We'll none of us die today. We'll be fine, an' home for spring plantin' afore long."

Andrew looked from Ciaran's pleading gaze to Dougal's narrowed eyes, and saw the image of his father again, dead in the mud. Andrew knew the truth. Dougal knew it, too. They would not be fine. They would all die. Their mother would be left alone to tend the fields.

"Dougal's right," Andrew said. "We'll be fine." He pulled Ciaran against him, then felt Dougal's arms wrap around them both, holding tight.

The stink of the smoke seeped into the mist, darkening the sky. From somewhere in the depths of the forest a lone piper pierced the air with an ancient call to duty, plaintive and powerful, lighting the fire in their blood. The Highlanders drew upon whatever strength remained and got to their feet. The chiefs raised their voices and called their clans, like fierce echoes of the Gathering. The men pounded their chests with their fists, harder and harder, grunting with the impacts, stirring their blood with the strikes. Their feet stomped the frozen earth until it was rock hard.

Then they followed their chiefs into battle.

Andrew's father and Uncle Iain led the MacDonnells, their black hair flying like battle flags as they screeched the clan's battle cry, *"Cragan an Fhithich!"*

"Cragan an Fhithich!" Dougal howled, then flashed Andrew a grin over his plaid-covered shoulder. They tore down the field after their father, shrieking like madmen. Seventeen-year-old Ciaran swallowed his terror and ran with them, leather targe strapped to his forearm for protection, readying a pistol in either hand as he ran. They charged blindly through the smoke and hailstorm of bullets, firing pistols, then tossing the smoking weapons aside or pitching them like rocks at approaching soldiers. It was how Andrew had been taught to fight—how they had all been taught. When a man went into battle, there was no time to reload, or even to holster a weapon after it was fired. Instead, Andrew reached for his sword. Its hilt was like the hand of an old friend, holding Andrew's grip as he crashed against the lethal wall of red coats.

The sound of battle was all around, but Andrew heard nothing save his own screams and the pounding of feet—or was that his heartbeat? A sword sliced the air beside him and Andrew lunged for it, striking its lethal edge away from his younger brother.

"Damn it, Ciaran!" he yelled over the noise. "Kill or be killed!"

He spun in time to block another blade, struggling to maintain his balance as his feet slid in the muck. He lunged against his attacker and plunged his sword through the bright red jacket. The dying man's screams were lost to Andrew as another screeching blade struck beside him. Ciaran grunted with effort and Andrew turned, ready to fight, but Ciaran's face was set with fierce determination. His sword screeched against his attacker's, he stepped to the side, then, with a roar, sliced his blade across the soldier's throat.

Blood sprayed from the man's neck, spattering Ciaran's cheek, and he wiped his face clear with his filthy sleeve. It wasn't the first time Ciaran had killed a man. His blue eyes caught Andrew's glance and the brothers had less than a minute to exchange silent words before the crack of a nearby musket cut the air. Ciaran's eyes flew open and he staggered backwards, hands pressed to his chest, mouth open in an expression of amazement.

"No!" Andrew screamed. He spun toward the soldier who had shot Ciaran and was now frantically pouring powder into his weapon. Grief grabbed Andrew's heart just as he twisted his dirk in the Englishman's chest.

Ciaran. Andrew was at his brother's side in an instant, the dead soldier's blood still glistening on his hands. Ciaran lay still, blue eyes open, lips relaxed into a soft line. He stared up as if the smoke were no longer there, as if he were seeing again the open skies of his Highland home.

Andrew had only a moment before the soldiers would overwhelm him. He knelt by Ciaran and took his brother's face between his blood-smeared palms. How could this be? How could he be holding Ciaran like this, knowing those eyes would never blink again? Why was it so much easier to envision his own death than that of his brother? And what of his other brother? Could Andrew survive if this day took Dougal as well? Dougal! The thought jerked Andrew back to the present and he laid Ciaran's head on the earth. He leaned in to kiss his brother's cheek and his thumb lowered Ciaran's eyelids, shutting out the sky forever.

"I will see ye soon, Ciaran," he whispered.

Andrew rose to his feet, spinning as he did so, just in time to defend himself against two oncoming soldiers.

"Ciaran!" Andrew screamed, feeling heat roar into his cheeks. "For you!"

The soldiers were well trained and healthy, but they were no match for a grief-stricken Highlander, no matter how exhausted he might be. When the men lay dead, Andrew strained his eyes through the fog and smoke, seeking Dougal. He saw instead the colour of the battle had changed. Barely defined shapes of men and boys from Andrew's childhood struggled, ran, and fell, their tartans falling under the sea of red coats and flashing silver.

The English kept coming in a relentless red tide. Andrew's strength waned and he thought of Ciaran.

"I will see ye soon."

He struck at swords, swerved around fists and feet, barely able to yank his exhausted legs from the muck. The dull ache of hopelessness seemed almost welcome. He was going to die here on this field. Today. He wanted to collapse to his knees, to beg for a quick and merciful death, but that would have taken more courage than he had.

Then he felt her, a presence that came from nowhere: a surge of warmth that stirred hope in his heart. He couldn't see her, but that wasn't strange. Often she came to him on the breeze. In a thought. A melody in the air. Now she entered his blood, flooding the labouring chambers of his heart. It could only be her. Nothing else could ignite his soul in that way. He felt her impulse and his body followed, spinning and deflecting sword strikes that should have killed him. She turned and he went with her, flowing with impossible energy. Even after her impetus faded, the power she gave him remained. Now he fought for her.

A young English soldier raced up the field, aiming his musket at Andrew as he ran. Andrew dodged the bullet and crashed chest to chest against the soldier, sinking all twelve inches of his dirk into the bright red coat. In one final, shocked effort, the redcoat lashed out, slamming the butt of his musket hard into the Scot's forehead. With that one motion, the worlds of both Andrew and the soldier suddenly went black.

CHAPTER 8

From Darkness into Shadows

Andrew lay unconscious but not alone. He felt a sense of comfort and encouragement, two emotions that held no place on this field of death. He wasn't surprised when the soft lines of the girl's face materialised. She had been with him through his life, and he had known she would be there when he died. So this was the end. He was glad she was the last thing he would see. He wondered if he would see her in heaven.

She smiled with such sadness. She held out her translucent hands, motioning for him to follow her, and though his body begged to remain where it was, his mind obeyed her as it always had, pulling him up to the surface.

He opened his eyes to the gray sky and felt her silky fingertips slip from his hand. The mist had stopped, and smoke from the battle had begun to clear. Raindrops shimmered in the grass, cobwebs glistened.

It wasn't the end, and he wasn't dead.

He needed to see the field, see how things lay, find life beyond the dead. Where was Dougal? Could he be nearby? Could he be alive? Andrew knew where Ciaran lay, or at least where he had last seen him. He knew his father was dead.

English soldiers wandered through the bodies, jabbing with bayonets, hunting for survivors. Their voices travelled across the field to each other, but Andrew didn't think any of them were close to where he lay. They would come for him, though. If he stayed here, he would certainly die. But his torn and weary body anchored him to the earth. He lay with his kilt draped over his thighs, crusted with filth. He closed his eyes again, wanting to be anywhere but here. Whatever light could filter through the dwindling smoke felt warm through his closed eyelids. His stomach rumbled, and he found it slightly amusing it could demand attention at a time like this.

He opened his eyes slowly. They burned. Shock began to lessen its grip, and Andrew became painfully aware of his many injuries. The worst was a deep slash through his thigh. He was relieved to see it wasn't bleeding anymore, but he tore a strip of cloth from his ragged sleeve and, grimacing at the pain, secured it tightly around his leg in case it started again. Over his left eye Andrew bore a solid red knot, courtesy of the dead English soldier, who now lay sprawled beneath a fallen Highlander, eternally oblivious to the dead weight.

Andrew's forehead throbbed with every heartbeat, but didn't bleed. He didn't think he could have done anything if it had. He was just so tired.

Then she was there again. Through the haze he saw her, motioning, urging him up. The familiar wave of her strength rolled through his body, and he used it to sit up, careful to stay hidden behind the remains of men.

The ground was littered with the fallen colours of the Highlanders, like autumn leaves in the spring grass. The prints of hundreds of bare feet, hooves, and leather boots scored the trampled earth. A set of bagpipes lay in the gore by Andrew's left hand, its vacant finger holes staring at the sky, its chanter shattered by a soldier's boot. The cords attached to the drones were tangled and choked with mud. What was left of the piper lay nearby. Andrew reached out and touched the pipes, trying to recall the joy the instrument had once brought.

At Andrew's right lay one of his cousins, his mud-smeared features relaxed and at peace, as if he could be sleeping. Andrew reached over to see if the man was still breathing, but jerked back, retching, when he saw everything below his chest had been obliterated. He spat to the side, then tried to conjure some sense back into his mind.

His hands were sticky with other men's blood, and he wiped them on his kilt while his eyes raked the field, taking in the devastation. Across from him a fire raged, its orange tongues dancing within billowing black smoke. The soldiers stood back from the heat, watching the burning pyres of Andrew's countrymen. This might be Andrew's only opportunity.

He rolled, snakelike, to his belly and dragged himself toward the trees. He knew the woods as well as he knew himself, and could find his way once he was rid of this cursed place. As he moved, he reached inside the sporrans that hung uselessly from the plaids around him. Inside some, as he knew there would be, were small bits of oatcakes, bannock, and dried meat. There wasn't much, though. He packed what he could find into his own sporran, silently thanking each man as he went, then rose to his hands and knees, gasping at the pain that shot from his thigh.

He could hear English voices falling short in the fog. They were closer than before, evidently having tired of the burning. He heard one voice clearly and squinted toward the sound while he edged forward. It was a young soldier, cursing and muttering to himself. Andrew kept moving, always alert. When he was ten feet from the edge of the trees, the soldier's boot struck a rock and he cursed again, louder this time. Andrew froze. Beside him lay the remains of two huge Highlanders Andrew recognised from the trek to England and back. Andrew wriggled under the folds of their plaids, barely breathing, counting the soldier's steps, waiting for him to pass.

After the sound of the soldier's leather soles had faded away, Andrew lifted his chin and combed his fingers through his rain-soaked hair, pushing clumps of filth out of his face. The soldier had changed course and was halfway across the field now, a safe distance from Andrew's hiding place. Andrew took a deep breath, stretching his rib cage with the effort. He peered around one more time and saw no close threats. It had to be now.

He pulled up onto his hands and knees, braced himself, then burst from the spot. He darted toward the trees, keeping as low and silent as possible. His leg burned as if freshly slashed, and cold sweat streamed down his face. It took all his restraint not to scream as the mud sucked at his feet, but he reached the trees and kept running, racing as far as his tortured legs could carry him.

He didn't know how far he ran before he finally slowed, wheezing through starved lungs. He leaned against a birch tree, trying to dispel the stars that circled before his eyes. He stopped panting long enough to listen, but there was no sound of pursuit. Sweat dripped from his brow when he leaned over, gripping his knees, bracing his body. Still breathing hard, he lifted his gaze and searched for some kind of shelter. A cluster of birch stood nearby: five in a row, like a line of sentries. A darkness yawned behind them, a tiny cave in a rock face. The cave seemed like it would offer space enough. He limped toward the wall, peeked inside, then squeezed in as far as he could.

The rock was cold, a soothing shock against his clammy skin. He curled up, his breath thickened by gasps of pain, and let himself relax into the blackness. There was comfort in the silence. He stared at the small pits and bumps inside the cave wall and breathed the damp air. His hands began to shake, hard enough that his arms twitched. A shudder started in his belly and spread as his body gave in to shock. The shudder rose and his throat thickened, burned, blocked his air until he surrendered. Tears he had held back for so long burst through and he buried his face in his arms, sobbing like a child. He cried for his father and for his brothers. He cried for his mother, and for the grief that might kill her when he carried home the news. He cried for the cherished pride the Highlanders had carried to battle that day, and lost on Culloden field.

CHAPTER 9

What Remains

Dusk settled over the drenched land as Andrew approached the outskirts of his family's property. The trees seemed to draw closer together as daylight faded, their newly budded branches reaching toward him like desperate arms. He followed the paths he and his brothers had cut as children, dimly recognising the rocks that marked the way.

It had taken two weeks to walk from Culloden, and the cold rain had fallen almost every day, stirring the rivers brown with mud. He had hunted and trapped enough to keep him alive, but hadn't seen one person the entire time.

Unease rippled through his belly when he didn't see the cattle. They often grazed within these woods, seeking tender hidden shoots that drew their strength from rotted logs. Andrew and his brothers had spent many hours rounding up the foolish beasts when they went too far, herding them to the safety of the family's field. But on this day he heard no familiar lowing, no crackle of underbrush beneath heavy hooves. Perhaps even more disturbing was the fact that no dogs bounded into the trees to lick Andrew's dirty face.

He stepped into the barley field, noting the spring shoots were untended and crowded by weeds. His mother would never allow the crop to fail. Not if she were able to do anything about it. His stomach clenched as he descended the slope toward his cottage.

The barn stood like an ancient castle at the side of the field, reduced to four stone walls. Its ashes had long since been pasted to the ground by rain. There was no more smokehouse. Even the privy had disappeared. Andrew sniffed, smelling the charred stink of the ruined building. He turned and hurried toward the cottage, passing wind-bleached skeletons of livestock left to rot in the yard.

"Mother," he whispered, and began to run.

He was surprised to see most of the cottage still stood. The second room had burned away, the one he had shared with Ciaran and Dougal. He rounded the corner of the cottage, trailing his hand against the familiar stone wall. A blackened bundle in the threshold propped open the door, letting the wind push the rain inside.

Andrew stood by the wall, afraid to go into the cottage. He clutched the doorframe and leaned heavily into his hands, trying to steady himself. Then he sniffed and stood straight, determined to ignore his fear. He looked down as he started to wipe his feet from habit and his gaze went to the shapeless black bundle blocking the doorway. He froze.

A dull glint of silver caught his attention, a bit of something small trapped beneath the charred cloth. He crouched and reached for the piece of metal, holding it between thumb and forefinger before letting it roll into his palm.

"Holy God," Andrew said, his voice catching.

It was a small ring, blackened by soot. His thumb caressed the silver, clearing away the dirt so he could see the tiny cuts in the metal he knew he would see. The light was bad, but he could still make them out: the letters of his parents' names, cut into his mother's wedding ring so many years before. The small bit of metal had fallen from his mother's skeleton, the blackened shape in the doorway. What remained was partially covered by a bit of soaked cloth the wind had caught and dropped.

There would be no welcoming embrace from his mother. There would be no glad tears of reunion. Her flesh was gone, burned off her bones, picked clean by wandering animals.

"Mother," he whispered, and dropped to his knees. His throat felt tight, but no amount of swallowing eased it. He needed to speak out loud. He needed her to hear him. "I'm so sorry. Ye shouldna have been alone. We shouldna have left ye." Tears cut dirty trails down his cheeks, and he let them roll down his neck. "Oh, Mother, could I give my life for yours this moment, I would do it. Wi' all my soul I would do it."

Ciaran's dead eyes gazed at Andrew from somewhere deep inside. Dougal's parting grin flashed in his memory; their father's voice echoed with rage as he charged the battlefield.

Andrew's head spun and he thought he might get sick. He leaned back against the rain-slickened wall of the cottage, sitting beside his mother, clenching her ring in his fist as if it was all he had left.

Everyone was gone.

Everyone except the girl from his dreams. He didn't know if it was even possible for her to die. How he wished she were there. She made him feel safe. Comforted. But his mind was too full of torment to welcome dreams.

Where would he go now? He couldn't live in the woods forever. Nor could he stay here, haunted by the cottage's stone walls. Half-remembered conversations and laughter were part of the mortar, pounded into the floor. Neither could he go to his Uncle

Iain's home at Invergarry Castle. In fact, Andrew would be surprised if the place was still standing. His Uncle Iain had hosted Prince Charles there before the war. The English would probably have destroyed the castle immediately after the battle, for spite if nothing else.

An icy gust jerked Andrew back to the present. He had to do something, else he would freeze right there. He heaved himself up onto his feet and stepped inside the cottage. Anything of any value was gone, furniture and dishes smashed and left in a heap. The cottage was as barren as he felt. Nothing but a shell.

Andrew crouched by the cold fireplace and let his finger follow the path to the darkest stone in the wall. As his father had so many years before, Andrew counted six stones from the left side and three up, then reached his fingers around the edges and pulled. The stone shifted slightly. He dug his fingers in harder and wiggled the stone loose, then reached into the hidden place in the wall: his family's tiny vault. Their life's savings. He pulled free a small leather sack and weighed it in his palm. His parents had hidden this money away in order to better their sons' lives.

"For the future," his father's ghost whispered.

Andrew slipped the little sack into his sporran and stepped back outside. The temperature was dropping and the wind picking up. It whipped past and between Andrew's legs, waving his filthy kilt, screaming through the trees. He wrapped his plaid over his face to ease the wind on his cheeks.

The land was littered by rocks, though many were shoved to the side in an attempt to clear more land. Andrew collected as many as he could find, then began the heavy work of building a cairn for his mother. He would lay her by the barn. She had loved the animals and they her.

When he was ready, Andrew knelt in the wet grass beside her, not wanting to touch the fragile bones, needing more than anything to hold her in his arms and weep. He gathered her remains to his chest, shuddering with horror and desolation, and walked to where he had set the stones. The wind shrieked past him again, biting his face and hands. He knelt again, laying her gently onto the ground.

"Beannachd leibh, a mhàthair. Gum bi Dia leibh. Tha gaol agam oirbh," he whispered in Gaelic. Good-bye, Mother. Go with God. I love you.

The stark contours of her skull faced skyward, and he tried to picture the soft pink skin that had once covered them. She should have a shroud, like a blanket beneath the stones. He needed to cover where her eyes had been, bring her some relief from the sights she had seen. He reached into his sporran for the sack of coins and poured the coins back in. He pressed the empty sack flat over his thighs, stretching it as wide as he could. Then he laid it gently over his mother's face and began to cover her with stones.

When he had finished, he stood back, surveying the land with weary eyes, letting them settle on the cairn. The gray faces of his mother's stones stared bleakly into Andrew's own—lonely markers of the family that had once laughed and loved and dreamed of a future.

CHAPTER 10

Survivor

Andrew hiked through the Highlands for a month. He followed deer paths, hunted small game, and searched for signs of humanity, all the while avoiding burnt-out homes and other signs of English brutality. He wanted to find someone alive. Anyone.

He was filthy and emaciated, covered in grime and dried blood. His hair and beard grew out of control, so that when he saw his reflection in a pool, he was reminded of a bear. Seeing his image in the water made him feel strange. He looked much older than he remembered. The easy smile of boyhood had leveled into a tight, grim line. His brown eyes seemed darker. More direct, as if they didn't trust what they saw.

At night he curled into his plaid, finding shelter wherever he could, and he dreamed. Most of the time the girl was there, and he could drift away with her, make believe the dreams were real, make believe he held her hand in his.

Almost two months passed before Andrew inhaled the musky

essence of peat smoke. He followed the smoke to a small white cottage, huddled in the centre of a ring of trees. No sooner had Andrew stepped out of the trees than a bearded man appeared in the doorway, staying dry under the overhang of his roof. He was huge, imposing in both height and breadth, and one large hand rested on the hilt of his sword. His copper mane flamed almost gold against the white wall, but his beard was dark and wild. The man was a forbidding sight, but he was someone. Someone was better than no one at all.

Andrew moved warily toward the cottage. He didn't blame the man for the suspicion in his eyes. There had been too much violence. Too much death. Trust was a difficult commodity to find. The sun was setting behind Andrew's head, and the big man squinted, trying to see his visitor's face.

Andrew raised his empty hands and slowed as he neared the cottage. When he was ten feet away, he stopped.

"*Dia duit.* Good day to ye, sir," Andrew said.

The man lifted his eyebrows and nodded briefly. He cocked his head to one side, as if listening for warnings in the breeze. "And to ye as well. Ye've come quite a ways, then, ha' ye?"

"Aye, I have," Andrew said. It was a relief to use his voice after being alone for so long. "I've been afoot nigh on two months. Yours is the first place I've seen in a very long time," he said.

After a moment of hard scrutiny, the big man stepped closer, chin lifted. *"Fàilte, a caraid,"* he said. Welcome, friend. His low, rumbling voice was noncommittal. "I've no' seen ye afore. From where do ye come?"

"From Invergarry. My name's Andrew. Andrew MacDonnell."

The big man frowned. "MacDonnell?"

Andrew nodded. "Aye. My father was Duncan MacDonnell, an' my Uncle Iain is—was chief. My brothers and I went with Captain

Scotus of MacDonnell to battle almos' a year past. I—I've been on my own awhile now, lookin' for others."

The shoulders of the big man relaxed just a little and he nodded slowly. "A pleasure it is to meet ye, Andrew," he said. He cleared his throat and seemed to come to a decision. "I'm Iain MacKenzie." He gestured toward the door in invitation. "*Thig a-steach.* I'd share a dram wi' ye. Been a while since I had company."

Andrew swallowed reflexively, the thought of whisky already warming his throat. He followed Iain inside and sat, dripping, at a small wooden table, admiring the carefully painted white walls and the few framed pictures that hung at random. All around the room were small feminine touches: a piece of framed embroidery by the hearth, a chair upholstered in a delicate floral pattern. But there was no woman anywhere to be seen.

The men sat by the fire for an hour or so, getting to know each other while they sipped rough whisky and tore pieces from a hard loaf of bread. Iain had also fought at Culloden, although he didn't remember much about the battle. Instead, he focused on the fact that he wasn't at home during that time. He hadn't kept his family safe in their little white house.

Once he began to tell his story, Iain seemed to forget he wasn't alone. Words tumbled through his shaggy beard like a river undammed. He had struggled home after the battle, tearing through the forests, his head filled with terrifying images of both where he had been and where he was headed.

"It was like I already knew," he said. His voice was tired, his eyes focused on nothing. "There were no way to get here any faster, but when I did, I saw there'd been no call for haste. My lass and the bairns was gone, the house bloodied and broke."

Iain's voice caught and he hid his face behind his cup. Andrew looked away, concentrating instead on the weathered wooden table-top before him. An ancient, meandering crack split the top of the table, threatening to extend from one end to the other. Iain's calloused fingers caressed the chasm, as if he could close the gap with his touch.

The moment stretched. Rain clamoured on the cottage roof in a soothing, persistent din.

"I'm leaving Scotland," Andrew declared, surprising himself. He'd considered the possibility over the past couple of months, but stating the words out loud felt final, and strangely satisfying. "If ye've naught to keep ye here, ye could come wi' me."

Iain stared at his big fingers where they fidgeted on the table, ragged nails dark with dirt. When he spoke, his words came from far away.

"Aye," he said, nodding and stilling his hands with the decision. "I'll go."

The rain eased and eventually stopped, and the men stepped outside. Iain carried some dry wood from inside and they lit a fire. The evening was blanketed by a light fog that drifted around the fallen tree trunks where they sat. The men didn't speak much, but the silence was comfortable. A large brown moth flickered past Iain's face, attracted to the heat of the flames. Iain trapped the creature between his cupped palms and held perfectly still. After a moment he lifted one hand and the moth appeared, motionless save for its twitching antennae, and the slow lifting and lowering of its wings. Iain raised his palm to the level of his chin and breathed against the moth's fragile body until it winged silently away.

Andrew stayed the night in Iain's house, supped on rabbit stew, and fell asleep on the floor. In the morning Iain suggested the next farm might still be functioning, so they set out in that direction. But the farm was abandoned. As were the next two. They walked on, determined to find some proof they weren't alone.

From the south edge of Loch Ness they headed west. The rough Glenmoriston trails led them along the banks of Loch Affric, whose water was a placid blue mirror reflecting lazy cumulus clouds. Over the next three hours, the clouds darkened and the rain returned. The men tucked their chins to their chests to keep the storm from striking full force into their eyes while they walked.

When they finally met with success, it amazed them. Hector MacLeod's thriving farm stood by the base of Glen Shiel, surrounded by cattle and a number of ponies. The family welcomed the visitors into their warm two-storey house, provided them with stools by the crackling fire, served bread and whisky, and asked for news.

The elder of the MacLeod brothers, Simon, was twenty, tall and well muscled from working the farm. He was dark, like his father, with short black hair that curled around his handsome face. His brother, Geoffrey, was a year younger, with straight, golden hair that swooped over his brow, partly obscuring calm, gray eyes.

Their younger sister, Janet, was lovely. Her hair fell to her waist in a cascade of black, and she studied everything through startling green eyes.

Hector's wife, Sorcha, fluttered happily, ensuring everyone had what they needed. It was rare that the family hosted visitors these days. While Sorcha worked, she watched her daughter, whose keen eyes were locked on Andrew. After the men were served, Sorcha went to her spinning wheel. Her eyes travelled between Janet and Andrew, then rested on the young visitor. When he glanced Sorcha's way, she turned back to her spinning wheel, her expression blank. But her gaze kept flicking back toward him.

"Andrew?" she said, lifting her voice over the whirring of the wheel.

Andrew turned toward her, and she inspected the tattered shirt he wore, the stained fabric taut against the press of his chest.

"Will I find ye a new shirt, maybe? That one's seen better days."

Andrew looked down at himself and she saw the tips of his ears redden slightly. His dark brown waves were pulled back into a neat queue, revealing a jagged scar on the side of his chin and another, more recent, over his left eye. He and Iain had trimmed and shaved their beards before the meal and their newly exposed skin glowed a faint pink.

Andrew gave her a weak smile. His thick eyebrows naturally arched up; as if he perpetually questioned his situation. They softened the intensity of his deep brown eyes.

"I'll be fine, ma'am. No need to trouble yerself."

She smiled. "No trouble at all. I'd no' have a guest in my house dressed in such a state. I'm certain I have something more suitable. I'll fetch it for ye, aye?"

"I'd be most grateful, ma'am," he admitted.

She stopped the wheel and attached a new bundle of flax to the distaff, then stood and shook out the folds of her skirt. On her way toward the stairs, Sorcha took a moment to observe her daughter. Janet stood between her brothers' chairs, joining in the conversation. Like her mother, Janet thrived on company. In the days when their home had buzzed with visitors, Janet's laughter had rung in the rafters. These days she paced almost constantly. She reminded Sorcha of a cat, restless and disinterested.

Andrew and Iain stayed for a few days at the MacLeod farm. They helped build an addition to the house. Andrew was tired at the end of the day, his arms and back aching with a delicious stiffness from the construction work.

On clear evenings the group settled on felled tree trunks around a blazing outdoor fire. This was the kind of life Andrew remembered, though it was a different fire, with different faces and stories. The night was clear and beautiful. The heat of the flames licked toward the men so their skin reddened with a pleasant sort of burn.

The MacLeods were a close family, and the discussions around the fire were always comfortable. Sometimes that bothered Andrew, and he knew exactly why. He was jealous. Hector hadn't followed his chief into battle, choosing instead to hide the family and livestock deep in the Highlands when the danger came too close. The decision had been hard on his sons, who had felt entitled to join the ranks of the fighting men.

Duncan had brought his sons to war. And now they were all dead. All but one.

Andrew recognised envy on Simon's and Geoffrey's faces. How ironic, he thought, that he envied them for the opposite reason.

Andrew closed his eyes, breathing smoke from the fire and hope from the air. Geoffrey lifted his fiddle from its case and played, feeding Andrew's hungry soul. He feasted until he could no longer hold his eyelids open, then went inside to sleep, and dream.

CHAPTER 11

A Cry for Help

The MacLeods were generous with their home. Andrew spent a fair amount of time in the stable, grooming, feeding, and caring for the ponies. He enjoyed the uncomplicated company of animals. When Hector suggested Andrew might like to ride up the mountain on his own, he was quick to accept.

A bay-coloured mare hung her head over the half door and nuzzled Andrew's hand when he came toward her stall. She seemed more than happy to escape the confines of the stable and stood calmly while he swung onto her broad back. When the fresh air hit her nostrils, she became restless under him, tossing her head and champing on the bit in anticipation. Andrew felt the same urge and looked forward to letting her run as fast as she wanted.

Andrew and his brothers had learned to ride at their uncle's castle in Invergarry. He had eventually become a groom, working with the *garrons*, the shaggy ponies of the Highlands. For Andrew, riding the animals was as natural as walking. He rode lazily through the trees, pushing aside the branches that stretched to touch him, until the forest opened to a wide meadow, flecked with purple blooms of heather and clumps of bracken as tall as he was. The breeze swept the long grass in invitation, and Andrew leaned into the pony's neck. He pressed his thighs firmly against her sides, and she raced across the field, her thick mane stinging Andrew's cheeks, her tail rippling behind her like a banner.

Partway across the meadow, the pony slowed of her own accord and Andrew relaxed along with her. She checked herself into a trot and finally into a rambling walk. He dropped from her back before she had stopped, and collapsed in the grass with a sigh of contentment. The meadow was alive with the constant buzz of bees at work. Their fuzzy bodies hovered anxiously when the pony lowered her head to graze, then returned to their duties. Andrew closed his eyes and draped his arm over his face to shut out the sun's glow. He relaxed into the bed of wildflowers and began to doze.

The moment suddenly shattered. Shards of panic shot through his body so that his heart raced and his fingers prickled with heat. He heard screaming, felt pain, terror—he struggled to escape its grip, but could do nothing. Slowly, like a figure emerging from a fog, the dream revealed itself and something in Andrew's mind realised it wasn't he who was trapped. He was only a stunned observer. His mind reeled. *She* was there. It was she who was screaming. He felt her agony as if it were his own. His mind pushed blindly to find her, to protect her. It was as if he were being tossed a precious parcel, but was expected to catch it without the benefit of light or hands.

When she finally appeared from the confusion, the clarity of the vision was like nothing he had ever experienced. His heart constricted at the sight of her. The brown waves of her hair were matted with leaves and filth, her eyes bloodshot, and the bruises on her face tracked with tears. He wanted to touch her, to hold her against him and protect her. He focused his mind on the core of her panic.

"Help me," she whispered, and he nearly wept at the sound. He had never heard her speak before.

But how to help? How could he possibly do anything? She needed a weapon. She needed some way to defend herself. His mind raced, searching. He had always been able to find hidden things and people. Now he focused his thoughts, demanding answers.

There it was. There, floating just out of reach, then suddenly in his hand: her salvation. An old hunting knife, abandoned long before by its owner, lay on a boulder nearby. He gripped the smooth wooden handle and felt the weight of the unfamiliar blade, then set it back down and gestured toward it with his open palm. He didn't know from where it might have come, but its savage blade was as solid as the rock upon which it now lay.

Something strange and exciting happened to Andrew while he lay there. It stirred his blood with its unfamiliar power, and he embraced the sensation. He felt as if he were no longer an observer, but a part of her. He felt the air she breathed, hot and dry, stirring the hairs on his arms. He smelled the trees above her, different from any he had ever seen. The ground was hard and dusty, choked with unfamiliar weeds and grass. Beyond the trees was the same sky, the same shining sun warmed them both, but what lay beneath was foreign. Where *was* she? It didn't feel like Scotland, but he couldn't be sure of anything. He lifted his hand and stroked her cheek, imagining he could feel the wetness of her tears against his palm.

"At the river," he murmured, having no idea where the words came from. "Look for me at the river."

He awoke slowly, rising from the dream as if fighting a strong current. One of his hands was vaguely stiff, the fingers curled from gripping the knife in his vision. He stretched his fingers and rubbed the sore knuckles. His nails had carved tiny half-moons into his palm.

His temples throbbed, and he pushed his fingers against them, trying to ease the pressure. The pony was watching, alerted to the unusual energy flowing around him. She swished her tail at a fly and nudged Andrew's shoulder. He groaned, but rose to his feet, still rubbing his temples.

"Ye're ready to go, are ye, lass?"

He stroked her velvet muzzle. Drops of moisture twinkled inside her nostrils. He leaned his face into the mare's neck, inhaling the tang of her dried sweat and hints of the straw she had left behind in the MacLeods' barn. He still saw the girl in his mind. Her tortured features cut painful lines across his heart.

The afternoon sun was moving on, the shadows of the trees lengthening into stark, black lines. Crickets would begin their chorus soon.

"Aye, all right," he said to the pony. "We'll head back."

He reached for her mane and hoisted his body onto her broad back. He smiled as they set off toward the MacLeods' home. Not even the shock of the dream had diminished the day. He had saved the girl in some way. She would survive.

CHAPTER 12

Entreaty

When Andrew reached the stables, Janet was waiting for him, a smile lighting her eyes.

"Ye had a good ride, did ye?" she asked.

"I did."

"Fognan's a sweet pony," she said, reaching up to stroke the smooth, russet neck.

Andrew swung off the pony's back and led her into the stable. Fognan walked into her stall, ears flicking with interest when she smelled fresh oats. Andrew latched the stall door on his way out, then went to where Janet leaned against the wall, watching him. She rubbed her palms on her long brown skirt, as if they were damp. He folded his arms over his chest and smiled expectantly at her.

"What is it then?" he asked.

"I was only wonderin'," she said. "Ye'll be off soon, won't ye?"

"Off? I jus' got back," he said, puzzled.

She shook her head and gave him a brief smile. "No. I meant ye'll be leavin' our home and movin' on."

"Oh, aye," he said. "I expect so."

She nodded and her cheeks suddenly flared red.

"Take me wi' ye," she whispered.

"Eh?" Andrew exclaimed. "I canna do that, Janet. Dinna be daft."

"Sure ye can. Please, Andrew. It's only—I canna stay here. I'll go mad," she blurted.

Andrew looked at her as if she'd just asked him to stand on his head.

"Why would ye want to leave here?" he asked. "'Tis a lovely place, an' yer family loves ye well."

"Oh, I ken that fine," she said with a sigh. "I love them, too. An' I like it all right here on the farm, but, well, 'tis only—I need more, aye? I need to see more o' the world, to do other things beside milk a cow an' mend torn britches. And I'd like someday to be marrit, wi' bairns. Most of the men around here died last spring in battle."

Andrew softened at the distress in her voice. "But why come to me? Speak wi' yer parents—did yer father no' mention ye've relatives in Edinburgh? Ye could maybe go there for a visit. Why me?"

Janet bit her lip and looked away.

"You are . . ." She looked back into his eyes and swallowed hard. "I ken I shouldna be so bold, but Andrew, ye're all a lass could ask for. Ye're handsome an' brave an' funny, an' ye dinna plan to stay put in one place yer whole life, like everyone else around here."

Andrew was taken aback by this. She was by no means a shy woman, but this was unexpected. Her eyes darkened as she spoke, softening into liquid emeralds. She stepped closer and reached up so that one small white hand cupped his chin. He had shaved that morning, but her thumb brushed the new bristles, tickling his cheek.

She blinked slowly, staring into his eyes. Without thinking, he bent down and kissed her, and felt her lips move against his own. He wrapped his arms around her waist so the ends of her hair tickled his hands. She wasn't the first lass he had held in his arms, but it had been a long time since the last one.

The need for physical contact was overwhelming, and he took what she offered. His fingers combed through her hair and he breathed her in, smelling the hay from Fognan's stall and a hint of the gravy she had prepared earlier in the day. She pressed her body against his then pulled her mouth away, searching his dark eyes. Her breath tickled his lips, fleeting as the wings of the moth Iain had held the night before, drawing him in like a flame.

She was tiny in his arms, delicate boned and at least a head shorter than he. He could feel the lines of her ribs through the soft linen of her bodice.

"Andrew," she whispered against his lips. "Take me wi' ye."

No, he thought. This could only end badly for both of them. His hands fell from her waist and he took a step backwards, but she held him, wrapping her arms around his neck.

"Stop, Janet," he said. "Let me go."

"Please take me wi' ye, Andrew," she pleaded. "Dinna leave me here. Take me wi' ye and I'm all yours."

He reached behind his neck and gently loosened her hands. He brought them together and held them against his chest, between their bodies, so they could both feel his heartbeat.

"I'm sorry. No," he said.

She suddenly seemed smaller, as if all the hope in her body had abandoned her. He fought the urge to kiss her again. Even in her unhappiness she was still the most beautiful woman he'd ever seen. But her expression turned swiftly from distress to animosity. The flush on her neck and cheeks that he had roused now darkened.

"Why not?" she demanded. "You and I, we could go away, start a life somewhere. I'd be a good wife an' ye know it. I'd be—"

He placed one of his fingers against her lips to stop her.

"Hush, Janet. No. I'm sorry. It's just that—there's someone else."

He heard a whisper in his mind. *Help me,* she had said, the words escaping through bloodied lips.

Andrew belonged, body and soul, to the girl from his dreams. He was hers and she was his, whether they ever touched or not. He needed to believe all these years of waiting, of wanting would eventually bring them together. Regardless, he would never truly love another. He couldn't.

He hoped Janet wouldn't ask anything more. How could he explain that he loved a girl he'd never met? Fortunately, she didn't.

"But—"

"I shouldna have kissed ye. Please forgive me," he said, looking into her closed expression and feeling wretched. "I'm sorry."

Without a word she turned on her heel and headed toward the house. She didn't speak to him for the rest of the day. He hated the silence, but there was nothing he could do.

At supper, Iain suggested it was time to continue the search for more survivors. Andrew was relieved. He had been growing restless. They agreed to head out the next day. Their party grew substantially as Hector decided to go along with them, bringing his sons.

In the morning the men set out on the ponies, loaded with supplies. Andrew looked back as they left the yard and saw Janet in the upstairs window, waves of shiny black hair framing her pale oval face. He turned back toward the path and tried to wipe the image from his mind.

CHAPTER 13

Rescue of the Innocents

By the second night the men had come across three abandoned homes deep in the thicket. The following day they discovered the remnants of a cluster of cottages built closely together for the safety they hadn't been able to provide in the end.

The ponies kept moving, plodding through misted game trails. Snatches of conversation between the men fell dead on the ground, smothered by shadows. Andrew and the others were worn down by the monotony and lack of success. They almost missed the small, shabby cottage that peeked from under a silver netting of mist, hiding amidst the trees.

Two children sat in the doorway, clinging to each other, their eyes huge in their grubby faces. They didn't move as the strangers drew near. It was apparent from their clothes they were a girl and a boy, somewhere in the vicinity of four and five years old. The little boy's filthy shirt was tucked haphazardly into his kilt. His sister wore a frock, so worn and dirty it was difficult to tell its original colour. Both had long red hair the rain had darkened to auburn.

Of the five men, big Iain was the first to reach the children. He crouched in front of them and looked from one tiny face to the other, speaking gentle Gaelic. The children stared, ingesting his voice, but saying nothing. He reached into his sporran and dug out two small pieces of bread. Their pale blue eyes followed the food.

"A bheil an t-acras ort, a chlann?" he asked. Are you hungry?

They responded by letting go of each other long enough to seize the food.

"Where are yer parents, *mo chlann*?"

The children said nothing. They simply chewed the bread and stared.

"Dè an t-ainm a tha oirbh?" But they kept their names a secret. Iain rose slowly, rubbing his fingers over the bearded line of his jaw.

"We're goin' inside yer cottage. To seek yer parents," he finally said. There was no reaction from the children.

Hector nodded to his sons. Simon and Geoffrey stepped around the little ones, and walked toward the door.

There was a horrible smell about the place, a stink so thick the brothers could almost taste it. The reek of rot, sweetened by the tang of old feces. Geoffrey left the door wide open to try and get fresh air into the cottage.

The pantry door was ajar, and the lowest shelves were empty. Other than that, the room was neat and tidy, seemingly untouched.

The only sound in the cottage was a buzzing noise that grew louder as Simon and Geoffrey approached the closed bedroom door. They exchanged a grim glance and covered their noses with their plaids before Simon unlatched the door. It creaked open at his touch, and the stench struck them with renewed force. The air inside vibrated with the wings of hundreds of swollen flies. Beneath the dining mass lay the corpse of a woman.

Batting away the winged army with one hand and covering his face with the other, Simon stepped toward the bed with his brother right behind him.

Not just a woman, they saw, but a pregnant woman, the bulk of her stomach obscenely round over her lifeless remains. From the blackened stains on the sheets, it appeared she had died in childbirth. Half-filled buckets of water sat cold and useless beside the bed.

The brothers burst out of the cabin, their pale faces set. Simon turned aside and retched while Geoffrey walked to his father, to tell him what they'd seen.

Iain helped the children to their feet, grasping one tiny hand in each of his huge paws. He led them away from the house, talking all the time in a low, reassuring voice.

Geoffrey turned to Andrew and jerked his head toward the cottage. "We canna leave the lass li' that."

Andrew shook his head. "No. You an' yer da ride back wi' the weans. We'll tend to this."

Hector nodded, then knelt in front of the children, who still held Iain's hands. He smiled gently. "Ye'll come wi' us now, aye? We'll keep ye safe in our nice warm cottage, an' ye can have hot stew an' pie."

The ground was hard and thick with twisted roots. It would take three strong men to dig the grave. Geoffrey and Hector could get the children settled by the time the others finished the foul work of burying the poor woman's body.

The men lifted the children and, meeting neither resistance nor questions, carried them to the horses. Iain passed the boy up to Geoffrey, who waited on a quiet mare. Hector, cradling the little girl against his chest, swung onto his mount. The children's bodies felt insignificant, soft and light as a pair of injured sparrows.

"Right then," Hector said to the men. "We'll have a hot meal waitin' when ye get back to the cottage."

"Fine," Iain said. "We'll be there soon as may be."

Andrew watched Hector and Geoffrey turn their ponies back onto the trail, their arms and plaids wrapped tightly around the precious bundles.

After the ponies disappeared into the trees, Iain went into a small shed beside the cottage. He emerged a moment later clutching two shovels, then walked to the edge of the wood, where he planned to dig the woman's grave. Andrew took one of the shovels and drove it into the ground while Simon collected large rocks to discourage scavenging animals. Mist sprinkled over the yard, adding to the misery of the day and the weight of the dirt.

When it was ready, Andrew motioned toward Simon with his chin. "Let's go an' fetch the lady, shall we?"

Simon nodded, though his lip curled with disgust.

It was difficult to look at the woman's body, or what was left of it. Death had molded her form into something vile. And yet her profile still offered a suggestion of her face, of the woman who had once watched her babies grow into children.

Andrew tugged her shift down, covering her nakedness and sending clouds of flies buzzing into the stifling air of the room. Simon moved past the bed and shoved open the latched window, as much to release the woman's spirit to the open sky as to aerate the room. The heavy wooden shutter swung open, creaking from disuse, and cool air flowed into the room like a river.

The men pulled the sides of the soiled sheet together and wrapped it snugly around the body. Andrew, breathing through his mouth, carried her outside. He laid her inside the shallow grave and they covered the site with dirt. Then they bowed their heads and clenched their hands behind their backs.

Iain's expression was miserable. More stricken than Andrew might have expected. The big man's eyes shone, but he didn't shed a tear as he murmured a blessing.

"*Bithibh aig fois le Dia a-nis,* lass. We will care for yer weans as they were our own. Rest and be wi' God now. Ye did yer best."

It was a moment before any of them moved. Andrew's eyes burned and there was a tightness in his throat, but his tears remained unshed. He wished he could cry for this woman. No one had. The children hadn't made a sound when they'd been placed on the horses. *Someone* should be crying, he thought.

As if they heard him, the heavens responded, turning the mist into a downpour. Water fell from the sky in silver sheets, and puddles danced at the men's feet. Andrew followed the others inside the house, where they stamped clumps of mud off their shoes and shook rainwater from their plaids.

The breeze did a fair job of freshening the air, but the cottage still smelled horrible. Andrew went back outside, preferring the rain to the stink. Behind the cabin he found a small patch of grass, slightly protected beneath a corner of the roof. He sat on the grass and leaned against the wall, not minding the dampness beneath his plaid. Iain joined him and they exchanged weak smiles. They said nothing, only rested deep in their thoughts, lulled by the random pattern of rain on the leaves.

The area was quiet and pretty. It seemed like a safe place.

Pat, pat, pat, pitter, the rain tickled the leaves. Andrew's dark eyes watched the drops roll on the shiny green surfaces, joining with others before splashing to the ground. It was hypnotic, watching the clear, perfect beads. He started to count seconds between drops, idly looking for rhythm in their dance.

Pat, pat, pitter, pitter, pitter . . .

His eyelids grew heavy, and he lowered his chin to his chest, gratefully surrendering to sleep.

Pitter, pitter, pitten, pittren, children, children! "Help the children! Help the children!"

The voice shook him within his sleep. *"The children! Help the children!"* she cried.

Two little faces formed in his mind. Their elfish noses were shiny with rainwater, pale blue eyes wide with fear.

"Help them help them help them," he heard, as clearly as if she whispered in his ear.

Andrew woke, gasping, and leaped to his feet. The sudden movement woke Iain, who automatically reached for his dirk. Andrew looked around the yard beyond the house, confused and disoriented. His eyes lit on a pony, and he ran toward her.

"Come wi' me," Andrew called to Iain. "We must catch up to Hector."

"What?" Iain exclaimed. "Why—"

"It's about the children," Andrew shouted over his shoulder as he reached the pony. "Hurry!"

Simon stared curiously as the other two sprinted past. Iain shrugged and hauled himself onto his pony.

"MacDonnell says we must go. Come on!"

Simon frowned, but mounted his own pony, nudging her into a gallop along the path.

An hour's ride at Geoffrey's and Hector's comfortable gait meant Andrew and the other men could reach them in half of that. The voice in Andrew's head still cried, *"The children, the children!"* and he pushed his labouring pony to her limit. The rain had stopped, but mud flew in wet slabs from the ponies' hooves, slapping against trees as they passed. Iain called out from behind, protesting the pace, but Andrew kept moving, with Iain and Simon thundering behind him.

Then they heard them: sounds they knew intimately, which made Andrew's stomach clench. The clashing of metal on metal. The grunts of men in the midst of battle.

The ponies streaked through the trees, slipping on the slick ground, recovering and still running. Andrew swiped a hand across his eyes to clear them of rainwater, and leaned lower over his pony's neck.

Andrew, Iain, and Simon crashed through the brush, and a half-dozen red-coated soldiers swung around at the explosion of sound. The Scots leaped from their ponies and joined the fight.

Geoffrey was blood-smeared and labouring, defending himself with desperate swipes of his sword. He looked up with relief when the other men arrived, but lost his balance and slipped in the mud, giving his opponent an easy target. The soldier stepped toward Geoffrey's prone body, sword ready to strike. Before he could attack, Andrew was at his friend's side and, using both hands on the hilt for strength, swung his own sword across the soldier's chest, slicing the army-issue shirt and the underlying skin to ribbons. The soldier's sword dropped into the mud and the man collapsed to his knees, clutching at his chest with both hands. Blood squeezed through his fingers and ran down his wrists, staining the white cuffs of his sleeves. Then he fell forward and his face hit the earth with a dull thud.

Geoffrey, weakened by exertion and injuries, dragged himself to the edge of the conflict. Beside him, paralysed astride two nervous ponies, sat the children, staring slack-jawed at the scene before them.

Hector had lost his sword to an English strike and now clutched his dirk as a last resort. As sharp a blade as it was, a dirk lacked the reach of a sword. Its strength lay in close combat. Hector was quick, spinning and ducking, somehow avoiding the soldier until the light English sword finally sliced deep into Hector's arm, just below his shoulder. Hector dropped to his knees, looking up as the soldier stepped toward him with the heady confidence of certain victory. Before the soldier had an opportunity, Simon flung himself at the man, roaring in a voice that couldn't quite disguise his youthful zeal. He stabbed his father's attacker, yanked his sword from the body, and ran to Hector's side.

Geoffrey had torn a strip of linen from his own shirt and tied it tightly around his father's injured arm. The blood flow slowed, but the wound was deep. Hector laid his head on the ground and breathed through the pain while his son tended him.

Across the clearing, Iain took charge. The fury he had kept buried since Culloden ripped through him. He growled at the British soldiers, flexing his back and shoulders, readying his muscles. A huge sword swung from his right hand and a dirk from his left. Without a moment's hesitation, he took on two soldiers at once. His sword caught one through the chest just before his dirk sliced through the other's throat. Then he was beside Andrew, standing against the final two soldiers. The Scots finished the battle quickly, using their hatred as a weapon, sharper than any blade.

Iain stepped around the bodies of the slain soldiers, reaching the children in three long strides. He lifted the girl from the saddle, and her arms and legs wrapped around him as if she were a spider. The little boy took a gasping breath, and Andrew collected him against his chest. Tremors shook the little frame until they finally burst through in a flood of tears. He clung to Andrew's neck with twig-like arms, and his tears soaked through Andrew's shirt.

"Hush, laddie," Andrew whispered. "Ye'll be all right."

The sound of crashing underbrush had them all suddenly alert and scanning the forest.

"There!"

Hector pointed at a flash of red tearing through the trees.

"I've got him," Andrew said, untangling the tiny hands from around his neck.

He placed the boy, still heaving with sobs, on the grass beside Iain, then ran toward the sound. The bright red uniform betrayed the fleeing soldier, and Andrew threw himself into the brush, racing after him, oblivious to the branches that whipped at his face.

Andrew's thoughts raced as quickly as his legs. The enemy soldiers had been on foot, not carrying much in the way of supplies. They had seemed well rested and their uniforms showed relatively little wear. That meant their camp was probably fairly close. If this one man escaped, he would head straight to the English camp, and the army would strike back at Andrew and his friends without mercy.

Andrew ran on, crushing roots under his feet, vaulting fallen trees. A branch caught his plaid and tore a jagged hole in the wool, but he kept running, catching himself when his foot slipped on a rock. The soldier had escaped into the trees long before the Scots spotted him, so there was a substantial distance between Andrew and his quarry. Andrew was already tired from the fight, his knees weak beneath him, but he couldn't give up.

For a moment, Andrew lost sight of the man. It was as if the soldier had simply vanished. Then the *crack* of a musket ball blasted a tree beside Andrew, sending shards of bark flying in all directions and attuning him to the source. He locked on to the bloodred jacket and aimed directly for it. He cut the distance in half, in half again, until the man was only a few feet ahead.

The soldier looked back to see Andrew and panicked. He tripped on a tree root, landed hard on his chest, and skidded across a moss-covered rock. He rolled over, grabbing for the pistol at his belt, but Andrew was faster. He leaped onto his prey, banged the soldier's head on the rock, then plunged his dirk through to the man's heart.

When the soldier ceased moving, Andrew climbed off and rose

wearily to his feet. He stared at the body and wiped his bloodied blade on his plaid. Something like regret flitted through his mind at the sight of the corpse. He was so tired of fighting, and now he had killed again. Then he recalled Ciaran's dead eyes. His mother's empty skull. The weeks he had spent alone, searching for someone. Anyone. His regret at killing this one man was short-lived. Andrew left the body where it lay and, gasping for breath, walked back through the woods.

His friends had dragged the bodies under a concealing screen of shrubs by the time he returned to the clearing. They had collected weapons and provisions from the fallen soldiers and packed them securely onto the ponies. Geoffrey held the reins of Andrew's pony, who stomped impatiently at a clump of damp, fallen leaves. Still breathing hard, Andrew nodded his thanks and swung up onto the animal's back. He reached down and lifted the little boy from Geoffrey's arms, letting the child's simple presence ease the fury that still pulsed in his bloodied palms.

The men headed down the trail in single file, Hector and his sons first, Andrew and Iain in the back, holding the children. Iain sat astride a stocky black pony, plodding behind Andrew's.

"MacDonnell."

Andrew turned to face his friend, whose expression was guarded. A sleeping angel drooped against the big man's chest, breathing noisily through her mouth, strands of copper hair hanging over her gaunt white cheeks.

"Aye?" Andrew asked.

He wants to know, Andrew thought. *He wants to know how I knew to come here.* He could see Iain trying to summon his question, but he must have changed his mind. Instead, Iain nodded and passed Andrew the shadow of a smile.

PART 3: MAGGIE

Changed Existence

CHAPTER 14

Into the Light

I pried my reluctant eyelids open and gazed at my surroundings, wondering if I were dreaming. An unfamiliar hum of voices bubbled around me, acquiring muted colours and taking on the shapes of women. If it was a dream, it was a good one. I blinked twice, proving to myself I was awake.

Most of our journey to this house was lost to memory. The Indian women had encouraged us to drink a strange-smelling tea, which calmed us. We lay on a travois the Indians had fashioned, then nestled into warm, creamy furs they tucked under our bodies. I was glad the tea muddled my thoughts. I couldn't think clearly, and didn't want to. I was beyond exhausted and needed peace. My visions had been absent throughout the rape. Without them I felt drained. The gentle jostling of the travois rocked me to sleep as we travelled.

* * *

I had no idea how long the trip had taken, nor how long I slept once we'd arrived. Now I woke to a completely different world.

My bed was a layer of furs, pillowed over feathery boughs of hemlock and broomsage. The woven pine walls of the house were cushioned by tanned skins, the roof layered by bark and thatch. Shelves along the windowless walls were filled with baskets and utensils, and a small open fire provided light, dimly illuminating dried husks of corn that hung from the rafters over my head. It also kept the building warm. The heat was almost stifling under the furs. A woman sat near the hearth, constantly feeding small sticks to the fire. Thin curls of smoke wafted upward and drifted through a rectangular hole above our heads, entering the atmosphere and disappearing with the breeze.

Adelaide slept beside me, her breathing regular and steady, if a little louder than usual through her swollen features. Her bruises brought back the events of the past two days, and I struggled to blur the memories. I didn't want to see, didn't want to remember. I closed my eyes again and lay in silence, blending my breaths with the Indian women's voices as they moved around the house.

But while I didn't want to recall anything from before, I'd had enough sleep for now. The sounds around me were inviting, and I wanted to see more. I sat up slowly, moving through the ache of my battered muscles. The buffalo blanket slid from my shoulders, and I realised my clothing had been removed and replaced by soft buckskin. My body was entirely cleaned of blood and dirt.

A slender girl in a pale doeskin tunic walked toward me, and offered a clay cup filled with some kind of tea. I took it, smiling thanks. She squatted in front of me, nodding and making small gestures with her hands to encourage me to drink, ignoring the ends of her long black hair as they brushed the floor around her feet. I sipped experimentally at the hot liquid. It was slightly bitter, but her smile helped me swallow. She stroked my hair, smoothing its brown tangles to mirror her own shining tresses. I smiled back but grimaced when my lip split with the effort. Without hesitation, she reached for a small bowl beside my bed and dipped in a graceful finger. She dabbed that same finger, topped with a brown tinged ointment, onto my lip and the pain was soothed immediately. I tried again, more successfully this time, to return her smile.

My expression encouraged her to open a one-sided conversation. I listened, but could make nothing of the strange syllables. That didn't seem to matter to her. She chattered happily, her hands and eyes dancing as she spoke. She touched me occasionally, patting my arms with friendly reassurance. Eventually she stretched out her hand and helped me to my feet. My legs were stiff, but it felt good to stand again.

I looked down at Adelaide, still asleep beneath her coverings. I would let her sleep. She needed to heal. The girl seemed to read my thoughts. She gestured toward Adelaide and nodded. She led me toward the doorway, talking all the while, and drawing pictures in the air with her long fingers. I shuffled behind, reaching for the wall for balance. The hum of the girl's words relaxed my mind into a familiar calm. I felt the energy of my dreams begin to flow again, tingling in my fingers, twinkling in my vision.

A large woman blocked the doorway to the outside. She was combing a nasty tangle out of a small boy's hair, and he winced with every one of her strokes. My new friend said something and the woman grunted, shifting her massive body to the side to reveal the outdoors.

When the first shafts of light blazed into my eyes, I felt as if I'd been blinded. But it was more than the sudden shock of going from dark to light. In that moment, my world spun completely out of control. I stumbled forward and slumped in the doorway, hands pressing against the sides of my head as image after image crashed through my mind. It wasn't painful, but the confusion was overwhelming. My knees collapsed and I hit the ground hard. Instinct forced me to concentrate on breathing, circulating sanity through my brain. My new friend dropped to my side and took hold of my arms, helping me sit. Images stampeded past me, and I could see nothing else but them. In desperation, I seized one image and held on tight.

The vision showed me a small Indian boy, lying at the bottom of a hill. He was curled on his side nearby, on the edge of the village. His knees were bleeding and his eyes were squeezed shut, his dark lashes resting on tear-soaked cheeks. I opened my eyes a crack, cautiously allowing light in. The women clustered around me, their curiousity blocking the direct sunlight. After a moment my eyes cleared, and I looked around the group. One of the faces caught my attention, and I looked directly at her. I don't know if it was her resemblance to the little boy or just the fact that I *knew*, but this woman was his mother. It had to be.

I hesitated before saying anything. My mind whispered my mother's words: *Keep quiet, say nothing.* I took a deep breath, released it, and rejected all of my mother's warnings.

"Your son," I said to the woman. "Your son needs you. He's fallen."

She stared at me, her soft brow creased, and I realised my English words meant nothing to her. I kept my eyes on hers even as she tried to withdraw from my unwanted attention. Grasping inspiration from the air, I folded my arms across my chest as if I were rocking a baby. The women around me murmured among themselves, trying to interpret my message. I rolled my hands to indicate someone tumbling down a hill, then pointed at my own injured knees. Finally, I gestured to a nearby hill. The woman blinked in bewilderment as

I repeated my pantomime and the others consulted each other in soft questions. Suddenly the woman's eyes widened, and she looked at me in surprise.

"Omnatea!" she cried. "Omnatea!" She tore herself away from the group of women and ran toward the hill where the little boy had fallen, calling his name as she went.

I looked from one face to the next, trying to read what they were thinking but getting nothing but a sense of wary puzzlement. The girl who'd brought me from the house sat very still beside me. After a few moments one of the older women turned to a younger one, barked a command, and waved her away. The young woman ran, obeying without question.

Had I made a mistake? Should I have kept my gift a secret? My mother, sisters, and I had never told anyone, afraid of the consequences. Afraid I might die on a burning stake like my grandmother. Here, surrounded by these strange people, my dreams had stepped into the sunlight, free at last. But at what price?

A new vision suddenly shoved its way into my sight: two little faces I had never seen before, deathly pale but for their damp red hair and terrified blue eyes. My arms felt the ache of physical combat; the clash of swords rang in my ears. The children were safe from the chaos, but still in the centre of my vision. What was this? Why was I seeing people I knew nothing about? What did this have to do with me?

My mind shifted naturally to the answer. Wolf. He looked tired. Yesterday he had led me to my escape, armed and protected me. Now I needed to ask him for more, and I wasn't even sure why. I couldn't know if my message would reach him or not, but I concentrated hard. I brought the children's faces into focus and pushed a silent scream toward his image.

The picture of the children disappeared as suddenly as it had appeared, leaving me dizzy and disoriented. My friend sat beside me on the dirt, drawing circles on my back with her palm until I relaxed. The other women had evidently lost interest, going on about their business and leaving the two of us alone by the doorway.

The morning activity in the village was a welcome distraction, constantly in motion. Small boys dressed in nothing but bits of leather around their waists laughed and squealed, kicking a cloth ball through the grass. In the doorway of the house next to ours, a tall, slender woman leaned into an even taller man, her eyes dark with suggestion. Beyond them a riot of dogs chased each other in circles, tails swinging with abandon. Casting a spell over it all was the magnificent backdrop of forest-covered hills, their mantle of green highlighted with gold by the day's early sunshine.

My life from before was over. My mother was gone, Ruth was gone. Adelaide suffered. My innocence was gone.

I had learned the darker side of men; I had killed a man.

I felt a soft touch on my shoulder and turned to see Adelaide, my only link to that life. She was barely there, barely solid enough to stand, but she was there, and she needed me. I stood up to support her, then folded her into my arms. She shook against me, and I held her tight.

From over her shoulder, I watched the village. Something about this place felt familiar. Comfortable. As if I had been here before. A breeze shivered the leaves on the trees at the outer bounds of the camp, whispering to me. It wound its way over the children playing ball and the young couple and the dogs, reaching out to ruffle my hair and cool my neck like water. It tugged me forward and I stepped into my new life.

CHAPTER 15

Communication

There were nights when I jolted awake, my heart beating madly and my body damp with sweat. There were also nights when it took a long time to fall asleep. How could I sleep when my mother's face came to me as soon as I shut my eyes, the bullet hole in her forehead staring like a third dead eye? And Ruth. Ruth was always in my thoughts: her golden curls bouncing around angel blue eyes, her soft pink skin torn to shreds, left to rot in the dark forest. Ruth had always been afraid of the dark.

Healing and encouragement surrounded my dear remaining sister and me. The Indian women cared for us as if we were members of their families. They washed our bruised bodies and provided us with doeskin tunics and leggings. They combed our hair until it shone and tied it like their own, in long braids that tickled down the centres of our backs.

The little boy, Omnatea, whom I had "seen" tumbling down the hill, had become my constant shadow, peeking through the longhouse doorway, watching me eat or sleep. His mother was usually with him, dark eyes just as curious.

One morning, the girl who had first arrived at my side came to escort me out of the longhouse where I slept. She carried out a detailed inspection of my appearance, flipping her fingers over the beaded tunic, petting my long brown braids. She talked and giggled and I nodded blankly in response. It didn't seem to bother her that no matter what she said, or how she said it, I didn't know what she was talking about. Her happiness was contagious. Today she seemed more enthusiastic than usual, and I got the impression that something important was about to happen.

She grabbed my hand, and I squeezed hers, feeling stronger with her beside me. She pointed at her chest with one finger and spoke slowly and clearly, as if I were a child.

"Kokila," she said, then repeated herself twice more. "Kokila, Kokila."

She watched to make sure I was paying attention, then pressed my hand against her shoulder and encouraged me to say the word as well.

"Kokila," I repeated dutifully, burning her name into my memory. "Kokila."

Kokila beamed, then tugged me outside. The air was heavy, still and quiet with the pressure of an impending thunderstorm.

Kokila spread her arms wide and, with a broad grin, indicated the entire village.

"Chair-oh-key," she said, "Chair-oh-key."

"Cherokee," I echoed, taking in the forty or so squat brown houses. I looked back at her and grinned. "Kokila," I said. Then I jabbed my finger into my own chest. "Maggie," I said.

She laughed and spun around. "Ma-kee! Ma-kee!" she chanted, emphasising the second syllable. I liked the sound of it.

I liked everything about this place. The last village or town I'd visited was the one where my sisters and I had, in another lifetime, traded eggs for cloth. The place had been far from welcoming, and my memories were coloured with an impersonal gray. Here among the Cherokee the colours of the land and the people spun together. There were no fences separating the long wooden houses.

I think Adelaide was content in the village, though we didn't talk a lot. She hardly spoke. Physically, she improved daily. But her eyes moved constantly, sweeping the faces around her, searching. She retreated into a glassy-eyed stare, focusing on monsters that lurked in her mind.

She knew our attackers were dead. We had both seen the remains of the camp. But their ghosts still haunted her mind.

Adelaide wasn't in the house when Kokila came for me. She had been spending more time with some of the women lately, so I assumed that was where she was now.

Kokila still held my hand, and began walking faster, probably hoping to outrun the storm. The wind had risen, easing the clouds past the mountains so they towered over the village, blocking out the sun. She led me toward the big house in the centre of the village: a long, seven-sided building I assumed was used for important meetings.

The wind swirled the ground beneath our feet, spinning dust through the village and chasing families into their homes. Fat, heavy raindrops began to dot the dirt around our moccasins. They drummed against the thatched roof of the house. Kokila and I ducked through the entryway just as the storm hit with full force.

It was dark inside, and very warm, as it was in all the buildings. A small fire burned at the far end of the house, and I could see the outlines of a few people sitting nearby. An animal hide hung partway over a hole in the ceiling, keeping out the wind and the rain, but letting out the hearth smoke. Kokila and I walked closer to the glow of the fire, and our eyes adjusted to the dim light.

I knew the woman the moment I saw her. She sat at the far wall, tiny and still. I had never seen her before, but her features were more than familiar. Her face was shrunken and wrinkled like a dried apple, and sparse gray hairs hung over ears that seemed oddly large for her head. Her body seemed to have collapsed in upon itself, but whatever strength it once held was now contained in her infinitely dark eyes, which were blazing and alert.

Three other women sat with her, cross-legged on the floor. One had narrow eyes that bored into mine, but friendly curiosity brightened the toothless smiles of the other two.

Kokila murmured something and squeezed my hand, then backed out of the house, leaving me alone with the women. One of them stretched out a thick, knobbly finger, indicating for me to sit. I did, and they examined me. Their eyes were keen and curious.

I was uncomfortable under their stares and tried not to squirm. Then I felt a veil of calmness descend over me, like a light caress. Without conscious effort, all of my thoughts melded, centred on the ancient woman I somehow knew. I felt drawn to her, almost physically. My body seemed to be vibrating—as if something crawled beneath my skin—and my vision narrowed so all I saw was her. Her lips moved and she hummed and spoke, hummed and spoke.

I was mesmerised. Somehow she was reaching inside me with her mind, seeking something within my thoughts. I could *feel* it. The air was taut, as if she held strings and could tighten or loosen them as she wished. I couldn't move, couldn't think; my senses were paralysed in fascination. Her mind wandered through mine, asking, answering, looking, and seeing. Without a single word I could hear her, and she could hear me.

Once I realised what she was doing, I relaxed and concentrated my thoughts toward her. Her reaction was immediate. She opened her rheumy eyes wide and sat up straight, heaving in a rattling breath. The deep lines of her face cracked into a smile, and her hands flew to her toothless mouth. She cackled and babbled to the women beside her, gesturing toward me with her gnarled fingers.

The women looked from her to me, interest brightening their expressions.

After a moment the old woman resumed her humming meditation, staring at me through her wrinkled old face. Her intensity blanketed me, almost smothered me, making me feel as if I had been drinking the hypnotic tea again. She appeared to me in constantly shifting patterns of browns and golds, and in the state I was in, I thought she actually floated a few inches above the woven rug on the floor.

The wind screamed and pellets of rain battered all seven walls, but I barely noticed. Why should I care what the outside world did? I had no intention of going anywhere. The sensations racing through me were amazing, flooding me with a rush of images. The woman showed me pictures from her past she wanted me to see, brief flashes of pain and joy she had experienced. I saw her face as it had been in her youth: plain, yet somehow more intricate than any beadwork. The woman in the vision laughed, held hands with a man, cried by the side of a roaring fire.

Flitting between the images, binding them together with silvery feathers of sound, came the syllables "Waw-Li," and I began to understand that these syllables were the old woman's name. Her thoughts began to shift into words, and I realised with mounting excitement that she was feeding me what she could of her own language. Words of her Cherokee tongue intertwined with English until I could pick out words and phrases. Sounds started to fall into place as if they had always belonged there.

Kokila, I suddenly thought, and knew that my friend's name was Nightingale.

The old woman's eyes opened wide and the thin line of her mouth stretched into the warmest, most understanding smile I had ever seen.

She said:

"*Osiyo, Mah-gah-ret. Tsi-lu-gi A-ge-yu-tsa guh-do-di A-s-gi Di-ka-ta.*"

And I heard:

"Hello, Margaret. Welcome, Girl with Dream Eyes."

I wondered how long she had been waiting for me.

CHAPTER 16

Cleansing

The rest of the village heard about my meeting with Waw-Li. She must have spread the message that I was different, and that she believed in me. Big smiles, encouragement, small tokens of beadwork and smoked meat greeted me everywhere I went. It was strange to be treated as if I were important, but it was exciting, too.

And now, incredibly, I could understand most of what the villagers were saying. Through Waw-Li's thoughts during our "conversation" the week before, she gave me an amazing gift. She had built a bridge that helped me understand the Cherokee language, and in turn, I helped Adelaide learn.

I flourished in the village, but Adelaide was still a shadow of the girl she used to be, weak and tentative about anything she tried to do. As spring blossomed into summer, I started to see Adelaide's strength grow along with the crops. Waw-Li and the old women in the council house spent time with her, slowly unraveling the fear and satisfying her need for reassurance. She learned to weave and bead, presenting her first completed creation to the woman who had taught her the art. The second was a beautiful necklace in vivid blue and green beads, which she proudly tied around my neck.

The village also knew of my dreams, because Waw-Li had seen them. To my relief, the women of the village came to me with eyes wide open, wanting to hear what I had seen in my sleep. Sometimes my dreams meant nothing to me, but my audience would nod and grunt in comprehension. It was unfamiliar and liberating, knowing people wanted to see what I had always hidden away.

Days turned into weeks, and as time moved forward, so did I. Kokila had a friend, a tall, lean young man with the difficult name of Eenuheegahtee Chawleegoo, or Tall As Tree. He and Kokila looked for any excuse to be together, so I often found myself alone. I began to meet more people and dared myself to trust again.

The women of the village were always happy to teach me whatever they were doing. When I was small, my mother had taught me about the healing properties of plants and herbs, but the Cherokee women knew much more. Waw-Li was the village wise woman, but her companion, Nechama, specialised in physical healing, so I watched and learned from Nechama. She was one of the two women who had rescued Adelaide and me that day in the forest, the first to help us rise from the ashes.

The village was always full of activity. I loved the feel of it, the constant movement flowing through the place. I loved to wade through it, watching what the villagers did so naturally. I sensed their purpose and pride.

In a clearing by the river one of the men worked alone, building a canoe, one that would carry up to ten men. He seemed oblivious to everything around him, but even over the crackling fire he burned to create the belly of the canoe, and the constant gurgling of the nearby water, he turned toward me in welcome.

The earthy scent of smoldering pine drifted on the breeze from one of the buildings, and I smiled because I knew what that meant. The women were firing dishes.

On the other side of the village, a dozen young men built a new home for a growing family. Their chests shone with sweat; their faces glowed with laughter and easy conversation.

I thought about my family's little house, with its lonely chimney poking through the roof. The tired, broken bits of clay that had held it together often surrendered to the elements, rolling off the roof and landing with a soft *thump!* in the tall bunches of switchgrass outside our window. The sagging roof always required patching before the winter winds began to blow. When rain fell, the water found every crack, forming small puddles on the uneven wooden floor of the parlor.

Now I lived among the people I had always been told were savages. The people who, it had been said, killed without mercy and conversed with the dead. I should have been afraid.

Instead, I felt envious. I had spent my childhood in a ramshackle house with a father who would rather not have had his offspring around. Here, children never went without food, shelter, or love. The entire village was a family, and the parents of one child felt responsible for every other child as well. No one was ever alone. Yes, I was jealous. But more than that, I was forever grateful at being accepted.

Summer was in its prime. Vivid green leaves quivered in the breeze, birds called and flew through the forest, bouncing from one branch to the next. Goldenrod and purpletop swayed within the grass.

Today, as I often did, I took the familiar walk to Kokila's house to enjoy the quiet transition from day to dusk with her. Adelaide was there already, so I sat beside her. We pulled shawls over our shoulders, not so much for the warmth—it wasn't too cool at night—but to discourage hordes of greedy mosquitoes. Kokila beamed up at Eenuheegahtee, who was joined by two friends. Wahyaw Gah-goAheesuh, or Wolf Who Walks, was one of them. He was tall like his friend, but broader in the chest than Eenuheegahtee. Wahyaw had a younger brother, Oohlaysaygee Soquili, or Dark Horse. They were all about the same age as we were, seventeen or eighteen, growing easily into strong, handsome warriors. Eenuheegahtee and Kokila were engrossed in each other most of the time, which left Adelaide, Wahyaw, Soquili, and me to get to know one another better.

It took a while before conversation between the four of us flowed. It wasn't so much a question of the language, because Adelaide and I became more comfortable with their tongue every day. But our trust in men had been shredded, and it would take more than friendly faces to patch up the damage.

Wahyaw wasn't a patient man. He was constantly on the move, pacing or abruptly leaving a conversation without notice, moving with the ease of a wild animal. When I spoke with him, his eyes always strayed just beyond me, but I was fairly sure he heard every word I said. He had a quick temper, but it was offset by a rich laugh that rolled through his chest.

Wahyaw was a beautiful example of a Cherokee man. The sides of his head had been plucked bare since childhood, as were those of most of the men. A thick, vertical comb of black hair protruded stiffly from the top of his skull, usually adorned with one or two feathers that hung loosely down one side. He rarely wore a shirt or moccasins, preferring only a breechclout. He wore cone-shaped earrings, and a ring pierced his nose. Black triangular tattoos, interlaced with images of running wolves, circled his muscular biceps. A red tattoo slashed through the right side of his face, running jaggedly down his high, bronze cheekbone. If I hadn't been adopted into this Cherokee family, the appearance of these men would have terrified me. As it was, they were becoming my friends. In fact, Wahyaw, Soquili, and Kokila were the first friends I'd ever had in my life, beside my sisters.

Soquili was about three inches shorter than his brother, which still left him almost a foot taller than I was. He was also very attractive, but his features were softer. Neither face tattoo nor nose piercing marked his face. His eyes focused on every sound I uttered. He hardly even blinked when he listened. Speaking with him could be a little disconcerting, but at least I knew I was being heard.

Occasionally the brothers took Adelaide and me hiking so we could experience our surroundings a little more. One morning they led us along a path we hadn't seen before, up a steady vertical climb. We walked in silence until we reached the top of one of the seemingly endless peaks. Centuries had rounded the shoulders of the hills around us, and they were blanketed by a patchwork quilt of green and gold. Wahyaw took us to the edge of a cliff, and the magnificent Keowee Valley opened below us. The Keowee River glittered under the sun, its waters a sparkling trail of jewels. Along its shores grew endless forests, coloured by trees of every kind.

Wahyaw heard something within the forest and, true to form, disappeared without comment behind the wall of trees. Soquili ignored his brother's apparent concern and came to stand between Adelaide and me. We stood for a while, lost in the view. Then Soquili spoke.

"The Cherokee believe the earth is a great island floating in a sea of water," he said, seeming to study the vista. He frowned and looked from Adelaide to me, making sure we were both paying attention.

"It is held at four points by a rope hanging down from the sky.

When the world grows old, the cords will break. The earth will sink into the ocean, and all will be water again."

We stayed quiet and he turned back toward the view. It was easy to believe his story when the evidence was spread out in front of us.

"Many years ago, before the Cherokee," Soquili said, "all of this was water. The animals lived above the water in Galunadi, beyond the arch." He raised an uplifted palm toward the sky. "It was crowded, and they needed more room. They wondered what was below the water. At last Daya Unisi, the Water Beetle, went to learn the answer. He dove to the bottom, and when he rose, he carried soft mud with him. The mud began to grow and spread on every side until it became the island which we call the earth."

Soquili's voice was full and rich, and I smiled at him in encouragement. His voice flowed with his words, his strong hands gestured, and his fingers drew in the air, moving like a dance.

"The earth was flat and soft and wet. The animals wanted to get to it so they sent the Buzzard to make it ready for them. This was the Great Buzzard," he clarified, making sure we understood the significance. "The father of all the buzzards we see now. He flew over the earth, near the ground. It was a long way to go, and when he reached the land, he was very tired. He flew lower and lower, and when he flapped his wings, they touched the soft ground. Wherever they struck, a valley was born, and where his wings turned up again, a mountain was created. When the animals saw this, they were afraid the whole world would be mountains, so they called him back."

Soquili's smile was peaceful. "That is what the Cherokee know," he said. "I will go and find my brother now, but I will not be gone long. Stay here and rest. Let the mountain speak to you."

The air was clear and fresh. The occasional gust of wind stirred the leaves, like a bird plumping its plumage. I walked to the edge of the cliff and inhaled, then glanced up when a raven flew low over my head, beating its wings in a wide *whoop whoop whoop,* as solid as a drum. It soared over the valley in a fluid arc, casting a shadow that stretched and shrank with the terrain.

Adelaide stood beside me, gazing with silent awe.

"Close your eyes and breathe, Addy," I whispered.

She did, inhaling the ripe scents of composting leaves, herbs and grasses, the pine sap, and even the water below us. I watched her face and saw the lines of fear and tension relax just a little.

Soquili emerged from the bushes beside us, quiet as a breeze. "Wahyaw is hunting. He doesn't need me. Come. Let us eat."

We followed Soquili away from the precipice, stepping over fallen rocks and trees, wary of the sharp drop beside us. He found a natural rock chair within a cluster of broken boulders and sat there in watchful silence while we settled beside him. Adelaide pulled out some biscuits and dried venison she had packed and handed them out. The climb had taken over an hour, so both the rest and the food were welcome. After a while, my sister lay down by the wide trunk of an oak and rested her head in a cushion of dry leaves. Her breathing slowed and softened, blending into the breeze. When I saw her like this, calm and peaceful, I hoped one day she might come back to me and be the happy girl from before. I missed her.

When she was asleep, I lay back into a cold throne of silver-gray rock. The chill of the stone was soothing against my legs and I yawned, closing my eyes and dozing.

Calm descended on me like mist, cooling and warming me at the same time. I was no longer aware of anyone around me, just a perfect merge with the air, earth, and water. My visions joined me, soothing as a velvet river, filling my subconscious with pictures, thoughts, and words. I coasted through them, recognising some, indifferent to others, floating in their existence.

My raft suddenly dropped anchor, and I knew my sleeping lips rose in a smile. Wolf lay in a field, sprawled peacefully among waving purple flowers. A dark woolen sash crossed over his shirt from one shoulder to his hip, where it pooled over him like a blanket. It was a deep green, darker than the grass in which he lay. The warm breeze tousled his hair, loose on the ground beneath his head. A short, stocky horse stood at his side, calmly mouthing the grass.

So often I saw him in times of crisis. Now he was at peace, and my entire being ached to lie next to him in the stiff stalks of grass. The need took over the vision until suddenly I was on the ground beside him, sensing everything he sensed, feeling the cushion of grass tickling my back and arms. I thought I could smell him, sweat and sun-warmed skin mingled with the scent of the earth. My fingers vibrated with a desire to touch him. I turned my face toward him, and he looked back at me with eyes that were just as astonished, and just as full of joy as my own. I sensed pressure around my fingers as he took my hand. His eyes were so close, so real, so much a part of my own being, I would gladly have melted into them.

"I will find ye," he murmured through soft, gentle lips.

I stared at him, mesmerised. There was a pleasant lilt to his voice I couldn't place. It drifted through me like a lullaby but woke every part of my body to an exquisite awareness. He lifted my hand and brought it to his cheek, where it hovered, a promise, a breath away. I imagined the warmth of his breath tickling my palm and my fingertips touching the bristle of a new beard. He watched me without blinking, then kissed the sensitive skin of my hand. A breath away.

"I know," I replied.

I did know. I had only to wait.

Suddenly, without warning, Wolf and the meadow were gone. I lay alone on a hard, gray stone that jutted against my back, rendering me numb from its cold, jagged edge. Soquili was leaning over me. His lips moved but I couldn't hear the words.

"What?" I demanded, angry at him for pulling me from the dream. If he sensed my irritation, he didn't show it.

"It is time to go, Ma-kee. It grows late."

He helped me to my feet and I stretched my back, still chilled from the stone seat. A storm was approaching, and the air cooled under the trees. Soquili was right. We had to go, although every part of me wanted to return to that meadow. I turned away from the stones, but the vision stayed with me. I could still close my eyes and see Wolf beside me, hear his simple words.

I will find ye.

CHAPTER 17

Restless Souls

Adelaide created beautiful crafts. I did not. I tried, but I eventually abandoned my tangled attempts and moved to tasks where I could be more useful: skinning, preparing food, and watching children for their busy mothers. That was one of my favourite duties. I ran and laughed with them, chasing and being chased. Fears and worries vanished when I joined their games. We took walks through the woods, collecting berries and nuts, picking flowers and herbs for Waw-Li and the other women. These were simple days of pleasure, filled with laughter and learning.

On other days, when I craved quiet, I knew where to go. Scattered around the village were numerous stone-covered mounds that marked burial places of clan members. The surrounding air quivered with restless death. Echoes of past voices haunted the burial mounds, whispering words never spoken. The ground beneath my moccasin-clad feet hummed.

For the Cherokee, it was comforting, I supposed, to know their ancestors were nearby. The only graveyard I had ever known was at an old church in the valley, hours from my home. The churchyard was dotted by wooden crosses. Our father was buried beneath one of those. We paid the church a fee we couldn't afford so he could lie there.

We were not a religious family. My mother read the Bible to us and told us stories of the saints, but we weren't given to much prayer or contemplation. Ironically, it was here, in a village that did not worship Christ, that I began to understand the power of prayer. The spiritual beliefs of the Cherokee gave me sanctuary. If, as they said, the earth connected us all, then my mother and Ruth were together right now, still connected to Adelaide and me. Sometimes I still felt them with me. My mother and Ruth deserved a peaceful burial spot like those I saw around the Cherokee village.

One day Adelaide came to sit with me on the stony riverbank, where the women went to do the washing. She needed to talk. I could see the lines of concentration on her brow. Ever since we had come to the village, we had avoided speaking about important matters. I suppose it was the fear of upsetting her that kept me from talking about those things, possibly opening a wound not quite healed. So it was a relief when she, not I, spoke first.

We dangled our toes in the cold running water and let the current tickle between them. She held a small chunk of wood in the palm of one hand and was slowly shaping it with a short, sharp blade that she held in the other.

"What are you carving?" I asked.

She held it up to eye level, considering. "I'm not sure yet," she said. She lowered it and resumed cutting into the soft wood. "Do you remember their faces?" she asked, eyes on her work.

I thought I understood whose faces she meant, but it didn't matter. I remembered them all. Strangely, the face I saw most clearly was that of the man whose throat I had slit by the river. I couldn't rid my memories of his stunned expression under thin red curls, darkened by sweat.

"Mm-hmm," I said.

"I sometimes have trouble seeing Mama's face," Adelaide said, her words barely more than a whisper. "I speak to her at night, when we're falling asleep. But sometimes, when I really want to, I can't see her face. Does that happen to you?"

I thought for a moment before I answered. If I closed my eyes, without concentrating, then yes, the soft features of our mother's face might escape me. But because of my dreams and their clarity, she was always with me. She and Ruth. I saw them from before, and I saw them as I hoped they were now: together, at peace.

"I think we're supposed to let them go," I said gently, my eyes trained on the tiny carving in her hand. There were no sharp angles cut into the wood, only curves and curls. Soft. Like Adelaide.

She turned toward me, gripping the small wooden figure in one fist until her knuckles whitened. She blinked quickly over unshed tears and her cheeks flushed. She looked much younger than her fifteen years.

"I can't," she said. "Maggie, I can't let them go. I won't. Sometimes I hurt *so much*. I need Mother so bad, and now when I can't see her, I get scared that I can't do anything without her. I'm afraid, Maggie. I'm afraid of *everything*."

I wanted to hold her. But there had been too many times when I had held her and taken away her fears. She needed to learn how to fight them on her own. I kept my arms at my sides.

"It's okay to hurt, Addy, and it's okay to be scared. Do you think I'm not? Ever since we were little, it was *you* who always showed *me* how we should go on when I was unhappy or frightened." I took a deep breath, then reached out and held her free hand. "We have to learn to understand our lives now, Addy. Everything is different. But they are our lives."

Her eyes were rimmed with red. She was trying hard to smile. "Help me, Maggie."

I held her then and thought I needed her as much as she needed me.

CHAPTER 18

The Green Corn Ceremony

Every few days the men of the tribe went hunting. They disappeared into the woods, each with a quiver of arrows and a bow slung over his back, a sharpened tomahawk tucked into his breechclout. Bronze, tattooed skin and dark eyes made the men as visible and *in*visible as the trees and shadows around them. They *became* the forest.

Sometimes they travelled on foot, sometimes on horseback. The Cherokee didn't use saddles, or even bridles. They rode bareback, their intuitive balance strong enough that their legs hung freely down the horses' sides.

The brothers, Soquili and Wahyaw, decided to teach Adelaide and me how to ride. As the summer wore on, I became more comfortable urging a horse forward, changing direction, and pulling my mount to a gentle stop using only my legs. I loved the movement, the sensation of flying a horse could give me.

Adelaide could ride, but didn't enjoy it like I did. She preferred knowing exactly where the ground was at every step. While she stayed in the village to sew or bead with the women, I often asked the brothers to let me go with them when they went hunting. Wahyaw was unsure, assuming I would somehow alert their prey. I persisted and promised I would be quiet, so Soquili persuaded Wahyaw to let me come once in a while, as an observer. Sometimes their father, Ahtlee-Kwi-duhsgah, or Does Not Bend, joined us. He was as powerful as a bear. An impressive fountain of feathers adorned his black comb of hair, still untouched by the white of age. His eyes flitted incessantly, constantly aware, like those of his elder son. He was a quiet man, issuing short commands only when necessary. His tall gray stallion had no patience for other horses.

More and more often, when the successful hunters emerged from the shelter of the woods, Soquili's eyes would meet mine. His dark brown gaze suggested he was interested in more than simply a friendship with me. I liked Soquili very much. We always seemed to have a lot to say to each other, and we laughed a great deal. It didn't hurt that he was handsome and cut from the rugged cloth of the bravest of warriors. I liked watching him move, and I liked the way he made me feel: confident and desired.

We spent the summer as friends, getting to know each other better. By August the corn had grown taller than anyone in the village and the stalks were heavy with fat, ripe cobs. The harvest heralded one of the biggest ceremonies of the Cherokee year: the Green Corn Ceremony. Soquili and Kokila told me what to expect over the four-day festival, but its reality still impressed me. Hundreds of Cherokee from other villages crowded into our longhouses, filling them with laughter until the early morning hours. The days and nights were filled with dancing, singing, and drums.

The festivities involved everyone, but the most obvious participants were the unmarried young people. It was impossible, in such a huge gathering of people, not to form new relationships, and not all of them were based purely on friendship. Anticipation of sex hovered like a cloud, low and thick in the air, adding heat to the fires where we all danced.

On one of those nights Soquili sat beside me and took my hand in his. He raised one eyebrow and grinned. Then he leaned forward and kissed my lips.

I wasn't completely surprised, but had no idea what to do or say. So I simply looked at him, smiling faintly, studying the tiny lines around his eyes, the soft pinkish bronze of his lips, the curl of his lashes when he blinked. I had noticed them all before. Now I took the time to see them.

My only other contact with the mouths of men had been brutal. This was a completely different sensation. Like a question, asked with intimate care. He reached forward with his free hand and placed it gently behind my neck beneath my braid. With smooth pressure he pulled my face closer to his and I closed my eyes. I felt the warmth of his breath touch my skin. Then his mouth was on mine, moving slowly, tenderly, not pushing but wanting. I could smell his musky scent under the smoky air. The taste of him was intoxicating, and the combination of his touch and the wildness of the celebration made me dizzy. I returned his kisses, giving in to the desire that tingled through me. His other hand released mine, and still kissing me, he moved his palm to the side of my face. He stroked my cheek, and his thumb traced the line of my jaw. His caresses were as soft as rabbit's fur, but unmistakably male.

I wanted this; I wanted to kiss and touch and feel and breathe him in.

But another layer of emotion emerged, one I had tried to ignore for the past few months. It bubbled up like sticky black tar: the fear, the outrage, the disgust, and the horror of my rape. The panic pushed upward in waves, and I shoved it back under. I trembled with the effort, and Soquili felt my movement. He pulled away.

"The night air is cold on your skin. Stay here, Ma-kee. I'll get a blanket for you."

He stood and smiled down at me, looking pleased with himself. Then he turned toward his longhouse, leaving me to my reverie.

The fire snapped in front of me, jerking me back to my surroundings. Across the flames from me, men and women huddled close together in pairs, smiling, touching, kissing.

The closeness they shared still reminded me of the men in the woods, and it terrified me. And yet I craved touch. I craved closeness. Would I ever be able to want a man like the girls across the fire did? Would strong, male hands ever soothe instead of panic?

Soquili strode back toward me, a blue woven blanket slung casually over his shoulder. He turned to laugh at something another man said, then swung back, still smiling, still walking with his dark eyes focused on me.

Suddenly my world dropped and I hung suspended in disbelief. I stared at Soquili, but it was no longer him that I saw.

In my vision, Wolf's hair fell in long, brown waves. His thick eyebrows were raised slightly in the middle, almost meeting under a well-defined widow's peak. His eyes were deep, flecked with gold.

Then he was gone, and Soquili stood in his place, draping the blanket over my shoulders. He sat beside me again and pulled in close, lifting one side of the blanket over his own shoulder so we shared our warmth. I smiled in gratitude, but felt empty inside.

I looked into the fire, forcing reality back into my head. Wolf wasn't here. Soquili stayed beside me, holding my hand in his.

Later that night, the longhouse was filled with women, babbling in girlish excitement. I slept on my regular pallet beside Adelaide, but my mind was elsewhere, floating by the fire, remembering Wolf's soft brown eyes. Every time I saw him in my visions, he seemed closer, but still so far away. *He is coming*, I told myself. *He has to come.*

In the morning I awoke feeling confused. It took a moment before I remembered why. Then the evening's intimacies raced back into my mind. Soquili. I liked Soquili a great deal. He was a good friend. His touch and his kisses felt wonderful. I wanted more.

On the other hand, I didn't want to hurt him. If I encouraged more than a friendship with Soquili, in the end I would leave him. My heart was already claimed, by a man I knew almost as well as I knew myself. By a man I had never met, but had to believe I would someday touch.

I dressed and stepped out of the longhouse, joining some of the others who were celebrating another day. Drums were beating already, hoarse morning voices beginning to sing. I told myself I would keep a friendly distance from Soquili, but as the day went on, it became apparent he was having none of that. He was with me whenever possible, holding me, brushing his lips against my skin and hair. His arms felt good around me, his sweet mouth warm and comforting. Despite my earlier conviction to avoid precisely this kind of attention, I did nothing to stop him.

Sometime after the midday meal, we walked through the village, holding hands, headed for the corrals. We wanted to escape conversations and other people for a while. He gave a low whistle from between his teeth, and our horses broke away from the herd. They walked toward us, their dark heads bobbing with every step, and when they were close enough, Soquili leaned over to help me mount. I stepped into his interlaced fingers, and he hoisted me onto my horse's back.

The day was hot and the breeze almost nonexistent. The sun

burned down, attracting flies to the horses so they shook their heads and whipped their tails. We guided the animals toward the trees and slipped into the forest. It was cooler beneath the oak and birch. Soquili turned his horse toward the sound of running water.

The path led up a hill, along a rough game trail that was too narrow for both horses to walk side by side. I followed Soquili, and from my vantage point I admired the smooth lines of his naked back as he flexed with his horse's movements. Soquili glanced at me over his shoulder, smiling and talking with his hands as well as his voice. I returned the smile, encouraging the stories as I always did. His voice was gentle but confident, and it flowed like syrup.

At the top of the trail, Soquili dismounted and held my horse while I slid off, then he led the way to a pretty little glen, flickering with yellow butterflies. Rocks and flowers were scattered around a tiny stream, illuminated into a golden ribbon by the sun. Soquili sat by me at the edge of the pool.

It was wonderfully quiet away from the village. Only the cheery sounds of birds and the voice of the stream met our ears. Soquili didn't speak, only leaned back against our shared boulder and closed his eyes.

A dead tree beside me gave no shade to the boulder. The brittle gray stubs of its branches extended like bleached-out bones, reaching for the sky despite the fact it no longer required the sun. A woodpecker hopped up and down the trunk, cocking his head at various angles, looking for food. A puff of wind fluffed the soft black and white down on his chest, but the little hunter didn't blink. He drew back his head, then hammered into the trunk with blinding speed, puncturing the still air. A moment later, a squirming insect hung from the long black beak. The bird glanced to his left then flew off, carrying his wriggling meal.

The sound of his flight brought back to mind another bird: the raven who had watched me that night in the forest as I lay tied and bleeding. At that time, I would have given anything for the power to fly. Now, as I breathed in the cool, clean air, gazing at Soquili and knowing he cared, listening to the unintelligible chatter in the trees around me, I had no desire to fly anywhere. My heart yearned to meet Wolf in the flesh, but I knew he would come in his own time. For now, this was my impression of heaven. I sighed and closed my eyes.

"Are you happy, Ma-kee?" Soquili asked.

"Yes." I sighed, not bothering to open my eyes. I was smiling, though, and I heard the smile in his voice when he spoke again.

"Ma-kee?"

"Mm-hmm?"

"Are you happy with me?"

The question was so simple, but finding the answer was not. I opened my mouth to speak, but he heard my hesitation. The tone of his voice changed.

"Have I done something wrong?" he asked.

I opened my eyes and turned to him. He was watching me closely, his dark eyes anxious.

"No, Soquili, you haven't done anything wrong. And everything about living in your village makes me happy. But . . ." I paused, not knowing if I should say anything more. No one knew about Wolf. No one but me. "There is something else, and I need to talk with you about it. It's important."

"What is it?" he asked. "Tell me what you need and you will have it."

"What I need, Soquili, is for you to listen and understand." I reached out and took his hands in mine. "It isn't something you can do or have done. It is something I have always known."

A flicker of unease crossed his expression. I squeezed his hands, feeling the warmth of his tough skin against my palms.

"I know it might be difficult for you to believe what I'm going to tell you. You can't see what I do. But I need you to listen and believe what I say. It is something I have always dreamed—"

"Wait," he said. He pulled his hands out of mine and sat up straight, evidently wanting to end the conversation. "Say no more."

"I have to," I said. "I can't let you think that you and I—"

"I want you by my side, Ma-kee. I would like us to be wed."

I took a deep breath and let it out slowly. His handsome features were drawn into a frown. Of confusion? Of anger? I couldn't tell.

"No," I said gently. "Soquili, the—"

"Ah, I understand," he said, his face suddenly brightening with an easy smile. "I know why you think this. It is because you consider yourself to be a member of our clan already and know we cannot marry within our own clan. You do not need to worry about that. The law is different because you are a white woman. We have brought you into our family, but you and I can still marry. I'm sure of it."

"No, Soquili. What I'm trying to say—"

He frowned again and looked down at his hands. "We can ask when we get back, to be sure, but I don't think—"

"Soquili, stop. I'm trying to tell you something. I'm trying to tell you that no matter what the laws of the tribe are, I cannot marry you."

There was a pause. I watched his expression go through a number of changes.

"You do not want me," he stated, his words falling dead on the rocks.

"That's not it, Soquili. What I'm trying to say is that my dreams—"

"Your dreams! Ha!" He slapped his hands on his knees and stood, towering over me. The corner of his mouth pulled in, almost into a sneer. "I knew it!"

I had never seen Soquili angry before. I didn't dare move. His black eyes flashed on me, and he spoke in a low, growling voice.

"Your dreams, your magic, your gift from the spirit world. Pah! You can make them say whatever you want. You do not want me, you blame the dreams. You are wrong about something, and you blame them, too. If you do not want to marry me, Ma-kee, you should be strong enough to say it. And if that is so, why do you kiss me and hold my hand? Why do you look at me the way you do?"

"I—" I said in a tiny voice, but stopped, having no idea where to start.

"This is what I mean," he fumed. "You cannot answer a question without consulting your dreams. You do not know what you want. I waited for you, Ma-kee. I trusted your eyes. Do not tell me some story about your dreams. Do not treat me like an idiot. The others may listen to every word you say, but I *know* you."

He disappeared into the trees, crackling twigs under his feet. I didn't watch him go, but stared at the dead tree beside me, feeling wretched.

He was right and he was wrong. To be fair, I did listen to my dreams, and paid close attention to them. But they didn't rule my every decision. I thought for myself and always had. The dreams only provided insight and guidance.

What hurt was when he had said I didn't know what I wanted. It hurt because in many ways he was right. I didn't know why I allowed myself to grow close to Soquili when my heart already belonged to Wolf. I liked being with Soquili, doing what we'd been doing. Before he came along, I had never felt protected or cared for by anyone other than Wolf. I had never expected to want to touch a man after what had happened to me in the woods.

I hated that I had hurt him. That he'd felt the need to strike out the way he did. I liked Soquili very much. But he had to understand I was never going to be his wife.

Birds began to sing after he disappeared into the trees, friendly chirps that sounded out of place after the harshness of Soquili's voice. I listened until their songs faded into the background and the quiet claimed me. My mind opened and the images of my dreams slipped through, filling me with peace.

Wolf's voice wove through my mind, caressing it with ancient syllables both rough and melodic. My heart reached out for more, needing to hear the words he whispered in his soft, curling accent.

As quickly as one might blow out a candle, everything went black. I was jerked from the warmth of my musings and plunged into an icy cold void. My fingers cramped around something hard and impenetrable—metal bars. The stench of death flooded my senses like water, and I thought it might be my own. Panic rose through me, and I knew I had to get out, I had to—

Soquili woke me, his hands tight on my arms as he shook the sleep from me. His eyes were concerned, his brow creased. I heard him call to me, but couldn't make out the thick syllables. As my mind cleared, so did his words.

"Ma-kee! Wake up! I am here, Ma-kee, I am here, *gugegui,*" he cried in halting English, using the Cherokee endearment for "love."

I awoke slowly, my eyes still blurred. I blinked up at him from where I lay against the boulder, not understanding.

"You screamed, Ma-kee. But you are safe with me."

He stroked my hair and freed it from the clinging sweat on my neck. I felt breathless, as if I'd been running for hours, as if I would never breathe deeply again. I raised myself to my elbows and looked into his eyes. I knew that fear dominated my expression. There was no way to disguise it.

"Soquili, something very wrong is coming. It is something I *know*, like when Grandmother Waw-Li knows something. It is coming and it is very bad, very *uyoi*."

He shook his head, brow creased, and tried to talk me off the precarious cliff where I teetered in my mind.

"There is nothing wrong, Ma-kee. There is only *dohiyi*," he said, trying to calm me. Peace. There is only peace.

But I knew otherwise. There was no peace in that silent black hole. I sat all the way up, and he put his arm around my shoulders for support. I was trembling. He must have felt it.

"Soquili, you know about my dreams."

He nodded and sighed. "Of course," he said, looking resigned. "Everyone knows. I do not wish to talk about them."

"I know that. But I need to. I can't look away from them like you can. They are real," I whispered. "What I see *will happen*."

He examined the broad palms of his hands. He knew he should believe. Everything in his culture taught him to accept what I was saying. After a moment he raised his eyes to meet mine.

"What did you see, Ma-kee?"

I paused. What *had* I seen? Nothing. It was what I had heard, what I had felt. The words rushed out.

"I saw black and felt death and it was cold. I was alone and—"

"You felt death? Whose?"

"I don't know. I think mine," I said, frowning and shaking my head. "But I couldn't really tell. I only knew it was something I couldn't prevent. Something very wrong. Something I . . ." I trailed off, no longer looking at him, trying to sort through the images.

He must have sensed my frustration because he grasped my shoulders and pulled me to him. He folded me into his arms and rested his chin on my head. His lips brushed over my hair and I closed my eyes, feeling the steady pulse that beat slowly in his throat. I wanted to cry from confusion; I wanted to be held. We sat silently like that, listening to the leaves and the water, waiting for my heart to slow.

"I will keep you safe," he told me. "We will not talk of the future today. But you do not need to feel fear. As long as you are beside me, no harm will come to you."

PART 4: ANDREW

Toward the Sea

CHAPTER 19

A Restless Peace

Sorcha and Janet MacLeod heard the jingling of harnesses and the slick whisper of ponies slipping down the muddy hill outside the cottage. They peeked through the door, wary of strangers, then flung it open when they caught sight of Hector, blood-soaked and white-faced. Behind him trailed the other men, their muddied ponies snorting at sight of the barn. And with them, two fragile children, pale as eggshells.

Sorcha was efficient. She assessed and treated her husband's injuries as well as she could, then coaxed him into a deep sleep on their bed. When she had finished taking care of him, she turned to inspect the other men. She checked Geoffrey's rough bandages, and sent Janet running for clean cloths and water.

"Who's this then?" Sorcha asked, bending over to inspect the children. They stared at her, blinking like owls.

Iain put a supportive hand on each child's shoulder. "We found these two orphaned in the woods. Have ye somethin' they might eat? I think another moment an' their stomachs will growl louder than my own voice."

"Of course. Come with me, children," she said. Clucking like a mother hen, she bustled them toward the table and brought steaming bowls of broth with currant cakes set on the side. The little faces stared in awe at the feast. Iain seated them on his vast lap and motioned for them to eat, then reached toward the bowl of broth Sorcha brought for him.

The huge fireplace took up the entire length of the west wall, burning fragrant peat. Janet sat on a bench by the fire, keeping to herself. She watched the guests and listened to their story, but kept her eyes averted from Andrew. Memories of their last meeting filled her with an unsavoury mixture of anger and shame.

When the broth and biscuits were finished, Janet set a chestnut pie on the table. When she placed Andrew's plate in front of him, he touched her sleeve and looked into her green eyes. He spoke softly so only she could hear.

"I thank ye for the welcome and for the meal. I'll no' trouble ye long. I'll be off in a couple o' days."

She frowned slightly and kept her voice just as low. She needn't have worried. Iain was engaged in hearty conversation with her brothers. Any private conversation wasn't likely to be overheard.

"Ye're always welcome here. Ye ken that well enough," she assured him. Her words were genuine, but spoken with a shadow of the warmth they used to hold.

"Aye, well, it's time I go," he said. His gaze flicked over the orphans. "I've had enough o' this cursed country. I've no' the stomach for it anymore."

Janet looked as if she didn't want to ask, didn't want to appear the least bit interested. But she asked nonetheless. "Where will ye go?"

"I dinna ken for sure yet. I'll head to the coast and go from there."

She nodded and a faint flush rose in her cheeks. She turned toward her mother. "I'll go see if Da needs anything," she said.

It was getting late. Geoffrey could no longer hide his yawns and retired for the night in one of the back rooms. The two little ones, already asleep on Iain's lap, were laid into a box bed, tucked against the wall. Even asleep, the children turned toward each other, coming together in a knot of tangled arms and legs. Sorcha pulled the curtain across, giving the children a safe cocoon in which to dream.

Iain and Andrew shared another room. Andrew could hardly wait to sink into one of the two small beds. He splashed his face with cool water from a basin and swished it around his teeth.

"Did I hear ye say to the lass as ye were thinkin' o' leavin'?" Iain asked.

Andrew turned toward the deep voice, seeing the profile of its owner against the flickering light of a candle. A clean cloth lay folded beside the basin, and Andrew used it to wipe the water from his face before it dripped onto his chest. He leaned against the wall and rubbed the cloth between his palms.

"Aye," he admitted. "I'm ready to move on. My family's gone, my home's gone. I'm tired o' fightin'. I'll leave when Hector's well."

Iain nodded, then muttered, "I've half a mind to join ye."

"Do it then, man."

Iain stood in silence while Andrew crawled into bed. When Iain spoke again, Andrew was almost asleep.

"I think I will," Iain said. "I'll join ye—wi' the weans."

Andrew smiled in the dark. "Aye. I'd no' expect ye to leave 'em behind."

In the morning, Iain and Andrew were up early. They headed into the woods and returned a couple of hours later, two rabbit carcasses dangling from each of their waists. Janet stood outside the door of the house when they approached, wiping her hands on her apron. Her brothers, still yawning, walked around her, headed toward the privacy of the woods.

"Good mornin', Miss Janet," said Iain. *"Ciamar a tha sibh?"*

"*Tha gu math, tapadh leibh,* Mr. MacKenzie. I'm quite well. And you—did ye sleep well?" she asked.

"Och, aye," Iain answered gravely. "That's a very soft bed your mother laid out."

As if she heard her name, Sorcha came out to join them, taking a break from the morning meal's preparations.

"Good mornin', Mistress Sorcha," Iain said.

Sorcha gave him a weary smile and reached for the rabbits. Her long black hair, so like her daughter's, was tucked under her cap. A few restless wisps escaped and fluttered in the morning breeze. She brushed them from her face with the back of one hand.

"An' to you as well, Mr. MacKenzie," she said. "This will make a lovely stew. I thank ye both."

"Did Hector no' sleep well last night, then? Ye look like ye were up most the night," he said gently.

"Oh, he'll do. 'Twas a long night, to be sure, but he'll do. I thank ye for askin'. And you? Did ye sleep well?"

They spoke of their plans for the day, and eventually came back inside for breakfast. Hector didn't join them, but Sorcha assured them he was sleeping comfortably.

After the two little redheads had finished their parritch and toast, they clambered off their chairs and wandered the room, ingesting every detail. They had been bathed and dressed in shirts that had once belonged to Simon and Geoffrey, and had begun to speak, a bit at a time. The little boy introduced himself as Peter. He was five. His little sister, Flora, had just turned four. Their mother was a seamstress. Their father had been a blacksmith until he'd left with the army.

The conversation inevitably led to the tragedy in the cottage. Peter stood by the fireplace and crossed his arms, refusing to take refuge in Iain's offer of a lap. He took a deep breath to steel his young heart.

"Mam was wi' child again," he said, "an' Da left wi' the rest o' the men, so he said as it was me what was the man o' the house."

"Ma and I wept when Da left," Flora added. "Peter said 'twas all right, that we'd do fine. But then the bairn started to come."

Peter nodded. "I carried water from the river, while Flora ran to fetch the midwife, but there was no one at home."

"There was no one anywhere!" Flora exclaimed.

"We was almos' home, an' we could hear Mam screamin' somethin' terrible. We was dead cold, so we run to the door, callin' to her," Peter said, "but all at once she quit her greetin' and there were nae sound t'all. I was scairt to go in, but we didna ken what else to do."

Peter looked at Flora, who stared at him with huge eyes. Peter cleared his throat.

"Mam was dead. We tried to give her a drink, we tried shakin' her, but she was dead, an' the bairn ne'er even born. Ever'thin' smelled so bad I thought I mi' get sick," Peter admitted. Flora nodded, her big eyes filling with tears. "So we went outside again to wait."

No one moved for a moment.

"What were ye waiting for, laddie?" Iain asked softly.

"Well," Peter said, looking at Iain with eyes round with trust. "I thought maybe someone would have to come sometime, aye? And I was right, was I no', Flora?"

He grinned at her and she gave him a smile that lit the room.

"Aye." She turned to Andrew, who was sitting beside her. "Peter's mos' always right," she said, as if that required confirmation. "We went in the cottage to eat, but we couldna reach the top shelf. We tried sleepin' in the kitchen, but the smell were too bad, an' then the flies started to come, so we took all the biscuits and jam outside. We ate all the tatties. There was no more food, an' we were hurtin' wi' hunger." She paused and turned toward Iain, pale blue eyes searching. "Did the faeries bring ye?"

"Why do ye ask that?" Iain asked.

"Because at night we asked 'em to find help," she said.

Iain nodded gently, cupping both little faces in his huge hands.

"Aye, the faeries tol' us where to find ye, *m'eudail.* An' they said 'twas up to me to keep ye safe from now on, so that's what I'll do."

He lifted them as effortlessly as if they were a handful of feathers. Andrew picked up a couple of bannocks Janet had spread with jam. He handed one bannock to each child as Iain swooped through the doorway with the children in his arms. Before long, Andrew could hear the children's giggles from the yard: silvery sounds falling like tiny snowflakes and melting in the warmth of Iain's voice.

Andrew remembered other days like this: sunny days that promised nothing but laughter. He had spent those days playing with his brothers, and the memory pushed a lump into his throat. He swallowed hard.

Sometimes Andrew swore he could still hear his brother Dougal's voice on the wind. He could see him clearly when he tried: long black hair and laughing eyes. He remembered Dougal's fierce expression on that last miserable morning in April, when Andrew had followed his brother into the moor and lost him in the mass of kilts and steel. He hadn't seen Dougal since that moment. He wished he could have at least embraced him before he died.

This sunny day, he decided, shrugging off his melancholy, would be spent in solitude. Having made up his mind to leave Scotland, he wanted time to reflect, to make plans. Ireland, maybe? Or perhaps try to find his way in France, where Ciaran had hoped someday to go to school?

Andrew went out to the barn, to where the ponies hung their heads over the half doors. He unlatched the door to Fognan's stall and she whickered, seeming happy to go with him. He led her outside, then Andrew swung onto the saddle and nudged the pony onto the same pathway they had taken before.

The colours of the meadow had changed since his last visit. Late summer had clothed it in a robe of lush green, speckled with purple and white flowers. Now early frost licked the fallen leaves, and their blackened edges crunched beneath Fognan's hooves.

Andrew loosened the reins and the pony wandered through the grass until they reached the centre of the meadow, where they'd stopped before. Andrew dropped off and lay on his back, but it wasn't the comfortable place it had been. September had cooled and stiffened the grass in preparation for winter, turning it a dull brown. It poked at his neck when he laid back his head. But the place was soothing, whether the pillow of grass was green or brown. He closed his eyes, craving the peace he had experienced before, and hoping to see the girl again. He drifted into darkness and blindly followed the dizzying path toward sleep.

It took a little longer for him to fall asleep this time. His thoughts were filled with the faces of those he knew: brief glimpses of the tiny children; deep lines of concern that creased Hector's wan face; Janet's faraway, green-eyed gaze; Iain's haunting expression of sadness. Into Andrew's mind flitted a surprisingly clear memory of his older brother, Dougal, giving him a wink and a grin. That one hurt the most, and yet he clung to it.

It was in that halfway world between consciousness and oblivion that Andrew saw her again. Her face seemed to float above him like a hovering bird. He studied it, burning every freckle and curve into his memory. Unlike the last time, when she'd been torn and defeated, now her cheeks glowed a healthy pink and her long brown hair was braided loosely on either side of her face. She wore a soft dress dotted with beads that clung to her skin and hinted at her curves. He ached to touch her.

In that moment she was there, lying beside him on the grass bed, closer than she had ever been. The image was so real he almost pulled away in surprise. Instead, he reached for her hand, and though they couldn't touch, he held it as if it had always belonged in his. The touch was almost real. Almost skin on skin. His palm buzzed with the contact, his fingers tingled. He wanted to keep her there forever. He wanted to stroke the soft curve of her face with his other hand, but he was afraid if he did, she would disappear.

"I will find ye," he whispered.

And then she spoke. Not a whisper, but a true voice. The most beautiful sound he'd ever heard.

"I know."

Then she was gone.

"I *will* find ye, lass," he promised.

CHAPTER 20

Plans

Long fingers of shadow stretched over the leaf-littered ground, but there was enough light that Iain sat on a log, elbows on his knees, absorbed in whittling a small piece of wood. He whistled to himself and nodded once when Andrew came to sit across from him. Iain's flaming mass of hair was tied back, affording Andrew a more detailed view of his friend's face than he was used to seeing. Not a handsome face, Andrew thought, but a kind one.

"Where be the weans?" Andrew asked, noticing their unusual absence.

Iain's eyes softened but he kept them on his work. "Sleepin'," he answered. "They just about wore me out, but I think I go' the best o' them after all."

"An' how's Hector?"

"Well enough."

"That's good." Andrew cleared his throat and his mind. "I'll go an' speak with him afore supper. Tell him I'm leavin' soon."

"Aye," Iain answered. His huge wrist rotated gently, changing angles to follow the wood. "The weans an' I will go wi' ye."

The little carving in Iain's hand was taking on the shape of a pony, its head and mane clearly defined. Andrew gestured at it with his chin. Iain shrugged.

"For the lass. She's taken a likin' to the beasts." He chuckled. "Sweet lassie, that one."

Andrew watched Iain's expression, then asked a question he couldn't hold back. "How old were yer bairns when ye went to war?"

The knife hand paused, hovering over its work. A shadow crossed Iain's face, and the gentle smile faded.

"About the same as these two." He lifted one corner of his mouth in a bitter smile and turned his face toward Andrew. "I couldna believe it when we found them there at the cottage, with their red hair and blue eyes. 'Twas like my own weans sent me for these two, God bless their wee souls."

He trapped his lower lip in his teeth for a moment before his eyes returned to his hands. The knife cut a careful curve in the wooden haunches, revealing a tail that waved with a flourish.

The connection between the giant and the red-headed pixies was as invisible, and yet as real, as the bond Andrew shared with the girl from his dreams. Andrew nodded, then hesitated, wanting to somehow comfort the big man, wanting to tell him he understood. Instead, he stood up and turned toward the house.

"Would ye think to travel to the colonies?" Iain said unexpectedly.

Andrew stopped, considering. "The colonies? Aye, well, it's certainly a good distance from here." He frowned at Iain. "What about the weans? Could they survive a voyage such as that?"

"They'd be fine wi' me," Iain assured him.

"The colonies," Andrew mused, then pictured the girl in her soft brown tunic, its beaded design like tiny flowers around her neck. "Aye. The colonies," he said with a smile. "I'd like that fine."

"Good then," Iain grunted, and returned to his carving.

"I'm off to speak wi' Hector," Andrew called over his shoulder. "I'll see ye at supper, shall I?"

There was no response from Iain. He had disappeared, melting back into his quiet world.

Andrew peered through the open door of the cottage and saw Janet, stirring the stew that bubbled in a black cauldron over the fire. The aroma rose through the room and caught Andrew as he entered, reminding him he had missed his midday meal.

Janet was frowning, her lips pursed together, having just sampled the hot stew.

"That smells fine," Andrew said as he walked toward her father's room.

Hector was sitting up in bed, reading, when Andrew came into the room. He didn't object when Andrew lifted the corner of the bandage on his arm, peered under it, then sat on a stool by the bed.

"It's lookin' well."

Hector smiled back. "Aye, it is, though 'tis fair to say I'd no' be here now if it wasna for you." He put his book facedown on the bed and frowned at Andrew. "I mus' tell ye, lad, I've ne'er been so pleased to see a fellow than when you an' the others came screamin' through the bush. What brought ye to us?" he asked, raising one eyebrow. "Ye couldna have heard the stramash from yon cottage."

Andrew didn't know how to answer. He never did.

"I just knew," Andrew said with a shrug. He cleared his throat. "I've come to tell ye I'll be leavin' soon. Iain and the weans are comin' wi' me."

Hector raised both brows this time. "Leave a man abed for two days and everything changes, aye?"

The afternoon sun arced just low enough to blaze through the window, momentarily blinding Andrew. He averted his gaze and turned so the sunlight warmed his back.

"Well, so." Hector tilted his head slightly. "What is it ye plan to do then, lad?"

"I'm tired o' this land. There are too many ghosts on it," Andrew said, looking at his feet.

Hector nodded. "An' ye've seen more than yer fair share." From the big room came the sound of Janet's voice, talking with her mother. Hector's expression looked sad as he gazed at the open door toward his women. "It's a hard life for us all," Hector said. "I understand. I'll miss ye, lad, but I do understand."

Andrew rose and turned toward the door. Voicing his plans to Hector eased Andrew's mind somewhat. For the first time he began to get excited about his imminent departure.

"Get ye up for supper then, auld man," he said, teasing Hector. "Else Iain will empty yer plate for ye this eve."

"Get on wi' ye. I'll be in presently." Hector paused. "Andrew?"

"Aye?"

"Ye're a good man. Your da'd be proud."

Andrew was in the doorway, but stopped where he was at Hector's words. He cleared his throat, but couldn't find words. His hand rested on the doorframe for a moment longer than it needed.

Hector watched him go. His smile of regret faded just as the sun's rays slipped beneath the window, leaving him alone in the quiet grayness of the room.

CHAPTER 21

Another Traveler

Andrew walked from Hector's room, through the kitchen, past Janet and Sorcha. The cooking fire sputtered under a drip from a roasting pheasant, which was flavouring the air and taking on a fine shade of deep gold. Janet stopped rolling out dough and cleared her throat when Andrew came out. She wiped her hands on her apron.

"Andrew, could I maybe speak wi' ye?"

"O' course," he said. "Will ye walk outside?"

He waited while she untied her apron and hung it over a chair. She cast her mother an apologetic glance, but Sorcha smiled and gestured for her to go.

Outside the cottage the air was crisp, the grass crunchy under their feet. They walked toward the firepit, where Iain had left a small heap of wood shavings lying in the ashes. Andrew sat in the spot Iain had left, and Janet sat beside him. She seemed agitated, frowning and plucking at her skirt, so he didn't rush her.

This was Andrew's favourite time of day, when day softened into night. He leaned back and closed his eyes, then yawned, filling his lungs with dusk.

"When do ye leave?" Janet asked. She picked up one of the wood shavings and stroked the edges with her thumbs.

"In the morn."

She nodded. They sat in silence for a moment, then she turned to face him.

"I want to go wi' ye," she said, daring him with a flash of green eyes.

"Oh, Janet. We've been over that," he said. "I tol' ye I'm not—"

She shook her head, biting her lower lip. "Nay, Andrew. I'm askin' if you and Iain are takin' the weans wi' ye, then can ye please take me as well. I'd be a help. I'd mind the weans, an' cook, an' whatever else needs doin'."

"And your parents?" he asked, returning her gaze. "Have ye spoken wi' them about this?"

She dropped her gaze to her skirt, where her fingers folded and refolded the material. She shook her head. "No' yet. I wanted to be sure ye'd say it was all right afore I asked them."

She waited and he saw the desperate hope in her expression.

"I dinna ken, lass," he said, and shook his head. "We've decided to go to the colonies, aye? 'Tis a savage land for a young woman."

"Andrew," she stated calmly, "I canna stay here. If I do, I'll die. The most excitin' thing I'll see here is the calving next spring. I've told ye afore, I mus' get out. If that means sailin' to America, I'm ready for it," she said. She reached for his hand. "Please, Andrew. Dinna leave me here. I promise I'll no' come after ye like I did." Her cheeks flushed again. "Ye can help me find a fine, rich husband where'er it is we end up."

Andrew laughed and gave her hand an affectionate squeeze.

"Whoe'er he is, he'll be a lucky man." He shook his head. "Janet, yer da will ne'er let ye go. He'll need ye here. He'll say ye're too young."

"Too young! Andrew, I'm no' much younger than you! And I could cook and take care of ye all. Please, Andrew!"

"I must say no unless he says it's all right."

She nodded, but her face turned a deep shade of red, her lips tightened in a straight line. He wasn't sure if she was going to scream or cry. He felt ashamed, and sorry he couldn't grant her wish.

Janet stood, feeling betrayed. She stared at Andrew, then turned and went to find her parents. They would be even more of a challenge, but she had to try. This was her only chance. She forced herself to calm down before she entered the cottage. Her father always said she had a wicked temper. It would do no good to lose control when she needed it the most. She took a deep breath and stepped through the outer door, into the cottage.

The air was scented with the spices of the supper she had helped prepare. It smelled delicious, but at that moment it seemed almost suffocating for her. She walked through the main room and past the kitchen, then knocked on her parents' door.

"Aye?" came her father's voice.

" 'Tis only me, Da," she said. "I've something I must ask ye, if ye've time."

"O' course. Come in, Janet," he said.

She lifted the latch on their door and stepped into the bedroom. Her parents were sitting together on the side of their bed, talking. Her father was dressed in a clean white shirt and wrapped in a dark kilt for dinner. Sorcha was laughing.

"Come in, *mo nighean,*" Hector said, smiling up at her. "What do ye need?"

Janet sat on the bed beside them. A cold weight landed in her stomach, and she realised she was too afraid to ask. They waited. She took a deep breath. No. She *had* to do it.

"I mean to go wi' Andrew and Iain when they leave."

There was an uncomfortable silence in the room. Everyone's smile faltered. Her father cleared his throat.

"What are ye sayin', daughter?" His voice was uneven with shock. He frowned as if she were telling a joke. "Ye'll no' be travelin' wi' those men. They've a great distance to go, and every mile of it dangerous. Yer mam and I need ye here."

Janet looked at her mother, then her father. Her eyes filled with tears, but she refused to shed even one. It would be a sign of weakness. She needed her parents to think she was strong enough to handle anything. She kept her voice level.

"I'm grown, Da. I'm seventeen. I've a life to discover, and I'll no' find it here. Ye know that as well as I. There's nothing for me here. The men were all killed last spring fightin' for bloody Prince Charles, so there's no one left for me to marry. Besides, I want more, Da. I want to see what I've read about in books. I want to learn things an' meet people. If I stay here, I'll never be happy. Ye know it, Da. Ye know it! I canna stay here."

Hector's lips tightened. "That's enough, Janet. Go now and forget this nonsense," he said and dismissed her with a jerk of his chin toward the door.

She hesitated, wanting to plead her case further, but his expression was set. Her mother's face showed little emotion, though her eyes looked sad. Janet backed away, looking at them in turn, searching for a crack in their wall. When she reached the door, she turned and walked out of the room, finally and quietly surrendering to tears.

Hector looked at his wife with his eyebrows raised in disbelief. He shook his head.

"Can ye believe that, Sorcha? Wantin' to leave like that? Leave us and go God knows where with those men we hardly know? Foolishness," he grumbled.

"Do ye think so, *mo dhuine*?" Sorcha asked.

He blinked. "What, do you not?"

"I think, my husband, that it is something we should talk about."

"How can ye say such a thing?" he blurted.

"How can ye refuse your daughter's wish wi'out stopping to think?" Sorcha touched her husband's face, cupping his rough cheek in her palm. "Ye ken she's no' happy here. She's bored, and she's lonely. Ye can see she wants more than this."

Hector stared at his wife as if she had lost her mind. Sorcha reached for his hand.

"Come now, Hector. What I mean is we shouldna forbid her wi'out thinkin' on it first. She deserves to be heard. If she feels so strongly, we owe her that."

Hector puffed air through his lips. "Ye canna be serious, Sorcha. Send her away? Put her on one o' them godforsaken ships and hope she makes it across to some piece o' rock somewhere? She just waltzes in here and says she's off? How can I condone that? What should I do, say, *'Ooh aye, Janet, lass. Have a lovely trip'*? She said it herself, Sorcha, she's only seventeen."

"Older than I was when I married you, Hector MacLeod," she reminded him. "I was old enough then to be your wife, to bear yer babes. She's a woman, *mo dhuine,* no' a wee lassie anymore." She paused. "Just think on it, Hector."

She kissed him lightly, then stood, dropping his hand. A calm smile still played across her lips and he saw, as he always did, how beautiful she was. They had lived a lifetime together, and she was every bit as lovely as when they had first met. And she had grown so much wiser over the years. She walked to the door and looked back, leaning against the frame.

"What am I to do, Sorcha?" he asked.

"Think on it," she repeated quietly. "*I'm* of a mind to let her go. But I'll say nothing wi'out yer blessing. Ye reacted quickly, and understandably. Now ye've had time to consider it. If ye say no, well, then I'll say no as well. But think o' Janet. Think o' what she'll do here. There's no' much future for her here. And out there," she said, gesturing vaguely toward the window, "she could find *more*. She could discover whate'er it is makes her happy." She sighed. "God knows I wish I knew what she wanted. I just know, Hector, you and I *both* know it's not here."

After Sorcha left, Hector sat for a long time, arguing with himself. His heart couldn't fathom losing Janet. His head couldn't imagine forcing her to stay. He walked to the window and looked out at his sons. They were talking with each other while they mucked out the stable and forked in clean hay. Hector tried to remember them as they had been ten years before. Young pups, laughing and pushing each other until they collapsed into a wriggling heap. Watching them now, he noticed things he hadn't admitted to himself before: their broad shoulders, the new suggestion of authority in their deeper voices, the shadow of beards on their faces.

They seemed happy. Hector didn't think they would leave. Not yet, anyway. They were Highlanders, content to be what they were.

But Janet—

He leaned his forehead on his hand, running his fingers under his hair. Aye, he'd think on it. His memory showed him a long-forgotten image of Sorcha on the day they had wed: her trusting eyes, her soft young body. Sixteen. Sweet Sorcha. How could it be his own daughter had passed that same age already?

When the meal was about to be served, Hector made his way to the table, heavily bandaged and bracing himself on his wife's shoulder. Janet was there, trying to hide her reddened eyes. She stared at her lap without saying a word.

The pheasant was delicious, and the pot of cock-a-leekie soup bottomless. Whisky and ale flowed easily throughout supper. Iain and the children carried on their own conversation, serious and laughing in turn. Spirits were high around the table. Nevertheless, tension hung in the air. After the meal, the women cleaned up and the men went outside to enjoy the evening. When the others gathered around the firepit, Hector pulled Andrew aside and led him along a line of trees that flickered with the firelight.

"She's only seventeen, Andrew," Hector said. He looked at his feet, not ready to meet Andrew's eyes. "She's headstrong and she's difficult at times, but she's my lass. I can see why it is ye're so drawn to each other, lad, it's just—"

Andrew frowned. "I'm sorry to interrupt, Hector, but what is it she said to ye?"

Hector raised his eyebrows. "She said she's leavin' wi' ye on the morn. Did ye no speak wi' her about that?"

"Och, aye, we spoke," Andrew confirmed with a wry smile that sparkled in his eyes. "I told her she couldna come."

"Ye told her no?"

"I did."

Hector thought this over. "And why is it ye said no?"

"I'm no' sure," Andrew said with a shrug. "I didna think ye'd agree to it, I suppose. We're headed to America, aye? A long journey, that."

"Aye, aye," Hector murmured, absorbed in his thoughts. They walked a little farther and Hector stopped, blocking Andrew's path.

"She'll never speak to me again if I dinna let her go," Hector said. "And I'll never see her again if she goes. It seems I canna win."

Andrew clamped his hand on Hector's good shoulder and smiled. "If ye trust Iain and myself to it, we'd care for her as if she were our own sister. I give ye my word she will come to nae harm."

"As yer sister, aye?" Hector asked, raising one eyebrow.

"Aye, Hector." Andrew grinned. "As my sister. Janet's lovely, and I'd be a lucky man, but it's not to be. I've another, aye? That I'm sworn to."

Hector's white linen bandage glowed in the night. The men stood in silence, digesting each other's words. Finally Hector sighed.

" 'Tis a shame, that, Andrew. Ye're a man of honour. She'd do well to marry ye." There was another pause. "I'll tell her yes, then, if it's fine with you, and wi' Iain."

Andrew smiled. "O' course, Hector. We'd be glad of her."

They walked a few more steps. The going was easier now the decision had been made.

"So, ye'll go to the colonies? Yer mind's set against Europe?" Hector asked.

"Aye. There's plenty o' land in the New World for men willing to work it. It's no' an easy way, but it feels right to me."

Hector looked dubious. He now had a personal interest in the direction Andrew took.

"They do say as there be great beasts and savages there, what eat men like you for breakfast. At least ye'd be safe in the streets of Paris."

"I think not." Andrew grinned. "Paris has its own predators, aye? Nay, I'll no' fool myself that life will be easy, but I dinna think it'll be as terrible as all that."

"Aye, well," Hector said softly.

They were across the clearing from where some of the others chatted around the fire. Janet sat off to the side, silently poking the ground with a stick. Andrew smiled. The lass was going to get what she wanted after all.

CHAPTER 22

Farewells at the Fire

Iain tucked the children into their box bed and wrapped a blanket around the two small bodies. They fell instantly asleep in a confusing array of skinny white arms and legs. He smoothed the hair over their foreheads with calloused hands that were larger than their faces and brushed his lips over their brows.

He stood for a moment, listening to them breathe. It calmed him to hear the little purring sounds that trembled through their throats, the occasional peep as something secret happened in a dream. He had done this every night with his own children. With them gone, it seemed so important that he stop and listen to these two.

He dropped his chin to his chest and stepped outside, latching the door behind him. Iain joined the others by the fire, where Geoffrey played his fiddle, accompanied by the songs of night creatures.

Andrew sat beside Iain and told him of his separate discussions with Janet and Hector. Iain raised an eyebrow but nodded. He was surprised she wanted to go with them, but he wasn't averse to bringing her.

A faint yellow glow spilled from the door of the cottage as it swung open. Hector and Sorcha stepped out, leaning against each other, Sorcha talking and smiling at her husband. He held her, letting her support him. They found a place among their friends, then Hector cleared his throat and began to speak.

"As master of the house," Hector began formally, letting his eyes meet those of Andrew and Iain, "I thank ye both for everything ye've brought to our family. It was a blessin' that ye came to our home when ye did. Ye brought my family laughter that hadna been wi' us for some time."

He glanced at his sons. "Simon and Geoffrey, ye've no knowledge of what I'm about to say, and for that I apologise. Things have come about very quickly in the past couple o' days, and I've no' had a chance to speak wi' ye proper."

Something about his sons' expressions caused a lump to rise in Hector's throat. When had they become men? He could remember the pull of Sorcha's apron against her growing belly as it held each babe until its birth. He recalled the days when his children had entered the world and how their tiny naked bottoms had felt as soft as dough, cradled in the palm of his hand. The memories made him feel old, and he found he needed the comfort Sorcha's hand gave.

"Mr. MacDonnell and Mr. MacKenzie are leavin' tomorrow. They're taking ship to—where is it? America?" he asked Andrew, who smiled in response.

Hector continued, his voice growing hoarse with emotion. "What I did no' find out until this day"—he paused and cleared his throat—"was that our own sweet Janet would like to include hersel' among the travelers."

The boys turned to their sister, who blushed and glared into her lap.

"Janet, look at me," he said, and she frowned at him. "Yer mother and I dinna want to see ye go, lass. I canna imagine bein' wi'out ye, to tell ye the plain truth of it."

He shook his head slowly, but kept his eyes on hers. "But ye're not a wee lassie anymore, as ye're keen to point out. Ye've nae fear, which is no' necessarily a good thing if ye're travelin' into the unknown. But yer mother and I have spoken about what ye said. We trust yer good sense. We shall pray for ye every day, and . . . and we hope ye find what ye seek."

There was a stunned moment of silence.

"What?" Janet squawked, bolting to her feet. "Ye're sayin' I can go?" She turned to the only one who seemed able to help her understand. "Andrew?"

Andrew grinned. "Aye. Yer da's lettin' ye go, and I'm lettin' ye come."

She whooped and flew across the clearing toward her parents. She threw herself onto them, thanking them, trying to reassure them through grateful sobs. Simon shook the surprise from his head and went to his family, leaving Geoffrey on his own.

"Who would've thought ye'd be the first of us to go?" Simon declared, his voice thicker than usual.

Janet turned from her parents and held Simon, then looked over his shoulder to where Geoffrey sat, elbows braced on his knees, face turned toward the flames. A lock of his golden hair, shining almost white in the firelight, hung over his eyes and hid his expression.

Janet released Simon and stepped toward her fair-haired brother. Geoffrey rose without meeting her eyes and disappeared into the trees. Her father shook his head.

"Leave him be. Give him time to deal wi' his grief."

Sorcha gave up trying to hold back tears. She pulled her daughter into her arms and held her tight.

Andrew glanced at Iain, who offered a weak smile and shrugged.

The conversation by the fire dwindled. It seemed there should be much to talk about, but suddenly it was hard to find words.

CHAPTER 23

Toward the Sea

In the morning Andrew found Janet and her brother Geoffrey sitting under a shared blanket, reunited on a log by the cooled firepit. That was good, Andrew thought. It would have been difficult for Janet to leave without Geoffrey's blessing.

After breakfast, the group quickly assembled everything they would need for the journey. Clouds hung low over Hector's farm. Andrew, Iain, Janet, and the children were eager to get as much ground behind them as possible before the storm hit.

They had a long way to go. Iain had made the trip years before, travelling with kin to a Gathering. He would be their guide to the major shipping port of Greenock, eighty difficult miles south of Hector's home. There they would somehow manage to purchase tickets and board a ship to the New World.

The plan was to hike the treacherous pathways inland, avoiding coastal areas. English dragoons still patrolled those routes in search of Prince Charles and the handsome price on his head. The soldiers wouldn't hesitate to confront any other Scots, Jacobite or otherwise.

Before the group set out, Janet turned toward her father and he placed his hands on her cheeks, raising her face to meet his. The knowledge that this would probably be the last time he ever touched his daughter made him feel strangely vulnerable.

"Ye've been my sunshine all o' these years, Janet. I pray ye find what ye seek. Always remember I love ye, *mo nighean*."

Janet blinked hard. Hector dropped his hands from her face and reached into his sporran, pulling out a small cowhide bag. He placed the bag into her palm, then folded her fingers over the gift.

"For yer journey," he explained. "Keep the lads well."

He pulled her to him and hugged her fiercely, then stepped away. Janet tucked the little bag into the depths of her bodice, unable to speak.

"Where's Geoff, Mam?" Simon's voice came from behind them.

"I dinna ken," Sorcha said. "He'll be here, though. Dinna fash yersel'. He'd no' miss this."

A gust blew across the yard, lifting hair and kilts, bending branches and shimmering leaves. As if drawn by the wind, a thin sound pierced the morning, plunging through their ears to grab at their hearts. Geoffrey, the quiet brother and son, the poet, the musician, emerged from the trees, eyes fixed on his sister's. His arm squeezed the bag against his side, and his fingers flicked over the small holes of the chanter. Even the children sat still, swallowing through their birdlike throats. Andrew's eyes stung as the pipes sang, wishing them well in their travels, wishing they would never leave.

The braes of Morar were steep and narrow. Iain led the group between rocky glens and under canopies of low-hanging leaves.

After an hour or so, the children were too tired to walk, so Andrew and Iain fashioned slings from their plaids and wrapped the children onto their backs.

Janet had difficulty keeping her eyes on the trail. The changing landscape captivated her. She had seen all of this from her childhood perch high atop Glen Shiel. It had seemed glorious, limitless, and free. Now she clambered amongst the reality of its sharp rocks and unforgiving braes, bruising her feet and legs. And yet she was happier battling the conditions here than when she had safely observed from a distance.

The storm was coming fast. The rising wind whirled between the trees, twisting through the travelers' plaids, making every step more difficult. Janet wound her *arisaid* over her head, cushioning her face from the force of the gales.

"Follow me," Iain bellowed over the wind. "I'll find a place to weather this."

The men pulled their plaids higher around their necks, and the children all but disappeared inside the fabric. Janet, Andrew, and Iain bent their heads into the wind, searching the hills for shelter.

Thunder echoed through the mountains, and dark clouds massed over the travelers. Andrew followed Iain up a crag, slick with pebbles, and Janet followed him. Her foot slipped and she caught herself on one hand, cutting her palm on the rocks.

"Are ye all right?" Andrew called, reaching for her. She nodded, but accepted his hand.

The clouds thickened, twisting down in black on black, their contours defined by an angry gray. A bolt of lightning ripped from the sky and struck close to where they stood and Janet caught her breath at its ferocity. The first padding sounds of raindrops hit the earth and when the thunder came, the children screamed. Tiny fingers emerged from within the plaids and clutched the weary shoulders that carried them. All at once the clouds yielded to the pressure, funneling rain onto the travelers.

"Oy! Here!" Iain cried, and they ran to catch up to him.

Iain led them into a cave that had been almost impossible to see along the steep hillside. They crowded in through the small opening, then spread apart in the open cavern and unwrapped the soaked coverings from their heads. They could see the downpour through the narrow entrance and hear the shrieking wind.

Janet felt around in the darkness, sweeping together a small pile of dry sticks and grass. Iain cracked his flint against it, shooting orange sparks into the blackness until the tinder caught fire. The glow of the infant fire lit the walls of the cave and drew everyone nearer. They fed it bits of wood and the small blaze licked at it, growing stronger with each flickering shadow.

The tempest continued to rage. The ragged land above their cave began to flood and collapse, plopping lumps of mud around the cave's entrance. Rain dribbled into the cave and pooled inside the entrance.

Inside, the travelers were relatively warm and very weary. The smell of wet wool rose from their plaids, mingling with the smoke. Janet spread her arisaid over the ground, hoping the heat from the fire might dry the skirt and bodice she wore underneath, then she leaned against the cave wall with a sigh.

When Janet opened her eyes a while later, she was the only one awake. The storm still raged outside, but there was no sound in the cave besides Iain's occasional snores. The children sagged in a boneless heap across her thighs. Andrew and Iain slept, spread out on their plaids.

The fire had faded into pulsing orange embers. Trying not to disturb the children, she fed it a few more sticks and stoked it back to life.

She stole a quiet moment to observe Andrew, reining in the impulse to stroke his beard-shadowed face. Her lips still remembered the tenderness of his kiss, the rough bristles that had burned her cheeks. She had never really kissed a man before that day. Not like that.

Janet reached into her bundle and brought out rolls and cheese. The need for sleep had been stronger than her hunger, but now her stomach growled. She chewed the bread and watched Andrew sleep, wondering at his dreams. He frowned in his sleep, and if she looked closely, she could see his lips move, as if he were speaking. She knew so little about this man whom she had dared to claim in that desperate moment.

Andrew stirred, rolling from his side onto his back. His kilt slid as he moved, revealing a jagged pink scar that stretched the length of his thigh. She shuddered, imagining what he must have survived to carry such a scar.

As if sensing her gaze, Andrew opened his eyes and his lips pulled into a sleepy smile. She looked away, not wanting him to know she had been staring.

"How are ye, lass?" he asked, keeping his voice low.

"I'll do."

"Did ye sleep a bit?"

She nodded and handed him a roll. "I did. 'Twas just what I needed."

Iain woke and sat up, rubbing the sleep from his eyes. Janet offered him bread and cheese, then brought out a bottle of ale. Iain nodded thanks, took a sip, then passed it back.

The rain slowed to a steady shower, then stopped altogether, though water continued to drip from the mouth of the cave. There was less need for the fire now that the sky offered glimpses of blue.

A small voice interrupted the quiet. "Are we goin' soon, Mr. MacKenzie?" asked Peter.

"Aye, lad," Iain answered. "We should see how far we can go afore night settles. Wake yer sister now an' we'll be off."

"Wait," Janet said. She handed Peter some food. "Eat a bit first. Give Flora some as well, aye?"

After the children finished eating, Andrew rose, wrapping the length of his plaid around his waist and over his shoulder. He fastened it at the front with a small silver brooch. Flora grabbed Andrew's hand and smiled up at him.

"Ready, lass?" Andrew asked, and she responded with an enthusiastic nod. He squeezed her little hand. "Be sure to hang on tight, aye? 'Tis slippery going now."

Andrew ducked through the cave's entrance and Flora followed, squeaking with surprise when her feet slid in the new banks of mud. Andrew held on to her and they walked on, their shoes making squelching, thirsty noises in the mud.

Janet emerged from the cave and snorted at the mess around them. The wind had felled a tree by the entrance, and hail had crushed a number of formerly defiant flowers. Below the travelers' path, mud and rocks had slid into a deep gorge.

The weather continued to be miserable over the next three weeks. The group plodded onward, singing or telling stories to help pass the time. Even the children contributed by gathering firewood and helping cook whatever game they caught along the way.

One day, as the wind rose in anticipation of another storm, the group came upon a quiet, windowless cottage in the woods.

"Halloo the house!" Iain called through cupped hands.

There was no reply save the wind in the trees, swaying the branches so they creaked like rocking chairs.

Iain called again, then stepped up to the door and knocked. When there was still no response from within, he unlatched the door and pushed it open. Andrew and the others followed Iain inside.

The cottage was neatly swept, the kitchen tidy. A bed of peat lay in the hearth, waiting to be lit, but there was no one home to light it. A layer of dust covered everything, suggesting the cottage hadn't been occupied for at least a month. Andrew went to the hearth and raised a flame so heat spread through the cottage and softened the clammy dirt floor. The group peeled off their soaked kilts and hung them on the available furniture in hopes the wool might dry.

While the others sat around the fire, Andrew went back outside to relieve himself. Twenty feet from the door, he stopped, frozen at the sight of a pale white hand, the fingers stiff under a pile of wet leaves. When he moved the leaves aside, he uncovered two bodies lying a few feet from each other. Their faces were unrecognisable, but the bloodstains on their clothing were all too familiar. Not even the steady impact of the rain could rinse the material clean.

Andrew stood beside the bodies, feeling sick. Then he turned back to the cottage, pulled open the door, and stepped into the doorway.

"Come in all the way!" Janet called. "No need to soak the floor."

"Aye, well," Andrew replied. "I'll no' come in just yet. Iain, could ye maybe come give me a hand wi' somethin'?"

Iain nodded. He left the children with Janet, who watched Iain shrug back into his plaid.

"What is it?" she asked.

Andrew lowered his voice and looked at Iain. "The people o' the house. They're no' coming back."

"Right, then," Iain said. Janet closed her eyes and sighed.

When the men were outside, Janet went to the pantry to see what food could be salvaged. The cottage was deserted, but not empty. The pantry held a treasure trove: golden strings of onions, a few cabbages, dried peas, and a large sack of potatoes. Two bags of oatmeal and one of flour sat on a lower shelf, but grubs had destroyed most of the flour. Dried mutton and fish were stacked in the shelves. And higher up, glowing with amber sweetness, sat two unopened jars of honey.

Janet was comfortable in a kitchen. This one beckoned and she set about preparing food for that night and the days to follow. She found a sturdy kitchen knife and chopped onions and potatoes, setting them to fry in the cauldron, mixed with lard and bits of dried meat. The aroma filled the air, and the sound of sizzling fat made everyone's mouth water. She added a little water to help everything soften, dropped in some peas, and let the mixture simmer. Off to the side she kneaded what clean flour she could find with lard, then sweetened the batter with honey. She set the bannock beside the fire to rise and bake.

Andrew and Iain disappeared into the woods to bury the bodies of their slain hosts. The rain turned the ground into a slimy base of mud, but death demanded respect. The men dug shallow trenches, lowered the corpses into them, then piled boulders over top.

"Tha sinn a' guidhe gun téid gu math leibh air an t-slighe chun na duais bith-bhuain," Iain murmured in formal Gaelic. We wish you well on your journey to eternal reward. And we thank ye for the bounty ye left for us in your home.

Soaked and chilled, Andrew and Iain went back inside to sit by the fire. Without a word, Janet poured each of them a cup of rough whisky she'd pulled from the pantry. Andrew inhaled its aroma, trying to clear away the stench of death.

Flora sat quietly in the corner, watching Janet work. The little girl's face was dirty, her eyes wide as an owl's.

"I'll go find a cloth for yer face, shall I, Flora?" Janet asked, turning toward the back room.

The room was crowded with two tick mattresses, made up with rough white sheets. A ewer and urn sat in one corner, a chamber pot in another, and at the foot of one of the beds stood a large oak chest. Janet pulled open the lid of the chest and found a homespun gown, towels, blankets, and a forest green length of plaid.

She hesitated. She felt awkward, helping herself to the clothing, but the owners were dead, and no one else had been in the cottage for a while.

They would want to help, she thought.

She removed everything from the chest and laid it all on the bed. She took off her gown, which was badly in need of a wash, and slipped the homespun over her head. The rough material hung loose on her small frame, but she belted it at the waist and approved of its practicality.

Janet took another peek inside the chest and spied a tiny rag doll lying in one corner. Its sagging head was sewn from an old stocking and stuffed with straw. Strands of blue wool hung down its back in place of hair. A layer of green tartan wrapped around its body, the same material as the larger plaid Janet had laid on the bed. She looked into the doll's face and its carefully stitched blue eyes. The doll stared back.

"I ken a wee lassie who would love to have you," Janet murmured to the doll, and tucked it into her apron pocket. Then she loaded herself up with towels and went back to the main room.

"Come here," Janet said, crooking a finger at Flora, who came to sit beside her. She dipped the corner of one towel into a pot of water on the floor, then dabbed at the little girl's face. "That's better. Let's take a look at your hair, too, shall we? Lean back. There. That's it."

Flora hung her head back so her long red hair dangled over the pot. Janet poured water over Flora's head, then scrubbed lye soap through the little girl's scalp and hair. When Janet was done rinsing out the suds, she pulled a comb from her pack and ran it through the little girl's tangles. Flora squeezed her eyes shut and squeaked at the tugging, but sat without squirming until Janet was finished.

Iain brought Peter to the tub, and Janet did the same for him. When they were done, the clean children stood side by side, smiling, looking quite different from how they had looked a half hour before.

Andrew sat close to the fire, trimming the scruff of his beard with shears so it fell into a pile of tangled curls on the floor. Janet moved her stool so it stood across from Andrew, then reached for his dirk.

"I'll do it," she said. "I've a better view from here."

He smiled and placed the worn leather hilt in her palm. She lathered her hands with soap and spread the suds over his cheeks and chin. Then she squinted and bit the corner of her mouth.

"I used to do this for my brothers. When they were being lazy." She scraped the blade with a steady pressure across Andrew's beard, cutting away the coarse hairs. "They had to behave when I held the knife."

Her lips shifted in concentration, and she sucked her cheeks tight as if she were shaving her own face. When she had finished, Andrew scrubbed the soap over his face, neck, and hair, then rinsed off the suds so he dripped onto the floor.

"Thank ye," he said. She handed him a towel, which he scrubbed hard over his face and hair. He grinned. "It feels fine to have that beard off."

"Wait," she said. She looked him over carefully. "Your hair."

He dug his fingers into the thick, wet waves. "What of it?"

"Ye look a fright. I'll fix that. Sit still a mite, aye?" She picked up the shears and trimmed his hair, adding to the pile on the floor. When she was finished, she sat back and eyed him critically. His dark locks fell to just above his shoulders, flicking into lazy curls at the ends. She was pleased they no longer covered his eyes. She nodded, satisfied.

"Done," she said.

"Your turn, lass." He smiled at her wide eyed expression. "Ye'll feel better once it's washed."

"If ye insist," she said.

She leaned back against the pot and looked up at the ceiling. Andrew gathered the thick length of her hair, knotted from weeks of walking, and let it tumble and darken in the suds. She closed her eyes as he poured the water over her, feeling the water trickle over her forehead and down her hair. Andrew was gentle but firm as he rubbed the soap through her hair, then rinsed it clean.

"I never thought I'd feel clean again," she said with a sigh. "Thank you."

He passed her his towel and she rubbed her hair, squeezing it between her fingers. She sat by the fire while she combed it out.

Using water from the same bucket, Iain sponged the filth off his face. Janet offered her assistance with the shears, but he waved her away. He clipped halfheartedly at his beard and scrubbed his hair, but didn't bother with a trim. Instead, he pulled it back into a tail and tied it with a leather thong from his sporran.

Now that the travelers were clean, warm, and dry, the mood was almost festive. Janet gave Andrew the plaid she had discovered in the chest. He gathered the material into pleats around his waist, then flung the end over his left shoulder and anchored it with a silver brooch on his chest.

The smell of dinner permeated the cottage. Janet took an experimental taste of the soup, then turned toward Iain, who waited for a sip. She raised the spoon to his lips, and he closed his eyes when he swallowed. A look of satisfaction settled over his face.

"Mmmm," he purred. "Thank ye, lass."

"I'm pleased ye approve, Iain," she replied. "Only a few minutes more. Then there'll be biscuits to go alongside."

They left the meal to simmer and went to sit with the children. Flora sidled up and leaned her soft weight against Janet's arm.

"I've a wee gift for ye, Flora," Janet said.

Flora looked up, her eyes even wider than usual. "For me? But it's no' my birthday," she said.

Janet smoothed Flora's damp hair. "Never mind that," she said. She tapped the little girl's nose with one finger. "A gift can come at other times as well. This one was waitin' here for ye."

Janet reached into the apron of her gown and pulled out the rag doll, then laid it in Flora's arms. The little girl's lips curled into a perfect circle, and a soft sound of pleasure escaped them as she stared at the gift. She caressed the woolen strands of hair as if they were silk.

"I'll call her Janet," Flora said, smiling into the doll's face.

"Come on," said her brother. "Bring her here. She can ride the pony."

He held up the carving Iain had made, and the children went off to the corner of the room with their toys.

Janet smiled. "Ye can play wi' yer toys after supper, aye? Come now and we'll eat," she said.

Supper was served and devoured. Afterwards, Janet poured oatmeal into the big cauldron, added stream water that Andrew fetched for her, then stirred it with the wooden spirtle as it boiled. When it thickened enough, she would let it cool. Then she would cut the hardened oatmeal into slices, and they would each carry some as their journey continued.

When their bellies were filled, the soothing rhythm of rain on the roof lulled the group into a peaceful quiet. Iain and Andrew dozed by the fire, comfortable among the folds of their plaids. Janet took the children into the bedroom, where Flora and Peter curled up on one of the mattresses and Janet took the other. Andrew could hear Janet singing to them, a lullaby he remembered in his own mother's voice. The little rag doll, mounted on the noble wooden pony, stood sentry beside the beds.

CHAPTER 24

Lochs and Glens and Leaves of Gold

November held fewer daylight hours and very little in the way of sunshine or warmth. The voyage took the group across a hopscotch of lakes and valleys, crossed by vast expanses of nothingness where ragged trees were the only sign of life.

They passed between sheer rock walls alongside Loch Hourn, the "Lake of Hell," where stubborn pine trees somehow kept a precarious footing. Loch Quoich lay silent to their west, harbouring small islands that rose through the surface in a line, like the knobbed back of an ancient beast.

The path turned to the southeast, but when Andrew and his group reached the Campbell lands and the outskirts of Fort William, they turned off, keeping a wary distance. By midday they had ventured into the eastern end of Rannoch Moor, where the desolation transformed itself into a thing of beauty. Rounded slopes rose from the shining loch, swaying with grass, peppered by heather. Across the moor the mountains faded into the distance: gray, black, and gray again, the taller peaks cloaked by snow. The water's flat surface gleamed on the moor, broken only by an occasional splash, hinting at the rich store of trout beneath.

Their midday meal was light, consisting of oatcakes and honey from the cottage.

Though he would never complain, Iain was as happy as the others to sit for a while, to soak up the sun without having to pound through its shadows step by heavy step. His fingers itched at the thought of fishing in this loch. He had done so once, as a boy, and had never forgotten the way the huge brown trout had risen so greedily to his bait. Neither had he forgotten the way their delicate flesh melted on his tongue. Later in the day, he told himself, he would take a hook from his sporran and drop a line into the cold, dark water.

For now it sufficed to watch the loch's feathered inhabitants as they floated across the water, paddling in haphazard circles. A pair of large goosanders drifted by, as calm as the surface that held them afloat. The dark green male's mate paddled beside him, bobbing her copper head under the water at intervals, trolling for a meal. A larger duck with eerie red eyes swam a bit farther out, preening its glossy black body. Something startled the bird and it exploded from the water, its plum-coloured neck stretched forward, feet streamlined behind him.

Andrew stood beside Iain, hands on his hips, gazing out at the ducks.

Janet ran in the near distance with the children, laughing and squealing as they chased her along the shore. "Ye'll never catch me!" she called, then turned and yelled, "Now I'm comin' for ye! Ye'd best run!"

"Right. Time for a swim," Andrew said. He unwrapped his plaid and dropped it to the ground, so he stood in nothing but his knee-length tunic. Then he took a deep breath, grinned like a madman, and tore off his last remnant of clothing, whooping as he ran into the freezing water. He dove under the water, barely causing a ripple, and bobbed back to the surface only to dive again moments later. He eventually emerged, still grinning, shaking the water from his head as if he were a dog. Then he grabbed his plaid and wrapped it around him like a towel.

"Now that," he told Iain, while scrubbing the end of the plaid against his hair, "felt good."

Iain grunted. "Bloody selkie. There's more ice than water in yer blood."

Andrew threw his clothes on again, then sat and wrapped his arms around his knees, observing the lines of the beach and the grassy expanses beyond Rannoch Moor. The distant landscape rolled with weather-softened mountains, but the terrain where he and Iain sat was level. Clusters of ancient gray boulders, their edges worn smooth by centuries, lay scattered among bursts of grass and shrubs.

All but one. An oddly shaped rock, as tall as a man's waist, stood alone, twenty feet from Andrew. It was darker than the others, and its sharp edges protruded from the earth at an angle which seemed to point accusation at the heavens.

Iain noticed Andrew's curious gaze. *"Clach na Boile,"* Iain said, though Andrew hadn't asked. "Stone of Fury. Have ye ne'er seen the wee stones?"

Andrew shook his head.

Iain squinted toward the stone. "There's magic in them, some say. Stones like that one are all over this land. Legend has it they communicate between themselves."

"What?" Andrew asked, frowning. "The stones talk?"

"So they say."

"Oh, aye?" Andrew said, rising to his feet. "And what is it they say to one another?"

Iain shrugged and reached into Janet's bundle of provisions, pulling out a handful of bannock and cheese. He bit into the bannock and spoke while he chewed.

" 'Tis said there are some folk who can hear them. No' me, though." Iain took a half bottle of whisky from Janet's pack. "Will ye have a dram?" he asked, raising a fuzzy eyebrow in question.

Andrew shook his head. Instead, he turned and walked toward the mysterious stone.

As Andrew drew closer, he thought he heard a low hum in the air, like vibrations from a beehive. Strange. There should be no bees in November. Nevertheless, the sound continued, growing louder with every one of his steps. He examined the thistles for fuzzy yellow bodies, but there was no sign of anything beyond the occasional hardy butterfly visiting the blooms.

Andrew had seen a lot of strange things in his lifetime. If he hadn't seen them for himself, he might never have believed them to be real. When he realised the humming was coming from the stone itself, he was more curious than shocked. He walked to the base of the stone and stared at it, looking for the cause of the sound. The breeze lifted his hair and bent the grass, so the long, pale blades appeared to point toward the stone. He hesitated for only a moment, then reached down and touched its cold surface.

The instant Andrew's fingers touched the stone, a bolt flashed through his body, hot and swift as lightning. The strike was sudden, but not painful, and his heart pounded madly. The sensation solidified, binding him to the stone as if it were a rope. He yanked his hand away in reflex, and staggered back, staring hard at the stone. It stood benign, as ordinary as any other feature on the blowing grass. Except it still hummed. Louder than ever.

Andrew looked toward the beach where his companions sat, eating and talking as if nothing out of the ordinary had happened. Janet and the children had come back and were sitting by Iain, laughing at something Iain had said.

So, he thought. His friends didn't hear the stone, and the land didn't seem to feel it. Could this possibly be a magic stone, as Iain had suggested? If it was, would Andrew be able to hear what the stone said? Maybe he could, he thought. His mind worked in strange ways sometimes, telling him things he shouldn't have known. He sat beside the slab and took a deep breath, then reached out and willed himself to touch the stone again.

The same heat shot through him, but this time he held on, riding the current as it raced through his body. He leaned against the stone while blurred images and thoughts bombarded his mind; none of which, he realised, were his own. His initial reaction was panic, but he forced his hand to stay pressed against the rock. As he grew more accustomed to the whirling sensation, he tried to relax and allow its energy to strike and bounce off him, to make an impact, yet leave no mark. He strained to pull the forces within him together, tried to focus them into a constant stream he could comprehend.

Then suddenly he knew the girl was there. He could *feel* her. He concentrated as hard as he could, harnessing his mind's strength until he was able to visualise her. He focused on her eyes, which held his like magnets. In his mind he saw her soft lips and slightly turned-up nose with the sprinkling of freckles across its bridge. He pictured the waves of brown and gold that framed her face.

The vision grew from his thoughts, becoming so clear it seemed she stood in front of him. Her eyes were round with wonder. She looked as surprised as he felt. She reached out her hand, close enough to touch him. Andrew's heart pounded and power streamed through him, fueled by the chunk of gray stone. He used all his strength to channel it through his arms so finally, impossibly, he reached her hand and gripped it between his own. He could feel the softness of her fingers, the warmth of her skin. He could smell her clean, earthy scent. And then he heard her.

"You can do this!" she exclaimed, her voice ringing like bells in his ears. "*You* called *me*! I thought only I . . ."

He couldn't help himself. He heard her voice and had to speak. "Sweet Jesus," he cried. "Oh, lass! To touch ye like this—I ne'er thought . . ."

"Your hands!" she cried. "They're so warm! I can't believe . . ."

"Ah, but ye must." He grinned, and squeezed the small hand he held. "Even if the entire world canna believe, you and I must."

He let go with one hand so he could trace the delicate curve of her cheek with his fingers.

"I dinna understand it," he said, his voice barely above a whisper, "but I feel ye all the time. I always have."

A smile lit her eyes, and two tiny dimples he'd never noticed materialised in her flushed cheeks. Just as he had, she raised her hand and touched his face, brushing the roughness of his sprouting beard. For a moment they stared at each other, neither knowing what to say. She broke the silence.

"My name's Maggie," she said finally, her voice sounding almost shy, and then, "Margaret."

"Maggie," he whispered.

The sound of her name escaped his lips like a sigh. He stared at her with an intensity anyone else drawing near might have been able to feel.

"I'm Andrew," he said. He shook his head like a dog, trying to clear his brain, but he immediately regretted the movement. His body was beginning to ache, stretched tight as a bowstring by the magic in the stone. The muscles in his back and neck were beginning to throb. "Andrew Adam MacDonnell."

"Andrew." She said his name slowly. Her lips formed a small circle he ached to touch, to kiss. "Where are you?"

"I'm in Scotland, but I'm leavin' here. I'm comin' to find ye, Maggie. Where do ye live?"

She grinned. "I'm in America. South Carolina."

Andrew nodded slowly, then stopped. The muscles in his neck protested, tightening until he could barely move his head. A burning pain ripped up the length of his spine, searing one vertebra at a time until it gripped his neck like a claw. Andrew pushed his mind against the pain. He needed more time.

"This is strange magic, Maggie. I dinna ken how long this will hold, but I"—he cleared his throat—"I need to try somethin', if ye'll allow me."

She nodded. "I think I know what it is." She leaned forward and kissed his cheek, touching him as lightly as a feather might brush against his face. He was overwhelmed by the feel of her lips, and seized her face between his hands, bringing her mouth to his. Her lips burned against his, and her curves pressed against his body. She knotted her arms around his waist, and he felt the delicious thrill of her fingers digging into his back. He gathered the soft brown waves of her hair, winding his fingers through it as he kissed her. His hands slid down to her shoulders and down the deerskin tunic, grazing the soft outline of her breasts, circling her waist. She pressed against him, needing more.

But the pain was impossible to ignore any longer. It was a demon, possessing his entire body so he could barely move. Where there had been a vibrating connection between himself and the stone, now there were sharp spasms, jabbing, pulsing inside his head. But how could he release her? After all these years, how could he let her go?

She pulled her mouth from his, gasping. Her hands flew to the sides of her head, and she squeezed her eyes shut against the pressure.

"What's happening?" she cried. "Do you feel that?"

He could see his pain mirrored in her eyes, and he knew he had to let go. Every one of his muscles strained until he feared they might snap. It was as if he were exploding from within.

"I have to go, Maggie. I canna stand it, and I willna suffer ye to bear it wi' me."

"Andrew!"

"Aye?"

"Find the Cherokee when you get here. They'll know where I am."

He clutched her hands and, fighting his screaming muscles, pulled her fingers to his lips. He filled his eyes with her. "I will be wi' ye every day, every night, Maggie."

His body convulsed and he lost her, disconnecting from the stone as if thrown. He lay on his side, writhing in agony. Iain and Janet were beside him in an instant, their hands flitting around him, looking for injuries.

"What is it, Andrew?" Janet cried. "What's wrong? Are ye damaged?"

They could see nothing. No wounds, no explanation for Andrew's suffering. Iain stared at him, watching Andrew's movements begin to slow, listening as his cries lessened. Only a moment before, Iain had seen Andrew leaning against the stone, napping; he could have sworn Andrew had been smiling.

The children sat nearby, watching in silence. For once, Iain wasn't paying attention to them. He was troubled. Was the lad ill? Had he eaten something that gripped his innards? He had seemed well enough earlier. And they had all eaten the same food. What then? Iain scratched his head, then glanced toward the stone. Could the legends be true? Could the stone speak? There seemed no other explanation for it, but—damn. Iain didn't want to believe it, didn't want to admit the possibility. He rubbed his hand over his face a few times, trying to think. Then he rose and walked to the stone, where it stood solitary and dull in the grass.

After a moment's hesitation, Iain laid his hand on the rock's face. And waited. Waited for what, he didn't know. Nothing happened. If the rock was cursed, if it was the thing that had paralysed Andrew, there was no evidence of its power now. And yet in that moment, Iain realised he believed in magic. He became aware there was nothing he could do to comfort Andrew. That knowledge frightened him.

The blazing fire in Andrew's head mellowed into a steady, crackling flame. With great effort, he uncurled his body and tried to relax his muscles. He fought to pry open his eyes, then squeezed them shut again at the sharp intrusion of daylight. Open or closed, the sparks of the sun shot through his lids, like needles of white heat.

Janet placed his sweat-dampened head onto her lap and poured sips of whisky through his lips. He choked but swallowed it down. She rubbed her fingertips in small circles around his temples and across his forehead, and he felt the taut muscles in his face slowly relax. Within moments he lost consciousness again.

Andrew slept for three hours. He lay on his back where he had fallen, arms splayed at his sides, face toward the sky. He didn't flinch when Janet moved his head from her lap onto a cushion of plaid.

When he awoke, his body was unwilling to rise. It felt weighted down. He wanted to breathe, *needed* to breathe. His lungs burned and his heart pounded in his throat.

"Andrew! Wake up!" the voice in his head whispered.

Maggie.

He cracked his eyelids open and tried to focus on a cloud floating overhead. His body felt stiff. Molded to the ground. As if he had lain in that spot forever. As if he lay cold in a grave. Every muscle screamed and his head pounded. His mouth was dry and tasted like blood.

Janet made a small sound of relief, seeing him regain consciousness, and her fingers stroked the hair from his forehead.

"Welcome back," she said.

She poured a sip of whisky through his lips and used her thumb to wipe a stray drop from the side of his mouth.

"Ye had us a wee bit worrit," she told him, "but never mind. Ye're back now. Can ye sit?"

Andrew considered her question. He didn't remember ever before having to ask permission of his limbs, but he did so now. Their response was noncommittal. The ground beneath Andrew shifted, and he stopped moving abruptly, waiting out a wave of nausea. Janet moved to brace his back, and he sat the rest of the way up, crossing his legs and hooking his hands under his feet to anchor himself there. He felt dizzy and let his head hang over his knees until he could control his balance.

He sat like that for a while, saying nothing. What could he say? He could offer no reasonable explanation. He gave Janet a weary smile.

"Hallo, lass."

The worry in her face melted at the sound of his voice.

"I'm that glad to see your eyes open, Andrew," she whispered. "I'm hopin' it wasna my bannock what set ye off."

She lifted a delicate black eyebrow, but Andrew only smiled.

"The food's no' the problem."

She waited, but he said no more. He scratched his head hard with both hands, trying to distract himself from the throbbing pain.

"I'm sorry to have scairt ye," he said. "Have ye a wee bit more o' that whisky?" He raised one hand to his brow and closed his eyes to the sunlight.

She reached for the bottle behind her and gave it to him. "Do ye think ye can walk?" she asked.

He took a sip, then wiped his lips with his sleeve. "Soon," he said. "Tell MacKenzie I'll be up presently. Just need to make sure my head stays between my shoulders."

She smiled uncertainly, and got to her feet. "Andrew?"

"Aye?"

"What happened?"

Andrew couldn't tell her. None of it made sense. He shrugged and shook his head. "I'm sorry to have scairt ye, Janet," he repeated, and left it at that.

He was left alone with his thoughts and the cold, black stone. He stared at its profile. It still buzzed in convivial invitation, but with less intensity than before. Andrew longed to reach out to it, risk the pain for the possibility of touching her again. But he knew his body couldn't stand the agony again. Touching the stone now would kill him.

Despite the waves of pain in his head, he warmed at the memory of her in his arms. He had kissed her. She smelled like grass and earth and wood smoke. The sound of her accent filled his ears.

And her name was Maggie.

CHAPTER 25

Greenock

By the time the group reached the slopes of Greenock, the wind had shifted so the salt air tickled their nostrils and kept their skin moist. They could look down over the town's narrow bay and see where it opened farther along the shore, clearing the way for a view up and down the Firth of Clyde. Along the water's edge lay a flat quarter mile of land, dotted by docks, streets, and buildings.

The town centred around the bustling activity at the docks. Ships were being built and loaded with everything from herring to cattle to whisky. And in the hold, if there was room, huddled a different sort of cargo: those of the human ilk, desperate to escape their present circumstances.

The travelers walked the main street of Greenock, stepping from quiet wilderness into mild uproar. Andrew's senses worked madly, adjusting to the confusing hive of people, animals, and buildings. The streets smelled horrible. Like the farm when it was time to slaughter pigs. In some places the thoroughfares were inches thick with dirt and waste, though the locals didn't seem to notice. Men and women made their way along the road, bumping against the visitors in their late afternoon rush. Bits of broken conversations filled the air. Everything was so much *more* than Andrew had anticipated.

Flora and Peter seemed oblivious to the mucky ground. They perched on the men's shoulders, chattering to each other, pointing and twisting to see everything. Flora's little feet pounded Andrew's chest whenever something excited her. Iain's glistening black eyes darted with purpose, searching for a tavern. When he found one, he and Andrew lowered the children to the ground and the five travelers ducked through the heavy wooden door.

The mingled smells of food, drink, and the unwashed crowd hit Andrew like a wall as soon as he entered. The evening oil lamps hadn't yet been lit, so other than a dim glow pushing through two dirty windows, the place was dark. And loud. Patrons and servers bellowed to each other, gesturing when their voices couldn't be heard.

Iain led Andrew and the others to a table against a wall. They crowded onto benches and lifted the children onto their laps. A waitress brought cups of ale, and with shared grins, the group lifted their cups twice in celebration: the first to mark their arrival, the second in anticipation of what was to come. They filled their bellies with meat and bread, cheese and broth, and for the first time since leaving the empty cottage, they slept on actual beds.

In the morning, Janet stayed with the children in a rented room while Andrew and Iain spoke with the tavern's owner, who claimed to know everyone in Greenock. At the docks, the coastal wind stirred the water and a half-dozen ships tied to the dock heaved against their ropes as if impatient to be on their way. At the far end sat the largest of the ships, the *Boyd of Glasgow.* She was set to sail to Virginia in two days' time. That was the ship Iain and Andrew were seeking. They moved among the sailors, asking for the captain the taverner had suggested.

The *Boyd of Glasgow* had been docked for two weeks, and although the crew enjoyed mingling with the townspeople and local whores, their home was aboard the worn wooden deck, rolling over the Atlantic. The unpredictable swaying of the sea was more familiar to them than solid earth, and they were looking forward to casting off again.

Four sailors stood at the slip where the two-hundred-ton galley was tied, happily leering at any woman who strayed in their direction. Andrew looked the men over with interest. Not Highlanders. He could tell from their swagger, from the images etched into their corded biceps, from the cocky teasing that darted through their mouths. He couldn't picture these men in the green peace of his homeland.

"Good morn to ye, sirs," Iain said, addressing the man who appeared to be in charge.

The man in question was taller than the others, though nowhere close to Iain's size. He wore an open vest, with nothing beneath, and his faded breeks hung loose around his hips. The sun had baked his skin to a dark leather, and both his face and the top of his bald head were covered by freckles. A gold hoop earring dangled from one ear, and there was a vacant space where one upper tooth should have been. His shoulders were broad and veins strained over the solid bulk of his biceps. His forearms were wooly with curly gold hairs.

"Aye, that it is. An' a good morn to ye as well," the sailor replied. "Be there somethin' I can help ye with?" He raised his eyebrows, cutting three large creases across his brow. They were the only hairs to be seen on the man's head. Andrew thought the man's expression held a glint of intelligence, but those of his companions did not.

"Aye, I expect there is," Iain said genially. "We're lookin' for passage to Virginia on yon ship. Who would we see regardin' that?"

"Be ye lookin' to work or just take a nice, easy ride?" the bald man asked, tilting his head to the side and lifting one corner of his mouth. "For one of the two will cost ye a pretty penny, aye?"

Iain crossed his massive arms and smiled, waiting for the other sailors to finish chuckling. Andrew stood at Iain's side, wary of the men's unpredictable reactions. The docks were full of sailors. If a fight broke out, he and Iain would be badly outnumbered.

Iain squinted at the sailors, then shook his head with apparent disappointment.

"If these be the size o' men what work the riggin' here, I'd say ye'd be needin' the two of us to make sure the ship doesna sink afore she leaves port," he said.

The three sailors' jaws dropped. The man in charge, however, hooted out a laugh that caused passersby to stop in surprise.

"Aye, 'tis so, we'd be glad o' yer braw," the bald man said, grinning. He thrust out a huge hand and Iain took it. "The name's Murdo MacKinley, first mate. These here are Cullen, Sparky, and Jean Paul."

"Andrew MacDonnell and Iain MacKenzie," said Iain.

"You'll want to speak with the cap'n, and he's in town at the moment. Oh, wait a mite, there he is now. Cap'n!" he called. "We've a couple o' men what want to work for ye."

Captain Ninian Bryce was a short, stocky Scotsman with a curly gray beard and a belly that made the captain's affinity for rich food obvious. His lips stuck out in a permanent pucker from under the beard, shaped for the moment around a weathered black pipe. His eyes were small, but in perpetual motion. They watched the men, the town, the ship, and the weather all at once. He tucked his thumbs into the waistband of his breeks as he approached the sailors and gave Andrew and Iain a shrewd frown, narrowing his eyes and puffing on his pipe.

"Do they? Do they indeed. Aye, well. Ye've braw enough." Smoke puffed through one corner of his mouth as he considered. "Have ye been aship afore?" he asked. He pulled the pipe from his lips and plucked a bit of tobacco from his tongue before continuing. " 'Tis a difficult voyage, this. I've no desire to carry dead wood."

Andrew spoke up. "We've no experience on the water, sir, but plenty o' time spent workin' hard."

The captain nodded, then seemed to spot something on the ground. "The sea's a wicked tutor," he muttered.

"We've need to purchase a cabin as well, sir," Andrew added. "No' for us, mind. For a lady and two weans. We've the funds to cover their passage."

The captain looked at Andrew with a new glimmer in his eye, suddenly more interested in the prospect.

"Aye? So I'll be thankin' ye for both yer coin *an'* yer backs?" The captain cleared his throat, then pulled his pipe from his mouth. He tapped the bowl against his leg, then turned toward his first mate. "Seems to me as we've a cabin no' yet filled. Is that right, Murdo?"

The bald man smiled. "Aye, sir. But we've interested parties to be sure."

"Have ye the passage wi' ye, sirs?" asked Captain Bryce.

Iain chuckled. "Not in my hands, no. We'll learn yer price an' be back within the hour, if you'll allow."

The captain nodded. "Aye. That'll be fine. We sail in two days, weather willin'. We've food and drink enough for the trip, lads, but if the good Lord should choose to change our course, we may have to cut back rations, so ye might tell yer lass to bring what else she can, an' keep it well hid."

"Aye, Cap'n," Iain said. "We'll do that."

Andrew wandered down the dock, leaving Iain to the practical discussions. He wasn't overly concerned about the amount of the fare. Beside the fact both Iain and Andrew were obviously fit workers, they had the money from his parents as well as Janet's.

The ship looked sound, he thought. Then again, he'd never seen a ship before, so he'd no idea what it should have looked like. But it looked sturdy, with a gleaming hull that was currently being painted black by two sailors hanging on swings. Three masts towered over the ship, looking almost overwhelmed by endless spiderwebs of ropes and ladders. The sails were bundled neatly; the deck's planking shone with a recent oiling.

Andrew took a deep breath. "All right," he said to the ship. "Get us there safe."

He turned back to Iain, who seemed satisfied with the business at hand. Iain bade the soldiers farewell and joined Andrew down the dock.

"Be ready to work like ye've ne'er worked afore!" called MacKinley, and they heard the sailors roar with laughter.

On the day of their departure the sun rose over a cloudless sky, the air cool with the aftereffects of rain. The wind dropped to almost nothing, which didn't bode well for sailing; however, the crew set to work readying the ship anyway. Andrew and Iain worked alongside the sailors, heaving cargo until their skin shone with sweat. After the hold was filled with goods and livestock, the remaining space was crammed with human cargo. When the hold reached capacity, the hatch doors were shut, the sun denied passage.

Thanks to Hector's purse, Janet and the children lived in relative luxury in a cabin, with two small beds and a table between. The men slept with the rest of the crew in another, larger cabin, sleeping in hammocks. Hammocks that were, in Iain's furiously stated opinion, far too small.

The *Boyd of Glasgow* was a massive ship. The creaking mast and spars hung with ropes as thick as a man's arm. Sailors hung from booms and dropped off rigging, hauled up sails, and waited for them to fill. MacKinley gave a piercing whistle to a boy aloft in the crow's nest. As if waiting for this signal, the wind swooped in and pushed into the mainsail, billowing it out into giant white squares. As they left port, the wind picked up strength and the men shouted and whistled, thundering across the deck to loosen cleats, open more sails, and tie down the ropes again.

Endless waves eased the ship into the infinite sea. Janet stood with the children at the rail, eyes squinted against the wind as Scotland's profile faded away. Andrew and Iain worked among the sailors, straining muscles and following orders, but when they could, they also faced backwards, their dark eyes seeing beyond the untidy buildings of the town, imagining the Highlands. The certainty of the past disappeared with each white-capped splash on the hull. The future stretched invisibly into the horizon, promising nothing.

The sailors plainly didn't see it that way. The sun was out and the wind had come up. The decks were scrubbed, and their clothes and bodies were relatively clean from their layover. They flew from rope to sail to mast as easily as Andrew might have skipped a stone across a stream.

The crew was a moving patchwork of old and young, wide and wiry, some bald, some with hair that hung in thick tangles. They wore breeks or kilts, many wore coats, some wore rough-hewn shirts that had seen better days, and a few stripped to bare torsos. Sun-darkened skin stretched over honed muscles, gleaming with exertion. Grime stained the sailors' hands and faces. Many of them tied rags in bands around their foreheads to keep the sweat from dripping into their eyes. A confusing medley of languages bounced across the deck: English, Scots, Irish, French, and another Andrew couldn't recognise. He thought maybe German.

And there was another sound. One that drew everyone to midship like a school of fish. Music. A lone fiddler stood by the bow, stomping a leather-clad foot in time to a jig. A wave crashed against the hull, showering the fiddler with seawater. The man laughed, throwing back his head as if waiting for more, but didn't stop playing.

Andrew leaned against the rigging with his arms crossed, slightly apart from the other crew members. When he saw Janet and the children, he smiled and cocked his head, inviting them to stand by him.

"He's mad," Andrew said, and she nodded.

"Aye. But he can play," she said. "Geoffrey would have liked it."

"What's 'at?" Peter asked, watching the fiddler with open awe.

The fiddler whirled toward them, dancing while he played, grinning from within his flaming red mane. His tunic was butter yellow, belted over black breeches, and he spun among the sailors, diverting them and spreading his enthusiasm. Before long most of the crew had joined in, clapping and whistling while the tempo built to a frenzy. At last the fiddler dropped his arms and bowed toward the company, shamelessly encouraging the burst of applause.

The captain's boot heels struck the deck like a soldier's drum as he strode toward the fiddler, thumbs in his belt. He stopped in the centre of the group, lifted his chin, and blew a stream of smoke into the air. He didn't look at anyone, only focused on the line of clouds overhead. His voice was genial, with an iron core.

"Am I payin' ye to be entertained, lads? Mr. MacKinley?"

MacKinley stepped out from where he had plainly been enjoying the music as well. "Cap'n?"

"If ye would be so kind?"

MacKinley bellowed, "Get yer lazy arses on deck, lads! This ship's no' goin' to sail herself!"

Andrew and the rest of the crew, cheered by the music and chided by the captain, returned to their work, muttering good-naturedly to one another.

After they'd left, the fiddler approached Janet, smiling under twinkling eyes. "Seamus Murphy. At your service, ma'am," he announced and bowed elegantly, fiddle tucked under his arm.

"That was lovely playin', Mr. Murphy," she said.

His ever-present grin widened. "Most gracious of you to say so, ma'am. I'll be guessin' this might be yer first time on a ship, am I right? I've a bit of experience I'd be pleased to share wit' ye, if ye're at all inclined. Yer accent tells me ye're a Highlander, are ye? From Dublin I am, sailin' to me fortune in America."

"Good luck to ye, Mr. Murphy," she said. Peter jerked on her hand and she nodded toward the fiddler. "If ye'll excuse me, I must go an'—"

"Och! And be these yer precious children? Or"—his pale blue eyes went wide with feigned wonder—"might they be faeries?" He stepped back to get a good look at Peter and Flora.

The two were struck dumb. They stared open-mouthed at the stranger. Seamus didn't wait for Janet's answer but returned his laughing eyes to hers.

"Have mercy on a wretched soul, I pray ye. I'm afraid ye've the advantage, for I've given ye my name. Might ye gift me with yours?"

He waited expectantly, wearing a genuine expression of friendliness on his face. Janet frowned. She wasn't used to strangers. And this Seamus fellow spoke so quickly it was difficult to understand a word he said.

"I'm inclined to keep that to myself, Mr. Murphy. Now, if ye dinna mind, I—"

"Oh, but I do! I do mind! A lass needs a proper escort on her first day aboard ship. How could I e'er forgive meself if sommit was to happen? It's yer lucky day, sure and it is, that Seamus Murphy is here, for I know the ship as if 'twere the back o' me own 'and. Allow me, miss"—he crooked his white-sleeved arm in invitation—"to give ye a tour—"

"The lady has said no, sir," came a low voice, "and I'll ask ye to respect her wishes."

Andrew appeared behind Murphy, and the Irishman stiffened, but quickly regained his composure. He winked at Janet before turning around to face Andrew.

"Seamus Murphy, sir, at yer service," he said, beaming at Andrew. "Am I to be acquainted with *your* name then, sir, as the lady isn't wantin' to tell me hers at present."

"Andrew MacDonnell. Pleased to make yer acquaintance, Mr. Murphy. The lady is wi' me, and ye'll mind yer manners around her."

Andrew kept his expression calm, holding the Irishman's gaze. He saw curiosity sparkling in Seamus's eyes. After a moment, Seamus bowed his head in good-humoured acquiescence.

"Sure, and I'll remember that. I'll apologise for any offense I might have given." He tipped an imaginary hat Janet's way, then turned back to Andrew. "I don't recall seein' you afore, Mr. MacDonnell. Is it your first time at sea, then?"

The fellow's energy was contagious. He reminded Andrew of his brother, Dougal, and he clung to that thought. Seamus seemed like someone Andrew would like to know. He was someone who knew nothing about his history—about the battles he had fought, the horrors he had left behind.

"Aye," Andrew said. " 'Tis my first journey across water. Did I hear ye say ye were familiar wi' this ship?"

"Sure an' I did, Andrew," Seamus answered in his cheerful lilt.

"Is it all right I call ye that? Andrew? I prefer the less formal in ever't'in', I do. Aye, an' I've been aship afore today, although I must admit I *might* have stretched the truth a wee bit wi' the lady." He grimaced and plucked one of his fiddle strings. "I've no' bin on *this* particular ship afore. How different can they be from one anot'er, though, I ask meself. Well, Seamus me lad, I says, let's find us a mate an' we'll go explore the ship. An' here stood this bonny lass"—he winked at Janet—"all alone wi' the wee ones. I t'ought to maybe cheer her up wi' a walk round is all."

Janet arched one cool eyebrow.

"Well, Seamus," Andrew answered, smiling and using the fiddler's first name. "I'd be much obliged if ye were to show *me* around. I dinna ken if the lady is of a mind to join us, though."

Andrew looked to Janet for direction. "Might I introduce ye?" he asked, and she pursed her lips, but nodded slightly.

"I'll do it myself. And I'll do it in my own time, thank ye. Mr. Murphy, I'm Janet MacLeod. At your pleasure, sir."

Seamus nodded formally in acknowledgment. "Indeed. And t'ese?" He looked down at the children, who stepped forward to touch the strings on the fiddle, cushioned between Seamus's arm and his side.

"These are Flora and Peter MacLeod," Andrew said. "We are takin' them to America since they've no kin left in Scotland."

"Ah," nodded Seamus. He frowned as he stooped and spoke to the children. "Not faeries after all then. For the faeries wouldn't be near so brave as you two."

Peter plucked one of the strings, then looked up at Seamus.

Seamus squatted so he was face to face with the little boy. "Have ye not seen a fiddle afore, lad? Well, an' t'at's a sorry thing to be sure. Tell me now"—he dropped his voice to a conspiratorial whisper—"have ye never afore met with an Irishman, either? Ah. Now *that's* a sin, it is. It's fine to meet you, sir." He offered his hand to Peter, who stared at it, then back at Seamus, who waited. The boy looked down at his own hand, then very gently placed it within Seamus's palm. Seamus nodded and shook the little hand. "Right, then. Let's go see the ship, aye?"

A smile lit in Peter's eyes that Andrew hadn't seen before. The little boy followed Seamus without a moment's hesitation, leaving Andrew and Janet slightly bemused in his wake. Flora clung to Janet's hand, but tugged on it, hurrying so she wouldn't lose sight of her brother.

The *Boyd of Glasgow* carried her passengers for three long months, holding together when massive waves dwarfed the ship and flushed gallons of freezing seawater through her cracks and joints. The wind was often brisk and the evenings sharp. The sky alternated between a gray expanse into nothingness and a blue so vivid it hurt to look into it for too long. At times it was easy to forget there was any land at all, so insular did they become on their floating home.

Andrew adapted easily to the rhythm of the sea, and worked harder than he'd ever worked before. Sometimes, when he took in the vast emptiness around him, he wondered at his decision to leave Scotland for this rocking, stinking craft. At other times he let the wind and surf pound at his body, slicking back his hair, burning his eyes, and he exulted in the fact that he had had enough courage to risk doing it.

It didn't take long for Andrew to get used to sleeping in his allotted hammock in the crew's quarters. It was different from curling up on a hard forest floor, but aside from the tight quarters and the stink of the neighbouring sailors, it wasn't an unpleasant change. On calm nights when it wasn't too cold, he lay on the deck, lulled by the lapping waves, admiring how the Milky Way smeared its translucent shine throughout the heavens.

One evening, in celebration of a particularly windy day, the crew broke out the whisky and danced to Seamus's fiddle. Andrew enjoyed the party, but the night was cold and he was tired. He headed down to his wool blanket and hammock, trying to ignore the dancing feet on the deck above his head and the raised voices of tone-deaf sailors. After a while, he rolled onto his side and folded his arm into a pillow, then, still smiling, closed his eyes and sank into sleep.

Maggie was there, waiting. Her blue eyes moved through him, warming his blood with their intensity. The soft line of her smile roused his own, although he still couldn't see her. He shivered at the hint of the breeze, believing it was her fingers on his ear, tucking the hair back from his face. It wasn't like the last time, when they spoke, when they actually held each other. This was more like a dream, reality twisted with his subconscious. But it was real all the same.

Then she was gone. The sudden loss awoke him, and he opened his eyes to the water-stained boards over his head. A tickle of sea air teased over his face, whispering through the vents in the cabin walls.

She had been there. The knowledge held him like an embrace.

PART 5: MAGGIE

Healing and Hurting

CHAPTER 26

Changing Leaves

The Cherokee village revolved around Waw-Li. So did my life. At first I approached cautiously, wary of her flame but needy of its heat. When I drew closer, she brought me in, making me part of her fire.

Waw-Li asked me to call her Grandmother, as the others did. She taught me many things, not least of which was the ability to calm my thoughts and drift into a place where my dreams could find me. She showed me how to ease myself into a trance, allowing me to direct my dreams, to use them and free them. At those moments I felt anything was possible. I lost all sense of time.

Every day for four months I walked from my house to the seven-sided council house, where each wall represented a different Cherokee clan. Waw-Li taught me all she could. One season passed into another, and our connection grew with each lesson. She asked me what I saw in my dreams, and I told her everything: what I heard and saw, how I felt. She interpreted what she could, building bridges between dreams and reality. She showed me the scars buried within me, and taught me how I could use them to strengthen my life.

She taught me the mysteries of animal totems, explaining to me why the shiny blackness of a raven always brought me comfort, why I always saw my world from a bird's-eye view.

"You are the raven," she said, her old woman's voice clear as spring water. She said shamans among the Cherokee often spoke through ravens. Some could change their human shape into that of the bird itself when it was required. The totem of the raven allowed them to pass between the worlds, between the veils of life and death, waking and dreaming.

"And there is a wolf that I see," she said. She opened her gnarled hands, palms up, as if accepting a gift. "This wolf is in your blood. He is with you awake or asleep. You must look for the wolf."

"Grandmother," I said. "I have found the wolf."

Waw-Li was the only person I ever told about Andrew. I told her how the mournful howl of a wolf brought me comfort. How I sensed the coarse fur brushing against my fingertips, but when I looked, there was nothing there. I always knew it was Andrew. When I glimpsed his dark shape treading through the night, the wary eyes softened as they met mine. I always felt safe when those eyes looked at me.

The old woman nodded, her eyes partially hidden by the slack skin of her eyelids. "The raven and the wolf," she said. "Power between the worlds. Strength of body and belief. Loyalty beyond all else."

A new world was opened to me through Waw-Li's teaching. For eighteen years of my life, things *happened*. No one ever asked the reasons. My true grandmother, with her many gifts, was an enigma no one in the family discussed. They had no way of understanding her, so they didn't try. My dreams were kept hidden within a blanket of secrecy, never surfacing until I arrived in the Cherokee village.

Now I lived in a world of magic. A world where animals and

people could exchange forms and powers. Where my gift wasn't merely accepted, but revered.

"What is it you want, Ma-kee?" Waw-Li asked one day. "What will you do now?"

I had wondered when she would ask me that. The question wasn't whether I would stay with the Cherokee. It was understood that wherever I chose to live in the future, I would always be one of them. No, this was different. She was asking about a practical use for my gifts. Giving something back as a way to thank the spirits. She was asking me to choose a direction. Once I did that, she would help me find the path.

"Do you have ideas for me?" I asked.

"Ma-kee, you have many gifts. Your ability to communicate with the spirit world will always be with you, and you will be a wise shaman with time and practice." She shifted on the cushion beneath her, then leaned toward me. "But there is more. The spirits blessed you with another gift. They dipped your soul into the pots of both white men and Cherokee, so you carry the minds of the two peoples. It came to me that your place should be between the two. I have asked Wahyaw to take you to the fort when he goes to trade. You will teach the white men about us, and us about them. If there is knowledge, there can be peace."

The thought of returning to the domain of white men stopped me. Waw-Li saw me stiffen and reached over to pat my leg.

"Do not let them frighten you, child. You must always be careful, but the men who harmed you and your sisters are no longer a danger." She brought her hand back onto her lap and smiled easily through missing teeth. "No one will make you go, Ma-kee. It is your decision."

My decision was to follow her lead, so when Wahyaw said we would leave in a week's time, I was ready.

Soquili wasn't coming. He didn't speak to me anymore. Not since the day I told him I couldn't marry him. I knew it was a good thing he was out of my life. I only had room for Andrew. But I couldn't help feeling an emptiness with Soquili gone. I missed him very much.

The day before we went to town, I went to join the other women as they bathed in the river. I laid my tunic on the grass and stepped in gingerly, hesitating as my foot touched the cold water. While I waited for my body to get used to the temperature, I stood still, examining the opposite bank where it rose toward a maple tree, shimmering with newborn green. Ripples of its reflection lapped the shore, ridged by pebbles that seemed to glow. I took a breath and held it as I waded into the deeper end of the pool, staying hidden and keeping quiet while I washed. I didn't want to interrupt the ritual exchange of gossip.

"Awenasa is with child," reported one woman.

A chorus of "Again?" danced across the water, followed by giggles and exclamations.

"I pray she receives the gift of a girl this time," said a small voice, and there were murmured grunts of assent.

"It is said Say-Lew Adsila found a new diversion for herself at the Ceremony. Is this so?" I peeked through the branches of a weeping birch to see Say-Lew's reaction. She was a jolly young woman with round cheeks and twinkling black eyes. She tossed her head back and laughed out loud.

"Ha!" she said. "The Ceremony is not just for prayers and dancing. Especially not when men like *that* come to our village!"

"There was one who had a sharp eye on our Soquili," someone said, interrupting the earlier laughter.

A chill tickled through me that had nothing to do with the

temperature of the river. I hardly felt the water as it licked my neck with its icy tongue.

"Yes! I saw that! The chief's brother's daughter! He could not do better," was one jovial opinion.

"Have you not seen? Soquili is already claimed! He loves the *o seronni* girl."

"Ma-kee has great power indeed," said a familiar voice, "but she has lost Soquili. He no longer looks her way. I do not think he will go to her again."

I closed my eyes and felt tears swim behind my lashes. This woman, Salali, would know better than anyone else. Salali was Soquili's mother. She gazed into the water, regret evident in her words.

"That is sad news for your house, Salali. She would have made a good wife for Soquili," said one of her friends.

There were quiet comments I couldn't catch, and a few brighter notes of speculation. I didn't wait to hear more. I emerged from behind the growth and their conversation ceased. Some of the women looked away, embarrassed to have been caught gossiping. But I smiled and shrugged.

"It wasn't meant to be," I said. I looked at Salali. "Don't be sad, Mother."

It was her sympathetic gaze that was my undoing. She reached out and I went to her, letting her fold me into her arms. The other women turned away, giving us privacy. I hid my face in her shoulder and wept. Soquili had been my protector and my friend. I had never been loved before. Not in that way.

But the tears I shed that morning were brief. They fell out of disappointment, not despair. The joy I awaited was on a ship somewhere, coming to me.

CHAPTER 27

From the Village to the Town

Wahyaw and five other warriors came for me the next day. Kokila said good-bye and reminded me she wanted stories about our journey when I returned. Adelaide stood beside her, staring at me with such intensity I almost turned back. She had used every argument possible to try and persuade me to stay away from the town and the white men in it. I wondered if she would ever trust another white man again.

The cool spring air roused our horses as they trotted from the village. I was glad of the furs we carried and wrapped a large deerskin around me for warmth, settling in for a long ride. Wahyaw said the journey would take three days if the weather held.

He rode beside me like a guardian for most of the trip. He wasn't much of a conversationalist, though when he did speak, it was obvious the words had been carefully considered beforehand. After an hour of silence, he cleared his throat and I realised he was about to honour me with one of his rare spoken thoughts.

"I am sorry for you and Soquili," he said, still looking straight ahead. I hadn't expected to hear a note of regret in his voice. "He had plans to wed you, Ma-kee."

"I know," I said. "He will find someone better suited."

We rode in silence for a while. A small brown bird swooped in low beneath his horse's chest, and the animal jerked its head up. Wahyaw didn't seem to notice. He was thinking. He squinted slightly, as if he were trying to look into the future.

"I think not," he said. "He would have been happy with you."

I looked at his profile, so handsome under the black comb of hair. The striking lines of his face were uncharacteristically soft with sadness. I felt an ache in my chest for him, and for Soquili. Wahyaw hated to see his brother in pain. I reached over and touched his hand where it rested on his thigh.

"He will be happy again," I said.

He looked at me, then frowned, considering. "And you?"

His concern surprised me. Tears sprang to my eyes, and I blinked them back. My words came out much more hoarsely than I had intended.

"I will be fine."

A rare smile slid across his face and rose to his eyes. He nodded once, then looked back at the path.

"Then it will be so," he said.

Fort Moore and its imposing fifteen-foot wall protected the trading post at New Windsor from marauders and other threats. A few soldiers looked up as we passed through the gates, but Indian traders were a common sight. With my long, dark hair braided and hanging over the furs, I blended in with my Cherokee companions.

Beyond the starkness of the fort spread the bustling town of New Windsor. Storefronts and alehouses welcomed people of all sorts. But the men with whom I travelled took no notice of those people or places. They stared ahead, following Wahyaw's lead, not meeting anyone's eyes.

I wasn't as disciplined. I looked everywhere, as fascinated by the bustle of a town as I had been as a little girl. The majority of the people in the street were white, but Indians gathered there as well. In some cases, their clothing was similar to what we wore, but their appearance varied. Hair length for one, and it was often adorned differently or covered by wide-brimmed hats. Some faces were tattooed with symbols and shapes I hadn't seen before. Some laughed as they stood talking with white men in the street. Others were pointedly silent, like my companions.

Wahyaw rode through the town until he reached a weathered cabin with a lopsided roof, standing at the end of the street. A number of men loitered outside its open door, standing in conversation or sitting on the dirt road. Most were Indians, but there were also white men who looked as if they had adopted the nomadic way of life. They wore buckskin, but it was, for the most part, dirty and tattered. Their beards and bushy hair made them appear more like bears than men. They were a sharp contrast to the Cherokee, who plucked their beards and scalps hair by hair as they grew from boys to men. I had grown used to the naked faces of my new family.

Our moccasins made no sound as we dropped from our horses. We tethered the animals to a post beside the cabin, then the men unloaded the furs and carried the heavy bundles toward the trader's cabin.

I was afraid of the men, of their voices, of their hands and intentions, but tried to keep my expression neutral. We started toward the door, and I tried to hide behind Wahyaw and his friends. Too late, though. The men spotted me, and the sight of a white woman entering the trading post with a group of Cherokee warriors sparked more than a little interest. Fear slithered through my belly, and I squeezed my sweat-dampened palms into fists as we walked past them. It wasn't the Indians who frightened me. It was the eyes of green and blue that glinted from under light curls, lips that smiled behind matted beards. The smell of whisky hung in the air around the doorway, and its odour reached through my nose to twist at my stomach. That smell . . . *ropes burning my wrists . . . legs forcing mine apart . . .* I flexed my hands, trying to contain their trembling.

"How much for the squaw?" one of them called.

Wahyaw didn't know the words but appeared to understand something of the meaning. He stared the man down with forbidding eyes. I looked straight ahead and followed the warriors into the fetid darkness of the trading post.

I stood in the doorway until my eyes adjusted to the light, or rather to the lack of it. We were in a single room, its walls lined with shelves, those shelves filled with boxes, bottles, blankets, and furs. In the centre of the room, a stick-thin man leaned back in his chair, his well-worn shoes propped on a desk in front of him. Crisp strands of hair were combed across his head, and his fuzzy gray beard was streaked with yellow from years of tobacco use. He chewed on a thin piece of wood, shifting it from one side of his mouth to the other. Standing beside the desk, speaking with the trader, was a very tall Indian who was dressed in clothing usually worn by white men. A dirty gray shirt was tucked into his pants, and a black tricorne sat at a jaunty angle over his cascade of black hair. His face was clearly that of an Indian, but his dress and manner were those of a white man. His ambivalence made me nervous.

We started walking toward the trader, who stopped talking mid-sentence to stare at me, as did the tall Indian beside him. Their expressions of surprise made it clear that women weren't usually seen in this building. White women were even rarer. I breathed in through my nose, filling my lungs with what I hoped was confidence, and immediately regretted doing so. The place reeked of old skins and tobacco. Bile rose in my throat.

"Well, now," the trader drawled.

He shifted the stick to one side of his mouth and, groaning with apparent effort, pulled his feet off the desk and stood. He stepped toward our group, pausing to spit a stream of yellow juice onto the floor beside my feet. I flinched, but didn't step away.

"What have we here?"

His eyes were small, their edges creased by constant squinting. His gaze dropped to my beaded moccasins, slid up my dress, then paused at the level of my breasts.

I was terrified. I fought the impulse to turn and run.

"Pay no attention to the pig," Wahyaw muttered in Cherokee. He stood beside me and crossed his broad arms across his chest. He stared at the trader with eyes dark and cunning as those of a wolf. And just as intimidating.

"We are here to trade," I said to the trader.

His mouth widened into an ugly grin. I saw why the little stick moved so easily within his mouth—he had no teeth to anchor it in place. I looked past him, wondering whether the tall Indian was a threat. I thought not. His dark eyes flicked between Wahyaw and me, taking in the scene, but he made no comment.

The trader sniffed, then spat again. "I'll take a look at them furs in a moment," he said. His lack of teeth caused "furs" to sound like "furth," a fact that didn't render him any less frightening to me. He hitched up his pants and stuck his thumbs into his belt.

"But I'll tell you what, girl. I'm wondering more what they'd take if I were to take you out back with me for five minutes," he said. The yellowed tip of his tongue snaked across his lips.

I glared at him. "We have brought skins to trade, sir. Nothing more."

He grinned, his toothless smile forming a strange, vacant hole. I shuddered.

"Injuns'd trade jest about anything for rum and guns, girl. You might want to ask your menfolk if they'd be interested in a couple of bottles in exchange," he drawled, winking at me.

The tall Indian said nothing but his eyes flicked toward the warriors behind me. My companions had understood none of the conversation. They waited in silence behind me.

"We have skins to trade," I repeated. "If you aren't interested, we'll go somewhere else."

He gave me a look of disgust and spat again. Wahyaw nudged me, inquiring. I turned my head and whispered into his ear.

"He wants to trade you a couple of bottles of rum—for me," I whispered flatly in Cherokee.

My protector exhaled in something close to a growl. The trader looked up into Wahyaw's furious black eyes, a foot higher than my own, and listened as Wahyaw unleashed a violent string of Cherokee threats and insults.

"Would you like me to translate my friend's words for you, sir?" I asked the trader, who flicked his eyes back toward me. "Or has he made his thoughts clear enough?"

The trader scowled, then sucked his lips in and out a few times while he considered what to do. "All right," he grunted. "Put them furs there. Ah'm payin' a blanket for fifteen skins, a rifle for twenty-five."

I had no idea what the furs were worth, but that seemed like robbery to me. The trader returned to his desk and had just started to sit when he noticed me shaking my head.

"That isn't good enough," I said. "We'll go elsewhere."

I turned to leave. Wahyaw and the others looked surprised, but stepped aside to let me through. Wahyah touched my arm.

"He isn't paying enough," I told him.

Wahyaw's jaw snapped shut, and he nodded.

"I ain't sure you wanna waste your time doin' that, little girl," the trader said. I looked back and saw he was still standing, his palms flat on the desktop. "You won't find a better trade anywhere."

I could hear the truth he was keeping from me. Like when my mother hid toys for me to find. I heard the numbers in his head, saw other deals he had made in the past. I pushed aside my earlier panic and stood up straight.

"You're lying," I said, gaining confidence. I saw again the numbers in his head, and applied them to our own deal. "You are offering too little. We will trade fifteen pelts for a rifle, not a blanket."

The trader made an irritated clucking noise with his tongue. Then he sighed.

"Injuns around here get that same trade every time. Don't you go and get difficult with me. I don't do well with girls what go against mah word."

Something inside me shifted into place, and my fear disintegrated. I strode toward the man, slammed my palms on his desk, and stared him right in the eye. To my great satisfaction, he flinched.

"I don't care *how* you do," I said through gritted teeth. In my mind I danced, so excited to hear the confidence in my words. It was as if I listened to someone else speak. "You take advantage of these Indians because they don't speak English. Well, I do. Make me a better offer, *sir*," I said, "or we will ride to the next post."

"Well, shit," he said, and spat.

He looked from me to the healthy stack of furs at the men's feet, lusting after the potential profit. He glared at me from under bushy gray eyebrows, then grunted in assent. He yanked open a desk drawer and pulled out his ledger book, then gestured toward Wahyaw with his chin.

"Tell yer dogs to lay them furs against the wall over there. Do you know how many they brought, or do I have to count 'em all?" he asked.

"Of course I know," I said, and listed off the various furs.

The trader wrote it all down, then looked up at me. A hint of a smile lurked at the corner of his lips. His mind, I could see, flickered with grudging admiration.

"You done yerself a good deal, girl."

The trader got up and trudged toward an open box filled with rifles. He checked my list against the guns, counting them out and setting them in a pile for the Cherokee, who inspected every weapon as if it were a legal document. He spat loudly and repeatedly throughout the trading process until Wahyaw put a stop to the habit by giving the man such a look of disgust I thought the trader might be afraid to do it again.

Two of the Cherokee nodded toward the cases of rum bottles lined up against a far wall, but Wahyaw dismissed the idea with a shake of his head. Instead, he headed toward another wall, stocked with various items for trade, and we followed him.

The trader waved his hand toward a stack of folded woolen blankets. "Gettin' cool at night," he muttered. "Got lots of blankets there."

The promise of warmth through cold winter nights drew me toward one, dyed in a cheerful red and white pattern. I brushed my fingertips over the rough fabric, but jerked my hand back as if I'd been stung. During that brief moment of contact, my mind had swirled with visions of the sick and the dying, lying in contorted shapes beneath this cloth. Disease crawled through the fibres. The air was thick with warning. Feeling slightly faint, I turned away and remembered instead the familiar comfort of bearskins.

The men appeared pleased as we left the trading post. Their arms were full of our half of the bargain: guns and ammunition, tobacco for council, a couple of iron pots for cooking, and some pretty shells and beads the women of the village liked for their embroidery.

We loaded the items onto our horses, then, our business complete, took a leisurely stroll to the edge of the Savannah River. I took off my moccasins and lowered my feet into the current, numbing my toes. The men squatted beside me on the water's edge and splashed their faces, cleaning off the dirt from the journey and the stink of the trading post.

I looked up at the sounds of voices, but there was no one but us at our little spot. I stood up to look farther and realised the words and bits of laughter were coming from a boat across the water. Wahyaw told me it was a ferry that transported people from one shore to the other.

I watched the tiny barge draw closer and thought of another ship, far away. This ferry was nothing like the ship on which Andrew sailed. Sails and nets shadowed his galley; hardened sailors manned its deck. I closed my eyes and searched for the comfort of his features and saw his face at once. He was standing by the ship's rails, wind whipping through his hair. The surf crashed around him, and the sails snapped as they gobbled up the wind. He was coming.

We set up camp just outside the wall of the fort. After the sun set, we ate around a fire, told stories, then bundled up in our blankets under a tarp. I couldn't sleep. I was unaccustomed to the late-night noises of a town. Even more disconcerting was hearing English spoken, after having spent so long with the Cherokee.

Out of habit, I translated the myriad of conversations. All the voices were male. Many of the words were rough and slurred, punctuated by random obscenities. Scattered bursts of laughter penetrated the darkness.

With a start I realised someone was discussing me.

"Yep, Ah saw her, too. Come marchin' outta the post there with them braves like she run the town," grunted one.

"How old she be, ye reckon, Henry?"

"Oh, I'd say no more 'an twenty." Henry paused, relishing the attention. I heard the sound of a pipe being puffed. "No. Less than that. Purty little thing."

"Whadda ya figure? She a prisoner?" came a younger voice.

"Nah," said Henry. "She looked like she *wanted* to be with them Injuns. Heathen, that's what she is. An' just beggin' for it if you ask me. She come back in here tomorrow, well, I'll—"

"I do beg your pardon, sir, but you'll what?" inquired a different voice. It carried a lovely, crisp accent. Henry hesitated at this interruption, but persevered.

"I'll damn well give her what she came for, that's what. Who the hell are you?"

"Captain John Quinn. At your service, sir," said the man.

"Well, Captain John Quinn," drawled Henry in a sneering voice that suggested he was sizing up the soldier, "what's this girl to you?"

"I am simply interested," came the smooth reply. "I heard others speak of a white woman who visited the town with the Cherokee today and was curious. Are they still nearby, do you know?"

"Got no idea," spat Henry. "Likely."

My curiosity was piqued. The captain sounded kind. I yawned widely and tucked my questions away, finally worn down by the day. I fell asleep.

That night I dreamed of the man in the blue shirt.

CHAPTER 28

New Windsor

The morning carried a drizzle over the river and left it sitting miserably overhead. The ground was relatively dry under our tarp so we were reluctant to emerge. The horses shimmied their coats against the wetness, twitching their ears as they watched us wake and roll up our gear.

Wahyaw led us to a tavern, looking for a little breakfast other than the bannock and dried meat we had brought with us. The air inside the building was ripe with ale and tobacco, the atmosphere still heavy from the night before.

There were other Indians within, all taking refuge from the foul weather. At the back wall sat the tall Indian from the trading post, watching everyone who came and went. Our eyes locked for an instant, and I was struck by the man's resemblance to a wall. Tall, broad, and impenetrable.

I looked away from him and followed Wahyaw and the others to a table. The dirty windows admitted little light, so the sunless room created shadows from candlelight. Wahyaw took the same position as had the big Indian: back to the wall. A position of defense and ready offense.

Breakfast was stew from the night before. It was a warm mush of carrots, potatoes, onions, and a tiny bit of beef, drowned in a murky pool of broth. I had eaten better food in the village longhouse, surrounded by better company, but the meal was satisfying and filled our bellies with enough sustenance for the day. At meal's end we left some coins on the table and left the tavern, anticipating the fresh, if damp, air.

Wahyaw was the first out, and I followed close behind. I was looking over my shoulder, listening to one of the others as I walked out the door, and as a result, didn't see where I was going. A wool coat slammed into me, its wet fibres rough on my face.

"Oh! Excuse me!" I exclaimed.

"Pardon me!" the stranger said at the same time, stepping back.

My first thought when I saw the man's clean-shaven face and long red jacket was that he had to have been the man I had heard the night before. The captain. My next thought was how intense his eyes were, staring at me from beneath his thick brown hair.

Wahyaw and the others stepped to the side, but were there, always there.

"Are you quite all right?" the man in uniform asked, frowning in concern. "Are you hurt? I do apologise. It was entirely my fault. My attention must have been elsewhere."

My face flushed hot and I hated myself for suddenly feeling shy. "No, no sir," I stammered. "I'm fine. Are you all right? I'm so sorry—I wasn't looking and I—"

He smiled, distracting me with a flash of teeth from within the angles of his prominent cheekbones. He was extraordinarily handsome. The only flaw in his features I could see was a long, well-healed scar on his cheek. The line cut straight down from just beside his eye, stopping at one edge of his full lips.

He gave me a quick bow. "No need for apologies. No need at all. Actually, this is a fine chance meeting," he said. "I had heard of your presence in our humble town and was hoping to make your acquaintance. So this is indeed fortunate—for me, at least."

"You knew of my presence?" I echoed.

"Indeed. It seems you are the topic of many conversations."

He extended one hand toward me. I wasn't sure what he wanted me to do, but I gave him mine and was surprised when he touched his lips to the back of it. They were wet and cool from the drizzle. My impulse was to jerk my hand back, away from the unexpected intimacy, but I didn't. In that brief moment I felt a jolt of something pass between us. Like a spark from my flint.

"Please allow me to introduce myself," he said, a small smile playing over his lips. He placed one hand across his waistcoat and issued a quick bow. "Captain John Quinn, at your service."

I stared, unsure. He raised his eyebrows and realisation hit me. "Oh! I'm sorry. I'm Maggie," I blurted, feeling flustered. "Margaret Johnson."

"An honour to meet you, Miss Johnson. And these fine gentlemen?"

He turned toward Wahyaw and the others and smiled. The warriors looked taken aback at the gentleman's interest in them, but nodded one by one as I introduced them.

"Osi-yo, dee gee naylee," the captain said, greeting them as friends in their own tongue.

Eyebrows raised in surprise, the Cherokee returned the greeting and appeared to relax their vigilance a bit. They stepped back, giving Captain Quinn unspoken permission to speak with me.

"I hope you do not find it too impertinent a question, Miss

Johnson, but I cannot help but wonder how it is you come to be here, in New Windsor? There are not a great many women who come to this place, fewer still who travel with the Cherokee."

"We came from the Keowee Valley to trade, sir," I said, beginning to overcome my shyness. "The Cherokee are my family, and they gave me the honour of speaking for them." I hesitated. "I'm glad I could help. The trader at the end of the road already tried to cheat them."

Captain Quinn nodded. "George Arnold. Yes, I know him. A swindler and a liar. I was told, however, that you handled him quite efficiently," he said. A slow smile spread from his lips into his sparkling brown eyes, and I couldn't help smiling back.

"You heard that?" I wondered where he'd heard it from. The big Indian? Maybe Arnold himself? "Well, I couldn't let him cheat my family," I said.

"Plainly not," he said without hesitation, his smile still in place. "And have you plans to stay for a while?"

"Oh, no. We leave tomorrow morning. We're needed in the village."

"Ma-kee," Wahyaw grunted behind me, speaking in Cherokee. "We must go. Adahy is restless."

"Might I be of some assistance?" Captain Quinn said, returning smoothly to Wahyaw's language. "I would be pleased to show you all around New Windsor. I have lived most of my life in the fort. I am well acquainted with the area."

Wahyaw's expression darkened. "We don't need a tour," he snapped. "We have been here before. Ma-kee," he said, turning to me with his mind obviously made up, "we are going now. There are people I would like you to meet."

Captain Quinn used my slight hesitation to step in again, offering a different option. He pushed the smooth brown curls back from his forehead and tucked the ends behind his ears. His red coat brushed against the tight white breeches as he moved. I was fascinated by the smooth look of him, by his confident manner.

"I would be honoured to show Miss Johnson around and deliver her to you afterwards. You need not worry for her safety. She will be well protected. My good name is known throughout the town."

Wahyaw looked painfully divided. He clearly didn't want to wander the town with this man. He also knew he should remain by my side. And from my expression, he gathered I wasn't interested in meeting more of his Cherokee kinsmen at that moment.

"I must apologise for my impertinence, Miss Johnson," said the Captain, returning to English. "I neglected to ask if you were inclined to spend the afternoon with me."

"I don't even know you, sir," I replied.

"No," Wahyaw decided. "Ma-kee, you will stay with us."

I thought I saw disappointment flit across the captain's face. The expression didn't detract from its perfection in the least.

"Perhaps we might meet for the evening meal?" he persisted, keeping his voice level.

He turned to Wahyaw and repeated the request. Wahyaw narrowed his eyes and turned to the other men. He sought resistance, but found none. The others were looking around, restless and uninterested, tired of waiting in the mist.

"Yes," Wahyaw said finally, sounding resigned.

Captain Quinn named the tavern and the time. We agreed, then parted. I watched him walk back toward the fort with his large hands clasped behind his back. The mist dampened his hair so it seemed almost black. Tiny droplets clung to his coat and shimmered in the silver light. I was struck by his resemblance to an animal with sleek, wet fur.

Throughout the day I was impatient to see the captain again.

Wahyaw shook his head with in disgust, but I scolded him into behaving. I reminded him that Waw-Li wanted me to help communication between the Cherokee and the people of this town. This was a perfect way to start, I told him. I suggested he didn't have to say a word at supper, if he didn't want to. He huffed through his teeth at me, but left it at that.

The captain's bright red coat was the only colour in the tavern when we met him there at the end of the day. He sat at one end of a table big enough for all of us. He stood and smiled when we came in, gesturing toward our seats.

The evening passed uneventfully; there was nothing of any consequence to discuss. I thought perhaps the captain wanted company, and my presence intrigued him. Wahyaw took me at my word and said nothing throughout the meal except to the other Indians. For the most part, Captain Quinn limited his attentions to me. I was unwilling to discuss how I came to be with the Cherokee, so he moved on to more basic questions: how I was enjoying New Windsor, the weather, and other trivial subjects. He listened carefully to every syllable I uttered. He laughed at any attempt I made at humour. It was flattering, but something about the way he looked at me, like he was trying to read my mind, made me nervous.

Despite this, I asked him about the fort, about the town, about anything I could think of. I was thirsty for knowledge, and he was more than willing to teach me. His voice was smooth, but I could tell that if circumstance required it, he could be heard clearly across a room. I got the impression he enjoyed hearing himself speak.

When the meal was over, the captain walked out of the tavern with us. The rain had moved on, lifting its wet blanket from the town's shoulders, leaving everything beneath soggy but optimistic. The evening air was a welcome relief after the tavern's smoky closeness. There were fewer stars visible than I was used to, but it wasn't the fault of the wispy clouds. The lights of the town had borrowed some of the stars' brightness for themselves.

"I hope we shall meet again when you return for more trading, Miss Johnson," the captain said.

"I'll ask for you next time, Captain Quinn. I enjoyed myself this evening."

"As did I. There's no need to ask for me, my dear. I am always around, keeping my eye on things."

As if in illustration he turned his face toward a group of people on the mucky street. He gestured vaguely at them with a dismissive wave of one hand and they crossed to the other side of the street. With a weary sigh, he turned back to me.

"I suppose you could say I am somewhat of a guardian of the town, you see. I know everyone that comes in, I know their business, and I know when they will leave. If I might say so, Miss Johnson, I am a valuable friend to have in this place full of rough, uncivilised men. You will never come to harm when you are with me," he said confidently. "Good night, sirs," he said to the others, returning to fluent Cherokee. "I wish you a safe journey, and I hope to see you again soon."

My companions nodded, grunting vague replies. Wahyaw offered a brief, forced smile that looked completely foreign on his face. None of the warriors tried to get along with Quinn, and he, after the basic introductions, showed no further interest in them.

I, on the other hand, spent the rest of the evening recalling every compliment the handsome captain had paid to me. It felt good to have a man look at me that way—as if I were a *lady*.

CHAPTER 29

The Darkness Within

That night I dreamed of the forest.

It was dark and I was running, dodging trees and rocks that appeared out of the blackness like ghosts. I tripped and stumbled as I fled, then was back on my feet and tearing through the underbrush again. Every muscle was tight, preparing to be grabbed by whatever breathed so hard behind me. I never looked back. I didn't need to. I knew there wasn't anything there for me to see.

I ran until I couldn't run anymore, until my escape was blocked by a tall stone wall. All I could do was turn and face my invisible pursuer. When I did, I saw, as I knew I would, nothing. I looked back toward the wall, and there he was.

The coyote bore a vivid white scar from a long-ago battle. It had cut through the copper red fur on his face, beneath his flattened ears. His yellow eyes focused on me while his tongue followed the points of his teeth.

He paced toward a large tree, watching my reaction with every one of his steps. A simple gold chain, like a ladies' piece of jewellery, hung from the tree above him, clasped onto one of the lower branches. The coyote lifted his leg and marked his territory, catching the tree, the ground, and the gold. The stench of urine filled my senses.

I stepped to the side and he mirrored my movement. He moved forward and I retreated. He grew as he moved toward me, as did the growl that vibrated through the furry throat. I blinked and the hunter's eyes became murky pools, simmering with madness. When I blinked again, he lay on his side, chest still, eyes glazed in a final stare. A dark stain spread over the plush whiteness of his breast. It stained my own trembling hands with blood that wouldn't wash away. He suddenly seemed very small.

I stepped back and everything disappeared. All that remained was the air. Even the solidity of the earth was gone. I fell down, down, down, my black wings beating madly in their struggle against the spiral. The wind sucked me toward a web of black fangs that stretched toward me, and I knew I was lost.

CHAPTER 30

Possession

Every time we rode to town, Captain Quinn was there. He always arrived so promptly it was as if he'd been watching the paths for us.

Wahyaw eventually, and reluctantly, permitted the captain and me to walk alone. Captain Quinn was very attentive, and his words were full of compliments and praise I'm sure I didn't deserve. It was all very flattering.

About six months after I first met him, everything changed.

The Cherokee and I had just ridden for three long days, then spent a half hour haggling in George Arnold's trading post. I looked and smelled appalling. Nevertheless, Captain Quinn was waiting for us outside the tavern, and he grinned when he saw me.

"Good afternoon, my friends," he said, nodding to each of us as we walked toward him. "You are all well, I hope? Miss Johnson, you are looking particularly lovely if I might say so."

I couldn't help laughing at that. "Oh, Captain. What a thing to say! I'm horribly dirty."

"Not at all!" he cried, beaming at me. "Not at all. It is indeed wonderful to see you looking so fine. The glory of the day pales next to you."

That was how he always spoke to me. It was strange hearing words like that, directed at me.

"Gentlemen," Captain Quinn said in Cherokee, "I do hope you'll excuse us this afternoon. I have something special planned for Miss Johnson."

Without waiting for their response, he ushered me into a tavern, which, owing to the late afternoon hour, was empty. Not even a waitress in sight. He led me to a table against the back wall, where we sat. He was still smiling, his eyes lit with excitement.

"What is it?" I asked. "What has you so happy today?"

From under his chair, Captain Quinn brought out a small package. It was wrapped in brown paper, bound with rough string that was tied in a careful bow. He balanced it on his palm, then stretched out his hand to me.

"For you, my dear," he said.

I stared at the package sitting on his palm. I had never received a gift in my entire life. Or at least nothing that had come wrapped. I touched the paper tentatively, not exactly sure how to proceed. He must have sensed my confusion. He placed the package in my hand and closed my fingers over its rounded edges.

"It is just a small gift, Miss Johnson, a token of how much I have enjoyed our friendship. I hope you will not find it inappropriate."

I pulled the loose end of the string until the bow unraveled and the paper escaped its bindings, revealing a small box. I lifted off the top and peeked inside, then closed it again in shock. My expression must have been comical because he laughed. He leaned toward me and opened the box himself, reaching in and pulling out a gold, heart-shaped locket, which he dangled from a delicate gold chain.

"Captain Quinn, I . . ." I stammered, feeling blood fill my cheeks. I had never seen anything so beautiful. I was almost afraid to touch it.

"Here," he said. "Allow me. These things can be difficult to manage."

He rose to his feet and took my hands so that I stood as well.

"Shh," he whispered and put his hands behind my neck to close the tiny lock.

The action brought his face close to mine, and I did nothing to push him away. His kiss was light at first, almost apologetic, but his confidence returned immediately. Heat rose in a wave from the depths of my chest, through my throat, up through lips and ears, even tickling inside my nose. He placed his hands on either side of my face to hold me there, and I was taken aback by the strength of his kiss, of the need that pulsed through him. He breathed heavily through his nose, sounding hungry. My lips and cheeks burned from his whiskers.

Curiosity and arousal shifted suddenly as fear flooded through me. I felt it bubble up in a sudden cold sweat which covered my entire body. Memories of men kneeling over me, of sheer helplessness in the face of primal violence.

"Stop," I said. "Please stop. You're scaring me."

He didn't seem to hear me. His voice, muttering what I assumed were intended endearments, sounded husky and unfamiliar. One of his hands gripped the soft flesh above my tunic, leaving red circles where his fingers pressed.

"No," I whimpered, struggling against him. "Please don't do this. Please stop."

I gasped when he pulled me in too hard and our teeth knocked together. His breath filled my mouth and tasted like onions. I tried to avoid his tongue as it probed and explored. My hands pressed against his chest to push him away, but he forced me back against the cold, stone wall.

I became very aware of the locket. The small, heart-shaped weight above my breasts increased suddenly, as if it grew in size. The chain dug into my neck. The locket was warm. No, it was more than warm, I realised. It was hot. And it *vibrated.*

"Stop!" I cried, but he heard nothing.

I jerked my face away from the captain's mouth, gasping for breath, but he sank his lips into my neck and travelled hungrily toward my breasts. Terror pulsed through my chest, and I felt myself being sucked back into that forest, back into the meaty grasps of the slavers, back against the sappy bark. I grasped within my mind for something to anchor me. My mind exploded in a storm of colours, whirling and shrieking, dragging me toward its eye. My visions barged in, and the locket pulsed against my flesh as if someone had jabbed me with a hot poker.

And I saw.

I saw a box on an earthen floor. Within its rough wooden sides lay small, incongruous trinkets: ribbons, a bit of lace, a small shoe, a button or two.

I saw the tightly woven grass bracelet I had tied around my sister's wrist so long ago.

I saw the blue hair ribbon that had once tethered my hair back.

And beneath that, I saw a much-loved rag doll wrapped in material from Ruth's baby gown. Its big, black eyes stared up at me, empty and lost.

I saw six girls sitting behind the box, leaning against the wall. Their long hair was matted and their faces were grimy, tear-streaked, and bruised.

The shock hit me like a fist. "Let go of me!" I screamed. "Let me go!"

The captain heard nothing but his own momentum. I felt the hard muscle, swollen beneath his immaculate white breeches, and I shoved against him with all my strength. His fingers gripped and bruised my thigh. My mind shifted back to that day, that moment when I had been forced to spread my legs for the first time, while a complete stranger shoved himself through my defenses. I was powerless again, unable to defend myself.

"No, no, no, no," I said, trying desperately to wriggle away.

The man wrapped around me was a stranger. A stranger who was somehow responsible for the deaths of my mother and my baby sister. I dug my fingers into his arms until my nails drew blood. I tried to kick, to raise my knees against his progress, but his hips held me pinned to the wall. Tears ran down my face, and sweat wound under my tunic. I heard myself crying out, telling him to stop, but my voice seemed very small, and very far away.

"His eyes, lass. His eyes!"

I had no time to question Andrew's presence. I did as he said. I put my hands on the captain's cheeks and jammed my thumbs into his eyes.

The captain howled and fell back, clutching his face with both hands. I grabbed for the knife I always carried in my belt. He lowered his hands and lunged at me, and my blade disappeared within his neat waistcoat. I yanked it out and he went down hard. His head hit the stone floor before the rest of him did, and he lay still. I stared at his body in horror, in confusion at the man who had called himself my friend.

"I'll head in to make the 'rrangements with the cap'n," Blue Shirt had said. His voice was so clear he might have been standing beside me, not lying dead by a stream.

My lips felt numb. The words tumbled out in a hoarse whisper. "Where are they? Where are the girls? What have you done?"

He didn't move, but anger shoved ahead of my shock and I dropped to my knees beside him. I didn't know what to touch, didn't want to touch any part of him, but I had to know. I slipped my knife back into my belt and pounded his back with my fists, needing a reaction of some kind.

"What—have—you—done?" I cried.

He gasped. A quick intake of breath, then a moment before he oriented himself. He turned his head to the side and rested his cheek on the floor. He was still handsome. Still Quinn. But blood was smeared across his face and his eye was unfocused.

"I beg your pardon," he said hoarsely. "I believe it is I who should ask that question."

"No, Captain," I said. "You tell me where those girls are."

"Have you killed me, Miss Johnson? Why would you kill me? I only loved you—"

"Stop it!" I yelled. I didn't bother fighting the tears. He was dying. I could see it in the fading light of his eyes. But he wasn't allowed to die yet. Not until I was finished. I lowered my face to his and spoke through clenched teeth. "You are the captain. You are the one in charge. You sent those men to steal my sisters and me from my mother. They killed my mother, did you know? Then they raped the three of us until we couldn't walk. And my baby sister? Who was ten years old. *Ten!* They raped her to death, Captain. And you paid them to do it."

A remarkable transformation came over his face. He turned his profile so he could see me better, and both eyes came sharply into focus. A dark red flush raced up his neck and mixed with the blood on his face.

"What are you talking about?"

"You know," I said. "Where are those poor little girls? What kind of man *are* you?"

He stared at me, his expression unreadable. I didn't need to read it, though. I saw his thoughts as if they were my own. Disbelief. Fury. *How could she know?*

His lips pulled back as if he were growling. "You know nothing," he hissed. "My personal business is entirely that. Mine."

I undid the locket from around my neck and dangled it in front of his nose. "Whose was this? How old was she? Did she fetch a good price?"

The little gold heart danced on the end of the chain, and he blinked. When he spoke, his voice sounded strange. Like the soft purr of an awestruck child.

"From the beginning I knew you were special, Miss Johnson." He dropped his cheek back to the floor. "So beautiful. So different from any other woman." His hand fluttered beside him, then stretched out, reaching for mine. But he would never hold it again. His voice changed again. "But you're not as smart as you think," he said. "You *could* have been smart. You *could* have stayed with me, where you belonged. But you'd rather spread your legs for those savages, wouldn't you?"

I had no words, only stared at him in horrified amazement. The man wore a complacent smile one might use on an obstinate child. He admitted nothing, and yet I knew it all to be true. Now he expected all to be forgotten, and worse, forgiven.

"Where are they?" I screamed.

The door slammed shut, and I realised a man had come into the building, apparently looking for the tavern owner.

"Have you seen . . ." he started, walking toward me. "Hey—what's goin' on here? What . . ."

He took one look at John's crushed nose, then stared with malevolence at the deerskin tunic I always wore. "Don't you go nowhere," he said. He turned and ran outside again.

They would be coming for me. I was going to be punished. They would call this murder, and in my heart I knew it was. I longed to smash the captain's head on the floor again, end it all, but I had to know the answer to my question. Or else Quinn would take the answer to hell with him.

"Where are the girls?" I demanded. "Where are they?"

"Forgive me," he said, his voice almost song-like. "Forgive me."

I stared into his eyes. "Tell me where the girls are, Captain Quinn. Tell me, and I will forgive you."

His expression transformed before my eyes. His gaze, liquid and pious, hardened. His face split into a smile that oozed blood over his teeth.

"I don't need your forgiveness."

For the first time it struck me how hard the lines of his mouth were. I glimpsed something deeper. Something feral. Something . . . canine was all I could think. In my mind his eyes began to slant and his teeth to sharpen. The white scar on his cheek seemed more obvious, as if it were exposed against a dark brown background. Like the colour of his hair. I heard Waw-Li's ancient voice wind like smoke through my mind.

"You know him, Ma-kee. The Coyote. The Trickster."

She had taught me so well. I had learned the totems, the lessons, the tools I needed to use my gift. She had shown me how the raven led me and how the wolf shadowed Andrew's soul. In front of me stood the one animal I should have seen immediately for his vicious potential. The one animal who had haunted my nightmares.

I slammed my palms down on his back so he grunted, then I closed my eyes. I reached for the faces I had seen through the locket. I reached for faces of children with deadened eyes. I saw Ruth. She tried to hand me the little rag doll she had carried the morning before she was killed, but her hands were empty.

"Find my doll, Maggie," she said, and Quinn died under my hands.

I was arrested for the murder of Captain John Quinn. When Sergeant MacMillan came for me, I let him tie my wrists together, then I asked if I could tell him my side of the story. He had kind eyes. I hoped I was reading them right. I'd started to doubt my intuition after the experience with Quinn.

"Of course," MacMillan said. "What is it you'd like to tell me?"

"It's a long story, sir," I said, "but it is all related to this horrible afternoon."

"Let's get a table then," he suggested. "I listen better when I'm sitting down."

There were other soldiers in the tavern now, and they were gathered around Quinn's body. They wrapped him up in a shroud and carried him out between them, shooting me furious glances as they went. It felt strange seeing them there. As if I were watching from outside myself.

MacMillan gestured toward the tavern owner, who brought him an ale. The officer was about the same age as my father would have been, but his face was gentle under his silver-streaked hair.

"I hope," he said after taking a sip, "that you have a good story. Because I assure you this is not a good situation. Captain Quinn was a powerful man around New Windsor, as well as in the fort. He had a great many friends. There will be a lot of talk."

I nodded. "I know. But if I can tell you from the beginning, maybe you could talk to whoever looks after these sorts of things."

"Of course," he said. "I will report everything you say to my superior, and he will pass it along to the man who will run your trial, Mr. Justice Schneider. That will ensure, as far as is possible, that you will receive a fair trial."

I told him everything, though I didn't mention either the death of Blue Shirt or my gift of Sight. He listened intently, nodding and shaking his head at intervals. When my story was done, when I finished with Quinn falling at the edge of my knife, MacMillan let out a long breath.

"Please tell me you have proof of all this," he said.

"Not with me, no," I replied. "But I know there is some. I just have to find it."

He scratched his head. "Miss Johnson, I will do what I can. You were right to come to me with this. But without some kind of proof, I don't see . . ." He shook his head. "I will do what I can."

He stood and beckoned to two soldiers, and I rose as well. They came over and stood on either side of me.

"You are to go with these gentlemen," MacMillan said. "I wish you the best of luck and promise to bring your story forward to the appropriate authorities. It has been very interesting speaking with you this afternoon. Please take care of yourself." He glanced briefly at the soldiers. "Treat her kindly, gentlemen. She has a long, unpleasant experience ahead of her." He bowed to me, and the soldiers took my arms.

They brought me to the fort and locked me within the black-barred jaws of the prison, the impenetrable black teeth of which I had dreamed.

I sat on a small bed and shivered. Everything was cold: the air, the floor, the walls, my heart. I clutched a scratchy brown blanket over me and curled up into myself.

The next day, two different soldiers came to my cell. They tied my wrists in front of me and marched me between them, as if I would flee. Maybe it was regulation. They must have been able to see I was too weak to try anything like that.

I was led into a large stone building and marched into a room with benches aligned in rows. The benches held probably twenty people, and they were all staring at me. The room went silent as I was ushered in. Adelaide's was the first face I saw. She looked pale. Beside her, Soquili and Wahyaw sat stone-faced. I smiled at them, but they didn't smile back. They were surrounded by a large crowd of townspeople. People I had never seen before.

An important-looking, white-haired man slid into the room carrying an armful of papers. He walked to the front and laid the papers on a large desk, then stared at me with venom in his gaze. I stared back and he looked away.

"All rise for Mr. Justice Schneider," he barked.

After a long pause, a large man who I supposed was Mr. Justice Schneider marched in and sat behind the desk. He didn't look healthy. His cheeks were bright red and spidered by blue veins, and they hung down in loose jowls. His nose looked abnormally round—too big for his face. He looked impatient and self-important. He glared down at me, lips pursed, then shook his head as if I were a nuisance.

"Read the charge," he said to the man in the glasses, who stood beside the desk.

"Are you Miss Margaret Johnson?" the clerk demanded.

I swallowed. "Yes, I am, sir."

"And where is your abode?"

"Um, I'm sorry?"

The clerk blew out his breath. "Where do you live?"

"In the Cherokee village. They took me in . . ."

"No other abode?"

"No, sir."

He coughed and made a note, then put both palms flat on his desk.

"Miss Margaret Johnson," he said. "You are charged with the willful murder of Captain John Quinn in that on the fourteenth day of June, in the year of Our Lord 1746, during the early afternoon, you did deliberately and with malice aforethought stab Captain John Quinn in the chest in the tavern popularly known as Squire Markworth's Tavern with the result that the said Captain John Quinn died forthwith of the aforesaid injury which he had sustained at your hand. How plead you, guilty or not guilty?"

I hesitated. I wasn't exactly sure of everything he'd said, but it sounded to me like he thought I'd killed Captain Quinn on purpose. That I'd planned to do it. Had I?

"How do you plead?" repeated the clerk, lifting one eyebrow. "Guilty or not guilty?"

I frowned. "I, um . . ."

Mr. Justice Schneider leaned forward, flaring his bulbous nose. "Speak up, Miss Johnson, and tell the court whether you plead guilty or not guilty. I take it that you understand the question."

"I did stab Captain Quinn," I admitted.

"Yes, yes. But do you plead guilty or not guilty to murder? We cannot proceed with this committal hearing unless you plead guilty or not guilty."

"I didn't mean to kill him," I blurted. "He attacked me."

Mr. Justice Schneider eased his bulk back in his chair and sighed. He seemed both bored and sorely tested by my apparent stupidity. "Guilty or not guilty?" he said in a singsong voice.

I bit my lip and steeled myself to make a decision. I had not planned to kill Quinn. I hadn't planned anything that day. It was Quinn's fault. He'd started everything with that locket. I'd finished it with my knife.

"Not guilty," I announced.

"So be it," declared Mr. Justice Schneider, making a note. "Is there anything else you would like to tell this court before I arraign you on a charge of the murder of Captain John Quinn?"

"Arraign me, sir?"

"Before I set a date for your trial on a charge of the murder of Captain John Quinn?"

I shook my head.

"In that case, I set your hearing for tomorrow morning. Are there any witnesses you would like to call in your defense?"

I looked over at Soquili and Wahyaw. Wahyaw looked pained and pretended to be watching something on one of the side walls. Soquili watched me closely, looking desperately unhappy. No, I had no witnesses. No one had been there. I had stupidly ignored all of Wahyaw's warnings and gone alone with Quinn.

"The man who walked in, looking for the tavern keeper, sir."

"Ah, yes." Schneider smiled unpleasantly. "He certainly saw what happened, much good may it do you. Anybody else?"

I stared at my feet. "No, sir."

"Louder, please, Miss Johnson."

"No, sir."

He motioned to my guards. "Take her away. Until tomorrow, Miss Johnson."

"Maggie!" Adelaide whimpered as they led me past her. I tried to give her a reassuring look, but I know I failed. I reeled against the soldiers' restraining hands and they shoved me ahead.

In the morning they led me back into the courtroom. Nothing seemed to have changed. The crowd seemed exactly the same, only louder, clustering together with anticipation. Adelaide, Soquili, and Wahyaw were there again, wearing the same expressions as they had the day before. I didn't bother to smile this time.

They brought me to the same seat as before, directly in front of where the judge would sit, flanked by two soldiers.

The man with the glasses threw open the door and walked briskly through the room. He shot me another piercing glare, then sat. A moment later he was back on his feet, bidding everyone to rise for Mr. Justice Schneider. Everyone rose as the judge came back to his desk and settled himself into his chair.

"Miss Johnson," asked Mr. Justice Schneider, "I take it that you continue to realise you are on trial for your life for the murder of Captain John Quinn?"

"Yes, sir," I replied.

"And do you wish to change your plea from not guilty to guilty?"

"No, sir."

A sly smile crossed his face. "I thought not. In which case, let us hear from Mr. Bryant, the lone witness of the crime."

As the witness made his way to the front of the room, the crowd started talking again, not bothering to whisper. I didn't need to listen. Their thoughts were loud in my mind already. I couldn't keep them out.

I hadn't known Mr. Bryant's name, but I recognised his face from the tavern. The man who had come in and seen me hunched over Quinn's body. My stomach twisted and I imagined I could feel the rough noose tightening around my throat.

"Mr. Bryant, could you please tell this court what you witnessed?"

Bryant looked up at the judge and smiled at him. Like he knew him. Like they were old friends, in fact.

"I saw Captain Quinn with Miss Johnson," he declared.

"Had you seen them talking before?" asked the judge.

"Many times, sir. Captain Quinn appeared most taken with Miss Johnson."

"On that afternoon, when you entered the tavern, were they merely talking?"

"Well, sir, here's what I saw." He puffed up his chest and frowned, seeming to pull back every memory of that afternoon. "See, Captain

Quinn was laying on the floor, on his stomach, like. That girl—she—Miss Johnson, I mean, she was on her knees beside him and she was punching his back with both her fists."

I saw it as he did, the back of Quinn's red coat dimpling under my fists, *"What—have—you—done?"* I had yelled.

The judge nodded. "Did she say anything in particular to him?"

"Yes, sir. She was yelling, matter of fact. But I couldn't make it out."

"Did you see anything more?"

"Yes, sir. I stepped closer and could see that Quinn—Captain Quinn, that is—he was bleeding bad."

"So Miss Johnson appeared to have stabbed Captain Quinn?"

I shot to my feet again, shaking my head. "But this man didn't see anything!" I shouted. "He saw what happened after, but not before. He can't say why I stabbed Captain Quinn. If he'd come in a few minutes earlier, he would have known Captain Quinn was attacking me. I was defending myself."

The judge watched me carefully, then turned back to Bryant. "Did Captain Quinn attack Miss Johnson?"

"No, sir," Bryant replied without a moment's hesitation.

"But he did!" I cried.

"Think carefully, Mr. Bryant. This woman's life is at stake here. Was Captain Quinn attacking Miss Johnson?"

Bryant shook his head vigorously. "No, sir."

The judge nodded, and a small smile flickered across his face. I suddenly realised what was happening. I had been set up. Bryant and the judge were working together. They had worked with Captain Quinn and his business. I could see them clearly in my mind. They were just as guilty as he had been.

"And then what happened?" asked the judge.

"Miss Johnson, well, she grabbed at Captain Quinn's purse and was about to run away with it, but I called the militiamen before she could get away."

"No," I said quietly. There was nothing I could do or say. Any objection was futile. My death order had practically been signed before I'd even stepped into this room.

"So, Miss Johnson was robbing Captain Quinn?" the judge demanded.

"Yes, sir. I think she had planned to do that all along. Flirting with him for months and all. She's just like the rest of them stealing Cherokee."

The crowd murmured unanimous assent.

Tears rolled down my cheeks. "You're lying."

The judge ignored me. Nothing I said mattered. Practically everyone in that courtroom believed I had set a trap for Captain Quinn. That I had killed him in order to rob him. If it hadn't been my life they were discussing, it might have been funny.

When it was my turn to describe what had happened, the crowd shouted me down. The judge, keeping up appearances, gave me plenty of time to argue my case. Why not? It was his courtroom and ultimately his decision. And now I knew the decision had been made much earlier. Probably at the moment Schneider learned I knew about Quinn's business.

For a moment I toyed with the idea of telling everyone in the entire room I could see their thoughts. I could prove it by telling them things no one could know. I could announce the name of the judge's mistress, perhaps. Declare myself, condemn them all in the midst of their friends and families.

And if I did that, they would condemn me as a witch as well as a murderer.

When I had finished, the judge stared me straight in the face and declared me guilty. He asked me if I had anything else to say before he passed sentence. I said nothing. He perched a piece of black cloth on his wig and sentenced me to death, to hang by the neck at a place of execution until I was dead. I was led back to my cell and left alone to ponder those words.

The prison was cold and dark. Like the dreams had foretold. But the loneliness was worse. No one was permitted to visit me. There weren't any other prisoners. The only person I ever saw was the jailer who brought me one meal a day. And he never said a word to me.

I couldn't find Andrew. The confinement sucked my dreams from me, stole my ability to see beyond the walls. If only I could have called to him. If only I could have seen him, but there were no images in my mind save memories.

No light, no conversation, no dreams. What do you do when isolation steals your soul?

I curled into the stone wall and let its pitted surface lower my body temperature. I felt hot and cold, sweating and shivering, but it wasn't a fever. It was worse in a way. It was fear. Within these walls, I could see nothing of my future. All I knew was I was going to hang. I thought suddenly of my grandmother and wondered how she had felt, all those years ago. Was it worse knowing exactly what would happen? She had felt it. She had smelled her own flesh as it sizzled and popped; she had felt her hair incinerate from her scalp. What would I feel? I touched my fingers to my throat and swallowed. The rope would go here, I thought, tracing a line under my jaw. It would go around, under my ears, then yank up high on my head. It would be a rough rope, but an old one, I hoped. The newer ropes had more spring in them, I'd heard once. They didn't kill a man—or woman—right away. The criminals dangled, kicking and struggling, as death slowly crushed their throats.

I wanted to be sure to braid my hair that morning, I thought, tucking the loose, tangled strands behind my ears. I didn't want the rope to tangle in my hair and make the pain any worse. Yes. Two nice, neat braids. And I would stand straight, shoulders back. I would say good-bye to everyone, and maybe, just maybe, when I climbed onto the scaffold, the air would bring me Andrew's face one more time. If I could die with his eyes on mine, it might not be so bad.

Sleeping without dreams was different for me. It should have been a pleasant experience—a full night's sleep—but it couldn't be. Not here. If the guard hadn't snored when it was night, I never would have known what hour of day it was. I missed the night. The crickets and the dew.

But when I awoke this time, I knew it was daytime because I wasn't alone. I couldn't see anyone with my eyes, but my mind felt him there. A little thrill ran up my spine at the realisation that my senses were still working, within the building at least. I couldn't see the man—and it was a man—because he didn't want to be seen. He sat down the narrow corridor from me, very still.

He had watched me sleep. He had stood there for an hour, watching me breathe, wondering who I was.

He wanted to know how I had become so beloved among the Cherokee. I saw them in his mind: the Cherokee, my family, who had been outside the jailhouse every day, in some form or another. Adelaide was always there. So was Soquili, my loyal friend. They had fought for me however they could, but had been cut off at every turn. As they had been banned from the jailhouse. But my entire being felt better, just knowing they were there. That they hadn't forgotten me.

I began to visualise the mysterious man in the jail with me. Dark in hair and skin, I could see. He was a very big man, and power flowed around him. And yet he was unsure. Confused. I disturbed his peace. His arms crossed over a broad, vested chest, his hair hung straight from under a tricorne. It was the tall Indian, I realised. The one who had always watched me.

Now I understood why he watched. He had run from his people, and I ran to them.

I settled back against the wall and closed my eyes, wanting to learn more.

Joe. His name was Joe. It wasn't his birth name, nor the name he'd received after his dream quest. It was the name the white people had given him as he worked his way into their society. There were those, like the jail guard, who feared him, as well they might, considering his size and his tightly restrained strength. There were those, like the trader, who used Joe's cunning mind for their own gains, and eventually realised they enjoyed his company as well. And there were those who still wouldn't look at him because of the colour of his skin.

Joe hated being in this prison. He felt trapped, though he could get up and leave at any time. He didn't mind so much being alone—in fact, he preferred it—but the tight enclosure made him very uncomfortable. He wondered if survival in this kind of enclosure might be easier for a woman than for a man. And whether it might be easier for a white man than for an Indian. I didn't think so, to either question.

Every fibre of my being wanted to reach out, to say something to him. I wanted to hear his voice, to colour this bleak existence with something other than gray. I needed a friend—or even a foe. Someone to keep me company. But Joe didn't want me to know he was there. If I called out, he would never come back.

So instead, I sang. Quietly, as if to myself, but I knew he heard me. He had hungered for my voice as well. I visualised him lying on his back, studying the intricate spiderwebs in the rafters overhead, soothed by my voice. It was better than being alone.

He came almost every day for six weeks. A few times I faked sleep so I could read his mind while he watched me. Joe was a tortured soul. I learned he was born a Choctaw, which was a relatively peaceful tribe. The Chickasaw had raided his village when he was a boy and enslaved his tribe. Joe spent ten winters with them, learning the arts of hunting and war, and was celebrated as a warrior of great strength and endurance.

The Chickasaw were an aggressive people. They attacked not only the other tribes but also the growing number of small white settlements that popped up across the land. Joe was reticent at the thought of slaughtering the pale-faced people without provocation. It seemed a waste to kill them without at least finding out how they did certain things, and why.

So Joe began visiting the white settlements on private scouting missions. He liked their practical approach to problems, their stubborn attitudes, their strange customs. He liked how no one spoke about spirits or totems or magic. He laughed more and learned things he never could have considered in the confining space of a longhouse. Something about the white man's way of life made more sense to Joe. In the end, he chose to live their existence.

It had been difficult, making his way into the outer boundaries of white society, but he had done it. He wouldn't go back to the nomadic way of living. After ten years, some of the whites actually recognised him as a man, rather than a barbarian.

He knew I was different. He could feel it. He could sense the connection I had with the Cherokee and the spirits, those same spirits he had discarded so easily as he had grown into a man. He knew I depended on the voices of the land and air to give me strength, and saw I was weak without them.

Joe was like a hawk. He floated silently over his quarry, watching and learning. Once he found what he sought, he plunged from the sky, grasped his prey within razor-edged talons, then disappeared from sight.

Right now he was circling over me, but had no idea why.

This morning, on his way to the jail, he had picked up a raven's feather lying in the doorway to the jail. Unable to completely dispel the lessons with which he had been raised, he picked up the feather and tucked it into his tricorne. He remembered that the Choctaw believed ravens spoke to the spirits. Despite his reticence at the old lessons, he hoped this feather might help him understand me.

Joe was feeling sad. Usually his emotions were unclear, but today I had no trouble feeling what he felt. He was depressed because I had less than a week to live, and he hadn't learned what he sought, whatever that was. He wanted more time.

So did I.

Sometimes Joe thought of Quinn. He had known the captain and never trusted him, but maintained an easy relationship. Quinn was a powerful man in the town. Or at least, he had been until I killed him. This morning, Quinn was on Joe's mind.

He took a deep breath that I heard down the hall. He probably thought I was sleeping, because he didn't bother to hide the sound. He blew the air out through his lips and showed me something he had never shared before. Something that froze my blood.

Joe knew about the girls. He knew about Quinn's business. He had never participated, but had stood by while Quinn profited. Joe didn't know that I knew. He had assumed only that I had done what I had said—killed Quinn in self-defense.

I had one week left to live. I had to do something.

I stood up and gripped the cold black bars of my cell, then called out a name no one could have known.

"*Onafa Hatak*?"

Ten years earlier, when Joe had left his family, he gave himself a new name. Onafa Hatak. Free Man. He had never told anyone that name.

I sensed his shock. As he started to think, I could tell he wasn't sure whether to freeze or bolt like a rabbit.

After a moment, he stood, brushed the dust from his breeches, and walked to my cell. He stopped in front of the bars and said nothing, only looked at me. I focused my eyes on his and felt him relax. He had knowledge I needed.

I squeezed one fist through the bars and held it in front of him. Then I opened my hand and showed Joe the thin gold chain I clenched within, and the heart-shaped locket that lay in the centre of my palm. The necklace meant nothing to him, but he listened.

"Where are the girls, Joe?"

That startled him. He wouldn't have been surprised if I had told him his future, his past, his darkest secrets. But he had never expected that question. How could I possibly know about the girls?

"It is not your worry," he said, not wanting to commit himself to any path.

"But it is," I whispered. "It is the most important thing in my life."

"Your life will be over soon," he reminded me.

"But it doesn't have to be over for those girls. Where are they?"

He shook his head. "It doesn't matter."

I grabbed his hand and clung to it. "I'll show you why it matters." I opened myself up to the memories of violence and violation. To the loss of my family. I focused all the images and pain through my hands, through his hands, and through his bloodstream until they reached his heart and squeezed. I felt him stiffen with shock. When the message was there, embedded in his mind, he saw me with new eyes. Softer eyes.

"Will you help me?" I asked.

"I know nothing that can help," he said.

Heat still flowed from my fingers, coursing through his mind, like fingers probing his secrets.

"Think, Joe."

I slipped the necklace between my hand and his. Joe's heart raced. Just as I did, he felt the locket *burn.* He longed to yank his hand back, but didn't. He squeezed his eyes shut while I stirred through his mind, dredging up memories, sorting through them, looking for the truth.

There is nothing in that cabin of any use to anyone, he thought. *Except the girls, of course. The place is four walls, nothing more. No chairs, no table, no window. The only other thing is—*

There. Joe's eyes snapped open. He knew the moment I did.

The box. The captain's strange wooden box. Like the skull collections the Chickasaw kept. Bits and pieces of every girl the captain's gangs had stolen. Souvenirs of stolen innocence.

His mind surrendered the cabin easily, with relief. Within its walls I saw the box. Within the box I saw the treasures that mourned their masters.

"Find my doll, Maggie," Ruth had said.

"I found her," I thought.

I let go of Joe's hand and he grabbed for the cell bars, bracing his weight when his knees threatened to buckle.

"You are a good man, Onafa Hatak," I said.

He snorted and shook his head. "I do not believe this is so."

I touched my fingers to his knuckles, which still clenched the bars of the cell. "You will know what to do," I said.

He didn't answer. He was confused and afraid, the words jumbled in his mind. As if I had seen his thoughts and he no longer could. He felt weak, and to his mortification, he felt like crying.

He turned abruptly and strode from the jail. I lost our connection as soon as he breathed in the outside air and shut the prison door behind him.

I knew where the captive girls were. And if I could get to that wooden box Joe had shown me, it would contain evidence of the captain's guilt.

I was alone again. But this time I held a tiny seed of hope in my heart.

CHAPTER 31

The Light of Day

Joe didn't come to see me again. But the following day, the world changed again.

I heard the jailer yell out, and scrape his chair across the stone floor.

"What's all this?" he hollered. "Can't a man get any sleep in this town? Hey, now what's all this?"

The door to the outside opened, and a tiny breath of fresh air trickled down the corridor to my cell. The sounds of the street and scattered thoughts from passersby trickled toward me. I heard a girl scream, and the sound was so familiar I jumped to my feet. She screamed again, calling for help, and I recognised my sister's voice.

"Addy?" I cried.

"Help! Can anyone help me? Please help!" she shouted, and I gripped the bars helplessly.

"I'm a-comin'," the jailer said. "Hold yer garters on."

I heard him step out onto the front doorstep, then a thump and a grunt. A fight? What—

Feet whispered down the corridor, and I heard the jingle of keys. I stared in amazement as Soquili charged toward my cell, his eager smile lighting the darkness. I had never been so relieved to see anyone in my entire life. He shoved the key into the lock and turned it. He tried to fling the door open with a certain amount of fanfare, but the ancient hinge only squawked open a few inches. I sidled out and grabbed on to him, wrapping my arms tightly around his waist.

"Soquili!" I sobbed. "I thought—"

"Shh," he said and pried my hands from his waist. He kissed my forehead. "We must go now."

"I heard Addy—"

"Shh. Do not think of that. Come now."

I followed him to the door, and was met by a crowd of Cherokee, all blocking the entrance and facing the empty inner circle of the fort's yard. They seemed content to stand there, apparently in animated conversation with each other. Wahyaw was the only one to look at me, and his smile was huge. At his feet lay my unconscious jailer, completely unaware of the jailbreak. Adelaide ran to me and we held each other for a moment, speechless.

Then she kissed my cheek. "I thought you were gone, Maggie. I thought I'd never see you again."

"Me, too," I said.

Wahyaw grunted from behind her. "Go. We can talk later. Go now."

Addy grabbed my hand and pulled me to the edge of the crowd. Everything felt unreal; even the warm dirt beneath my feet felt foreign after the past two months. The sky was an amazing shade of blue, like the beading on Adelaide's new tunic. She yanked me farther into the sheltering crowd of Indians, and I saw three horses tethered to a post. Soquili tugged the knots free and tossed me onto one horse. He unpacked a heavy fur from our horse's pack, then passed it up to me. He climbed up behind me and, though it was a warm day, wrapped the fur around my body, partially covering my face. Soquili tucked one arm around my waist and urged our horse forward. I felt his breath on my neck when he leaned in and spoke in my ear.

"You feel small, Ma-kee," he said. "We will feed you soon."

The horses walked sedately through the fort to avoid notice. Wahyaw went first.

"Not too slow," he muttered over his shoulder. "They will discover you are gone soon. If we can get through here, we will be fine."

The horse hair was rough but comforting on my calves. The sounds of people talking, of dogs barking and babies crying—every noise pushed the isolation of the cell farther away. I leaned against Soquili's bare chest and smelled his scent. I never knew anything could smell so good.

Other than the noisy crowd of Cherokee, there was very little movement within the bleak walls of the fort. I supposed in times of battle, this area would swarm with bright red uniforms. But whenever I'd been here, there had been no sign of a regiment, other than the occasional soldier wandering through the grounds or carrying supplies. Occasionally there was a guard or two set up at the other entrance, blocking the archway we now approached, but not very often.

I was hot inside the fur, and it itched terribly, but when I shifted, Soquili tightened his grip.

"Be still," he said.

The horses' steps thudded against the earth as we drew closer to the archway. And suddenly my heart began pounding and I broke into a cold sweat.

"We're not going to make it, Wahyaw. Run!" I said quietly.

Wahyaw nudged his horse into a canter, and we did likewise. But it wasn't fast enough. I felt it coming, the pressure of pursuit building in my head.

If they caught me again, they would hang all of us.

"Wahyaw—" I said, but was interrupted by a shout somewhere behind us. The fort soon filled with men's voices, raised in agitation.

Wahyaw kicked his horse hard, and we roared toward the entrance. I leaned around Soquili to see what was happening, and was amazed by the number of soldiers I saw. All this time I had assumed the fort was empty, or nearly so. Now they flooded through every door, guns in hands.

Two guards were stationed at the archway. Even if they hadn't heard the warning, our mad gallop would have given us away. They aimed muskets directly at us and fired. And missed. We kept running, outpacing the shots that came from behind, thundering past the guards as they tried to refill their muskets. The brothers whooped as we burst from the fort, and pushed the horses toward the relative safety of the trees. No one knew these woods like my Cherokee.

The soldiers weren't prepared. Their horses still lazed in their stalls. So we went unaccompanied into the woods. But they would come soon. One didn't need to see into the future to know that.

We rode for an hour, barely speaking. Eventually, as the sun began to set, we slowed and Wahyaw dropped from his horse. He reached up to help Adelaide down, and Soquili did the same for me. Then I stared at them all, and they stared at me. I smiled. Even my smile felt foreign.

"Thank you," I said.

Adelaide flung herself on me and we started to cry, talking nonsense between sobs. Over her shoulder I saw Soquili smile before he turned away with Wahyaw.

She led me to a log, where we sat and kept talking. I didn't want to talk about the jail, but couldn't seem to stop. Except really, there wasn't much to say. She heard me repeat how cold it was. How dark. How lonely. How sad. But I didn't mention the absence of the dreams. We'd barely spoken of them before, and I didn't want to start now. I listened to her talk about the difficulties they'd faced trying to see me. About how Waw-Li had shut herself into her house with the elders and they hadn't come out for days. About how Wahyaw and Soquili finally lost all patience and broke me out of jail the only way they could.

While we talked, the brothers set up a tarp and laid out furs where we would sleep. They lit a small fire and roasted roots and small birds over it. When the evening was over, Adelaide and I snuggled together under the furs.

The air, the beautiful air, breathed life back into my dreams.

Andrew, I thought. *Please, Andrew.*

He came into focus slowly, as if he had to find his way. When his face appeared, my veins seemed to pulse with liquid fire. How had I existed without him?

"Maggie!" His eyes were shadowed with concern. "Where have ye been? It's been weeks since—"

"I know. I'm so sorry."

"But where were ye? Wha' happened? I've had the worst dreams of late."

I held my hands up and he took them in his own, intertwining his fingers with mine, warming my hands with his invisible blood.

"Where are you?" I asked. My story was so long, and I knew our time was brief. The dreams were always too short, always ending when I needed him most.

"I'm here. I'm close." He stepped closer. "Are ye all right, *mo nighean*? Are ye no' well? Ye're pale, Maggie. Very pale."

He caressed my cheek with the backs of his fingers, and I leaned into them. If only I could stay like this forever, safe in his mind.

"Don't worry about me," I whispered.

"How can I no'?"

"I have a lot to tell you, but I don't want to squander this time talking about it. I just want to feel you. You have no idea how badly I've needed you, Andrew. I felt empty when I couldn't dream of you."

He frowned. "You couldna dream?"

I shook my head. "Nothing," I said. "For almost two months."

I was thinking, *Hold me,* but he was there before I could say the words. He wrapped his arms around me, pulling me in tight. His tunic was a faded white, stained and smelling of earth and sweat. The wool that was always draped over his shoulder scratched my cheek and I nuzzled into it, wanting to relish every stubborn fibre. His breath was in my hair, warm and delicious. I lifted my chin to kiss him and felt his lips touch mine for a heartbeat before I was shaken awake.

"Ma-kee," Soquili murmured. "The soldiers have come. We must go."

It was still very early. The calls of birds were still unpracticed, the odd starling calling for a friend. Adelaide silently rolled up the furs and passed them to Wahyaw, who packed them onto the horses. Soquili hoisted me onto our horse and slid on behind me. We set off into the rough deer paths.

"What's happening?" I whispered to Soquili. "How did they find us?"

Soquili leaned forward and rested his chin on my shoulder. "They have a scout."

Our horse lurched over a dip in the path, and we swayed forward with the momentum. Soquili was already warm in the predawn chill, and he wrapped himself around me. He sighed in my ear, a perfect sound of satisfaction.

"Soquili—" I said.

"Shh," he replied. "I am only keeping you warm. Never be afraid of me, Ma-kee."

We rode on and I let myself be cradled against him. I closed my eyes and tried to disappear into the world I had missed so much. I wanted to *feel* again. I set my mind free to travel the trails, and they brought me back the image of Joe.

He was in the forest, too, I realised. He turned and spoke with someone, and I saw a red coat behind him. He was their scout. It made sense. Joe, I knew, would be able to find us. Of anyone, he was the most dangerous. But I understood him now. I had been in his mind and seen the confusion that influenced his thoughts. I had travelled through his past and seen who he was, though he didn't know himself. I could reach him again.

"Joe," I called to his mind.

He stood straight and looked up, his eyes raking the shadowed leaves, hunting for the source.

"You know I'm not there," I said.

I felt the fear in him, and understood. Joe had felt me in his mind before, and he knew what I could do.

"Let us go," I begged.

His mind flickered with red coats and a sense of responsibility. He had a duty to lead them to us, to see justice done.

"It's not justice," I told him. *"You know it isn't."*

Thoughts of the white world he had wanted for so long sat heavily on his heart. If he caught us, he would be lauded as a hero among the white people. Or so he thought. If he let us go, he would be nothing to them.

Then his thinking softened. He remembered our moment in the

jail, when our minds had merged. He had had time to reflect on that. He still found it funny that I called him a good man.

"You will prove it to yourself, Onafa," I said, and he snorted.

"Did you say something?" Soquili asked, bringing me back to the moment.

"I don't know," I said, turning to smile at him. "Did I?"

Wahyaw shot us a look, and we were quiet again. I watched little things scurry through the forest, creatures I might never have seen again if the judge had gotten his way. The army following us would be hungry. They needed to please Schneider. I felt for Joe and his divided loyalties.

The path eventually opened into a huge field, ringed by trees. It looked as if it might have been cleared years before by a farmer, but left barren since then. To Wahyaw the open space was an invitation to run. The horses picked up his cue and started trotting to stay together. Adelaide grinned at me, bouncing up and down with the horse's gait.

It took no more than a tiny metallic click to alert us. It came from the right, from within the trees. We were instantly on guard.

"Joe?" I called in silence.

Joe's jaw was set, his expression an uneasy blend of pride and shame. He wasn't surprised to see me this time. It was as if he'd known exactly where I was. That was when I realised my thoughts had acted like a beacon. He had led the army to us, and we were surrounded.

Wahyaw let out a piercing shriek and the horses leaped into action, racing across the open meadow as muskets began firing all around us. Soquili reached behind him and pulled out his arrows as we went, shooting blindly into the trees. We hadn't gone more than a hundred feet before I heard Adelaide's scream.

The musket ball hit her and sent her flying from her panicked horse. She landed in a motionless heap, and I could sense nothing from her.

"No!" I screamed. "Turn around, Soquili! Get Addy!"

Wahyaw yelled something to his brother, but I missed it.

"Soquili! Go back!" I cried.

"I must keep you safe, Ma-kee," Soquili said, and kicked his mount forward. "My brother will go for your sister."

I twisted around him, craning to see through tearing eyes. "Turn around, Soquili! Turn around!"

Wahyaw raced through the musket fire, bent low over his horse's neck. The soldiers were emerging from the trees, and I felt a sense of helplessness as the big brave leaped from his horse and grabbed my sister over his shoulder. He suddenly swerved sideways and I saw he'd been shot in his arm, but it didn't stop him. He was mounted and running again as if nothing had happened, Adelaide leaning against him.

Behind us, the soldiers had gotten onto their horses.

We plunged into the trees, hoping to hide again, but I knew Joe would be able to track us anywhere. The cavalry thundered behind us, crashing through trees, hunters intent on the fox. There was nothing I could do. I wanted to call back to Wahyaw, to see if Adelaide was all right, but couldn't chance being overheard by our pursuers. I couldn't even look behind Soquili without toppling us both from our horse. So I leaned low against the horse's neck and let Soquili take care of us all.

He had a goal in mind. I could tell. I felt it in the set of his body against mine, the concentration that kept his breath silent.

Wahyaw was behind us, with Adelaide slumped in front of him. I had never been able to read Wahyaw's thoughts. He was a blank wall almost all of the time. But I sensed a crack beginning to spider from one corner. He had taken a bullet, and it took all of his power to focus away from the pain. I wished I could do for him what I could do for Andrew, give him my strength to fight against it, but I couldn't. Wahyaw was on his own, as he always had been.

"Hold on," Soquili whispered in my ear, and we dove down a steep hill, both of us leaning back to help the horse's balance. The mare's front hooves slid down the muddy hillside, but she caught herself and kept going. At the bottom of the hill raced a river, maybe twenty feet across. It curdled with excitement, white water swirling over hidden rocks and caverns.

Our mare hesitated at the bank, but Soquili didn't. He kicked and moved his upper body, urging her forward, and she trusted him. Wahyaw's mount did the same, plunging into the water upriver. I could see Adelaide now, curled against Wahyaw as if she were sleeping. Wahyaw saw me glance over and smiled. He nodded. He thought she would be all right.

Our horse arched her neck, concentrating on the hungry current. She stumbled on the uneven riverbed and threw her head up with concern, but Soquili spoke to her, his words encouraging. She seemed to take strength from him, and stepped with more confidence into the foamy water.

All at once the earth vanished from beneath her hooves. We dropped until icy water licked at our necks, and I felt the churning, panicked power of the horse's legs beneath us. I visualised her muscles, bunching, flexing, struggling to cut through the current, and tried to blend my thoughts into her body. I imagined she felt me there, though I could never know if she had.

"Don't let go," Soquili said.

Beside us, Wahyaw's horse laboured, but seemed to maintain a better footing. Wahyaw's jaw was clenched, but his arm was tight around Adelaide, his eyes blinking away the mist of the rapids.

When our mare struck ground, we were jerked upright so suddenly we grunted. We ran, streaming water, back into the forest. Shots rang out behind us, splintering trees and cracking against rocks, but we kept on. We had to get away, but stop soon, to rest the horses.

The sound of pursuit ceased after a while, so we rode a little farther, then stopped.

Wahyaw slipped off his horse and pulled Adelaide against him, then carried her to a shaded spot where the forest floor was patched with soft moss in brilliant shades of green, yellow, and pink. I ran over the spongy plants and knelt beside her while Wahyaw straightened and went to his brother.

The bullet had caught her between her right shoulder and her neck. I couldn't see the ball, but saw the bloodied path it had taken. I pressed my hands hard over it, concentrating on the injury as Waw-Li had taught me, focusing on the source, the severed blood vessels, encouraging Adelaide's heart to slow the blood flow.

"There is another way around the river," Wahyaw said behind me.

"I know," Soquili said. "But their tracker will need time to find it. They cannot follow us now or their gunpowder will be soaked."

"Can we stay here for the night?" I asked

Wahyaw grunted, then nodded. Soquili frowned and touched his brother's arm.

"They shot you?" Soquili asked.

"Twice," Wahyaw said, then spat into the moss with disgust.

"I can't believe you got out of there alive," I said, turning toward them. "Thank you, Wahyaw. Thank you for saving her."

He didn't like the attention, but when he shrugged, I saw him grimace with pain. "It would take more than an army to take me down," he said, and I snorted.

"Come here," I said. "Let me see your arm."

"It's fine," he replied tartly, then settled stiffly on the grass beside me.

"Come here. Soquili, would you press here on Addy, please? Just for a moment."

Soquili took over for me while I inspected Wahyaw's shredded skin. The bullets had made a mess of him, but the injuries didn't go deeper than his skin. He would heal as soon as the bleeding stopped. At the moment it ran down the side of his body in long, dark trails. He glared at me when I reached behind his neck, but his expression softened when he realised what I was doing. He wore a leather thong necklace, weighted by a bear's tooth. I untied the necklace and cinched it around his bicep to stop the bleeding.

I went back to Adelaide's side and Soquili stepped away. Her bleeding seemed to have stopped. I would have to go after the bullet soon.

"Will they find us here, Soquili?" I asked as Wahyaw disappeared into the trees.

He rose and squinted in the direction of the river, which we could no longer hear. "It will depend on their scout. I have seen him before, in the town." He nodded. "I believe he can find us. We will have to move on soon. There is an easy way to cross the river, but it is maybe two miles upstream."

Then it was up to Joe.

Poor Joe, the soul whose heart battled constantly with his head, his aspirations smothering his beliefs.

I needed to know what he was thinking. If I called out to him, he would know where I was. But if I didn't, would we lose the tenuous connection we had built? Would he turn away from thoughts of me?

"Joe?" I called silently.

He had been waiting for me. He opened the door to his mind and welcomed me inside. I said nothing, only watched.

The soldiers prepared to hunt us down. Powder was checked, horses were watered as the captain, brisk and efficient, walked toward Joe, looking for guidance within the deep woods.

I saw Joe's regret, the understanding that this was the moment when he would have to choose. He had seen Adelaide fall, and had been relieved at her rescue. His thoughts filled with questions and answers, and a sudden understanding of me. Warmth swirled through his chest and he stood straighter. Something within him reached out and my own heart beat faster. I understood. He honoured me. He respected my right to be free.

He met the captain halfway, then made a circular motion with his hand, pointing downstream. The opposite direction from Soquili's easier passage. The men discussed Joe's plan and there was much nodding before the captain turned away to speak with the soldiers under his command.

Joe would lead them the wrong way. He would get them hopelessly lost, and then he would disappear. Joe was good at disappearing.

PART 6: ANDREW

Resurrection and Resolution

CHAPTER 32

Another Life

It was near midday when the ship landed in America, dropping anchor at Chesapeake Bay in Virginia. Andrew, Iain, Janet, Seamus, and little Peter and Flora all clustered together at the rail, kilts fluttering like flags, watching the unfamiliar landscape loom up before them.

Noises from the shore carried across the waves: chickens in crates, seamen whistling and yelling incoherent remarks, dogs barking, hooves clopping like rapid hammer blows. Ragged children ran amongst the boxes and people, playing, laughing, picking pockets.

Andrew ran his hand over the bristles covering his cheeks and chin, and thought how nice it would be to bathe properly. With a good, thick cake of soap. He breathed in, savouring the stink. The ship's decks were cleaner than the streets, but the travelers had been on the sea for so long they drank the pungent town air as if it were ale. Gulls circled overhead, shrieking at the ship that bobbed beneath them, a treasure chest of food.

A raven cried out from the shore. It circled low over the docks, a black giant among the gulls. It flapped toward the ship and looped over the mast before returning to land, its wings caressing the sky like a lover's touch. Andrew had the impression the bird had looked him in the eye. If it had, he wouldn't have been surprised. Ravens had always come to Andrew in dreams. They visited him still, whispering messages from Maggie. He smiled at the thought of her, barely noticing the gust of wind that whipped his hair across his cheeks. The New World. A new life. Maggie was here.

The ship pulled alongside the dock, and the seamen heaved massive mooring ropes across to wind around cleats. A gangplank was lowered, bridging the pier and the ship. Andrew had visited the purser earlier in the day, and for his three months of labour he had been given two pounds, five shillings. Fair compensation, Andrew thought. He hadn't hoped to become a rich man by working on the ship. The coins could buy a few things, beginning with a good night's food and lodging. Andrew aimed his worn leather boots down the gangplank and finally stepped onto American soil.

He attracted the attention of more than one woman as he stepped off the ship. He was a large man, over six feet tall, with a ruggedly handsome face the sun and wind had darkened to a dusky bronze. His muscles were solid beneath his shirt, defined and stronger than ever from working the ship. He walked up the main road, feeling the heat of the sunshine on his back and thinking this warmth was one aspect of the colonies he already preferred to the perpetual mists of Scotland.

Andrew's destination was the closest tavern. He needed a cup of ale to wash away the salt of the sea that had coated his throat throughout the journey. Real ale. Not the swill from the ship. He turned to wait for his friends, just coming off the gangplank, and they hurried to catch up.

"I was thinking," Andrew said to Seamus, "we'd stop in at—"

"Say no more, my friend," Seamus answered in his laughing Irish lilt. "A tavern was my first thought as well." He gave Andrew's shoulder a companionable smack.

Peter was perched on Seamus's shoulders. Flora enjoyed the view from Iain's. The group walked past a few unmarked doors until they arrived at one that practically vibrated with sound. A trio of men stood outside the door, teasing two women, who giggled in response.

"Seems as good a place as any," Iain said, lifting Flora down and setting her on the ground.

Andrew pulled the heavy door open and, with a gallant bow, swept his palm across his body, ushering his friends ahead of him.

The pub was dark and smelled of spilled ale and unwashed bodies, but Andrew and his friends grinned as they stepped inside. It was crowded and noisy, men trying to yell over each other. Serving girls winked and flirted while they worked, delivering ale and meals through the comfortable pandemonium. Seamus, Andrew, and Iain moved into it with ease, Janet squeezed between them. Flora clung to a handful of Iain's plaid, and Peter trotted to keep up with Seamus. The Irishman parted the crowds with a few words from his quick tongue and led his friends to an empty corner table.

Andrew couldn't wait for a barmaid, so he sidled up to the weathered pine bar and ordered an ale. After the barkeep handed him a cup, Andrew turned and leaned back against the bar, sipping at the warm amber liquid as he perused the crowd.

The tavern's patrons were mostly scruffy, unshaven men, and an occasional woman in subdued browns and grays. The men carried fatigue in their posture as well as in dark circles around their eyes. From what Andrew could surmise, most of the men were Scots. He didn't recognise any of the faces, but saw reflections of himself in their eyes. Many of them, talking Gaelic from behind grimy beards, would have been Highland warriors who had fled their homeland after last April's battle. Like Andrew, so many defeated men had risked their lives and those of their families for the opportunity of a better life. Only time would tell if the risk had been worth it.

Andrew enjoyed the noise of the tavern. Unlike Seamus, he wasn't one to demand attention. He preferred to experience its buzz from a distance. The sights, smells, and sounds of the place enveloped him like a blanket, smothering the relentless chill that had gripped his bones throughout the sea voyage.

From his observation post against the bar, Andrew watched a waitress bring ale to his friends' table. He grinned as she gave Iain a beguiling smile, leaning over the table so her generous bosom was displayed to its best advantage. Iain took no apparent notice. The waitress nodded at something Janet said, then turned and waddled back to the bar, her pudgy arms balancing the tray she carried while simultaneously shoving customers aside.

Most of the conversations going on around Andrew focused on this land. He listened for a while, gleaning information. The farmland in the colonies was said to be second to none, and if one were brave and hardworking enough to settle deep in the backcountry, the government was giving away grants of land for next to nothing. That promise made it easier for newcomers to overlook the endless stretches of hostile forests before them.

Andrew ordered another ale and went to join his friends at the table. He sat, leaning against the wall with a sigh of contentment, always watching the crowd. The waitress returned, carrying a tray of meat and cheese.

After swallowing a mouthful of surprisingly tender meat of some kind, Andrew told his friends what he'd learned from the tavern chatter. "So it seems we should travel the coast on one of the local flat boats," he said. "It'll take us to Cross Creek, in North Carolina. We'll get a wagon there an' go to Charleston."

"Oh aye?" Janet said. "An' what's there?"

Iain cleared his throat. "Is that no' where land permits are handled?"

"It is," Andrew said, smiling. "Our own property. Think o' that."

"So it is, so it is," Seamus said with a nod. He took a gulp of ale, then sat back. "And enough trees an' rocks to keep a fellow workin' for a lifetime. It's not going to be pretty, lads. But," he said, smothering a burp, "I've nothin' else planned for me day." He grinned. "Let's have another ale," he suggested. Seamus was just putting up his hand to attract the waitress's attention when his fiddle was spotted.

"Oy!" shouted a burly, cheerfully inebriated fellow. "Let's 'ave some music!"

Seamus, always happy to be the centre of attention, grinned and stood up. He opened his worn leather case and lifted out the fiddle then plucked at the strings and adjusted the tuning pins while he spoke to the man.

"Sure an' I'm happy t'oblige. What'll it be, sir? Let me see."

The patrons howled with enthusiasm, and fists hammered on the tables in encouragement.

"That'll do, lads," Seamus said. "Now hush if you'll care to hear it at all."

The level of the din lowered, and all faces turned toward the Irishman. Seamus cleared his throat and began to play and sing.

What Cato advises
Most certainly wise is:
Not always to labour but sometimes to play.

He paused and grinned around at the men, who cheered and raised their glasses. Seamus sang on.

To mingle sweet pleasure
With search after treasure,
Indulging at night for the toils of the day.
And while the dull miser
Esteems himself wiser,
His bags to increase while his health does decay,
Our souls we enlighten,
Our fancies we brighten,
And pass the long evenings in pleasure away.

The waitresses were suddenly busier. The bartender, thrilled with this unexpected boon, filled drink orders and encouraged the revelers to throw a few pennies in a cup for the entertainment.

Andrew sat back and smiled, watching his friend. It had been a long voyage, and there was a long road ahead, but for now Andrew was fed, comfortable, and content. The flight from Scotland had been a desperate attempt to save his sanity and his life. Sitting here, with an ale in his hand, he was glad he had come all that way. Here was hope and anonymity. The exhaustion of the past year began to peel away, revealing a tentative core of excitement.

And Maggie was here. He was sure of it. From the moment he stepped onto the soil, he could feel her.

After a few songs Seamus placed the violin back in its case, apologising profusely to his protesting audience. If it had been up to the tavern's patrons, he would have performed all night. But even Seamus was tired. He nodded when Andrew motioned with a quick wave toward the door. Their group rose and went with him, but before they reached the door, the bartender grabbed

Seamus's shoulder, spun him around, and thrust a bag into the fiddler's free hand.

"An' what's this then?" Seamus asked, peering into the bag. "Ah! Treasure for me hard work. I t'ank you all from the bottom of me Irish heart, I do." He gestured his thanks over the noise, then joined his group as they left the building.

Evening was settling over the land, and with it came a darker populace. Earlier in the day Andrew had asked where a decent inn might be found and had been directed toward The Swan, where they now stood. Iain knocked, and a round woman in a stained apron pulled open the door and scowled at the visitors.

Andrew followed her substantial hips up the stairs and turned toward one of the two rooms she indicated. Both rooms were furnished with two small beds, a ewer, and a chamber pot. A closed window overlooked the street. Iain settled a sleeping Flora into one of the beds and was backing out of the room as Peter climbed in beside his sister. Janet would sleep in the other bed.

The men retired to their room across the hall. Seamus lay fully clothed on one of the beds, his hands clasped behind his neck as he stared up into the rafters.

"I was t'inking perhaps I'd take a bed if ye'd no' mind, lads. Ye see, what happened was I sat down and now me legs won't be bothered to get up again."

He grinned at the other men, looking for opposition, but they only shrugged.

"It's you who's payin' the bill tonight, is it no'?" Andrew said. "You take the other, MacKenzie. I'll claim it at the next inn."

"Ye're a fine gentleman, MacDonnell," Iain replied. "I'm happy to accept. 'Tis a joy to see a bed an' not a wee hammock. Och, I barely slept a wink on that damn ship."

Iain blew out the solitary candle in the room, and they were plunged into darkness. Moments later the big man's snores rumbled through the room. Andrew took off his boots, bundled his plaid under his head, and fell asleep on the floor.

For much of the sea voyage Andrew had suffered from nightmares. Before long it became apparent they had followed him to shore. They were always the same, or at least variations of the same dark theme. In the black and gray depths of sleep he was running, twisting through trees and rocks, his feet jamming into impossible crevasses as he climbed. His lungs felt tight, straining for air. Maggie was somewhere ahead of him on the rough path, but he couldn't see her. She was in danger. He had to get to her, but every time he caught a glimpse, the distance between them seemed to double until he couldn't sense her anymore.

In tonight's dream, though, the threat of malevolence seemed less. For the first time, his torn feet had a destination. They carried him to a spring in the midst of a tall stand of birch, where he stood, chest heaving. The air was clear of threat. All was calm. He knelt at the water's edge and leaned in, filling his hands with the cool water. The reflection of his face, clean shaven, peered up from the clearing ripples. Behind him stood Maggie. Her long brown hair tumbled toward him, almost close enough for him to twine within his fingers. Slowly, afraid to disturb the peace of the moment, he turned from the pool to face her, but she was gone.

The next morning Andrew was awakened by Seamus's shoe as it bounced off his head. The Irishman had been awake for a while and was impatient to set off. Andrew sat up, frowning and rubbing the spot where he'd been hit. He yawned, then threw the errant footwear back at its owner, who caught it deftly in one hand. Iain rolled over with a groan, scratching his big hands over his face as if to wake it.

Andrew stood, stretching to his full height so his fingers

brushed along the rough slivers of the rafters. He stared into a small looking glass propped by the ewer but barely recognised his reflection.

The travelers moved quickly, finding a flat boat to take them to Cross Creek, then using some of Hector's money to purchase what they thought they might need for the journey to Charleston, including a horse and a wagon. The horse was nothing special, an ordinary gelding of about eight years, strong enough and not fussy about who led him. Andrew liked to look at the horse because he was so different from what he was used to. He stroked the animal's long russet neck, admiring the smooth texture. The hair on Highland ponies was coarser—as were their personalities, generally speaking. This horse was larger than the ponies in both height and breadth. As great a beast as he was, Andrew admitted, he would never have been able to keep up with his stout cousins among the crags of the Highlands.

When they arrived in the streets of Charleston, the atmosphere was brisk but cheery. Voices called to each other and bounced down the road like pebbles. The group walked toward the Court House: a fine, stone building at the end of the road where optimistic travelers could petition for land. They had arrived on an opportune day: the magistrate was going over petitions and, being in a cheerful mood, was handing them out like candy. The royal officials granted the land free, subject only to a small surveying and transfer fee: four shillings proclamation money per hundred acres.

When they swung out onto the crowded dirt road a few hours later, all six of them were smiling from ear to ear. Even the children tried to look as if they knew what was going on.

They wandered to the side of the road and sat on a patch of grass. Iain cleared his throat and read the land grant document aloud.

CERTIFICATE OF LAND GRANT:

George the Second by the Grace of God of Great Britain France and Ireland King Defender of the Faith & c

To all to whom these presents shall come—Greeting

Know ye that we for and in consideration of the rents and return therein reserved have given and granted and by these presents for us our Heirs and successors do give and grant unto Iain MacKenzie, Andrew MacDonnell, Seamus Murphy a Tract of land containing 100 Acres of land . . . in our Province of North Carolina . . . as by the plot hereunto annexed doth appear together with all woods waters Mines minerals Hereditaments and appurtenances to the said Lands belong or pertaining (one half of all Gold and Silver mines excepted) to hold to him. . . . In testimony whereof we have caused the Great Seal of our said province to be hereunto affixed Witness our trusty and well beloved Gabriel Johnston Esq Our Captain General and Governour in Chief at Bladen County this third day of April in the twentieth year of Our reign, Anno Domini 1747.

CHAPTER 33

Almost Home

All the way up the Cape Fear River, Andrew and his friends met with migrant families who provided food and lodging whenever possible. The new buildings they passed were completely different in construction from the dark peat cottages of Scotland. Homes and barns were built from the towering pines dominating the land, and their floors were wooden planks instead of dirt. They had occasional windows and chimneys. Here in North Carolina, sweet-smelling smoke from the hearth curled up through chimneys and over shingled roofs. The insides of homes were no longer blackened by smoke and soot.

Scots had established themselves along the route to the Keowee Valley, where Andrew's group planned to eventually build their home. The terrain constantly changed as they travelled north. Beneath massive sandy hills stretched acres of freshly turned earth, planted with Indian corn and grains. Thickets and canebrakes surrounded the cleared land, and towering above it all were hills and pine trees. There were so many trees the limbs crossed each other, over and under, forming a natural thatched ceiling, beneath which nothing grew. Scaly, reddish bark protected their inner gold mines, the source of turpentine, rosin, pitch, and tar.

There were a few similarities between this new land and the one they had left behind. The hills and ridges, and the rain, for example. But there were constant lessons to be learned. Unfamiliar threats presented themselves every day. Not the least of these were the Indians. Andrew hadn't seen any yet, but had heard stories about the savages while he was onboard the *Boyd of Glasgow*. As Andrew's group came into contact with other settlers, he discovered many of the stories had been fiction. The Cherokee, while unpredictable, were *not* cannibals, nor did they usually attack without provocation.

Even if they had been the barbarous creatures he had heard about, Andrew would have sought them out. Maggie had said: *"Find the Cherokee,"* so he would.

It took weeks for Andrew and his group to fight their way upriver to their land claim. The farther west they went, the less travelled the road. Settlements became fewer and farther apart as they moved deeper into the backcountry. When at last they stepped onto their own land, it was as indistinguishable as any other piece of rough, uncleared forest. But according to the map, it was theirs.

They lived for a while in a rough, temporary structure by the river, spending their energy clearing land enough for planting. Without crops, they would starve over the winter.

With the help of a few neighbours, they raised two houses and a small barn, infusing their lives with the soothing scent of pine. The first home was built for Janet and the children, but eventually Iain moved in with them, constructing a separate bedroom just for him. His imposing presence essentially guaranteed their safety. Theirs was the larger of the two houses. It had a spacious cooking area, with room for a pine table and six chairs, as well as a spinning wheel, for which they had traded in the nearby town of New Windsor.

Seamus and Andrew shared a smaller house, but they, too, built a wall between their bedrooms, giving them privacy for the first time in their lives. It was a strange sensation, not hearing the soothing rhythm of the other's breathing at night, but it wasn't entirely unwelcome. Seamus was quick to make all the furniture for both houses. The only other person Andrew had ever known who could work so easily with wood had been his brother Dougal.

When they had cleared enough brush, they discovered their new home was at the top of a slope, uphill from the river. Winding green vines climbed the trees on either riverbank, then arched over the water, dangling clusters of succulent blue and white grapes. They built their houses away from the riverbank to avoid any possibility of flooding, but close enough they had easy access for filling the cauldron that hung over their hearth. When they stooped to fill their buckets in the stream, the water flashed with the silvery scales of perch, pike, and rockfish. Iain spent many days casting his line, and countless fish suppers were served at their table.

Spring and summer flew by, hastened by exhaustion. Lazy evenings filled with the serenades of crickets turned to longer, darker nights, when the prevalent sound was the wind shuffling thousands of fallen leaves. Autumn heralded the harvest, which provided no relief in the way of rest. There was canning to do, honey to collect from nearby hives. The men brought home rabbits, wild turkey, ducks, partridges, and fish, and occasionally a deer. All the meat that wasn't immediately used was hung and smoked. Janet wove baskets for the children so they could gather berries. Hours later, they returned home with purple hands and faces. What berries made it back from their outings were stirred into pies and jams.

When nights became too dark for outdoor work, Andrew was

drawn to the hum of Janet's spinning wheel. Sometimes he sat by her after the children had gone to sleep, watching the golden-brown flax twist into a fine thread between her fingers, flickering by the light of a lantern.

"What do ye think of as ye spin?" he asked her one night.

Without taking her eyes from her work, she smiled and said, "Oh, naught of any great importance. My family, I s'pose. I wonder how my brothers fare, an' my parents. An' you? What is it ye think of when yer mind wanders?"

He tilted his head to the side and shrugged. "This and that." He paused, then a small smile lit his eyes. "We've come a long way, you and I," he said.

She nodded and made a quiet sound of assent, still tapping her foot on the treadle. "And now?" she asked. "What will ye dream of next? Yer no' the kind to sit still for too long."

Again he shrugged, then leaned forward so his elbows rested on his knees. A dark lock of hair fell forward, and he tucked it behind one ear while he watched the spokes blur.

"Aye, well," said Andrew. "This is a good life. A man could be happy if he were to live his life here."

"But you're no', are ye? Ye've somethin' on yer mind. Tell me if I'm wrong."

He grinned and sat straight, rolling back his shoulders and flexing his back.

"Ye're no' wrong," he admitted. "But I'm happy this eve. I'm a lucky man. What I'm lookin' for will happen, mayhap no' on the morrow, or the next, but it's coming." He paused. "I'll let ye know then, shall I?"

She laughed. "I'll ken when that time comes by the look in yer eye. Now run along. Ye look like ye need the sleep, an' I've just dropped my thread again. I'll have a time tryin' to fix it while I'm paiterin' on wi' ye. Good night, Andrew."

He stood and kissed her on the forehead. Janet couldn't know how right she had been. Andrew did need the sleep. His nights were filled with lonely, uneasy dreams. In the silence of the night, in the solitary existence of his bed, the colourful North Carolina days faded into flat gray images, eclipsed by Maggie's empty eyes. His dreams conveyed a sense of hopelessness he had never sensed in her before, and it frightened him. If she had been in pain or if she'd been afraid, he might have known how to help her. But she sent no clues as to what held her in this mysterious purgatory. It had to be that she was trapped somewhere. The confinement was draining all of her energy as if it were water. She had nothing left with which to reach him.

Winter drew closer, but the climate remained temperate and there was a lack of truly cold winds, since the surrounding mountain ranges served as protection. If it rained the air cooled, but rarely, if ever, did it become that bone-chilling sleet so common in the Highlands.

Once the harvest was in, the group began to explore the land around them. The grant extended far into the backcountry, and now that they had some leisure time, they wanted to see its boundaries. Some days the paths were awkward and crowded with brush and fallen trees, discouraging further progress. On others, they followed deer trails and discovered wide open areas where they sat, enjoyed picnics, and told stories. One day, as they trudged up a hill through the trees, Iain stopped them with the wave of a hand. They stopped in their tracks and followed the direction of his gaze. Ten feet ahead stood a six-point buck, stretching his golden neck to pluck a cluster of leaves from a branch above his head. Andrew was close enough to see the animal's jaw shift sideways as the big molars crunched the leaves. His glistening black eyes stared straight ahead, unaware of his audience.

Flora coughed. It was a tiny, muffled sound, but the buck heard it and froze, meal forgotten. His nostrils flared, sensing the breeze, but Flora was silent and downwind. After a moment, the buck flicked his white paddle tail, dismissing the sound, and reached to pluck something sweet from a nearby shrub.

There were times when this fine specimen would have provided meals for a very long time. There were also times when it was right just to stand and watch.

When the buck moved on, so did the group. They climbed in silence, enjoying the tiny sounds of crackling leaves and chattering squirrels. They moved west, exploring an area they had visited only once before. At the top of the incline they looked over a rock shelf and breathed in the green and gold valley spread like a feast below them.

Janet stood beside Andrew, arms folded across her chest. She sighed.

"Like home a bit," she said, and he nodded.

"Aye, I suppose so. But better. I've no' buried a body since I've arrived. Nor have I raised a sword to anyone."

"True enough," she said. "Though I'm pleased to see ye armed all the same. Some of the ladies the next farm over said only a galoot walks this way wi'out his blades. Ye've heard the painters at night, have ye?"

Andrew nodded, hearing the soulless screams of mountain cats in his memory. It was almost impossible to sleep after waking to that sound. Andrew automatically scanned the thick branches of trees above him, half expecting to spy one of the huge tawny bodies, tail twitching from side to side.

Seamus approached from behind them, shuffling in the leaves.

"Have we a supper with us, Miss Janet? Could that be what's weighin' down yon basket?"

Janet grinned at him. "As a matter of fact, I've brought a fine wee supper. Where shall we go to eat it?"

"Here's good for me," Seamus said, rubbing his stomach.

Iain cleared his throat. "There's a better place a bit farther that way. A place to sit where the weans willna fall off a cliff," he said. "And a wee pond for a drink."

"A pond?" Seamus asked with a look of dismay. "Have we no ale?"

"Of course we've beer," Janet said. "Come on."

They turned in the direction Iain indicated, but had gone only a few feet before Iain stopped them all again. He squatted and crouched behind the foliage and the others immediately followed suit, respecting his skill at hunting and sensing danger. Iain motioned for Janet and the children to stay hidden and the three men crept forward, approaching a game trail they hadn't noticed before. Andrew couldn't see anything. He glanced sideways at Iain, checking, but the big man was straining to hear, eyes narrowed, looking left down the trail.

Then Andrew heard it. Two men's voices, and they didn't sound friendly. They didn't sound as if they were speaking English, either. Andrew walked silently back to Janet.

"Take the children from here," Andrew told her. "Seamus'll go wi' ye."

"What is it?" she asked.

"Indians, I think," he said. "Now go."

She kissed his cheek. "Be careful."

Seamus, looking slightly disappointed at having to leave the possible excitement, joined her. They took the children's hands and headed back down the trail.

Andrew joined Iain behind the brush. The voices were getting louder, and their tongue was definitely foreign.

The branches across the way shook suddenly, shaking loose a dozen golden oak leaves. Two Indian men stepped through the leaves, engrossed in conversation. They looked to be the same age as Andrew, tall, muscular, and menacing. One had an injured arm—blood had dried in a black line down his side.

Andrew looked at Iain, who shrugged. Their priority had to be protecting Janet and the children. If that meant engaging these two, they would. Andrew stepped to the side to get a better view—and a twig snapped beneath his foot.

The Indians froze. In one movement, one of the warriors grabbed his bow, fitted it with an arrow, and aimed the point smoothly around the trees, searching. The other gripped the ax that was hitched in his belt.

Iain nodded, a slight, almost invisible movement. It was habit, Andrew supposed, for men to suspect anyone and everyone of being the enemy. Hard experience had made it impossible to trust without reason. Andrew's chest tightened at the sound of Iain's sword sliding from its scabbard.

Iain called out and an arrow immediately pierced a tree beside him. Iain burst from the trees, sword at the ready, and Andrew stood by his side. The lithe bodies of the Indians swayed as they watched Iain and Andrew run toward them. When Iain didn't slow, the taller Indian, the one with the injured arm, gripped his ax and roared toward him. They slammed together, metal to metal, and Andrew turned to counter a similar strike from the other Indian.

It was too fast. The Indian was too close for Andrew to use his sword. He dropped it and reached for his dirk, gripping it across his chest, blade turned for a lethal swipe. The Indian's eyes were black on his, teeth bared. The men came together with a grunt, grappling for each other's weapon, snarling and ripping at whatever they could grasp. They hit the ground and Andrew punched the Indian's jaw, then used his weight to hold the man under his hands, but the Indian rolled away and sprang back in without hesitation, shrieking, blood running from his nose.

A few feet away, Iain grunted and growled. The steel of his sword rang against the ax's blade, echoing against the forest wall.

The Indian facing Andrew held a knife in one hand and an ax in the other, and looked to be equally efficient with both. He smiled at Andrew, his eyes wild, blood from his nose painting his teeth red. He rushed toward Andrew, a shrieking gust of unstoppable fury. Andrew pulled back and tried to shift sideways to throw the man off, but the Indian matched him step for step. Andrew needed a new tactic. This man was too good. He stopped, bringing his attacker up short, and swung his dirk close enough to the Indian's neck that he felt the man's breath on his skin. But not close enough. The Indian leaned backwards to avoid the blade, then lunged forward.

"No!"

The scream cut through the forest. All four of the men froze, then turned to stare. The woman stood at the edge of the forest, her face white with panic. A woman Andrew had known his entire life. He couldn't look away.

The Indian took advantage of Andrew's hesitation. He bowled Andrew over, then knelt on top of him, knife raised. He screamed something Andrew couldn't understand, and Andrew knew he was about to die.

Then Maggie was there. She grabbed the Indian's arm, yelling, pulling him off balance. He shouted back and shook her off, then stabbed at Andrew, cutting a glancing blow off his ribs before Maggie was there again, shoving the Indian away. She threw herself over Andrew while the other men gawked in confusion.

"No! No! No!" she cried.

Maggie pressed hard against the slice in Andrew's side, and he felt again the energy that had flowed through the mystical rock on Rannoch Moor. The heat was almost overwhelming, like a wave shoved through him, and it sent his mind reeling. Her small hand pressed on his wound, and his entire body surged with power. Again he was bombarded by unfamiliar images and thoughts, but he knew how to focus his mind this time, and he pulled toward her.

"I feel ye, Maggie," he said.

She jerked up onto all fours and stared down at him, as if she were surprised to hear him speak. Then she leaned forward so her hair touched his shoulders and her breath tickled his cheeks. "Tell me you're all right," she whispered.

He chuckled and took her face between his palms. She melted into them, and he felt her swallow a sob.

"Oh, Maggie," he assured her. "I'm more than all right."

CHAPTER 34

Andrew

Soquili stared at me as if I'd lost my mind. As well he might. He had been battling these strangers to the death, bent on protecting Adelaide and me. I had been with her, but she was sleeping soundly, having survived the rough operation I had performed to remove the bullet.

The commotion in the forest brought me running. I raced through the branches, leaping over rocks and logs, feeling strange. As if I ran in a dream. As if my feet didn't touch the springy moss under me. As if the air didn't exist.

I burst into the small clearing, and there he was. No longer the wolf, no longer the dream. Andrew stood chest to chest with Soquili, shoving apart from him, fighting for his life. I screamed and everyone stopped moving. They looked at me, then turned back to the battle—everyone except for Andrew, whose eyes were locked on mine.

I don't remember attacking Soquili. I don't remember anything but lying on top of Andrew, feeling his heart beat beneath mine, feeling his breath, feeling the solid truth of him. I pressed against the slash on the side of his ribs and felt his blood run through my fingers. I pressed harder, concentrating on the injury, and felt his heat rise to meet mine. It swelled like a river overflowing its banks. I wanted to drown in it.

"I feel ye, Maggie," he said, and my world started to spin. I leaned over him and searched his eyes.

"Tell me you're all right," I whispered.

His hands were warm and he laid them against my cheeks. I wanted to disappear within them, dissolve into his skin. His smile was so soft, his eyes wet with unshed tears.

"Oh, Maggie," he said in his deep, curling accent. "I'm more than all right."

Wahyaw stood off to the side with Andrew's friend, no longer interested in the fight. Soquili sat beside Andrew's prone body and frowned at me.

"What are you doing, Ma-kee? Who is this?"

I had broken Soquili's heart before. If only I didn't have to do it again.

"This is Andrew," I said. "This is the man I have dreamed of my entire life."

He stared at me, then frowned at Andrew, who gave him a vague smile. Soquili snorted with disgust. "The man you spoke of so many months ago? This is him? How did he come here?"

"She called to me," Andrew said. "O' course I came."

Soquili hissed at him to be quiet.

"It's true, Soquili," I said. "I tried to tell you. Everything I have ever told you is true."

Soquili's eyes flicked between the two of us, and I could almost see the questions and answers flowing through his mind. He shook his head and stood up.

"It is all true," he said. "It was true all along."

He backed away, then disappeared into the trees.

I sat up and stared at Andrew's chest, at the stain that bloomed across the side of his white shirt. "You're not all right," I said.

"I am," he assured me. He pulled himself up so he sat with a grunt, then yanked the bottom of his shirt up so we could see the wound. He was right. It wasn't bad, but he would probably need me to stitch it.

His skin was warm beneath my palm, soft yet taut over his muscles. I felt dizzy at the sight of his skin, of the sparse black hairs that drew lines over his chest and belly. I touched his side, near the cut, and gasped at the contact, no weaker than it had been a moment before. He felt it, too, and stared at me in amazement.

"Skin to skin," I said quietly.

He took my hand from his chest and held it to his lips, then tugged me closer. I don't remember moving toward him, but I was there, and he was kissing me, our bodies feeling each other as they always dreamed they would. His lips were warm, and he smelled of sweat and dirt with a hint of fresh blood. He tasted . . . like nothing I could describe. He tasted like Andrew. His fingers were in my hair, strong and sure. He drew away from the kiss far enough that we could look into each other's eyes.

"My God, Maggie," he whispered.

Tears poured down my cheeks, and he wiped them away with his thumbs. His lips brushed my cheeks, my neck, my eyelids, my forehead, my lips. I lost track of everything around us. I had no idea if it was day or night, and I didn't care. I was in Andrew's arms. He was all there was in the world.

He pulled away again, holding my face in his hands. His smile was beautiful, his cheeks wet with our shared tears. The dark eyes I had seen in my dreams danced.

"Come away," he said. He stood up, wincing only slightly as his wound objected, and pulled me to my feet. "Let's go home."

"Home?"

"My home," he said, then gave me a wry smile that raced through my senses. "*Our* home, if ye'll have me."

I laid my palms on his warm, solid chest and felt whole. Complete. Every question answered. Finally, after everything, I felt at peace.

"Tell me you're real," I whispered.

"I'm as real as ye are, Maggie. An' I'll spend every day of the rest of my life provin' it to ye."

CHAPTER 35

Resolution

At first, Andrew didn't understand. He had her. He had Maggie in his arms, safe and warm and real. But she said they couldn't go. Not yet.

She led him by the hand, deeper into the woods. "My sister is back here," she explained.

Adelaide was awake but lying still as a fawn in the grass. When she saw Maggie, she sat up slowly. She offered a small smile, looking curiously at the man who held her sister's hand.

"How do you feel?" Maggie asked, kneeling beside her.

"I'll be fine."

"Addy," Maggie said, her face lit with joy. "I never told you something."

Addy waited.

"This is Andrew. This is the man I have always known in my dreams."

Addy looked confused, but not overly surprised. She knew her sister well enough to know it was the truth.

Maggie turned to Andrew, who sat in the grass beside her. "I never told anyone about you," she admitted. "I didn't want—"

"Nor did I," he assured her.

Andrew studied the slight blond version of Maggie. So alike, he thought. And so different. Like his brothers and him. He felt a twinge of regret. Maggie would have liked Dougal.

Iain and Wahyaw, looking more than a little confused, joined them, and Andrew introduced Iain to Adelaide. Wahyaw glared at them all. Soquili understood English and spoke a little, but Wahyaw had never learned. Adelaide began to translate, and his expression relaxed. He nodded with understanding as Maggie explained.

Maggie's gaze was weary. "There's one more thing I have to do. If they never see the proof about Captain Quinn, I will spend the rest of my life running."

"Tell me what to do," Andrew said. "An' I'll do it."

"There is a box," she said slowly. Her fingers tugged at the grass by her feet. She ripped out one piece at a time while she spoke. "It's in a cabin near the fort. That cabin belonged to Captain Quinn. He . . . he brought girls there. Girls his men stole from their homes and did terrible things . . ." Her voice caught and she grabbed a handful of grass, but didn't pull.

"It's okay, lass. Take it slow," Andrew murmured, resting his hand over hers until it relaxed.

"How is it ye ken these things?" Iain asked.

"Because . . ." She stopped, unsure.

"It's all right, Maggie," Andrew said. "He's a friend."

Maggie's chin quivered slightly. She looked up and met Andrew's eyes. The air between them thickened, and for a moment, Andrew forgot anyone else was there.

"I know because Addy and I were two of those girls," she said softly.

For a space of a breath, the only sound came from the tall pines whispering overhead. Then Addy sniffed and Iain cleared his throat.

"And the evidence, lass? What's in the box?" he asked.

"Quinn took something from every girl. He put those things in the box. There are ribbons and lace and shoes and . . . and dolls . . ."

Maggie closed her eyes, and Andrew felt the air change again, as if it drew him toward her. He held her trembling hand tighter, and she showed him the six beaten girls in the cabin, and the worn wooden box off to the side.

"Please, Andrew," she said silently.

"Where do we go?" Andrew asked.

"I've only seen it once," Maggie admitted. "But there is someone else who knows."

CHAPTER 36

Guardians

Joe had known it was coming. From that moment in the prison when she'd entered his mind and discovered what he knew about the cabin, he'd known she'd need him again. He felt her now, as he stepped out of the woods and through a field of knee-high grass.

The soldiers were miles behind, having eventually accepted his apologies for having lost the fugitives' trail. In fact, he thought smugly, he could have followed them with his eyes closed. Theirs had been a desperate escape since both the girl's sister and the big warrior were injured. Their track would have been obvious. But no one questioned Joe when he led them down the line of the riverbed, in the opposite direction.

She needed the box. He had wondered how she would manage to get it. She knew there were captives in the cabin. She had shown him that. She most likely knew the place was guarded. But what she didn't know was the exact location.

Safely away from the army, Joe skirted the fort and headed toward

Quinn's cabin. The building was buried deep in the brush, a delapidated four walls and a roof. That was all Quinn had required for storage.

Joe sat hidden among the trees, watching six shabby men loll in the clearing. Usually only two stood guard, and under closer inspection Joe saw that only a couple of them carried pistols. Another had a musket. So two, maybe three were guarding. And the others? Why would men make their way out this far if it weren't for the girls in the cabin? Joe's gorge rose and he spat into the leaf mold beside his feet.

The men appeared to have finished what they'd come to do, and now relaxed around a small fire, laughing and talking. Nothing much to hold Joe's attention. He lay back in the dry autumn grass and waited for Maggie.

It didn't take long. *"Joe,"* she whispered.

He knew she would follow his mind as easily as he had hers. All she had to do was hear his thoughts and she'd know exactly where to go. Her gratitude wrapped around him like an embrace, and when it was gone, he felt alone.

The sun was high in the sky, filtering through the canopy of the forest, dotting Joe and the leaves around him. The man with the musket stood up, brushed off his trousers, and nodded farewell to the other men. Joe slid soundlessly out of view and watched him head down the path. Now there were five outside the cabin.

Maggie was close. Almost close enough he could hear her if he tried. Joe peered around the area until a quick movement caught his eye, and he spotted Maggie's group. The two Cherokee were there, and it looked as if the warrior's injury had been well tended. Joe could see no trace of blood. Two other men had joined them. Large white men. Scottish Highlanders, from their dress. Joe had seen quite a few Highlanders in town recently. He got along with them, for the most part. They weren't so different from the Indians in some ways. They lived off the land and they were not a people to suffer provocation in silence. Maggie crouched behind with her sister, as if they were protected by the men's shadows.

Joe had no intention of fighting. Today he was merely an observer. He had brought her here. He had given her what she needed, and in return she had given him something he couldn't name.

There was a *thwick! thwick!* as arrows cut through the air and plunged into the two armed men. They fell to their knees without a sound, and their cohorts stumbled backwards with surprise, then grabbed their knives and scanned the line of trees.

The Scots downed the first two, and the uninjured warrior sliced the third man's neck with unerring skill. They left the bodies where they lay, then strode toward the cabin with one Cherokee in the lead. The injured warrior stayed behind to watch over the sisters. Joe wasn't surprised. From everything Maggie had shown Joe back in the prison cell, he imagined she had no desire to step any closer to the cabin.

The sound of heavy breathing alerted Joe. He sat up straighter, always hidden. Ten feet in front of him hunched the man who had left earlier, adjusting his position amongst the fallen leaves. The man must have heard the noise of the short-lived brawl and come back. The barrel of his musket followed the midpoint of the smaller Scotsman's back as the group walked toward the cabin.

Joe slipped through the crackling brush as silent as a snake, until he was close enough to smell the man's scent: musky and aroused. Joe knew many men who reacted the same way when they killed another man, as if it were a sexual act. Joe had never felt that. He accepted that causing death was part of his life. An unpleasant part, but one he understood.

Joe's huge hands clamped on to the man's face from behind. The musket dropped to the earth with a dull thump in the split second that Joe held the man's life in his hands. Then he jerked his grip with precision, disconnecting the man's neck from his spine.

Joe dropped the body and ground his jaw forward and back as he considered what he had done. He couldn't know whether or not he had ended his own life through that quick twist of his wrists. He would be put to death if his action was discovered, yet his heart felt unusually light.

She had been right. He had known what to do.

CHAPTER 37

Lost Voices

Andrew hadn't known what to expect when they stepped into the cabin. Soquili moved aside, probably feeling his appearance would frighten the girls more than theirs, but Andrew wasn't sure if he was right.

He glanced over his shoulder toward Maggie, but couldn't see her.

"It will be over soon," he told her, and relief tickled through his mind like a spring shower.

Iain knocked on the door. There was no response from within, but they hadn't expected one. After a moment Iain opened the door.

Six girls huddled together in one corner of the room, their eyes huge with fear, their meager dresses torn and bloodstained. The air was heavy with a nauseating blend of sweat, stale sex, urine, and fear. Iain dropped to a crouch, as he had when he first met Peter and Flora in the woods. The girls watched him, but their gazes flicked behind him, at the imposing profiles of Andrew and Soquili.

"We're here to set ye free," Iain told them.

The girls stared, mute.

"We'll take care of ye now," Iain said.

One girl pointed a trembling finger at Soquili. "He's an Indian," she said in a terrified whisper. Soquili rolled his eyes, annoyed. Andrew hid a smile.

"Aye, he's that," Iain assured her. "But no' the kind of Indian ye need fear. We'll help ye from this place an' have ye cared for. Ye've nothin' to fear from any of us."

One of the girls began to weep, and another joined in. Their sobs tore at Andrew's heart, and he remembered Maggie's bruised, tearstained face on that day so long before. His Maggie had lived through this as well.

"I wasna wi' ye," he thought.

"You saved me," she whispered back. *"Now you can save them."*

"Come away," Andrew said softly to the girls. "We've food an' water, an' horses to carry ye to a good bed. No one will touch ye unless ye need help."

The girls rose slowly, leaning on each other for support. Andrew, Iain, and Soquili stood back and let them pass, ready to catch the fragile creatures if they lost their balance.

Maggie stood at the edge of the trees, watching. When the girls came outside, she ran toward them and offered whatever comfort she could manage. Tears had dried on her cheeks in little trails, but she smiled encouragement to each tortured face.

Andrew turned back inside and found the box in the corner of the single room. It was weathered and nondescript, not much more than two feet by three feet, not quite as high as his knees. Andrew knelt beside the box, wedged his fingers under the bottom, then stopped as his head filled with the voices of so many young girls. He felt their terror, the pain, the despair, felt it shudder through his entire body. He let go and stared at the box, then touched it again.

"We will do all we can to bring ye justice, though it is far too late. May ye find peace where'er ye are," he said, and the frenzy of pleas began to slow.

Andrew left the box closed and cradled it against his chest. He carried it out the door, toward Maggie. She was kneeling beside a girl, wiping a cool, wet cloth over a dirty brow. When she saw Andrew, she rose and went to him, her steps unsure.

She stared at the box, and he sensed her dread. He set it on the grass in front of her, then stepped away, wanting to give her room to breathe.

"Stay with me," she whispered, sinking to her knees. Adelaide joined her on the grass, and the sisters stared at the box.

Andrew walked around so he could touch Maggie's back, offering support. He knelt behind her and kissed the side of her neck, feeling goose bumps rise on her skin. She trembled under his fingers, and he felt her urge to run, to forget the pain in the box, to escape with him and never dream of it again. But the voices called to her as they had to him, needing to be heard.

Maggie unhooked the clasp and lifted the top. She reached within the worn planks and Andrew's fingers tingled, as if the girls held his hand, and he knew Maggie had opened her mind to share everything with him. The first thing Maggie pulled from the box was the blue ribbon that had been yanked from her hair so long before. She drew it loose, flattened the length of it between her fingers, then wrapped the ribbon loosely around her neck and tied the ends into a bow. She took another breath, then withdrew Adelaide's bracelet and gave it to her sister. Adelaide slid it over her wrist without a word. Then

Maggie rested her forehead against the edge of the box and reached for Addy's hand. She forced her other hand back into the box and closed her fingers around the waist of a little rag doll. The tiny body shook as Maggie lifted it, then held it to her chest. Her grief seized Andrew and whispered in his mind.

"My sister, Ruth."

CHAPTER 38

Life Continues

Iain rode to New Windsor with the evidence.

Maggie had told Iain everything about Captain Quinn and his business. Iain listened with unswerving attention, the changing expressions on his wide, bearded face reflecting strong emotions. She told him there was only one man she trusted with the evidence: Sergeant MacMillan, the officer to whom she had confessed immediately following Quinn's death. There were men of power in the town who would want to seize the incriminating evidence within the box, and Iain would have to be on guard for them.

No one would get in Iain's way. Andrew felt confident the evidence would be presented, the story told in all its horrific detail, and Maggie would be vindicated. It wasn't going to be an easy process, since the judge and other prominent figures were involved in Quinn's business. But there were too many witnesses now, witnesses who were more than willing to stand up and point accusing fingers.

That was why Andrew hadn't let Maggie go with Iain. The army was scouring the forest for her, Soquili, and Wahyaw. They wouldn't hesitate to pluck the three off the street and drop them behind bars.

The rescued girls yielded to Iain's soft promises that the Cherokee would not hurt them. They rode back to the village with Wahyaw and Soquili, where they would be tended by the healers. The Cherokee women would do what they could for the broken bodies, but the girls' spirits would require more time. Two of the girls were very ill, their bodies torn, their eyes deadened. Andrew wasn't sure they would survive.

Maggie, Adelaide, and Andrew walked to his home a few hours away. They took their time, depending on Maggie's strength, stopping often to rest. When at last they reached the tiny settlement, Maggie took Andrew's hand and squeezed it. He smiled, but a flurry of nerves bubbled through his chest.

"Would ye be happy livin' here?" Andrew asked.

"Yes, of course. Why?"

"I mean, to leave the Cherokee an' all—"

"Oh. No," she said, her eyes glancing appreciatively around the houses, barn, and sheds. "I won't ever leave them entirely. But I want to live with you. I want to be with you, in this house you built. It already feels like home."

He squeezed her against his side and thought: yes, now that she was here, it did feel like home.

Seamus opened the door and discovered Andrew with two unknown women. They joined him inside and warmed themselves by a snapping fire while Andrew explained as much as he could. The children buzzed around him like flies until he told them where Iain had gone. Janet hung on a pot of stew over the hearth, brought the sisters something clean to wear, and checked Adelaide's injury.

"Ye're healin' well," she remarked.

Adelaide smiled and nodded. "Maggie's a healer."

"Oh, aye?" Janet looked impressed. "Lucky for you then. She's done a fine job."

Maggie took a sip of ale and smiled at Janet. "Thank you. And thank you for taking care of us."

"We're happy to have ye." Janet turned to Andrew. "Andrew, if ye'd no' mind, could ye maybe come wi' me an' bring in an armful o' wood?"

Andrew glanced at the neat stack of wood by the fireplace, then at Seamus, who shrugged. "Aye," Andrew said. "Let's go."

He squeezed Maggie's shoulders and followed Janet to the tall stack of wood by the house. A step away from the woodpile, she turned on her heel and stared at him, hands planted on her hips.

"She's her, isn't she?"

Andrew blinked. "She's who?"

She shoved at his arm. "Dinna fool wi' me, Andrew. She's the girl ye spoke of to me, so long ago. The girl ye're promised to."

"How could ye ken that?"

Janet's smile was warm with pleasure for him. "Oh, Andrew. 'Tis written all o'er yer face. Ye're the happiest I've seen, an' you wi'out a bite to eat yet. Normally if ye're no' fed, ye're no' happy. But this Maggie—I think ye could go a week wi' no meals an' ye'd still smile."

"A lifetime maybe," he said, grinning helplessly.

Janet shook her head, watching him with wonder. "She's a lucky thing, she is," she said.

They headed back inside, arms full of kindling, and listened to Seamus entertain the girls with his endless chatter.

The fire burned low and warm, soothing as a soft blanket. Maggie and Adelaide were yawning behind their hands by the time the crickets started up their evening songs. Andrew suggested they stay in his room that night, and he would sleep by the fire.

They followed him to the bedroom, and Andrew watched Maggie's reaction as she took in his meagre possessions, his unassuming bed, and the small table and chair by its foot. She closed her eyes and breathed in.

"It smells like you," she told him.

That startled him, and his cheeks flared red. "Oh—shall I clean it then? I'm sorry. I ne'er expected—"

She turned toward him and put her palms against his chest. Her eyes were tired, but her giggle rang like little bells. "You smell wonderful," she said.

Adelaide stood beside her sister, a curious smile on her face. "I'll just go to bed now. You come in when you're ready, Maggie. Thank you for letting us use your room, Andrew. And Andrew?"

"Aye?"

"Thank you for today. Thank you for everything you've done for us. If we hadn't met you—"

"We would have met him eventually," Maggie told her. "I always knew we would."

Adelaide frowned, then shrugged. "Anyway," she said. "Thank you."

"I'm only glad we could help," he said. "Sleep well. In the morn we'll head to the village to see how the wee girls fare. Ye'll need yer sleep for that."

Adelaide nodded, then rose up on her toes and kissed him on the cheek. "Good night," she said, and shut the door behind her, leaving Andrew and Maggie standing in the hall.

"Come outside?" Maggie asked.

"Ye're no' too tired?"

"Just for a bit. I don't want the day to end yet."

"Nor do I," he admitted. He grabbed a blanket before following her outside, then wrapped it around them both as they sat on a felled tree trunk. It was a cool, crisp evening, and the sky was alight with stars. Maggie snuggled closer.

"I just need to touch you," she said. "So I know I'm not dreaming."

He kissed the back of her hand. They stared at the stars in silence, and Maggie caught her breath when one shot across the sky, then vanished just as suddenly. Andrew rested his cheek on her head and watched for the next shooting star. Then he heard:

"Can you still hear me?"

He turned and grinned at her. *"Aye, I can."*

Her eyelids fluttered closed, and she smiled like a satisfied cat. "Good," she said out loud. "I was hoping we could still do that."

Andrew hooked a finger under her chin. He lifted her face and kissed her.

"I dinna mind so much," he murmured. "As long as we can do that."

When he thought she could stay awake no longer, Andrew gently lifted Maggie and carried her inside, where the dying embers of the hearth fire bade them good night. Adelaide was softly snoring when they opened the bedroom door, and Andrew kept very quiet as he laid Maggie in the bed beside her.

"Sleep well, my Maggie," he said in his mind.

She blinked heavily and gave him a sleepy smile that made him want to kiss her again.

"I will dream of you," she said.

"And in the mornin' it will all come true, aye? Good night, Maggie." He gave her one more kiss, then left her in the darkened room, knowing she would be asleep in a few breaths.

His dreams were smooth and joyful and full of her. He slept deeply, knowing his waking moments would be the same.

In the morning they set off toward the Cherokee village. Andrew was concerned with Maggie's health and wanted to get her to the healers as soon as he could. She had slept well, but was emaciated and exhausted, needing comfort and rest as well as food. The messages that flowed constantly between them were there, but her voice seemed weak.

Andrew spent every moment with her, awake or asleep. He watched Waw-Li and learned from the shrunken woman, fascinated by her powers. The old woman barred other men from her house, but she enjoyed having Andrew there. She often said how the spirits had blessed her indeed, to have brought both the Raven and the Wolf to her.

Every day brought new colour to Maggie's cheeks, more spring to her steps. When she spoke in his thoughts, her voice rang clearly again, and every word was like a touch of her lips on his skin.

It was over two weeks before Iain returned from New Windsor, looking tired, but satisfied.

"All's done," he announced to Andrew. "Or as much as can be done for now. A lot of folk are none too pleased wi' that box, aye? Like Maggie told me. But 'tis done now. She's no need to run. Nor do the Cherokee lads."

That was cause for celebration among the tribe. The big fire near Waw-Li's seven-sided council house blazed so fiercely that the night burned as bright as day. There was a feast, and no Cherokee feast was complete without dancing. Maggie and Andrew sat together, watching everyone, seeing no one but each other. She leaned against his arm, her forehead on his shoulder, and he tilted his head so his cheek rested on the soft bed of her hair. Every dream, every breath had led to this moment, and he felt completely swallowed up by the sounds and the silence, the dark and the light, the warmth, the warmth of her. He stared into the fire and saw her before him, though she sat at his side. She was beautiful. She smiled at him as she so often had, reaching out and touching his cheeks with her translucent fingers. He turned to her, sitting beside him, and she laid her own cool fingers, solid and real, on his face. He wondered if it would always be like this: living somewhere between dreams and something better than dreams.

"Marry me, Maggie?"

"Silly question. Of course."

Neither said a word out loud, but matching smiles stretched across their faces. He kissed her, tasting her joy, knowing he had given it to her. His calloused fingers curled around the slender curves of her ears, and his thumbs stroked her fire-reddened cheeks.

"I do love ye, my Maggie," he whispered.

Her blue eyes were slightly unfocused as she blinked up at him. "I have always loved you."

Later that evening, Andrew walked toward the forest, needing to relieve himself, and was surprised to hear the near-silent footfalls of Soquili behind him. The men walked toward the trees, and when they stopped, Andrew said nothing. He hadn't asked Maggie about Soquili, but knew the warrior was deeply hurt, and Maggie treasured him as a friend. Andrew admired him as well, but didn't know how to speak to him. He thought any words of apology would come out wrong, and he didn't want to insult Soquili. So he was relieved when Soquili spoke first.

"Ma-kee is very special to the people," Soquili said, looking into the trees. His voice was stiff, and Andrew realised this was the first time he had spoken with him directly.

"She's a very special woman," Andrew said. "To me as well."

Soquili nodded, chewing on his lower lip as he considered what to say. Ecstatic howls erupted from the fireside behind them, and Andrew peered over his shoulder. Sparks flew and fell in a fountain of fire. Maggie sat near them, laughing at her friends, then gazed toward Andrew.

"I will take care of her," Andrew promised, looking back toward the forest.

A frown darkened Soquili's profile, but he nodded and it disappeared. "I know you will do this," he said. "And I will apologise to you now."

Andrew turned with surprise. "Apologise? Whatever for?"

Soquili took a breath, then spoke quickly, "I thought to make her my wife, and she said she could not. She said she waited for you. I did not believe her and I was unkind to her. Now that I meet you, I know she speaks the truth, and you are here for her." Finally, he turned toward Andrew. "I love Ma-kee," he said, standing tall. "I will always love her. But I do understand this, I think. And I welcome you as a brother."

EPILOGUE

The blanket of fur had been replaced, laid over my body while I slept. It wasn't the temperature that had prompted Andrew to cover me, but a sense of protection. That, more than anything else, warmed me.

Andrew was an early riser. I imagined that, before I came along, he was a busy man, tending to chores from the moment the day began. He was a man who thrived on accomplishing things, by assuring himself all was as it should be. Now he came back in, balancing a mug of steaming tea in each hand, as he did most mornings. The sun arced over his profile, tracing the line of his hair and shoulders, continuing down the long, lean muscles of his body. Low in my belly a tingle started, spreading through my body at lightning speed as he set down the drinks and settled under the furs with me.

" 'Twill be a lovely day, Missus MacDonnell," he said. "Shall we chance leaving our bed for a change?"

His voice was matter-of-fact, with teasing woven through it for my enjoyment. I loved the vibration of that voice, the fact that his words were for me, and only me.

"I don't see any reason to hurry, do you?" I mused. "After all, we were up late last night . . ."

He chuckled and rolled toward me. I tucked a strand of his hair behind one ear. I wanted to tell him how happy I was, how fulfilled and excited for our future. I wanted to sing and laugh and dance around the room like a child. But his eyes, those dark pools I had always seen, said so much more than I ever could.

I reached for his face and he brought it to me, touching our lips together once, twice, until they molded with a need neither of us could manage on our own. The air felt alive when we were wrapped together like this.

The first time we made love, he knew I was afraid. He caught glimpses of my memories and I, in response, felt his helpless pain.

"No one will ever hurt ye again, Maggie," he said. "No one."

And he kissed me. Slowly, slowly, he taught me how to leave the past behind. He showed me pleasure I had never imagined, gave me moments when I could no longer tell the difference between dreams and reality. But when all was done, when we both relaxed into a sluggish stupor, he tucked me against him so we lay back to chest, my thighs on his, my feet twisting over the hard bones of his shins. And we slept.

I craved his body and his touch. In my dreams I had always reached for him, and that didn't change now that he was with me in the flesh. There was rarely a moment when I didn't consciously touch him in some manner, even if it was just pressing my thigh against his while he slept. And he reached for me. I woke once to discover our fingers woven together, and him still asleep.

The dreams didn't end, but they changed. In the past, when their violence ripped me from my sleep, loneliness haunted me like clinging smoke. I was often afraid, but the fact that I was alone in the knowledge of what lay ahead made it even more frightening. Now, with Andrew here, I shared everything but the loneliness. We were together, awake or asleep, and when I saw the worst, Andrew was there to hold me close and understand without speaking.

We made love slowly that morning, subsiding into oblivion at the same moment. The tea sat untouched and cooling as we drifted back to sleep.

The dreams were murky at first, a confusing, rolling texture moving closer with every heartbeat, and I felt an unaccustomed flutter of fear. Without warning, my belly clenched and I curled instinctively around it. A searing pain cut through me, sharp, with a brutal, relentless urgency. I reached for Andrew, and felt him beside me, but he was an undefined shape, though I sensed his concern. His hand held mine, anchoring me, refusing to let the pain take me from him.

"You said no one would hurt me!" I screamed, resentment boiling in my thoughts.

"I canna take this pain from ye," he answered, *"but I willna leave ye alone wi' it."*

My body burned, my skin tore, and yet I could see nothing of the source.

"I can't! I can't!"

The pain eased a bit, and I realised he was stretching his mind toward me, his strength a cushion, a place I could feel safe. Then the agony was back, and I was certain my body had burst into flame.

"I'm sorry, Andrew! I'm dying! I can't! I can't!"

Relief came unexpectedly, leaving a hollowness I was afraid to trust. Sleep still trapped me, but Andrew's face was clear to me now, drawn with concern. His breath touched me from far away. I ached for him. *"Andrew! I don't want to be alone!"* I cried, but heard another voice singing through the dream instead of my own. The sound of a bird, harsh and sweet, calling in persistent squawks. A weight in my arms, a warmth . . . Andrew's tears, his handsome face alight with joy.

"She's beautiful," he said.

She was hot in my hands, wet and slick with my blood. Her tiny limbs flailed like windblown branches as she greeted us. Her shocked expression blurred behind my tears.

"Ruth," I said.

We woke then, our eyes blinking open at the same time. We stared at each other, our heartbeats eventually slowing to a shared rhythm.

"Are ye afraid?" he asked.

"Yes," I admitted. "The pain—I don't know . . ."

He pulled me into his chest, and I breathed in his sweat. His scent was reminiscent of fear, but fresh now with relief. He kissed the top of my head, then spoke into my hair.

"Aye. But ye will survive. Ye will. I will hold ye an' keep ye safe. And ye will wake as ye did just now, holding our child in yer arms when ye do."

I sniffed. "I have a better idea. Maybe you could do it, and I'll hold your hand instead. How would that be?"

He smiled. "Ye're a brave wee thing, my Maggie," he said, sweeping damp hair back from my brow, "an' I love ye wi' all my heart an' soul."

I sighed and snuggled tighter against his warmth.

The dreams may never stop, but I'm not alone anymore. Nor is he. Never again.

Before death comes silence. It hovers during the final heartbeat, in the moment between the screams, moans, whimpers of the dying and the final puff of air. A breath suspended, waiting, held in expectation or discovery. Silence is the last sound a dying person hears.

Dougal was no stranger to the voices of the dying, but he had never heard the silence within himself. Not yet. The tones and timbres of last words and final pleas were familiar, though. He had heard them countless times as they slashed at men's hearts and bodies, separating souls from skeletons.

Dougal was a warrior, born and trained to kill. Death was simply part of his life. In the heat of battle, blood roared so ferociously through his head he barely heard the men's voices anymore as they screamed defiance or whispered frantic prayers of disbelief, crying of futures never met.

But on this bloody morning in April 1746, one voice cut through the curtain of noise, yanking Dougal from his battle frenzy. The sound was small, almost buried beneath the misery of it all. Still, he heard it: a particular voice. A voice he knew so well, distorted by grief and pain.

His father had known this would not go well. Before the butchering began, Dougal had looked into Duncan MacDonnell's liquid blue eyes, tearing from the cold, and had seen the knowledge. He focused on the words in his father's mind, hearing them clearly, though they were more of a prayer than a thought. When Duncan gathered his sons to him for what would be the final time, Dougal saw defiance in the set of his father's chin. He also saw the sweat of fear on his brow.

"I'm proud o' ye, my lads," Duncan said. "An' I'm proud to be here wi' ye."

Dougal remembered the weight of his father's hand as it had clapped onto his shoulder. Then the cannons had started up and the hand was gone, grabbing for pistol and sword.

"Where are th' others?" his father had hollered, meaning Dougal's brothers, Andrew and Ciaran. They had vanished, swallowed up by the smoke-heavy mist.

When the battle began, they'd gone in together as they always did, the four of them. Andrew always ran at Dougal's right flank, his father and their younger brother, Ciaran, at his left. The MacDonnell men always fought in pairs. He and Andrew had trained to fight side by side, covering each other's more vulnerable points. Together they were an invincible force. Since Ciaran was the youngest, he and their father fought together, Duncan taking Ciaran's weaker side. But when Dougal looked beside him now, he saw his father, not Andrew. The English had managed not only to decimate the entire Scottish army, as ragtag as it was, but to fracture his family's tiny battalion.

Dougal glanced around, seeking his brothers, and spotted

Andrew, leaning in to take a swipe at a redcoat. Ciaran was a few steps back, watching, sword at half-mast. Andrew finished defending his younger brother, then swung around and yelled something Dougal couldn't hear. But in Dougal's mind, Andrew's thoughts were clear: *Kill or be killed, Ciaran! Fight, damn it!*

"There, Da!" Dougal yelled, pointing across the field. "Andrew's just saved Ciaran's arse again."

His father nodded shortly, his face haggard behind a shaggy beard. "They'll do. Let's you and I go then."

The two roared into the thick of things, black-haired demons with fury burning in their eyes.

But the fire had been extinguished from his father's. One minute he was beside Dougal, cursing the English in furious Gaelic, hacking through them as he would swing an ax through trees. Then he was on his knees, gaping into the victorious expression of one of them. The soldier's bayonet was sunk deep in Duncan's chest, and Duncan's filthy hands, emptied of their own weapons, clutched at the blade, heedless of its edge as it sliced through his fingers.

Despite the chaos, Dougal heard the blade go in, cutting through the thick blanket of tartan, carving into his father's body like a knife into meat. He heard Duncan's tortured scream at the initial pain, then the gurgling sobs that began to seize him. The soldier shoved Duncan backwards with the heel of his muddied boot, yanking the bayonet from the kill, and Duncan's voice suddenly seemed much younger. As if he were a child, a youth, surprised at being cheated.

Dougal thrust his sword through the soldier's back in a reflex action, then fell to his knees at his father's side. He didn't hear the soldier die. Didn't care.

"Da?" he cried. "Da!"

Duncan's eyes had begun to glaze into an opaque stillness Dougal had seen too many times. Blood snaked from the corner of his mouth, but he tried to smile, pulling back his lips and showing teeth dark with blood.

"Proud o' ye, son," he grunted.

"No, Da! Hold on!"

But Dougal knew, as his father knew. Nothing could be done for Duncan.

They were in an area to the side of the main field, slightly out of the way of the oncoming missiles of grapeshot and cannonball. Dougal dragged his father out of the way, avoiding the relentless tide of foot soldiers. His father needed him, needed *someone*, and everyone else was gone. Dougal hunched beside the shuddering body, bracing his father with one arm, gripping his sword defensively with the other. Just before he had to rise and fight, he heard his father's last breaths, a weak gasp, then a lifeless whistle as his lungs released air for the final time.

"No!" Dougal cried, feeling rage and grief roar like flames in his chest. He set his father gently onto the ground and bent over the still chest, breathing quickly, forcing his tears to stay within. There was no time for them now. "I fight for you, Father," he said, then leaned forward to kiss the clammy brow.

Turning away, Dougal threw himself into the battle like a man possessed. These men would pay. They would pay with their meaningless lives for the only one that had mattered. Dougal was a *ban-sidhe*, a whirling monster sick with rage, black eyes burning through a face smeared with filth and blood.

Such was his trance that he didn't notice the five sweat-soaked redcoats surrounding him until the black mouths of their muskets yawned at his head.

"'Allo, you scum-suckin' toad," yelled one over the battle noise, peering at Dougal through his sight. He took a moment to spit to the side and peruse the fallen bodies at Dougal's feet, then set his chin back to the handle and squinted. "We'll 'ave yer 'ead for all this mess, we will."

Dougal stood panting, his face twisted with fury, each hand clenched around the hilt of a different sword. He drew a blackened arm across his brow to clear his eyes of stinging sweat, lifting his upper lip in an instinctive display of teeth. "No' one of ye to pull the trigger? Go on then. Afraid I'll come back from the grave to haunt ye? Clever bastards, ye are. For I will. I will remember each of ye. I'll tear yer hearts through yer own teeth while ye watch."

A cannonball ripped through the air twenty feet away, crashing through trees, men, mules, anything in its path. Muskets flashed, men shouted, but the nervous glance exchanged by a couple of the soldiers seemed more related to Dougal's threat than to the obvious physical one. They shuffled nervously, and two musket barrels wavered, but at a grunt from the lead soldier the men snapped back into position.

The first soldier smiled and gave Dougal a knowing wink. "You ain't comin' back, mate. Where you're off to, they don't let you come back. Tell you what, though. We won't kill you just this minute. We'll 'ave a bit of fun with you first, right? And when we're done, I'm willing to wager you'll wish one of us 'ad shot you. An' then maybe we'll just take you wif us when we go 'ave a little visit with your mother and sisters, shall we?" He nodded at Dougal's two swords, dark with blood, held in readiness at his front and side. "Drop those, would you?"

"I won't," he assured him.

The soldier shook his head with apparent disappointment, as if Dougal were a child requiring discipline. "Oh, you will." He jerked his chin toward a soldier behind Dougal. On cue, the second soldier slammed his musket into the base of Dougal's skull.

When he woke, he lay on his stomach, unable to move. He

opened his eyes but kept his head down, leaving his cheek to chill on a bed of mud. The air was still, its quiet engulfing the ringing in his ears. Battle sounds had ceased. It was done. The back of his head felt as if a horse's hoof had dug into it with the weight of the beast behind it, and his eyes throbbed from the pressure. His shoulders ached. He tried to bring one palm to his forehead but discovered his hands were tied and bound behind his back. His feet were tied as well.

So, he thought. *My head isna the worst of my worries.*

He wasn't alone. He lay among others of his kind, all similarly trussed, most groaning with pain. From his vantage point, facedown in the dirt, Dougal didn't think any of them seemed too badly injured. That meant, he assumed, they were to become prisoners of the damn English dogs, slaves to their demeaning whims. Dougal knew some of the men here would rather die than face that prospect. Rather slit their own throats than submit to English rule. But Dougal had other thoughts. He would survive, if only to make the English regret everything they had done to him. To his father. To his brothers.

Where were his brothers? Not here in this writhing mass of captives. He studied the group as closely as he could, checking each dirty face, listening for familiar voices, but found nothing of them.

Very carefully, ignoring the crushing agony at the back of his neck, Dougal turned his head so he faced the battlefield. As he'd thought, the fight was done. A pall of thick smoke still hung in the mist, stinking of sulphur and death. Wincing at the pain, he peeled his cheek from the wet ground so he could see farther. He narrowed his eyes, watching dark, red-tinged figures wander through the field. Occasionally the sharp crack of a musket cut through the fog. Putting the badly injured out of their misery, he figured. Maybe that was a blessing, to end the suffering. If they weren't hurt too badly, it appeared they ended up here on the ground, tied like a beast.

Dougal's gaze picked out two of the distant soldiers and followed their movements. They walked, stopped, then leaned down, jerked back, and repeated the motion. Strangled sounds of men were cut suddenly short. Dougal shuddered and thought of his brothers again, this time with more urgency. *Please, God*, he prayed. *Don't let them be lying injured on that smoke-shadowed moor. Not shot to pieces and still breathing.* Because those poor souls were being systematically dispatched by English bayonets.

"Wherever ye are, brothers, I go wi' ye in spirit," he murmured, then lost consciousness again.